Bad PRINCESS

THE NEW AMERICAN MAFIA

—BOOK 1—

N. E. HENDERSON

This book is a work of fiction. Names, character, places, and incidents are the product of the author's imagination or are used as fictitiously. Any resemblance to actual events, locales, or persons, living or dead, is coincidental.

Publisher © N. E. Henderson Books

Editor: Charisse Hankins

Beta Reader/Editor: Tesha Cupak

Proofreaders: Nikkita McDuffle, Amber Reid, & Rosa (My Brother's Editor)

Cover Art: Jay Aheer

Photographer: Wander Aguiar

Models: Pat and Dina

Paperback ISBN-13: 978-1-948539-14-2

DEDICATION

Maddy.

You were the first to love them after me. Thank you for reading this story, offering feedback, and continuing to message me, asking for more chapters. You made me stay accountable to the end. This book is for you. — Love, Nancy

CHAPTER 1
SIENNA

I slap the button on the gear stick of my gray, Mercedes AMG GT Coupe into park harder than it deserves. I've been fuming since I received a text message from my brother, Ren, fifteen minutes ago. As a result, my poor car has taken the brunt of my anger since I left the gym in a haste.

Luckily, I hadn't gotten as far as the women's locker room, so I hadn't changed out of the clothes I'd dressed in this morning. *Thank fuck for Vin, too.* It's the only reason I was able to beat my brother here. God, I hope Dad only sent Ren and not Dom too. I can sway my twin much easier than I can our older brother.

A shiver runs down my spine at the thought of what Domenico is going to do when he gets his hands on Vin. *How could he be so stupid?* I wasn't even supposed to be at the gym this evening, but I missed my early morning training session. It's the only reason I was as close to where my moronic friend hangs out.

Closing my eyes, I wrap both hands around the steering wheel, squeezing the leather as I pull in a long, slow, calming breath through my nose. As I release it from my lips, my day mask sheds, letting the *other* Sienna Caputo make a public appearance. Slowly lifting my lashes, I glance in the rearview mirror, looking at my dark brown eyes and the black eyeliner coated thickly around them, the perfect wing end completing my look.

I am just as mentally and physically strong as my brothers, I chant to myself, seconds before pressing the button to turn off the ignition and climb out of the car. *I am, dammit, and the whole goddamn world will see that one of these days.*

Perhaps in ten short weeks, whether anyone likes it or not. That's a promise to myself I intend to keep. I parked in an open spot directly in front of the single-door entrance to Raymond's; a dive bar on the outskirts of town in one of the more seedier communities of Long Island.

Yanking the glass door open, I step inside a dimly lit open room. The bar is to my left against the wall, tables and chairs with patrons scattered about litter the main area in front of me. All of them men, shooting the shit with their buddies after work before they go home to wives, girlfriends, families.

A couple of pool tables and a dartboard line the back of the place. I see Vin almost instantly, but he's yet to see me. "Jesus Christ," I mutter under my breath when I spot Matteo De Salvo sitting to Vin's right and Levi King in front of Matteo at the four-top table. I'm not surprised to find Matteo here. I know he frequents this bar; he has since before it was legal for him to drink. I know this because my brothers used to come here for the same reason—easy access to all the booze underaged patrons could ever want; perhaps even more than just alcohol lurks among these walls.

What I didn't know was that Matteo and Vin are acquainted,

or maybe even friends. Why I didn't know is the current question ping-ponging around in my head. Calvin—or Vin as I know him—and I have known each other far too long for me not to know that he's friends with *the* Matteo De Salvo—the current world heavyweight champion of boxing.

You'd think with someone of Matteo's stature, he'd find better places to hang out than here among questionable individuals. *I'm judgy, I know.* Him being here fucks with my state of mind.

As I stalk toward their table, fire licks the skin underneath my black leather jacket the closer I get. The knife I keep concealed inside my right sleeve itches against my wrist, wanting to join the party. Vin's already in deep shit over Levi. If Vin brought Matteo into his mess, I will make him bleed from every pore on his body until he begs me to turn him over to my father, Antonio Caputo. Domenico won't even get to lay a finger on Vin if I find out that's the case—and it better not be the goddamn case.

My father is *the* Boss—or the Don, or even capo dei capi, if you prefer the television version—among the Italian-American Mafia. The latter was placed upon him many years ago by the media before Domenico was born. My grandfather and great-grandfather also adorned that eye roll worthy of a title once upon a time. It sounds stupid to me; though I've been told my great-grandfather loved seeing it next to his name in newspapers back in the day.

My dad usually goes by Tony or Boss, nothing too formal, but Don Caputo isn't a term unheard of in my house from time to time by associates of his. He reigns over the northeast and Midwest region of the United States, after all—a rank he doesn't take lightly. Soon he'll own the southern region and then only the west remains left to be claimed.

My gaze roams to my left, catching the bartender's head as it snaps up at seeing my presence. Bennett's eyes meet mine for all of two seconds before I hear a curse slip from his lips. Glancing down, I witness the draft beer he's dispensing into a pint glass overflowing, the amber liquid running over the top of his hand about the same time Matteo and Vin see me approaching their table. The dumb-fuck in front of Matteo is oblivious to my approach, and continues to run his mouth when the other two at the table have stopped talking, their gazes tracking me.

I don't bother asking if I can take a seat before I wrap my left hand around the top of the chair to Levi's right, snatching it backward, the legs making a scraping sound as I drag it against the dirty concrete ground. Vin's hazel eyes narrow when they reach my irritated dark gaze. It could be the dim lighting in this bar, but they appear light brown today, like muddy water.

"What's up, Sienna?" Vin asks, a cautious undertone evident in his question while his eyes are silently saying, *what the fuck are you doing here*?

I sit my jean-clad behind down, placing both of my elbows on the table, ignoring the way the top tips toward my side at the unevenness of either the floor or the table legs. My eyes never veer from Vin, both of us silent for at least ten seconds before his mouth goes to open again.

"Don't," falls from my lips. "I told you, Vin. I told you on four different occasions not to bring Levi into your business, and four times you said, 'fuck you, Sienna.'"

"Stop right there," he spits out, his face heating. Vin has blond hair with a touch of red—or maybe it's strawberry-blond—with fair skin. The tiniest amount of irritation always makes his face flush, his skin reddening like the snap of fingers. "I never said—"

"Your actions say otherwise," I fire back, cutting him off. "You may have not verbally said the words, but how else should I take it when I explicitly told you that he was going to fuck you over, and you disregard my warning?"

"What the fuck, you little bitch? If you have a problem—" The sound of King's voice amplifies my rage, but to the naked eye he wouldn't realize that; none of them would. I'm good at hiding what I'm feeling. It's a skill I've perfected over the years; training that my father personally taught me from a young age.

My eyes can't help themselves as they flick to Matteo at *that* very thought. Our gazes briefly meet before I turn my head, my dark irises hardening when they land on the lowlife sitting next to me.

"Don't speak to me," I warn Levi with a quick shake of my head, cutting him off before he finishes a sentence that's bound to spike my temper even more than he already has.

Before I can open my mouth to continue my conversation with Vin, Levi decides to say 'fuck your warning' by opening his trap again. "Look, cunt—"

My left elbow lifts off the table, connecting with his mouth, physically not allowing him to finish his sentence. The impact sends a jolt of pain through my upper arm and over my shoulder. My ass is out of the chair the next second, my fingers plunging into his mop of dirty-blond hair as my nails claw at his scalp. I tighten my grip, fisting my hand around a chunk of his greasy strands. With force, I slam his forehead down on the hard surface of the table, making their pint glasses tip over and crash to the ground.

"I said, don't speak to me. That wasn't a request. It was an order, you stupid fuck," I seethe, inches from his ear.

I really hate men like him—pathetic waste of air.

The silence inside the bar is deafening, but no one intervenes to help Levi. Matteo's expression doesn't go unnoticed from my peripheral. His mouth wide from shock, his jaw damn near sits on the table. *Yeah, I bet you never saw violence coming from me*. He doesn't know everything about me; not that he ever tried to get to know me in the first place, because he didn't. In fact, he refused to do just that.

"Jesus, Si," Vin breathes out my name. "Was that really necessary?"

The fact that he has the audacity to ask that after his pissant brother-in-law just called me a cunt has me questioning our relationship. Vin is a friend; not a close one, but still a friend, nonetheless. That's all he is and that's all he'll ever be.

There was a time he wanted more, but I quickly set him straight—he isn't my type and that will never change. I have one type and he doesn't fit the bill. Once that was cleared up, he and I found out we got along quite well. We met my freshmen year of college at the campus gym and we became workout buddies that first day.

I retract my fingers from Levi's head, shoving him as I take my cell phone out of the back pocket of my jeans with my clean hand and wipe my other off by running my palm down the side of my pants. When it's as clean as it's going to get short of washing it, I take a seat again. My eyes go to my phone, bringing it to life, then I locate the text message I got from my brother. After I have it pulled up, I tap on the photo Ren sent, then I place the phone down on the table, sliding it in front of Vin.

"I don't know, was that necessary?" I grill, leaning my back against the chair and then fold my black, leather-clad arms over my chest, my eyes on Vin as he picks up the phone, staring at the photo. I feel a set of ocean-blue eyes on me that heats me deep inside my core, but I stay still, fighting the urge to squirm in my seat. It takes more effort than it should to force my eyes to remain rooted to Vin's face.

Vin's brows crease between his eyes as he scrutinizes the picture of Levi shaking hands with Fredrico Romano—or Rico "the rat" Romano, as he's known among the families on this side of the country.

Matteo's uncle, Giovanni De Salvo, is serving a life sentence because Rico testified against him in a murder trial. God only knows why Rico isn't dead for that deed, and now Vin's sister's good for nothing husband is caught in a photo with the rat himself only a couple of months after my father put Vin on his payroll.

Vin's head snaps up, his wide eyes first locking on mine and then going to Levi's. "Are you fucking kidding me?" he barks out, snapping his jaw closed as he stares his brother-in-law down. About the time his face reddens with anger at the realization that Levi has fucked him over, the sound of screeching tires from outside makes my body tense, knowing whoever walks inside isn't going to show the least bit of sympathy for Vin, even if he didn't know Levi was involved with Rico.

My head swings from Vin to Matteo. "Whatever happens, I need you to *not* react. Don't say a word, Matteo. Don't even move a muscle."

"What's going on?" Matteo inquires in a calm but cautious tone. I don't get the chance to answer his question before I hear the bell on the door jingle, signaling someone has swung it open.

"Trust me," is all I have time to say and I pray he hears the plea in my voice.

"Sienna," Vin whispers, pulling my attention back in front of me as a set of heavy hands land on my shoulders.

"You shouldn't be here," Ren muses, making me relax for the first time since I arrived. *My twin*. Ren isn't just my brother, only older than me by two minutes, he's my best friend too. Him, I can work with. Vin might have a chance at surviving the night. It's a small chance, but a chance, nonetheless.

"Go home, Si." *Fuck!* Domenico.

"I'm good." I reply, my eyes finding Matteo, issuing a silent order not to make one move. His life depends on it.

"You broke my fucking nose!" Levi finally sputters out.

Dark, sinister laughter comes from behind me and Ren squeezes my shoulders, as if to say, 'way to go.' "Motherfucker, you're lucky that's all she broke. Let me guess, elbow?"

Dom lets a snicker slip past his lips as he comes to stand to the side of the table between Vin and me. "Definitely an elbow. Left one at that," Dom responds. "If it'd been her right cross, he wouldn't have any teeth left."

"Yeah," Ren agrees. "I've been on the receiving end of her knuckles. Not something I recommend if you can avoid it."

I tip my head backward, looking up at my brother, and give him a *fuck you* stare right back. Lorenzo will never get over the fact that I knocked out two of his teeth—baby teeth—once upon a time. He's such a whiner.

"Take him," Dom orders to someone I can't see with Ren blocking my view behind me. Vin starts to rise but he's met with resistance when Dom places a firm hand on his shoulder, shoving him back down into his seat. "Him too," he says, and I realize he's motioning to Matteo.

"He stays," I breathe, the fire in my voice coming out as a warning to whichever one of my father's men that's approaching.

Ren's eyes dip down to mine and then skate over to Matteo's. It's only a second, two at the most, before he realizes *who* is sitting next to Vin.

Matteo De Salvo isn't a "made man," though his father grew up in a "connected" family. His mother didn't want that life for herself or her family. I'm guessing his dad didn't either. Matteo grew up somewhat normal, but that doesn't mean he isn't a force to be reckoned with. He's a boxer, the current reigning world champ at that, the same as his father once was years ago, only Matteo is three times the fighter his old man was.

Dom holds up his hand, halting one of the men. I have to give it to Matteo, he seems to be listening to me, though there is no doubt that he knows who my brothers are. Even someone like him knows you don't come out the winner going up against a Caputo.

Dom's chin dips, his eyes meeting mine. The three of us have our dad's dark brown eyes, but Domenico's are a shade darker, almost appearing black. Everything about Dom is darker than Ren and me. His olive skin, a tint darker no matter how much sun I get. Even his black hair looks blacker, shinier than Ren's and mine. "Don't you think you're a little too old for a schoolgirl crush, little sister?"

"Sister?" Matteo questions, opening his mouth for the first time.

Bet he didn't see that coming either.

I didn't attend the same private school my brothers did. My parents thought it would be safer for me to go by my first and middle name—mom's maiden name—instead of the last name on my birth certificate, and that if I attended public school then no one would realize I was the only daughter of Antonio Caputo.

And it worked.

To the outside world, I was Sienna D'Angelo. It's like everyone forgot Tony and Ari had twins. That was until I graduated high school and wanted in, the same as my brothers—well, as *in* as Dad would allow.

I don't respond to Dom's question; not like he expected me to. "He stays," I repeat.

"The boss said to bring everyone back," Dom argues.

"The *boss* can take it up with me if he has a problem with *my* decision." Dom arches an eyebrow. "We both know you aren't going to go against me on this, Dom." I look up once again. "And neither are you, Ren."

That's the thing about my brothers and me. We'll beat each other up until we're black and blue and bleeding and feeling like we're five minutes from death, but we'll also back each other up against anyone, including the boss.

"What the fuck?" Matteo spits. I don't hear the knife slip from Ren's sleeve or realize what he's doing until the blade digs into the flesh below my jaw. I didn't need to either. I knew it was coming. Ren is predictable with certain things, but only to Dom and me.

We love making each other bleed. It's sick, I know, but it's what we've been doing since we were kids, and I'm the one that started it. The first punch I threw when I was six years old was the beginning of my addiction to violence. It's an addiction that grew, but I was forced to hide it. As siblings, we never had to hide that part of ourselves from each other.

"Trust me, Matteo," I insist, my eyes never leaving Ren's. The movement of my jaw causes the blade to nick my skin, and that irritates Ren because he isn't the one to make me bleed—I am.

There will be a cost to me saving Matteo's ass and this is just the start. Later tonight, when I step onto the mat with my brothers, the cut under my jaw is going to split open at the first hit Ren lands with his knuckles.

I don't let my brothers treat me like some weak little princess they have to protect. I'm perfectly capable of holding my own and protecting myself. Our dad made sure of it after someone invaded our home and beat our mother to death when I was a kid. The attack was personal. She was brutalized and then shot in the chest. Ren and I were seven and Dom was eight. Dad hasn't been the same since.

"See ya later, *princess*," Ren taunts, using our father's nickname for me. He shoves off me and I hear his boots retreating toward the exit.

"Let's go," Dom orders, fisting his fingers around the material of Vin's shirt.

"Word of advice, Vin." I meet his worried stare. "Don't beg and look him in the eyes."

Dom jerks him up and out of his chair. Within seconds, Vin is escorted out of the bar and into Dom's awaiting Range Rover that's no doubt double parked in the middle of the street like he's the authority in this city. Then again . . . maybe he is.

He is my father's second-in-command, the underboss. Technically, our grandfather is third, but none of us see him as such, so to my brothers and me, Ren being third and I'm fourth. Very few people outside of my father's organization know that—and that's exactly how Daddy likes it. *His little chameleon, his little Mike Tyson as he sometimes calls me.* I manage the money and other aspects of our businesses. Never have I gotten my hands dirty like Dom has.

"What the hell just happened?" Matteo's lethal voice assaults my ears, but the sound is so unwelcome that I don't acknowledge his question.

What would I say anyway?

Blowing out a breath, I let my forehead fall against my left hand where my elbow rests on the aged wooden table. My middle finger rubs away the tension between my eyes—or attempts to without much success. I just sent my friend to the slaughterhouse. *What kind of person does that make me?*

A Caputo. That's who I am, after all. I'm headstrong, stubborn, set in my ways—the same as the men in my family. I'm just like them down to the marrow in my bones.

"Sienna!" My name comes out of Matteo's mouth like a hiss. It's the first time I've ever heard him utter my name. Ordinarily, I'd be shocked.

I'm about to tell him to fuck off when movement to my right catches my attention, putting my body on guard. My eyes fly up, meeting Bennett's. He may be the bartender here, but I've known him since elementary school; nearly as long as I've known Matteo. He was the only one in school that knew my real identity, and to my knowledge, never breathed a word to anyone else about me. His father was an associate of mine, so . . .

"Drink it, Si." He shoves the tumbler into my palm as his hard eyes bore down on me. Without breaking our stare, he wraps my fingers around the glass. "You need it." With a sigh, his light brown eyes soften a hair. "You've never let anyone, including me, see you shake. Don't start now."

My jaw locks, my teeth grinding together when I realize there's a slight tremble coursing through my body. It pisses me off. Lifting the glass to my lips, I knock my head back, swallowing the amber content in one gulp, enjoying the burning sensation that goes down my throat before warming the pit of my stomach.

It's rare that I drink, but sometimes this life gets under my skin, like today. I'm just usually better at hiding it.

"How are you a Caputo?" Matteo demands.

So, he finally put that together.

My eyes land on Matteo, but I don't answer this question. He should be thanking me for saving his ass, but I'm not going to point that out. Instead, I stand and walk out the same door that I entered.

Fuck him. I didn't exist to Matteo De Salvo in elementary school. I didn't exist to him in junior high or even high school, so I might as well not exist to him now either.

I refrain from throwing my middle finger in the air for good measure.

CHAPTER 2
MATTEO

How the hell is Sienna D'Angelo—the good girl that used to stare at me nonstop all throughout school like a little creeper—a Caputo? Is she adopted? A long-lost relative that was sent to live with them?

Nothing that just transpired makes a lick of sense. And what has Vin gotten himself into? What did he almost get *me* put in the middle of? That's what I want to know.

If Sienna hadn't shown up, it was clear the Caputo boys would have tried to take me when they took Vin and his shit for brains brother-in-law, Levi King. I don't know what would have happened if she hadn't been there or spoken up. The Caputo brothers weren't alone either. They had three goons with them. I'm a damn good fighter—some would say the best that there is—but I don't think I would have been able to take on all five of them. One thing is for sure: they wouldn't have gotten me out of this bar without dragging my unconscious body out of here.

Sienna D'Angelo, or is it Sienna Caputo? Hell if I know. One thing I do know is the woman that sat across from Vin tonight is not the same girl I remember from North Montego High. The girl I remember was a mouse. The woman I saw today was a force to be reckoned with.

She ordered Tony Caputo's two sons to stand down and they obeyed her. Granted, Lorenzo pulled a knife on her, but she wasn't afraid. If anything, her eyes lit up the second the blade met her silky, olive skin.

Fuck me. I'm getting a hard-on remembering the way she looked when Ren held that knife to her flesh. Jesus, I'm sick in the head. But then, I've always known that.

There was more to Sienna than her muted beauty that drew me to her. Maybe it was the way I'd catch her staring at me or the subtle blush she'd get when she realized she had been caught. Like I said, she was a mouse. She dressed like a proper girl, an innocent little thing. To my knowledge, she didn't date in high school. She was plain and stayed under everyone's radar. I didn't understand why my own eyes would drift to her more often than I care to admit.

I hated that I'd get a chub in the middle of class when the teacher would call on her and Sienna's rich, buttery voice would respond. It made zero fucking sense, because I'm not attracted to the good-girl type. They do nothing for me.

Sienna did.

Now I'm wondering what I missed.

Is there more to Sienna D'Angelo—if that's even her real last name—than she let on?

"You ready to tab out or do you want another beer?" Bennett questions, bringing me out of my thoughts. My eyes flick up to where he stands on the other side of the table, the same place Domenico stood minutes ago before hauling Vin off to God knows where.

"What do you know about Sienna D'Angelo?" I probe.

"Do I look like someone that wants to be on the Don's radar?" His brow arches. "You want information on Sienna, ask Sienna." And with that, he tosses my tab on the table in front of me and walks back to the bar, not sparing me another look.

That's my cue to get the hell out of dodge.

Maybe he's right.

Maybe I will ask Sienna.

Maybe I'll get my dick wet in the process and her out of my system at the same time.

Throwing three twenty-dollar bills down to cover not only mine but the others' bill too, I stand, shoving my chair back and then I step from behind the table.

That sassy mouth of hers would fit perfectly around my cock.

The thought of her on her knees with my hands in her long, black locks, while shoving myself down her hot throat until she gags makes my boy twitch from inside my pants at that very image.

If I didn't have to meet my ex at my place in half an hour to get my daughter for the weekend, I'd hunt that pussy down tonight and get the deed done. But alas, I have responsibilities, so it'll have to wait.

CHAPTER 3

ANTONIO

Eighteen Years Ago

I have twenty large on Pete De Salvo, and though he is the brother of a man known to be my sworn enemy, the bastard is too good in the ring not to bet on him. His opponent doesn't have a shot at winning the heavyweight title from De Salvo. Everyone thinks Ron Hogan got lucky when he knocked out Johnny Montaigne last month, but I know different.

Luck didn't have jack shit to do with Hogan's win. Montaigne took a wad of cash to go down in the third round. Only a worthless piece of shit does that, and although I haven't been on friendly terms with anyone from the De Salvo family since I severed a friendship, that's not a term I would use to describe any of them.

Pete, just like his brother, will fight for the win every single time. I'd bet my life on it, because it's what I would do. In many ways, Giovanni and I are a lot alike. There was a time we were best friends, then he was witnessed going after something I'd already claimed, and that was the end of a sixteen-year friendship.

A small shadow pulls my attention away from the match when her tiny body blocks my view of the television screen.

"Daddy," she calls out as her small hands plant on her hips. Her nightgown makes her look every bit of the princess my little girl is, and I can't help the curve my lip forms at the sight of her and her unruly jet-black locks that fall to the middle of her back, much like the Asian girl on her gown from one of her favorite movies.

"Yes, princess?" I ask, setting my tumbler down on the end table to my right. Opening my arms, I silently beckon her to climb onto my lap. She continues standing there looking at me until her head twists and she briefly looks over her shoulder at the boxing match broadcasting on the TV behind her. When her head comes back around, she steps forward, doing as I request.

"What's that?" she inquires, her innocent brown eyes set on mine as she nods her head back toward the television; eyes I pray are never tainted by the world we live in or the life she was born into.

"The men fighting on the television?" I ask for clarification, and she nods her head. "It's a boxing match. What they are doing is called boxing."

"I want to do that," she tells me with the most serious expression I've ever witnessed on her pretty face. I quickly bite down on the inside of my cheek to keep myself from laughing.

"Princess . . ." I draw out the nickname I gave her seconds after she was placed in my arms on the day she was born. She was born last, only two minutes after Lorenzo, but a baby she has never been. Not that I can tell Domenico that. I swear that boy has been fiercely protective of the twins since the day he met them. "You're a young lady. You should be playing piano or taking singing lessons or dancing. Your mother wants you to do ballet. Don't you want to be a ballerina like other little girls your age?"

"No." She shakes her head and crosses her arms over her chest, giving me the same look she's developed over the years that often matches my own—determination. Without a doubt, I already know my little hellion is going to prove herself one way or another. "Ren!" she yells her twin's nickname so loud I cringe at the piercing sound. How someone so small can make that much noise is beyond me.

Within seconds I hear the tell-tale sound of little feet barreling down the stairs. My six-year-old son comes running anytime his sister calls him.

"Yeah?" Ren asks as he makes his way over to us, barefoot with dark-colored pajama pants and lacking a T-shirt.

"Stand right there," Sienna orders as she begins to crawl down from my lap.

What is she up to now? One never knows with Si.

"We're supposed to be in bed, Si. Ma is going to kill us if she catches us up this late." Ren isn't wrong. Ariana will tan their hides if she walks in and finds the kids in here with me past their bedtime. She may even throw a few swats my way for not ordering them up to their rooms, but the way I see it is if the kids want to tempt fate, then it's their little asses that'll pay the consequences if Ari catches them.

Sienna rolls her eyes and purses her pink lips like it isn't a big deal. My little rule breaker.

"We'll go to bed in a minute. I just need to show Daddy something first," she tells him. Her eyes flick up to mine, making sure I'm watching. "Don't look away, Daddy," she directs, the command rolling off her tongue like an order, making my lips twitch.

If this kid only knew—no one gives orders to Antonio Caputo and lives to take their next breath. Well, no one except my wife, that is. Ari has always gotten her way, but she is the love of my life, so her requests rarely feel like orders when coming out of her sexy-as-sin mouth.

I lean forward, my jaw coming to rest in the palm of my hand with my fingers splayed out, covering my lips and cheek and giving my daughter my full attention. To hell with the match I have twenty thousand dollars riding on. The scene in front of me screams all kinds of entertainment is about to go down.

Sienna takes a quick look at the television screen and then my eyes widen when I realize she's balling up her right fingers, making a fist.

"Prin—" I start to call out to stop her actions, but I'm not quick enough. She swings, her knuckles connecting with Lorenzo's jaw, sending my son to the floor. My jaw drops, but then I can't control the way the corners of my mouth curl up in a proud smile.

"Sienna D'Angelo Caputo!" That smile quickly vanishes at the sound of Ari's reprimand. "What in God's name were you thinking?" my wife scolds.

Sienna, on the other hand, just sighs and then turns to face me. "See, Daddy. I can do boxing." Her little brow lifts as if to back up her words.

"Tony!" Ari breathes, her tone coming out as lethal as my own when I'm pissed.

"Yes, wife?"

"You *let* our daughter knockout our son and did nothing to stop it?" Ari's tone is an accusation.

"He's not knocked out." I lift my arm, my elbow coming off the armrest as my index finger points toward Ren. "See. He's getting up."

Jesus fucking Christ, did that just happen?

"What did you do that for?" Ren asks his sister, looking up at her from where his ass still sits on the carpeted floor. His little brows crease, then his eyes round. Lifting his arm, he brings his hand to his jaw and I can see his tongue feeling around in his small mouth. "You knocked out my teeth!" he screams, and then tears spring to his eyes.

Well, shit.

I'm going to get my ass handed to me for this fuck-up.

"Oh, please," Sienna chimes. "They're just your baby teeth. You should be thanking me. Now you don't have to wait for Mom to pull them. And you get money." Sienna refuses to call her mother by the traditional term of "Ma" when referring to her mother. The boys call her Ma, but Sienna goes against the grain; always the one to be different.

"Sienna!" Ari fumes. "Get. To. Bed. Now. I'll deal with you tomorrow, but let's get one thing cleared up now, young lady. If you think for a second that I'm going to allow you to box or hit your brothers, or anyone else for that matter, you're dreaming. It isn't going to happen in this lifetime."

"That isn't fair," she throws back, stomping her feet.

"Do as you're told, princess," I intervene.

"Daddy!" she calls out, turning to face me, her hands going to her hips and her brows set with a deep line in the middle of them. "You can't—"

"Do not make me tell you again." Pushing out of my chair, I stand to my full six-foot-two height, cutting my daughter's words off as I take a step forward and grab her chin gently between my fingers. She's only six, and I'd never harm one of my kids, but this has gone too far. She needs to be put in her place. I run this house and that's the way it'll always be.

Squatting down to her level, I look my daughter in the eyes. "If you think dealing with your mother tomorrow will be bad, wait until you suffer my wrath. I don't think you're ready for that yet." I apply the smallest amount of pressure, attempting to place the fear of God in her more so than causing any amount of pain.

It must have worked, because her brown eyes double in size and then she starts to nod her head profusely, tears welling in her lower eyelids.

"Go to bed like your mother told you to do," I order, my tone harsh.

"Yes, sir," she squeaks out, pulling out of my hold. Without another word she turns, and I watch her as she races up the stairs as fast as her feet will take her.

"What about my teeth?" Ren cries out.

I flick my eyes to him. "Be a man and suck it up, Lorenzo."

"Tony!" Ari huffs out a breath before bending down and lifting Ren into her arms.

"I didn't know she was planning to go all Mohammad Ali on her brother, Ari," I plead to my wife as Ren sniffles, trying to control his emotions. *Good boy, Lorenzo.*

"Tomorrow, she is starting ballet whether she likes it or not. I'm not raising three boys. She's going to act like the girl she is, do you hear me?"

"Yes, of course, baby. Whatever you want." I smile down at my wife, then wrap my hand around her upper arm and pull her into me for a kiss.

"Ewww," Ren whines, but I ignore my son, finishing the kiss I started before pulling away and looking into his mother's eyes.

"What I want is for her to stop trying to outdo her brothers at boy things. She's a girl." Irritation mars Ari's beautiful face, but I'm smart enough not to dispute anything she just said.

Ari and Sienna are polar-opposites when it comes to things that interest them, but similar in the way they stand their ground. I'm not about to tell my wife that watching our daughter throw her first punch might be one of the proudest moments of my thirty-two years. "I'm sure she'll learn to love dance. Now, go put Ren down and come to bed with me."

She smiles up at me and nods, before heading in the same direction our daughter did moments ago. I watch my hot wife's ass sway from side to side, forgetting our daughter's drama when I realize exactly what Ariana is doing.

If she wants my dick, who am I to deny her? Maybe a fourth hellion is what my wife needs, because something tells me Ari is going to have one hell of a time molding Sienna into the proper princess she wants her to be.

Sienna is too headstrong for that. She's a Caputo, after all.

CHAPTER 4
SIENNA

Present

Walking into my father's home office, I shut the door behind me and see his head snap up, looking over his iMac at my approaching form. He'll be fifty in a couple of months, but he doesn't look a day over forty. There isn't one strand of gray to be found in his styled jet-black hair. He works out as hard as my brothers and me do. To the outside world, I can see why men tremble in his presence. He really can come off scary.

"Take a seat, Sienna," he orders, his tone already attempting to chastise me.

"Yes, Daddy." I comply, my voice sugary sweet, and I'm rewarded with an arched brow. "Oh, sorry. Of course, Boss."

"Acting like a brat is beneath you." He stands, folding his arms over his broad chest. He's dressed in his usual—an Armani five-piece suit. Tonight being no different from any other day or night, he's adorned in a black-as-night jacket with matching pants and a pressed black shirt and black tie. Dad hasn't been seen in any other color since the day before my mother's funeral.

People say his soul died the day she did, but I know differently. He just hides it from the world, the same way he made me hide my real identity for years. I know deep down he's afraid the same thing that happened to her will happen to me. It won't, but there's no telling him that. It's the reason seeing me with a cut on my jaw and a bruise forming around it gives him peace of mind.

He's okay with my brothers beating my ass and me kicking theirs. He's not okay with someone else hurting me outside MMA. God forbid anyone try. The devil himself might even fear the wrath of Antonio Caputo.

"Is Vin alive?" I inquire, sitting in the chair in front of his desk.

The way he stares at me makes my palms sweat, but I force my eyes to stay locked on his dark glare. Sitting back down, he steeples his hands together and leans forward. "He's still breathing." That confirmation relaxes my shoulders. "It's like he was coached on how to pass his test. Was that your doing, princess?"

I shrug. "And Levi?"

It's like a flame of fire ignites through his eyes at the mention of his name. "What do you think?"

Yeah, that bastard is probably at the bottom of the Atlantic Ocean by now; no doubt the fish are making a meal out of him. I shouldn't laugh at that thought—it's morbid, after all—but I don't give a fuck either. That dickwad got what was coming to him. You don't fuck over Tony Caputo and live to talk about it.

I told Vin on more than one occasion not to let Levi King in on anything my father's men told him or instructed him to do. When Vin found out I was Tony's daughter a year ago, he started begging me for an introduction, an interview to discuss working for my dad.

Why anyone on the outside would want anything to do with our world is beyond me. It got my mother killed. The mafia is nothing but living through blood bath after blood bath. It's not a life at all. It's a life sentence. I learned that at a young age, but when you're born into this life and it's all you know, you deal with it. You suck it up and move on. You even learn to like it in ways.

That's my motto.

"I heard Matteo De Salvo was there with them and you wouldn't allow your brothers to take him." It's not a question, which means I don't have to answer. I also know my brothers didn't rat me out, so it was one of the men on his payroll that's afraid of him.

I may have to find out who that was and properly introduce him to the *real* Sienna Caputo. It had to be one of the younger guys trying to impress my father. Little do they know rats aren't welcome in our family; especially if they're ratting out a Caputo.

"You're not to beat Paul's ass, Si." It's me who arches a perfectly sculpted eyebrow this time. "That's an order."

"Accidents happen, old man. I can't always be held responsible for who falls into my fist."

"Your mother would be ashamed of the daughter I raised." He sighs out a tired breath.

"Nah, she's probably wishing she could throw a punch as effectively as me right about now." *Oh, fuck. Did I say that out loud? Shit. Shit. Shit.* By the look in his eyes, Levi isn't the only one he's going to murder tonight. "Daddy, I didn't mean that the way it came out. I'm sorry," I say, trying to backpedal my way out of this mess.

The silence in his office is so deafening that I can hear my own heartbeat pounding against my breast plate.

The heat in his stare finally dies out, but I continue holding my breath. "In hindsight, Si, I wish I had made your mother learn self-defense. Knowing that you could probably kick my ass helps me sleep easier at night."

"Wanna find out?" My eyes light up at that very thought. I should feel ashamed for even thinking about wanting to go toe to toe with my father, but I'm not. In fact, the thought is thrilling.

"Do not look so happy at the thought of beating up an old man, princess." His brows dip and his lips purse. It's a much easier demeanor to sit in the presence of than the lethal one I just saw.

"Dad, you're not old," I chime back, relaxing in our usual father-daughter banter.

"And your little ass better not forget that either." One side of his mouth tips up in a rare smile. That's probably the biggest thing I miss about my mother. She made my father smile daily. He was happy when she was alive. Now he just goes through the motions of everyday life.

"We just need to find a hot little number to keep you in check. That's all." My own lips crack a smile at the way he cringes.

"Please do not ever say that again." I can't help the chuckle that fills the air between us when I know I've just grossed out the most dangerous man I know.

"Am I free to go now?" I ask, hoping I'm out of whatever hot seat Paul put me in. Dad is delusional if he thinks my hands are staying off his man for ratting me out. In fact, I might bring Ren and Dom in on it with me. If they find out what he did, his ass will be grass before I can get to him. My brothers are awesome like that.

"Am I going to have to order you to stay away from De Salvo?" He leans back in his chair, crossing his arms over his chest. It's meant as an intimidation tactic, but this form isn't so effective with me. It only works on Lorenzo.

"Why would I have anything to do with him? It's not like we run in the same circles, Daddy." *Not like Matteo has ever given me a second glance.* But I don't say that.

"Then why did you feel the need to protect him a few short hours ago?" he inquires, and I see the genuine curiosity in the eyes that's trying to see into my soul.

"Matteo isn't known for doing what he's told. Plus, he has a kid. I didn't want her to become fatherless tonight if Dom and Ren decided to get a little handsy."

He gives off a look that says he knows my answer is a stretch. Even he knows Matteo could take on Domenico and Lorenzo and likely come out on the winning end. Matteo is *that* good; even Dad bets on him in every one of his fights.

"We're done, daughter."

"What are you planning on doing about Rico?" I probe, even though I know I should have kept my mouth shut and left when he dismissed me. But I'm too curious. It's too much of a coincidence that Vin started working for my father and then his sister's husband is seen accepting money from a dirty rat like Fredrico Romano. Rico is up to something and I know my father aims to find out what that is.

"That's for me to know, and if I deem it necessary for you and your brothers to know also, I'll inform you all. Until then, behave and stay out of trouble."

"I'm a princess." I shrug, laughing. "What kind of trouble am I going to get myself into?"

"The same kind of trouble that you're bound to get your brothers into as well."

I stand, shaking my head. "Not *me*, Daddy." Smiling, I lean over his mahogany desk and place a kiss on his cheek, and then turn, making my way to the door to make my exit.

"Sienna," my father calls as I reach for the handle. I open the door but look over my shoulder before exiting his office. "Stay the fuck away from De Salvo."

"Yes, sir," I respond, like I'm the obedient princess he knows I'm not.

CHAPTER 5
MATTEO

"My dad's a badass."

I hear my daughter's voice ring through my thoughts, and I whirl around on the mat so fast I don't take the time to see the figure squatted down beside her from where she sits against the wall.

"Brooklyn," I scold. "Language! You do not repeat cuss words. Do you hear me?" I command, fuming that curse words fall from her lips like it's no big deal. I make it a point not to say those words in front of her, but her mother, on the other hand, does nothing to curb her foul language around our impressionable daughter.

"Well, it's true, isn't it?" Brooklyn doesn't wait for my reply, turning her attention back to the person next to her. "He's never lost a fight."

That's not exactly true, but it has been a long time since anyone has managed to knock my ass to the floor.

"I'm a lot more of a badass than he is." She throws her thumb over her shoulder, pointing at me, and something about her sassy voice sounds familiar—and sexy. "I could beat him."

"You're a girl. He doesn't beat up on girls," Brooklyn tells her, and I can't help but give a satisfied smile. She's right. I won't hit a woman, not even her mother, no matter how much I want to strangle that bitch.

"Too bad," the woman says, and I let my gaze fall to her. She plops down on her ass and twists around so that her back is to the wall the same as Brooklyn's, and it's then I realize who it is—Sienna D'Angelo, or Caputo. I still don't know which, nor have I thought of her again until now. "I could totally take your dad."

"Keep dreaming, lady."

"Wanna bet on it?" Sienna nods her head and then twists back to her knees. "How much money you got in that bag?"

"I got ten dollars," my daughter tells her.

"So, if I get him on his ass, that ten bucks is mine, right?" Sienna confirms.

"Can you not cuss in front of my kid, please?"

"What?" Sienna shrugs. "She dropped the ass bomb before I did."

I put my wrapped hands onto my hips and stare at the adult making bets with a five-year-old. Sienna pushes off the ground and stands up. I can't help but take her in. Her dark hair is pulled up into a high ponytail on her head. She's wearing a white rash guard that appears to be soaked in her sweat and glued to her fit body. I'm almost certain I can make out the outline of her nipples through a very thin sports bra, but I force my eyes to move on, not lingering like I'd like to. Her thick, muscular thighs are cased in red and white shorts that hang loosely, stopping mid-thigh. They have slits sewed into each side that allow for easy leg kicks.

Bet she takes kickboxing for the fitness aspect of it. And from the looks of it, it's done her body a world of good. This gym caters to anyone into serious MMA training to people looking to get in a great cardio workout.

I watch as her bare feet step onto the mat as she stalks toward me.

"You might as well give my kid the ten dollars. I'm not going to pretend to let you knock me out, babe."

Her mouth opens and a giggle rumbles out. "I didn't ask you to pretend, De Salvo."

She stops in front of me and I have to drop my eyes to meet hers once again. She's not quite a foot shorter than my six-foot-four height, but I'd be willing to bet she stands at five-foot-seven or eight inches tall. "Then would you like me to go ahead and put you on your back to get this over with?"

Her brown eyes track mine as she starts to walk around me. I follow, moving my feet and turning with her. "I'll have you on your back way before you have me on mine," she taunts.

I smile, because it's cute as shit that she believes the words that came tumbling past those plump red lips of hers. She doesn't have a stitch of makeup on, and she doesn't need any. Her lips are already stained such a deep red that it looks like she's wearing lipstick, yet she isn't.

"Baby, don't kid yourself."

"I'm not your baby, De Salvo," she challenges with a little too much venom, insinuating that's exactly what she wants to be—my girl. She used to watch me with those dark eyes way too often to have not had the hots for me. Domenico's comment about her schoolgirl crush comes back to me.

Yeah, she had a thing for me all right.

It's okay, though, because I'm pretty sure I have a thing for her right now too. She looks like a fucking panther the way her eyes track my movements. We're going around the mat in a circle and it's like I'm her prey. I'm not used to being anyone's prey; it's usually the other way around, but I guess this one time won't damage my reputation too bad.

If anything, I'll get some entertainment out of it, and maybe I'll pin my body to hers on the mat and feel what she has to offer. Sounds like a win-win to me. "You can be. If you want." My lips spread. "At least for a night."

"Trust me, De Salvo. You couldn't handle the wrath that would come from . . ." Her eyes skate over to where my daughter watches us, then Sienna's dark irises flick back to mine and she mouths, "fucking me," so that Brooklyn doesn't hear her, before continuing in a sassy tone that I'm beginning to like a little too much. "You can probably take my brothers, but my father is in a league of his own."

"So, you are a Caputo."

"All the way down to the marrow in my bones," she admits.

"Neither one of you looks badass from where I'm standing." Brooklyn sighs out a dramatic breath.

Lifting my arm, I snap my fingers and point toward my daughter without taking my eyes off Sienna.

"She's a mouthy little shit," Sienna whispers.

"Yeah." I break my hard stare, cracking a smile as I glance over to where Brooklyn now stands with her hands on her hips. "But she's a cute mouthy little shit."

"We doing this or what?" Sienna asks, stopping with her back to Brooklyn. A crowd has started to form near my daughter; mostly people that workout here, and a couple of the trainers seem to have taken an interest in me and the Caputo princess.

I wonder why I never knew that? Her brothers went to private school. Why didn't she?

Looking over Sienna's head, I see Michael, one of the Muay

Thai trainers. "Bring me my gloves," I yell, looking at him. He nods, turning to go locate my gym bag that's by my daughter's feet.

"We both know you only use gloves when you're in a sanctioned match. This is just for fun, De Salvo," Sienna says.

My eyes dip back down to hers. "You seem to know a lot about me. Still like watching me, do you?" I taunt.

That wiped the smile right off her face, which was exactly what I wanted to happen, and to prove what I already knew—she was a creepy little stalker back in the day. Guess she still is. That should work in my favor, though.

I'm caught by surprise when her hands suddenly grab me by the shoulders, and before I know it, I'm taking a knee to my lower abdomen; too close to my goods for my liking. Within a three-seconds span, she steps back, her foot lifts and push kicks me in the stomach—hard I might add—shoving me backward, and then Sienna advances, kicking again. Before I can defend myself, I'm on my back staring up at the ceiling.

The motherfucking ceiling.

That bitch put me on my back. How the fuck . . .

"Are you kidding me?" I hear somewhere off the mat, my daughter's voice laced with shock and perhaps a little pissiness—probably from realizing she just lost her first bet. On her dad of all people, the fucking heavyweight boxing champion of the goddamn world.

I finally raise up, propping my elbows onto the mat and stare up at Sienna's smug form. I swear my dick swells to twice its normal girth, and I don't even give a fuck that everyone, including this hot as fuck chick, can see it.

Go on, baby, look between my legs. Take in every inch of it. It's going inside you later.

She smirks and then turns her head to the side. "You owe me ten bucks, kid."

And that kills it, deflating my package in an instant. "Son of a bitch."

"I heard that, Daddy!"

Pursing my lips, I keep looking up at Sienna. Her demeanor is still smug; so smug that whatever is knocking around inside her head has her so engrossed that she doesn't see me flick my foot out, connecting it with the back of her Achilles heel, dropping her to the mat beside me.

Once I have her on the floor, I quickly move to straddle her hips, pinning her body to the mat with some of my weight. I'm pushing two hundred and fifty pounds, so I don't sit completely on top of her. I don't want to crush her; though something tells me she could take it and that has blood rushing back to my dick.

Leaning down, I cage her in by pinning my forearms to the mat next to her head. "Who's on their back now, baby?"

"Doesn't matter, Matteo. I got you first." Her eyes light up, and that paired with the sound of my name on her lips is beautiful—and confusing as hell.

"Siiiennna!" Her name is drawn out with so much venom it sounds murderous. That pulls both of our attention. Sienna's body shifts beneath mine as her head tips farther back. My gaze follows hers until they land on a middle-aged man wearing a designer suit. He's encased in all black, adding to what is supposed to be a scary-as-fuck look.

To most, I'm sure it is. It should be to me too, but I haven't met a person on this earth that scares me—not even the Boss himself.

I should lean down and capture her lips with mine just to piss him off, but Brooklyn is here, and I'm not going to confuse my daughter or let her watch her dad get killed in the same breath.

CHAPTER 6
SIENNA

I've never been more thankful for my poker face than when I was lying on that mat with Matteo's semi-hard erection growing while he was on top of me. I know he was holding back most of his weight as he straddled me, and I'm fortunate for that. It would have only amplified how turned on I was getting.

I'd worked up a sweat when I was sparring with Dom, so the wetness that had gathered between my thighs could have been played off as the liquid layer I already had coating me.

Jesus, it's been fifteen minutes since I hightailed it to the showers and I'm still hot and bothered. The look on my father's face was priceless. He totally wanted to murder us both. Matteo on principle and me because I had defied his request to stay away from the man. *As if I do what I'm told on anything else*.

Dad should know by now that telling me to stay away from Matteo is only going to make me want him more, and I've wanted him for a very long time.

Too long.

So long that I'll be damned if I give myself to Matteo now. He may be the hottest man I've ever laid eyes on, but there is one thing that even Tony Caputo can count on: I'm not easy. Matteo will literally have to pry my legs apart if he wants a taste.

I slap my wet hand against the tile wall of the shower as a moan rips its way up my throat and past my lips. "Oh, God!" *Oh, Matteo,* is what I really want to say, but I keep that locked inside my head as an orgasm rocks through me.

"Jesus, can't you do that shit at home?" I hear outside the shower stall I'm currently occupying.

I really have no shame, but hell, I needed that release, so whoever that was can fuck off. We're all adults here, except for Matteo's daughter—who he obviously brought in while he works out, and that was only because of *who* he is with it being an eighteen and up facility. If I need to masturbate so I don't get stabby, I'm going to do it.

After I shampoo and condition my hair, I soap up from head to toe, rinse, and then towel dry my body with a white, fluffy towel. Once I've pulled on a pair of distressed jeans and a black tank top, I slide into my boots and grab my gym bag with my dirty clothes and head out to find my father.

He's not hard to spot. He's the only man in this place dressed in a suit. He looks like he should be sitting behind a desk in a corporate office, and to most, I'm sure that's what they see when they pass by him on the street. My father prefers to drive himself wherever he's going rather than having a chauffeur like one would think.

Other than our two housekeepers, the only service people employed by my father are the men that work for him and the five tech geeks. Some of the smartest hackers in the world are on his payroll. They spend hours scouring the dark web and the worldwide web looking for anything and everything on people with power.

"I'm done," I announce, interrupting his conversation with Tim, the gym manager.

Dropping my gym bag to the tiled floor, I'm silent as my father eyes me from top to bottom. His dark irises finally land on my matching set and he blows out a breath, fanning me in the process. "You're wearing that?"

I glance down and then back up to the irritation marring my father's features. "What's wrong with the way I'm dressed?"

"You're not wearing that attire to Casa dell'Ariana."

"It's just dinner at a restaurant you own. What's the big deal, Dad?"

"It's a business dinner, Sienna, and I expect you to dress the part of a grown woman that's in charge of this family's money. Capisce?"

Well, when he puts it like that . . .

Casa dell'Ariana—or House of Ariana as I like to call it—is hands downs the best Italian restaurant I've ever eaten at. It's also the most expensive and lavish establishment not only in Great Neck, New York but all of Long Island.

After my mother's murder, my father moved us out of the city and over into Great Neck, just under an hour's drive to Manhattan. One year after her death, he opened his first restaurant; the one in which he named after his late beloved wife. Since opening the restaurant, my father is here at least twice a week, sometimes more.

He's dabbled in many businesses over the years, but Italian eateries and fitness establishments seem to be the most profitable. He owns a line of fightwear too, but only an elite few know this tidbit of information. His name isn't associated with the company, but my brothers' and mine are—D'Angelo. Putting the company under D'Angelo was an easy decision since the three of us share the same middle name.

I'm in charge of what comes in and out of all the businesses financially speaking. In other words, I'm the CFO and business manager if you want to throw out titles and shit. I was shadowing my father long before I received my business degree last year when I graduated college.

Dom, like our father, has a law degree and handles all the legal stuff that gets thrown my father's way. Domenico is smart, genius level smart. He's a lawyer by day and computer whiz at night. He graduated high school two years early and then got his undergraduate degree before entering law school. Dom's passion is computers; he only sought after the legal stuff to make sure the family's ass was covered. He passed the bar exam last year. Ren just entered law school at the beginning of this year and still has two and a half years left since he just wrapped up his first semester. My twin is the one that has a real interest in the legal mumbo jumbo.

Our father didn't force these duties upon us. In fact, he made us think long and hard before he allowed any of us to go down the paths we've chosen.

The thing about Dom, Ren, and I is that we're just as headstrong and stubborn as our old man; perhaps more so when you consider all three of us together. It made our dad happy that we all chose to work for the family. There is no one he trusts more than his three kids. We may be the only people on this earth he fully trusts, except for his father, our grandfather.

That doesn't mean he tells us everything, because he doesn't. And I hate that more than I care to admit. *Bet Dad tells Grandfather everything*.

I think of Grandfather as Daddy's counselor, his therapist, his advisor. The old coot can't keep his meddling hands out of shit, even though he hasn't been in charge for nearly thirty years. Grandfather had a stroke years ago, and at the age of twenty my father became the head of the family.

Grandfather eventually recovered, but Dad didn't step down. I don't think Grandfather liked that, but no one speaks much of it. Dad took over and that was that.

I'm not my Grandfather's biggest fan; only my brothers know I secretly can't stand the old bastard. They don't care for him either, but they respect him.

I don't.

I can't respect someone I don't trust, and there is something sinister about that man that I haven't quite figured out. He's the only person whose voice makes me tremble in fear, and even that doesn't make sense. I could take his old ass down in a heartbeat; probably before he realized what was happening.

My father changed the game when he took over. He has all legit and profitable businesses now. That doesn't mean he isn't also a criminal. He did murder a man last night, after all. Tony Caputo is a ruthless king who bathes in the blood of others, but he's not all bad. He uses his position, his money and power, to keep corrupt law enforcement and politicians in check. *Someone's got to do it*.

There are far more evil men and women in the political game than there are mobsters on the street.

"Antonio, when are you going to find a suitable man for our little Sienna?"

It takes everything I have to restrain my reaction to his question. As if to silently say, *fuck you*, I don't even look up from my phone to acknowledge the bastard is talking about me.

"Si isn't ready for a husband, Father," my dad replies from his spot at the table to my right. From my peripheral, I see my father pick up his glass of cabernet sauvignon, taking a small sip before setting it back on top of the white linen tablecloth. "She has too many responsibilities to this family."

"And the right man could take on those responsibilities for her," my grandfather adds from where he's seated across the table from me. I feel his hard gaze on me, but I continue scrolling down the page.

"Trust me, Father, I'm actually doing the men of the world a favor by keeping her busy." One side of my lips tip up at that remark. "It took her brothers three hours last night to make her tap out. She would walk all over any man, and then I'd be forced to put a bullet in his head for being a fucking pussy. So, I see no point."

A full-on smirk is displayed across my lips now as I scan the cost report from my inbox on the latest sales data from DEFY Gear and Apparel, our fight gear company. "Maybe if you'd sent her to an all-girls school, she'd act like a proper young woman instead of some butch broad that goes around beating up men to prove she's just as tough."

"There's nothing butch about me," I finally chime in. Glancing up, I look at my father. "I clean up quite well, don't I, Daddy?"

"You do, princess." He smiles, cutting his eyes at me, and they are full of life tonight; a rarity these days. "A far cry from what you had on an hour ago."

My father isn't big on informal attire. If there's one thing he could change about me, it would be how I dress. Dad would prefer me to wear expensive business-like suit dresses instead of my normal jeans, fitted tank top, and leather jacket paired with biker boots. Even though I enjoy dressing like the badass bitch I am, I can easily soften my appearance with a designer dress and heels.

I'll never admit it to anyone, but I like looking sexy, and I love the gazes I pull my way from men when I do dress up. Like tonight, half the patrons in the restaurant have cut their eyes over to our table more than once; though, that could have something to do with the fact that I'm sitting at a table with not only Antonio Caputo, but Raffaele Caputo as well.

My grandfather still has quite the reputation. He became a widower when my father was in college, but from what I've heard, he wasn't a faithful man to the grandmother I never knew. It's another reason I'm not fond of him. He's seventy-five for Christ's sake, yet he's still photographed with women that are younger than my twenty-three years.

There is a big gross factor to that.

"Besides," my father continues, "it makes me proud to know that she can protect herself. In the world we live in today, a woman needs certain skills. As a father, I like to think I've made sure Sienna is adept at anything she may need to handle herself."

Our waitress stops next to my father, and without speaking a word, she tips up the bottle of wine in her hands, refilling my father's glass. She then smiles, meeting my eyes.

"No, thank you," I say and then pick up my glass, taking a sip of cool water.

"It's unnatural as an Italian to not drink a glass of wine with dinner, Sienna," my grandfather comments while waiting on his own glass to be filled. "Seriously, Antonio, are you even sure she's yours?"

I swear I can see a dark fire ignite behind my father's eyes over my grandfather's rhetorical question. I place my hand over my father's wrist, squeezing, but Raffaele Caputo's words hit their intended mark as he locks his jaw.

Anything that can be construed as ill-advised remarks regarding the subject of my mother should be avoided at all costs. Everyone knows that Ariana D'Angelo Caputo was the love of my father's life. Though my brothers and I have no issue with our father dating again, he never will. We know that. Hell, my grandfather even knows that.

"Why don't we get back to the reason we're all here. I have the data for the first quarter and the projections for the second. Would you both like to hear them?" I ask, before my father has a chance to open his mouth.

My mother is the only topic they've ever argued over to my knowledge. It's been almost eighteen years since my mother's death and my grandfather still can't help himself. Just another reason not to like the cocksucker. He's disrespectful in regard to the dead.

"Sure, Sienna," my father answers, his jaw finally unlocking.

"We took a loss in the first quarter with the launch and how much we placed into marketing. Of course, we knew the likelihood of that going in. We are, however, projected to make back three times our investment next month at quarter's end."

"I like that. Good work, Si."

"Why are we even in the clothing business?"

"It's more than clothing," I clarify. "And we're in talks with martial arts gyms across the nation and Canada to supply them with anything from boxing gloves to Jiu Jitsu Gi's to T-shirts and other fight clothing."

"You think just because you can scrap, that you now know something about fightgear?" My grandfather shakes his head.

"She can do more than scrap, and if you want to see for yourself, you can watch her in her first sanctioned match in July, Raffaele." My dad only calls his father by his given name when he's on the verge of losing his temper which often has to do with me. My grandfather hates the fact that I'm a woman who is a full-fledged member of this family with actual say in what goes on—to an extent, of course. When it comes to money, Dad listens to me over his own father when they disagree, which is a lot. But I haven't steered my father wrong yet, so until I do, I'm going to soak that shit up every chance I get.

"Sienna!" I hear my name being yelled in a close enough range that I turn, seeing a little girl launching herself at me. My chair scoots back, as if on some type of instinct, and the next thing I know, I have a brown-eyed, chestnut-haired girl in my lap.

"Uhh, hi," I say, looking down at her and not knowing what to do with a kid on my lap. *Do I hug her? Do I push her down? What the fuck am I supposed to do right now?*

"Jesus, Brooklyn," he scolds. When I glance up, I see Matteo standing in front of us, dressed in black pants paired with a black dress shirt. No tie is present, he has the top two buttons, with a hint of his chest tattoo peeking out. He and my father are dressed similarly, but it's Matteo who has me drooling, because let's face it, drooling over my own father would be all kinds of wrong. But here I sit, mouth hanging open and trapped by a tiny human on my lap.

Fuck. Me. He's positively delicious.

"Yeah, I don't usually say this, but okay, I guess I am. I'm sorry for the intrusion." His stare goes from awkward to pissed. "Brooklyn," he admonishes. Another aspect he and my father share. Dad often says my name as if I'm being reprimanded. "Come. Here."

"No, Daddy." She shakes her head and rolls her eyes at the same time. I can't help the snicker that escapes my mouth. Brooklyn twists her head around, looking back at Matteo. "I want to hang out with her. She's cooler." Her soft eyes slide to mine. "You got me in trouble for saying ass, by the way."

"I have a knack for getting people in trouble." My arms go around her to keep her from pushing my dress farther up my thighs. "Stick with me long enough and your backside will stay black and blue."

My gaze flicks over her head to see Matteo's expression, but his eyes aren't on either one of us. They're on my exposed flesh, and the way his hungry stare is eating me up, I'd say his meal wasn't very satisfying—that is if he's already eaten.

"Princess, you're done here, so you're free to leave," my father chimes in. His eyes go from me to the kid on my lap and then to Matteo's. "De Salvo." My father picks up his napkin and wipes the corner of his mouth with it. "I'll accept your apology if you take my daughter home for me. She's finished and I have other business to attend to."

"Of which I'm sure you require your business manager," I add, because . . .

What the fuck?

I literally take a double look at my father's easy form. Only a couple of hours ago he was angry that I was within Matteo's breathing vicinity and now he's asking him to escort me home?

"I don't, Sienna. You can go," he retorts, not giving Matteo another glance or seeing if he agrees.

"Oh, goody. Thank you, Mister," Brooklyn squeals with giddiness in my father's direction, then turns her head to look up at me with a big, bright smile. "You can come home with me. Do you like Barbies? Xbox?"

"My granddaughter wouldn't know what a Barbie was if one fell into her lap."

"I would too." I stand, gathering Brooklyn up, and place her on my hip. Turning toward Matteo, I'm caught off guard again when I take in the strange look on his face as he eyes me, or his daughter, or both of us. "You heard Daddy. You're taking me home."

"My home," my father clarifies from behind me.

"Tonight just got way better," Brooklyn hollers, and the whole restaurant looks our way.

I can't help but laugh as I pass Matteo, who still hasn't said a word. "Maybe, kid. Just maybe, it has."

Six years ago

The back of my neck tingles when I sense someone watching me.

It's her! I know it's her. It's always Sienna D'Angelo.

She looks like a choir girl in her knee-length dresses, a white cardigan draped over her shoulders, and her wild black hair pinned back with a barrette. She does her Italian heritage an injustice by dressing like a forty-year-old schoolmarm.

Then again, maybe she's related to Principal Harkins. Or maybe she was adopted by an old couple. I've never seen her parents at school functions. My mom is at every school activity, which forces me to be at them too. Never seen little miss goody two-shoes at one—not that I've looked for her, because why would I?

Leaning back in my school desk, I roll my head to the right and glance over my shoulder. *She's quick, I'll give her that.* Her eyes avert, but not before I saw her head bend forward like she was reading her textbook. She wasn't. Her dark stare was solely on me, like always.

It was weird in elementary school, somewhat intriguing in middle school, but in high school it's gotten a little creepy. It's like I have a stalker that I can't confront or beat up. Even I have my limits, and hitting a girl is one of them.

Fingers slide over my shoulders and down my chest, her arms wrapping around me, and then I feel Kennedy's lips next to my ear. "She's watching you again, Matty. It's annoying me."

"It annoys me every time you call me that. It's not my fucking name," I bark out in a low tone.

"But I like it. It's mine, and you're mine," she coos from behind me.

Kennedy and I have dated on and off since ninth grade. We're currently on again, but as our senior year draws to a close, so will our relationship—she just doesn't know it yet.

"Miss Sellers, please keep your hands to yourself and get back to your schoolwork before I move you," Mr. Pacini calls out from where he's seated at the front of the classroom behind his desk.

Her hold slips as she releases me, dropping her hands, but I still feel her head close to mine. "Do something about the little freak. Or I will," she threatens, and then drops back into her seat, leaving me with a thought.

Maybe Kennedy is my answer. She's not above getting into someone's face and tends to be intimidating. I bet all she'd have to do is threaten Sienna once and that would be the end of her weird obsession with me.

Sounds like a win-win for me.

I tip my head backward, looking at Kennedy upside down while giving her a lopsided grin. "You'd do that for me, baby?"

"Yes, Matty, I would."

My smile drops. I'd take D'Angelo's eyes on me every minute of every day if it meant that I would never be called by that stupid-ass name again. My mother doesn't even call me that, and she's the only woman I'd allow to get away with it.

Righting my head forward, I feel *her* again, but this time I ignore the pull I always get when she's watching me.

Present

FROM WHAT I'VE SEEN SO FAR, SIENNA no longer wears those church dresses she used to wear in school, but tonight, she is a far cry from the hot as fuck chick that walked into Raymond's like a badass yesterday. She's still hot, but she's more beautiful, sexy even, dressed in a cocktail dress and five-inch heels. I can't seem to keep my eyes off the way her hips glide from side to side as I follow her and Brooklyn to the elevator.

Casa dell'Ariana sits at the top of a thirty-eight-story plaza hotel. The space is surrounded by floor-to-ceiling windows on all four sides. You can see the north and south bay as well as Manhattan, depending on where in the restaurant your table is nestled.

I'd like to say high-end restaurants aren't really my thing, but I'd be lying. I like good food. That's not to say all expensive establishments produce palatable meals, but this one does, and growing up in an Italian family, this food not only nourishes my body but my soul too.

This place has also become a Saturday night tradition when it's my weekend with my daughter. She's my regular dinner date, and I don't ever plan on giving that up. Besides my mother, she's the only other person to own my heart. The day she was born, I became a man and a father all at the same time. A girl I dated from time to time back in high school got pregnant. Although I never once considered making Kennedy a permanent fixture in my life, that changed the second I held my daughter. Even at nineteen I knew I'd do anything for those big round eyes that were staring back at me.

The elevator ride to the underground garage is silent until Brooklyn finally opens her mouth. "Can you teach me how to beat my daddy up?"

"Uh, yeah." Sienna bobs her head. "Piece of cake, kid."

"Hold up, you two. First, I did not get beat up today. Second . . ." I look at my daughter, waiting until I have her full attention. "You are not allowed to beat anyone up. And third, she tripped me and got lucky." I laugh. "Beat me? Me?" I flick my gaze over to Sienna's. "Not in this lifetime, sweetheart."

"Wanna go again?" Sienna deadpans, her right eyebrow arching.

"No!" I blow out a sigh. "Sorry, but I don't beat up girls."

She steps forward, Brooklyn still held securely in her arms. "I'm not a girl, or whatever it is you have in your head that I am, Matteo. It's like I'm always talking to a brick wall with you and you never actually hear me. So, hear me now, because apparently you've taken too many blows to the head. I'm not the woman you think I am, so stop assigning labels to me. I'll only rip them apart." She steps away, stopping when her back meets the shiny metal wall inside the small space of the elevator.

I'm left wondering what the hell that speech meant when the elevator stops and the doors open.

"Which way, De Salvo?" she calls over her shoulder as she steps out into the dimly lit, muggy, parking garage.

"Right," I reply.

Once I take Brooklyn from Sienna, I buckle her into her booster seat in the back of my black onyx Lexus LX while Sienna makes her way over to a car only a few feet across from mine. I'm too busy watching her backside as she ducks her head inside the backseat that I couldn't even tell you what make or model the machine is, and I have a perfect view from the back glass.

"Daddy, can we take her home with us?" Brooklyn asks, pulling my attention down to hers.

"No." I lean forward, pressing my lips to Brooklyn's forehead. "She's a bad influence," I say, pulling away.

When I'm in the driver's seat, I start the ignition as Sienna slides into the passenger seat with an overnight bag and her purse. She places both down on the floorboard between her legs, then she pulls the seatbelt across her body. When I hear the click, I know she's secure, and I reverse the vehicle.

"What's a bad influence?" Brooklyn asks.

Sienna twists around in her seat to look at my daughter. "Someone who teaches someone else to do wrong or have wrong thoughts." Her head cocks. "Why do you ask?"

"Daddy said you're a bad influence."

"Did he now?" There's humor in her question.

"He said I couldn't take you home with us."

"But what if I want to go home with you." I feel her eyes, and from my peripheral, I see her lips tip up on the sides. "Didn't you say you had Barbies for us to play with?"

"Yes!" Brooklyn squeals from behind my seat. "You really want to come play with me?"

"Of course. Sounds like the best Saturday night ever." Sienna sounds like a bratty teenager, making me grip the steering wheel, squeezing the leather as I pull out of the parking garage.

"No," is all I say, not addressing anyone in particular. They both heard me, and my word trumps theirs. I don't care how fucking hot this chick is. There is no way in hell I'm bringing her to my townhouse. For years she was weirdly obsessed with me, or something along those lines. For all I know, she has psychotic tendencies. If her actions yesterday are any indication of the type of person she is, then psychotic sounds like an appropriate term for Sienna Caputo.

And that's another thing—she's a Caputo. The mob. The mafia. Bad fucking people that I don't want my kid anywhere near. So really, that's the end of that. This broad is not coming home with me under any circumstances. I shouldn't even be giving her a lift home in the first place. *And why the fuck am I?* is a better question.

My eyes skate to the right, and though it's dark inside my SUV, those thick, tan thighs are on display in a way that my mouth practically waters at the thought of them wrapped around me. "Where to?" I ask.

There's silence as I pull to a stop at a red light. It gives me enough time to roll my head to the side, my arm stretched across the steering wheel as I look over to Sienna. Her arms are crossed over her chest, but those dark eyes have me at center focus. "Today would be nice."

"Maybe you should have asked my father before you carted me off."

"Real adult of you." The light turns green and I accelerate, driving through the intersection.

"I agreed to come over and play Barbies with a what?" She glances to the back seat. "A five-year-old?" She doesn't wait for my answer. "I'm not exactly on an adult level at the moment, Matteo."

"But you're going to tell me where you live, right?"

Her sculpted eyebrow arches, but no words fall from her lips.

"Yay!" Brooklyn breaks the silence. "Sleepover at my house."

"I don't think so." I look in the rearview mirror, giving her the same look that I give my opponents in the ring. She just grins even bigger, in no way intimidated by me like two-hundred-fifty-pound men usually are. "No, Brooklyn. It's not going to happen."

CHAPTER 8
SIENNA

Who would have ever thought Matteo De Salvo would end up wrapped around a girl's finger?

At best the kid is forty pounds soaking wet. With her big, round, ocean-blue eyes, she's cute, I'll give her that, but it's more than that. She seems to have some type of superpower when it comes to her dad. Is it just that she's his kid? Is that all it takes to get 'The Beast'—as he's called in the boxing ring—to bend to one's will?

He's different with her, but then again, my dad is different with me than he is with my brothers. I got away with much more shit as a kid than they did. If Dom or Ren had pulled the same things, they would have been beaten within an inch of their life—or so my dad sometimes threatened in order to put them back in line.

Threats never worked with me; still don't.

It's interesting to watch Matteo with his daughter. From

where I'm perched against the arm of his plush, oversized couch, he almost seems touchable, like I could walk up to him and run my hand down his arm without him flinching. That used to be a fear, and maybe it still is.

I watched him a lot when I was a teenager; even during my younger years, but never once did I have the confidence to put my hands on him. Even now, I still feel that pull. My palms itch at the thought, at the images I've conjured up. I don't want to want him, yet I want him all the same.

"Do I have to?" she whines from where she's craning her neck back to look up at Matteo. "I wanna play, Daddy."

"And you can once you take a bath, Iron Girl." Her eyes light up and her lips spread into a grin at the nickname her dad used. It seems to satisfy her, because without another word, she prances down the hallway that I'm sure leads to a bathroom.

"Iron Girl?" I question.

Matteo laughs, watching her. After a beat, he finally turns his head, his eyes meeting mine. "Just wait until she's done playing dolls and pulls out her favorite superhero costume. For the past year, she's been adamant that she plans to marry Iron Man when she grows up, so according to her, she needed a superhero name too."

"And is she?"

"Is she what?" His eyebrows scrunch together.

"Going to marry Tony Stark?"

"Over my dead body." His sudden seriousness has my shoulders shaking and a laugh rattles out of my throat. "So . . ." Matteo pushes his hands into the pockets of his black slacks. "Where's Vin?"

"Probably nursing his wounds if I had to guess." I haven't

called him today. I'm giving his stupid ass time to process how badly he fucked up by trying to bring Levi in. I told him no, but he kept letting his brother-in-law tag along on jobs anyway. It's not that he ever did anything illegal, and he wouldn't have. My father doesn't allow anyone but himself and Dom to do dirty work.

I'm not naive. I know certain shit goes down in my father's line of business. He typically keeps Ren and me out of it. Dom being the oldest, he's privy to things my twin and I aren't. The only reason I knew Levi's life was going to come to an end last night was because Tony Caputo doesn't allow loose ends or men on his payroll that have ties to families we're not on good terms with.

He doesn't take chances—not anymore.

Just because my father does less than honorable things doesn't make him a bad person. Like I said, he's ruthless in his pursuit of the truth. *A truth I'm not sure any of us will ever find out.*

"And the other guy you bloodied up? What happened to him after your brothers dragged him out of the bar?"

I shrug, not giving him an answer. "How do you know Vin anyway?" I ask, because it's something I've been wondering since I walked into Raymond's yesterday.

"I've known him for a few years. We met my senior year of high school. He started training at this MMA gym I'd been going to since I was a kid. Said he wanted to box, but after a month or two he just up and quit. He wasn't very good, and I guess he knew that too. Now I just see him from time to time when I go into Raymond's for a beer."

"Hmph."

"What?" Matteo asks, his eyes scrutinizing my thoughts.

"When I met Vin, he told me he'd never boxed or kickboxed

and didn't have any interest in it whatsoever. I met him my freshman year of college at the university's gym. He liked the weight machines, so did I, actually. That was the only thing I used there, and it was just to keep my strength training up since I couldn't train often during the week with my workload."

"Like I said, he wasn't any good. Vin probably didn't want to mention that he sucked at it."

"Maybe."

"The way you say that makes me think you don't buy it."

"Just cautious of people's motives."

"Does your brother put a blade to your throat often?" Matteo's face hardens like he's suddenly pissed off. "That cut wasn't that wide or bruised when you left Raymond's yesterday."

I can't control the slow smile that spreads across my face. I'm sure I'm giving the Cheshire Cat a run for his money. I'm good with makeup and I have it mostly covered with concealer and foundation. He'd have to look hard to see the blueish coloring or the cracked skin underneath my makeup.

"Why is your elbow bruised? It's not the one you used on that guy," he keeps going, and I'm guessing he takes my silence and smile as playing it off. I'm not. I'll tell him the truth. I'm not ashamed; quite the opposite.

"This," I start, pointing to the skin under my jaw on the left side, "was courtesy of Ren. He wanted to see his cut bleed more. The elbow is from hitting Dom in the back of his hard skull."

"Your brothers fucking beat up on you?" He sounds exasperated.

"No." My nose scrunches up and I shake my head. "If anything, I beat up on them. A lot of times it's equal blows—them not being pussies and all."

"So, you just like hitting men then?"

"I just like hitting period. And kicking." God, do I love the feel of my flesh hitting other flesh. It's like an itch I need to scratch. If I leave it be, the itch only intensifies. My brothers know this, my dad even knows this, so they give me an outlet.

Flipping my wrist, I eye the time on my smartwatch. "Do you have a second bathroom where I can change out of this dress?" I ask, grabbing my tote bag from where I placed it in the corner of the couch.

"You're not staying the night," he deadpans.

"I'm not staying the night," I mock. "I'm meeting my brothers in an hour and a half. Don't worry, Matteo, I'm not going to rub off on your little angel in that timeframe. Jeez."

"Brooklyn is no angel."

"But I'm the Devil?"

"Aren't you the product of the Devil?" My eyes flash with fire, his words hitting a mark I don't like. My father may have questionable morals to some—not me—but he'll never belong in the pits of Hell.

"Careful, De Salvo. You wouldn't like for your little girl to see me take your ass down again, would you?"

"Did I hit a nerve, *bad* princess?" He smirks, and it makes me want to wipe it right off his too-sexy-for-his-own-good face.

I lift my butt off the edge of the couch, standing, but as I take a step forward, his daughter runs in the living room—buck naked—stopping me in my tracks.

"Brooklyn!" Matteo scolds. "Go put your clothes on."

"I was making sure she was still here." She places her hands on her hips, but I turn my head, trying not to stare at little girl parts. "I'm ready to play now," she says in a much sweeter tone, and I know she's addressing me even though I'm not looking at her.

"Not until you put something on," Matteo fusses.

"I gotta change too, kid," I say, holding up my bag to show her. "You throw something on while I use your daddy's room to change. Okay?" I ask, bypassing her and heading down the hall. I don't ask Matteo which way. It's not a huge house. I'm sure I can find his room or the bathroom on my own.

Anything to get away from wanting to wrestle her dad to the ground while straddling him at the same time. Why I find that man hot, I have absolutely no idea; none whatsoever.

CHAPTER 9
MATTEO

She came out of my bedroom half an hour ago dressed in skintight jeans that had rips in the knees and up the front of her thighs, a pink racerback tank top and I swear to God she isn't wearing a bra, but I didn't see her nipples, so I'm guessing she has on those adhesive nipple covers that go over them. As slinky as her shirt is, there are no lines on her back indicating a bra—and yes, I looked.

She is so fucking hot. All I want to do is shove her curvy body back through the door of my bedroom and peel every layer off in an agonizing, slow manner, before sheathing my dick with her pussy.

Sienna didn't spare me a glance before she turned down the hallway and entered Brooklyn's room. I never heard Sienna's voice, but Brooklyn being Brooklyn, has been giggling the whole time. As much as it pains me, my daughter can go from fine one minute to low in the next breath. She's the same way with her highs. Like most parents, I want my kid happy, and it hurts my heart when she's having an episode. I'll take her highs over her breakdowns or distraught behavior any day of the week.

The lows are rare, but they still happen more often than I'd like. I can blame Kennedy all I want, because she didn't breastfeed our daughter, and I doubt she took any of the vitamins that women are supposed to take while pregnant. She smoked and she drank from time to time too, but then again, maybe Brooklyn is just Brooklyn and her behavior or emotions aren't caused by any of her mother's actions while she was pregnant. Maybe the way she is, is the way she was meant to be.

I try not to think too much about it. I love my daughter and I'd do anything in the world for her—except be with her mother, though I know she wishes we were together. She hates it when I drop her off. She begs me to stay every time. I've thought about it, but I can't stand the sight of Kennedy, and I'd kill her if I had to spend any more time around her than I already do.

"Matteo, are you listening to anything I'm saying?" Tristen asks from the other end of the phone. My promoter called me five minutes ago and has been going on and on about my next fight.

"Yeah, of course I am."

Nothing has been announced, but the rumors have already started. It's just the way the boxing world works, any fighting sport really, including the fake wrestling shit.

"I just told you to eat my nuts and you said, yeah I'm on that. You aren't listening. Also, you aren't a liar, so let's not become one tonight," he adds. "What has you so distracted? Got a hot piece of ass tonight?"

"Yeah, but she isn't on my dick like she should be. She's in my kid's room playing Barbies or some shit."

"You're not in the market for a stepmom for Brooklyn, are you?" His tone has turned serious.

"Hell no," I affirm, setting him straight. *Where the hell did that question come from?* "Do you ever see me settling down? Don't be fuckin' stupid, man."

"No, and I want to keep it that way. You being unattached is good for your image. I don't need some bitch sinking her claws in my paycheck."

"Thanks, brother. Tell me how you really feel."

"I do. I'm your promoter, not your manager. I don't kiss your ass like that fat fuck does. You make money, I make money. It's that simple. That lard ass just cares about the shit he shovels down his throat or the fat pussy he somehow pulls from being connected to you."

"Yeah." I chuckle. "And just how much pussy do I bring you?"

The sound of someone knocking on the door pulls my attention from the phone in my hand. I'm not expecting anyone, but Sienna did say she had a ride picking her up, so this must be it.

"Hey, Tristen," I call out, interrupting whatever it is he's rambling on about. "I gotta let you go. Someone's at the door. Can we finish this Monday?"

"Yeah, man. I should be at my office, so just stop by or text me and I'll meet you for lunch."

Pressing end on the call, I toss the phone to the middle of the couch I'm sitting on and stand. Once I get to the landing that leads to my front door, I jog down the stairs. After unlocking the deadbolt, I pull open the door wide.

"Yeah?" I greet him. He's a young guy, probably my age with extra meat on his husky form. He's wearing a rumpled blue T-shirt and baggy jeans with his hands shoved down into the front of his pockets.

"I'm the Uber driver. Been waiting on some chick for like ten minutes."

"Oh, okay." I laugh under my breath. *Good fucking luck handling her*, goes through my head. "Hold on. I'll grab her for you." I shut the door, leaving him standing outside on the concrete step, and take the stairs two at a time back up to the main level of my townhouse.

"Hey," I call out as I walk down the hall toward Brooklyn's bedroom. "Bad Princess," I singsong. "Your ride is he—"

I stop in my tracks, my feet still outside the threshold of my daughter's room. Sienna is lying on her back, but asleep. Brooklyn is half draped over her side with one hand wrapped around Sienna's loose curls and her other hand tucked underneath her body with her thumb in her mouth. It's a bad habit she has yet to kick. Sienna must have been reading a story, because there is a book facedown on her leg.

I can't begin to describe what I'm feeling as I watch the two of them. It's foreign, yet I don't dislike it. Kennedy never did this with our daughter that I know of. Brooklyn is sassy and can come off tough, but she's extremely affectionate. Oftentimes, when she's with me, this is exactly how I get her to crash out. Other than my parents, I've never witnessed anyone else cuddle with her.

Backing up a step, then another, my eyes don't leave their resting form. After a beat too long, I turn, leaving them be before I can do something like join them on Brooklyn's full-size bed. I'm a big guy, but I could still squeeze my tall, broad form in that bed with them.

The question is why do I suddenly want to?

Quickening my pace, I take the steps back down and open the

door again. "Look, man, I'm sorry." I pull out my wallet from my back pocket as I continue. "She fell asleep and I'm not going to wake her. Will this cover your time?" I pull out two twenty-dollar bills and flick my wrist toward him.

"Yeah, sure." He reaches up, taking the money. "It's cool. Thanks." I go to step back inside when he gives me the look I'm all too familiar with. "Aren't you that boxer? Matteo De Salvo, right?"

"In the flesh," I tell him. When I won the Heavyweight Championship title eight months ago, my face became recognizable on the streets. Sometimes it's still weird, like now. I don't know what to say to people. I'm just a guy; the same as this guy standing in front of me, but I try not to come off like a douchebag. He could be a fan for all I know.

"That's cool. Nice to meet you, man."

"You too." He nods, but doesn't say anything else before he pivots on his feet, heading back to a small car parked in my driveway behind my Lexus SUV.

Closing the door, I turn, but I don't head up the stairs. Instead, I stand here looking up and not knowing what to do.

Do I leave her be?

Do I move her to my bed and sleep on the couch?

Do I move her to my bed with me in hopes she wakes up handsy? Nah. My mom would beat my ass if I pulled that shit on a woman, even if that woman is connected to the very people she despises—the mob.

If there is one person in my world that I actively try *not* to piss off, it's my mother, Martina De Salvo. She may not be a part of Sienna's world—whatever world that really is—but she is an Italian woman through and through and you don't fuck with her or get on her bad side. Nothing good ever comes from that shit.

And if she knew a Caputo was in my house, let alone in her granddaughter's bed, she'd have my balls. I like my junk intact and unharmed, so, there is no telling my mother about this little change of events tonight.

I do, however, go back up and grab an extra blanket from the hallway closet, one big enough to cover them both.

I guess the princess is here for the night.

And with that thought, I head to my bathroom for a *long* hot shower. Of course, at this rate, it may not take long to get off from the image I saw walking out of my bedroom earlier.

I want to fuck her six ways from Sunday—and I plan to. Even if it's just to get her out of my system.

Until then, bad princess. Until then . . .

At some point, I fell asleep on the oversized couch in my living room. I didn't want to be down the hall, closer to where Sienna is lying asleep in Brooklyn's room. I wanted to be closer to the door in case she decided to sneak out.

I don't even know why I care if she did.

Don't I want her to be gone? Hell, I didn't even want her here in the first place, but I can't seem to tell my daughter no when she's excited over something.

Noise jars my body upright and my eyes fly open. There is sunlight shining in from the sheer curtains hanging in front of the bay window that overlooks the small front yard. It's morning, and it seems to be early. My head swings around when another round of banging sounds from down the stairway. Whoever is beating on my door is about to get his ass kicked. The fucking neighbors can probably hear the person hammering down on my front door.

Jogging down the stairs, I flip the lock and then swing the door open. My face is a fury of heat and my body itches to lay this fucker out when my forehead is met with cold, hard steel as my eyes connect with Tony Caputo, the Boss himself.

"Where's my daughter?" he demands, not a lick of friendliness in his tone to be found.

"You mind removing that gun from my head," I spit out.

"I do mind. Don't make me repeat myself." His voice is calm, but it's laced with more venom than a cobra.

I sigh out a breath, knowing that if I don't tell him something, he's liable to pull the trigger.

"If I had to guess, I'd say she's still asleep," I answer. I don't like guns or knives, or any weapon for that matter. My fists have always carried enough punch to do the job.

He doesn't retract the weapon; instead, he presses it harder against my skull, no doubt leaving an indent. "De Salvo, I wouldn't give *you* permission to date my daughter, much less bring her home with you to bed."

I stay silent. It's on the tip of my tongue to inform him she didn't sleep in my bed or with me, but my mouth suddenly won't open. In fact, it's sealed fucking shut. *Permission, my ass.* That woman doesn't give two shits about asking permission for anything.

Shuffling from behind me makes my body aware that someone—Sienna being the only likely one—is coming down the stairs. Brooklyn can't make that much noise.

"Daddy, stop pointing a weapon at Matteo." There's no heat behind her words. She isn't worried for me, so does that mean I shouldn't be either or does she simply not care if her dad fills me with lead?

"Get in the car, Sienna. Do as you're told for once," he demands, his eyes never veering from mine. I have to hand it to Tony, he's more intimidating than any fighter I've been in the ring or on a mat with.

"I'm twenty-three," she points out on a huff like it's something he doesn't realize.

"I don't give a fuck if you're thirty-three, forty-three, or fifty-fucking-three. Go get in the goddamn car, Sienna." Tony finally flicks his dark eyes to his daughter. Sienna stopped next to me on my left side just inside the doorway.

She turns her body and tips her head back. "You're on your own, big guy," she mutters, as she pats my bare stomach with the back of her hand before stepping around her father. Her touch makes my abdomen flutter with something I can't quite decipher, and right now isn't the time to do so.

"The next time I tell you to escort my daughter home, take her the fuck home. And De Salvo, don't let me catch her here again. It won't end well for you." With those final words, the barrel of the gun is removed from my head. He pivots, walking away from me, then inserts the gun inside his designer suit jacket, looking every bit of the mobster he's known to be.

As much as I want to coat my dick in the juices from every orifice on her body, even the Caputo princess isn't worth all this trouble. Pussy is pussy where I'm concerned. It certainly is not worth receiving a gunshot wound—or death.

That ship just sailed, folks.

CHAPTER 10
SIENNA

Dad was *pissed* when he picked me up from Matteo's Sunday morning; so mad that he hasn't spoken a word to me in two days. This is the longest he's ever gone without speaking to me, and it's fucking with my head. I don't often have tiffs with him, but when I do, it's usually over in a matter of minutes.

In our family, we talk problems out. When talking doesn't settle it, we use our fists and knees and elbows to get our message across. The one that taps out first loses the argument. That's just the way it is—as it should be. We don't bitch or whine. We make each other bleed.

And we do whatever it takes to win.

Like right now, I'm barefoot in the boxing ring of the gym I work out and train at for my upcoming match, pacing back and forth. I have too much pent-up aggression and frustration running through me. If I didn't let it all out, I swear my head would blow up from everything that's constantly turning over and over in it.

This gym was the first business my father purchased when my brothers and I were still in diapers. Dad doesn't workout here since he has a home gym and a personal trainer that comes to him five days a week, but he used to train hard at this very gym when he was younger.

Tony Caputo isn't your typical forty-nine-year-old man with a Dad bod. When he's dressed in his designer suits, one may not necessarily notice he's athletic. Sure, he's trim and tall and that's easily seen with the naked eye. It's what's hiding underneath all his layers that people should fear. He's a viper full of venom. If he strikes, you might as well hang it up. You're done for. It's over.

"This is the dumbest idea you've ever had, Sienna." I ignore Lorenzo from where he's seated with his legs crisscrossed off the side of the ring with his back against the painted black wall. My personal trainer is out today. His wife, Jennifer, is out of town on a business trip and their son is sick, so Kevin is at home.

He'd be spouting off at the mouth, same as Ren, if he were here. I know this is dumb. Totally idiotic actually, and I'm acting like a punk kid.

So what?

It's Dad's fault. He is the one that's giving me the cold shoulder, not the other way around. It's not like I slept with Matteo, and he knows it. I told him. Besides, I'm certain if he actually thought something had happened between us, Matteo would probably be swimming with the fishes. At a minimum, he would have obtained a non-career-ending gunshot wound somewhere on his sexy frame of a body. The latter is more likely. I don't think my father would end Matteo's life for fooling around with his daughter. He respects him as a fighter too much, and betting on his fights is one of my father's simple joys in life.

One of his only *joys in life without Mom around.*

I don't think of my mother as often as I should. If I'm being honest with myself, I make more of an effort not to think about her, or the day she was killed. A shiver runs up my spine at the thought, reminding me why I avoid letting my mind go there.

"Nah," Domenico chimes in. "This is the most entertaining idea she's had in a long time."

I flick my eyes to my older brother, giving him a *go fuck yourself* look. He smirks as he leans his left shoulder against the wide opening of the room that houses two boxing rings and four heavy bags that hang from the ceiling.

Our father steps from behind Dom, entering the space. It's not often you see Tony Caputo dressed down. This is probably his everyday workout attire, but I've never seen my father workout with his trainer, or even when it's just him alone in his personal gym. His frame adorns a plain black T-shirt and black fight shorts with red trim that reach his knees. The material is loose, the same as mine, but I needed a lighter color today that didn't match my sour mood. My shorts are white trimmed in red with a matching racerback tank top over my sports bra.

Walking toward me, he stops outside the ring to climb up. Once he ducks his head and slides his body inside the ring, he stands to his full height–all six feet, two inches.

Crossing his arms, he stands there looking at me. No words leave his lips, and his dark eyes don't give anything away. Those eyes are hard, calculating, maybe even devious. The eyes on me right now are not of a father staring at his daughter, but of a man in charge of a lethal organization. This is the Boss, here to teach me whatever lesson he deems necessary.

Ren loves to say that I have our father wrapped around my finger, but that couldn't be further from the truth. The only woman, or person, that ever achieved that feat was our mother.

"Daddy." I greet him with a smile, but it does nothing to defrost his ice-cold features.

He steps forward, his pace slow and steady. Even though his chocolate brown eyes haven't left mine, I feel them everywhere, and it makes goose bumps break out along my arms. *I'm in such deep shit right now, I don't think I'm going to be able to crawl out of this one.* I don't let that thought show, though. That would give him too much satisfaction, and I'm the one that asked him to come, not the other way around.

He's mad, or furious. I don't know which. I figured we would do what Dom, Ren, and I do when we get angry at the other. We fight it out.

There is no doubt in my mind that the man before me can take me down without barely working up a sweat, but there is that part of me that wants to know for sure. I act a lot tougher than I actually am. You have to in my world. I'm the only female, and I'll be damned if I let dicks run all over me.

"So," I draw out, rocking back and forth on my heels. "How do you want to do this?"

His hands aren't wrapped. He's not wearing any boxing gloves either, but neither am I. Muay Thai is the sport I favor, but I've dabbled in a few different styles of MMA training. I started out with Brazilian Jiu-Jitsu and did it for five years. After that I got into kickboxing, which brought me to Muay Thai. There are too many rules in kickboxing that I don't care for. Fighters are too limited, which is why Muay Thai fits me better. Plus, an elbow to the head is the most satisfying move there is, and you can't do that in kickboxing.

My father may have a love for the sport of boxing, but he spent his youth doing jiu-jitsu—hence why my brothers and I started BJJ when we were little kids. Even boxing is limited. I can't for the life of me understand why Matteo loves it when all you're allowed to do is punch. He should try ramming a knee into some guy's gut so hard they feel it in their spine. Once you knock someone out, it's over. Where is the fun or challenge in that?

My brothers, like our father, love ground fighting, but I prefer to be on my feet. That doesn't mean I'm not good at grappling. It's just not as much fun in my opinion, and I simply love to throw a punch or kick the fuck out of someone.

My father's head swings to his left and his body turns. "Gloves," he seethes, the word coming out like an order.

Michael appears out of nowhere, walking up to the ring with two sets in his hands. He tosses my father his gloves and then looks at me, waiting until I walk to the edge of the ring closest to him. Holding the other pair up, I take them. They're my gloves, so he must have grabbed them from my bag.

"Back out, Si," Ren calls out to me. "It's the smart thing to do."

He's probably right. Okay, I know he is, but this is the only option I can think of that might get me back into Daddy's good graces. I'm certainly not going another hour without him speaking to me. He only does this to get a reaction out of me, and it works, every freakin' time.

"Stop ruining my entertainment," Dom chimes in. I don't bother acknowledging his comment this time. This is between Daddy and me. They didn't need to be here. I didn't tell them, so our father must have.

Walking back to my original spot, I shove my hands through

both gloves and use my teeth to pull the strap around my wrists, my eyes never leaving my father's, and his never leave me. He steps toward me, but once his gloves are secured around his wrists, he stops, leaving four feet between us. "Your brother is right, you know. You can back out." He tips his head to the side, his neck cracking at the forced movement.

"And you go back to giving me the cold shoulder?" I cock an eyebrow. "I don't think so." I'd rather get my ass served up on a silver platter than choose that option. And Daddy knows I won't back out. I asked for this. This is what I want. Once it's done, whatever shit he's holding against me will be over. Life will be back to its normal peachiness.

"Had I not found you some place you shouldn't have been, we wouldn't be here in the first place."

"Yeah, yeah." I roll my eyes. "My fault." I give him a snide smile, knowing damn well I'm acting like a brat.

"Tsk. Tsk." He shakes his head. "That's going to cost you, daughter."

I should shut up and take my punishment. It really would end better for me, but I've never chosen the easy way out of anything. Always the opposite.

"You sure you still got it, old man? Seems like you're doing more talking than actually doi—" Advancing in one quick stride, his heel hooks behind mine and he jerks my feet off the ground, knocking me on my ass. "Son of a fuck," I yell, and then snap my mouth shut.

"Keep running that mouth and using foul language . . . You're going to get your little ass dragged to the bathroom and your trap washed out with soap."

Laughter hurls out of both my brothers' lips.

Planting my palm on the platform of the ring, I push back to my feet.

"Where's your mouth guard?"

"I don't need one," I say, instead of answering the question.

"Put it in."

It's in the small pocket inside my shorts and I'm sure he knows that which is why he's ordering me to, but I make no effort to grab the flexible gel rubber piece that will help prevent my dad from knocking my teeth out. I don't like being told what to do. He could've asked nicely or he could have reached for his and in doing so, suggested I use mine too. But did he do either? No.

"You first."

"Another comment, Sienna, and I'll make you wear headgear too." He cocks an eyebrow in challenge, then smirks when I grind my teeth. I'm mouthy. I'm not stupid. I know when to keep my lips sealed and pushing Daddy any further than I have will only end badly for me.

Pulling one hand out of a glove, I reach into my shorts and retrieve the mouth guard and shove it in, then I squeeze my hand back into the glove without unwrapping it.

He just wants to shut me up. That's the only reason he wants me to wear it. Yes, a fighter should always wear a mouth guard when fighting, but even I know my father isn't going to go balls to the wall with me. Though, there is no doubt in my mind I'm going to lose.

In Muay Thai there are five rounds with each round lasting three minutes and a two-minute rest period between each round. Typically, there can be no more than a five-pound difference between fighters, but this isn't a regulated fight or a competition. This is Tony Caputo's form of discipline, so the weight class is out. There are usually judges that give scoring too, but I know my dad is going to make me tap out—probably within the first three minutes if I had to place money on it.

Lifting his gloved hands in the air, he stretches his arms out wide. "Waiting for you, daughter."

He wants me to come at him first, giving him the advantage. Daddy has enough of an advantage on his side. He's a more experienced fighter than I am and he has twice the number of years fighting than I do; not to mention at least seventy-five pounds on me. Plus, he has the height and reach advantage too. The chances of me knocking my father out or having him tap-out before I do are slim. All he needs to do is lean backward to be out of my range.

I shake my head in slow succession. Daddy's lips tip up.

Bringing my feet and hands together in front of me, I give him a slight bow, nodding my head out of respect, and he does the same. We're both right-handed, so getting in a stance, I step my right foot backward, putting most of my weight on my right leg. My left leg is out front, and my heel is lifted off the floor. Bringing my arms up, I ready my stance, my father doing the same.

It's hard not to be intimidated by the man standing in front of me. I've always looked up to him, and there is no doubt in my mind that I always will. He's the strongest person I know, both mentally and physically. Okay, maybe he's not technically the strongest, but through my rose-colored glasses he is. Matteo isn't called a beast for no reason, and ever since he won the heavyweight title two years ago, he's still undefeated.

But through my eyes, no man is bigger, tougher, or fiercer than my daddy. He's my king, and I will always be his princess.

The ball of his left foot bounces against the floor of the ring, the same as mine. My eyes are on his, but I need to pay attention to every one of his limbs at the same time. I can't allow one thing to distract me or I'll leave an opening for him to strike.

Daddy is the first to make a move, advancing and attempting a strike to my thigh with his right shin. I jump back, but the top of his foot nails his target. I don't wince, though it hurts like a motherfucker. This is a welcome pain, though I can't explain why. I love this, and I can't stop my lip from lifting as I walk the pain off, stepping to my right with my elbow still lifted, my guard still up.

Flicking my hip forward, I throw a cross punch, but Daddy dodges it easily. I follow through with a jab at the same time he dodges, nailing his gloves, but I'm not done. I lift my knee and snap my leg up, but he's quicker than me, and before I know it, he kicks his leg out, his foot connecting with my heel. My other foot comes off the ground and before it sinks in, my back hits the floor.

Fuck.

I try to verbalize the curse word, but because of the mouthpiece, it comes out like a frustrated breath instead. From the smirk on his face, he likely deciphered it anyway.

"Get up, daughter," he orders, and beckons me with the flick of his gloved wrist.

Blowing loose strands of my hair out of my eyes, I jump up, getting back into a stance once again. This time I wait until Daddy comes at me. We go back and forth longer than three minutes, longer than ten minutes, and at some point, he thrust kicks, nailing the fuck out of my hip. By the time I go shower, a bruise will be forming.

I get a hint of gratification when I nail him in the jaw with a jab that surprises him. After the shock ebbs away and after he stretches his jaw out, his smile is one of pride, and that warms my heart.

Knowing I can make my Daddy proud is one of the best feelings. It makes me feel stronger than I really am. His pride makes me feel invincible.

Of course, on the tail end of his "punish Sienna for not obeying," I feel as small as an ant. He takes off his gloves, throwing them out of the ring, and I follow, knowing I am about to get my ass handed to me, but I go in eyes wide open anyway.

We are done with standup fighting. It's time for the ground. It is time for Tony Caputo to show me what he is made of. And that is exactly what he does.

Daddy gets me into side control while I'm on my back. I manage to get an under hook around him, thinking I'm about to turn this around when I turn up onto my side. He can't see my face, but I'm sporting a smirk, knowing I have him exactly where I want him; I'm about to dominate my father.

It's my cocky attitude that does me in, but I don't realize his arm has gone underneath mine until his thumb is behind my head. The smile is wiped from my face and my eyes get big. In the blink of an eye, he's onto his feet. He moves, pushing my arm inward. I try to escape, arching back, but Daddy is much stronger than me and I don't have a chance in hell of getting out of the D'arce choke he's put me in.

I tap out without thought and he releases me, jumping up as I suck in a breath of air. He stares down at me as I stare up at him. His mouth is shut, but his eyes are saying, *lesson learned.* I'd grit my teeth, but I'm not stupid enough to make the slightest move.

"See you at dinner, daughter." And with those words, he exits the ring, not a drop of sweat on him, whereas my body is soaked.

Sitting up, I take notice of the crowd that's formed around the ring. *Great*. Everyone witnessed me get my ass beat by my father. *Fucking perfect*.

As my father is walking out, not acknowledging anyone, I watch him trip, nearly planting his face on the ground, but his hands shoot out, bracing his fall. Gasps echo off the walls and it's the only noise palpable in the room.

My mouth drops open, and that's when I see Brooklyn standing next to my father while he's on the ground. "My Daddy said boys aren't supposed to hurt girls." She crosses her little arms, purses her lips, and juts out her hip while her tiny brunette eyebrow arches high on her forehead.

I'm so stunned I can't even laugh.

"They're not," my father deadpans, lifting his head and taking in Brooklyn's form. Her head swings toward me as if to call him on his bullshit. "Disciplining a child is not the same thing as hurting one, little girl."

"She's no kid, Mister." Her nose scrunches up, and I must admit, it's cute. A smile forms on my lips as I push up to my feet.

"Oh, she's every bit of a kid; the same as you are. Don't let her age fool you." Planting his palms on the floor, he pushes himself to stand up. Once he's at his full height, he's at least three times as tall as Matteo's daughter.

"What did she do?" Brooklyn asks as I climb out of the ring, jumping to the ground.

"Brooklyn," Matteo barks out his daughter's name, and I'm not sure if he's scolding her or warning her to shut up. My eyes snap to where he's standing against the wall near Domenico. He's got a pissed-off look going on, but at the same time, he seems to be holding himself back too, his body rigid.

"She stayed somewhere she wasn't supposed to," my father tells her.

"Well"—her eyes squint and I have to bite back a laugh—"you're just a big meanie."

"Brooklyn Martina!" Matteo bites out.

I stop next to my father and Brooklyn. "Squirt," I greet her, smiling down. "I'm touched that you're coming to my defense."

My eyes shift to Matteo, noticing that his breathing is coming in and out of his mouth in a slow but hard rhythm, which makes me think he's about to lose his shit. Pushing off the wall, he storms out of the room, leaving Brooklyn here by herself, and I'm not sure if that's because I'm here with her or if he really did have to get away before he lost it.

My father bends and grips Brooklyn by her chin, his hold firm but still gentle, and tips her head back. "I can be a very mean person, little girl, but"—he lets a slow breath flow from his lips—"I've never once been mean to Sienna, and I never will. She's my little girl, the same as you are your father's."

"Awww, Daddy," I draw out in the girliest voice I can muster, and then I place myself between my dad and Brooklyn, causing him to release her chin. Stepping into his arms, I wrap mine around his waist and squeeze. I hope it'll show Brooklyn that my dad isn't the bad guy she's formed in her head. "I love you, too."

He kisses the top of my sweaty forehead, and then he leaves without another word. "So," she says, gaining my attention. "If he can beat you up and you can beat my daddy up, does that mean your daddy can beat up my daddy?"

I smile, because this little girl still believes I whooped Matteo's ass. I find that hilarious. Squatting down in front of her, I lean in so that only she can hear my words. "No one can beat your daddy's butt," I admit, curbing my language. "Not even me. Your dad was just playing around the other day. He didn't really get beat, *but*," I stress, "let's keep that secret between us. Capisce?"

Standing back up, I grab her hand, but before I lead her off to find Matteo, a strong arm wraps around my neck. I get a glimpse of a crown tattoo on the inside of his left forearm, telling me it's Lorenzo just before he tightens his hold, pressure squeezing my neck and fusing my back to his front. "Bet you'd like him to *beat* something of yours, sister," he whispers so only I hear him, and then his arm is gone just as quick as it appeared, laughter falling from his mouth. Walking off, he turns, walking backward. "You think he pounds *that* just as hard as he does his fists?" Ren cocks an eyebrow and I glance down at Brooklyn, praying that she has no idea what my brother is insinuating.

She isn't paying him any attention, thank God. Her gaze is staring out toward the open gym, and I'm guessing she's searching for Matteo.

"He tries that shit and he won't be the one doing the pounding," Dom chimes in, following Ren. "I will."

"You realize I am an adult, right?" I yell at their backs. Dom shrugs, but continues walking away without another word. Looking down, I tug on Brooklyn's hand. "Let's go find your dad."

CHAPTER 11
MATTEO

Disciplining a child is not the same thing as hurting one, little girl.

Those were his words only moments after locking *his child* in a goddamn choke hold. I throw my right fist into the heavy bag hanging in front of me, and then I follow with my left, my knuckles stinging from the lack of material that should be wrapped around them.

I have a fight in less than two months. I shouldn't be putting this type of strain on my fists. If my trainer, manager, or even my promoter saw me now, I'd catch an earful on how I could damage my hands. They're only worried about losing the money I line their pockets with, not my fucking flesh.

She stayed somewhere she wasn't supposed to.

Last time I checked, she wasn't underage, so it isn't like she needs permission to stay at a man's house. What is this, the fifties?

Stepping backward, I lift my right elbow and swing it across my body, nailing the leather bag and sending it swinging. Elbows aren't allowed in boxing, but it's something I've always got a thrill out of doing. Today, the usual adrenaline isn't coursing through my system like it normally does. Anger, on the other hand, is very much front and center.

She stayed somewhere she wasn't supposed to.

Who does that motherfucker think he is? It's not like I fucked her; not that the thought didn't cross my mind, because it had several times that night. I had to jerk off to her image in the shower after her father dragged her out of my house.

Even if I had fucked her, she is an adult. Does he really think she could still be a virgin? Has the man not seen her? Now that thought is laughable—a virgin in her twenties.

"Hitting that bag mighty hard, big guy." Speaking of the fucking devil herself . . . A sigh leaves her mouth from behind me. "I think you left something in the other room," she says, prompting me to grab the bag with both hands, stilling its movement, then I turn.

Sienna stands three feet from me with Brooklyn on her hip much like she was a few nights ago when we left the restaurant. "Looks like she found me."

I shouldn't have left my daughter alone with her father, but had I not walked away, I'm certain I would have lost my shit on the man, and I'm not stupid enough to believe I would have walked away from that situation alive, so I walked to the other side of the gym where the other set of heavy bags hang and started punching out my aggression. Not the smartest thing I could have chosen, but it's my go-to to let off steam, and it *usually* works. Today, it doesn't seem I'm that lucky. My body is tight from my neck down to my calves.

"Nah," she tells me, a lopsided grin ghosting her lips. "I had to snatch scrappy up to keep her from trying to take out my brothers like she did my dad." Sienna laughs like it's a joke, and to her, I'm sure it is, but to me it's not, and that only fuels my fire more; so much more, in fact, that I twist back around, throwing my right fist into the bag as hard as I can. "Whoa, big guy. What's up with you?"

"Daddy is mad, Si." Brooklyn purses her lips. "Your daddy beat you up. My daddy doesn't like when boys are mean to girls."

"My daddy didn't beat me up. Didn't he explain things back there?" Sienna throws her thumb over her shoulder.

"Just like you didn't beat my daddy up," Brooklyn follows up, and I roll my eyes. The fire coursing through my veins seems to settle the longer they're standing here.

"Oh, I totally whooped your dad's butt." Sienna chuckles, her chest jumping up and down.

"If anything," I chime in, "I let you take me down to the mat."

This time it's Sienna with pursed lips as she cocks an eyebrow. "You still trying to play that angle, huh?"

"No angle, babe. Like my kid said, I don't hurt girls."

"I'm not a girl, Matteo." All playfulness in her tone is gone and that makes me eye her harder. Is she trying to tell me she's a woman or is she saying she's as tough as a man? Maybe both. Who knows? What I do know is that she is definitely a woman and the majority of them don't make a lick of sense most of the time.

"Daddy, I'm hungry," Brooklyn whines from where she's perched on Sienna's hip.

Looking at my daughter with Sienna's arm wrapped around her back, I'm struck once again with the same odd feeling I had the last time I watched them together.

Maybe it's that they're both mouthy shits who act like they're cut from the same cloth. But is that really it?

"Daddy," Brooklyn draws out. "Did you hear me?"

"Yes," I say, my eyes cutting to hers. "But I told you I have to get in a workout and . . . didn't you just eat before we left the house?" I ask, reminding her and knowing damn well she can't be starving. The kid doesn't weigh shit but eats like a grown-ass man.

"I can take her across the street to Mario's while you work out if you want?" Sienna offers, catching me by surprise. Si is grown, but no young adult wants to deal with a kid that isn't theirs. Then again, she was just over at my house playing Barbies with her and reading stories, so maybe Sienna is different—not your typical twenty-three-year-old that's looking for the next party or club to hit up.

If not, why isn't she?

If given the chance and I didn't have Brooklyn or a strict training regime, I'd like to think I'd be one of those twenty-something-year-old partiers. But I never got that chance. I didn't even get to go to college. Once Kennedy got pregnant, I had to look for a job that paid well and I had to figure it out fast. I thought for sure my boxing dreams would crash and burn.

"That doesn't sound good." Brooklyn scrunches her nose and shakes her little head, her brown locks swinging in her face.

"It's pizza, kid," Sienna says. "If you tell me you don't like pizza then we can't be friends."

"I love pizza," Brooklyn beams, her eyes and lips simultaneously widening. Her head swings toward me. "Daddy, can I go? Please say yes!"

"I'm taking you to your moms in an hour. Can't you wait?"

"But pizza!" she exclaims, her jaw dropping to the floor, waiting on my response.

"Matteo," Sienna starts, "she'll be less than five hundred yards away. You can work out in peace. Seems like a win-win to me."

"Do you not have anything better to do than hang out with a five-year-old?"

"Guess not," she deadpans as she hikes Brooklyn higher on her hip.

"No friends your own age?" I ebb.

"Careful, De Salvo. My friends are the weapon-carrying kind," she sneers at me like it's supposed to intimidate me. It doesn't. If Antonio Caputo or his sons wanted me dead, there is no doubt in my mind that I'd be a cold stiff right now. Apparently, either they don't, or I'm low on the Boss's hit list. Then again, perhaps he expects his daughter to walk the straight line he thinks he set her back on.

"Are you even supposed to be talking with me?"

"Who says it's you I want to talk to?"

"I'm hungry," Brooklyn interrupts, irritation evident in her tone.

"Well, it seems your daddy doesn't want to let you go eat with me."

"Daddy," she stresses, cocking her head to the side. "Come on. I want pizza. You want to hit things. Please," she draws out.

"Fine. Pizza at Mario's but nowhere else. I'll be over once I've finished and showered."

"Grazie," Sienna says thank you in a tone filled with so much attitude that it makes me want to teach that mouth of hers my own form of a lesson. I wonder how she'd like me punishing her throat with my dick.

She smirks, rolling her eyes at the same time she turns, walking away from me like she could read that very thought. We'll see what she thinks when my cock is sliding past her lips. My lips tip up, watching her leave.

I'm still smiling half an hour later after I've pummeled the heavy bag until my knuckles are bleeding and streaks of blood are running down the leather. I'm going to catch hell for this shit, but oh well. I can handle anything my team throws at me. It's *my* fists that line their pockets with cash, so they can take their words and choke on them for all I care. Put any boxer in a ring with me and I will still be standing at the end of twelve rounds, unless I knock the fucker out before it gets that far, of course. Most say I'm cocky, and at times I am, but really, I'm just confident in myself.

My phone chimes with a text message that's likely from Kennedy, so I grab it, but instead of checking, I shove it in my pocket and head for the locker room in need of a quick shower. Pizza sounds good right about now. I'll deal with Brooklyn's mother later. I have another woman on my mind, and doing everything I can to get my junk inside that sassy mouth of hers. Trust me, it's going to happen.

That's another thing I'm sure of—my ability to get any woman I want on her knees.

Being the eldest child of Antonio Caputo, I have to have eyes in the back of my head. I have to have eyes on everything and everyone, including my siblings, but especially my sister.

My father would have my ass if I didn't.

I'm his second-in-command, the underboss if you want to get technical. I'm the one he tasks with the jobs he doesn't want anyone else to know about, the jobs he doesn't even want Ren or Si involved in. I agree with him in that aspect, and I respect him more for wanting to protect them from the ugly things my father sometimes has to carry out.

He's not a bad man, though he has to do bad things more often than he wants to. He doesn't enjoy the life he lives, and a large part of that is because it cost him his wife, my mother. She was the love of his life; his other half so to speak. I knew that early on in my youth. It was easy to see and he didn't have a problem showing anyone what she meant to him. That was his biggest mistake; not the loving my mother part, but displaying his emotions for the world to see, for his enemies to witness, and he knows it.

It's why people outside of our family only see how hard he is on us, like today with my sister. Everyone else sees a controlling hard-ass, but to his kids, Antonio Caputo is the best father. That's not to say he isn't hard on all three of us, because he is; more so with Sienna than Lorenzo and me.

Our father made sure all three of us could protect ourselves if the need were to ever arise, but even knowing Sienna could bring down a man twice her size, he's still terrified that something is going to happen to her like it did our mother.

He watches her like a hawk.

I also watch her like a hawk, but what my father doesn't realize is that he still shows his hand. His ruthless reputation may hold strong in every circle it needs to, but his love for his children breaks free from his cold, hard eyes anytime we walk into a room.

That's where my father and I differ. He doesn't enjoy hurting another human being, but he'll do it in a heartbeat if the need arises. I, on the other hand, love inflicting pain. The twins enjoy it almost as much as I do, but they're up front about it. I'm not. I hide my need well, and being the enforcer in the family, that need easily stays hidden.

Only my siblings know my true nature. It's likely why Sienna engages me as often as she does. Whereas Ren and Si's need for fighting is more to relieve the buildup of pressure, a way to calm them when they get out of control, my need is more often about euphoria and pleasure. I get off on others' pain, they don't.

Believe it or not, our father is the more normal one of all of us.

My eyes are on the muted baseball game that's playing on the screen, but they also track Matteo De Salvo as he slips out the door, leaving the gym with his gym bag slung over his shoulder.

The front of the gym is lined with floor to ceiling windows, so it's easier to track his movements once he's exited the glass door. He doesn't head to his SUV that I know he parked down the sidewalk. Instead, he jogs across the street, going into Mario's pizzeria directly across from the MMA gym.

If I were in a joking mood, I'd laugh at the name. Mario isn't Italian. The owner's name isn't even Mario. It's Kevin. An average white guy with a beer belly and thinning hair on top of his head. But even I have to admit the pizza there is the best I've ever placed on my tongue, so really, who gives a fuck that he isn't Italian? Pizza is pizza. His is authentic.

"Watch her." His order hits my ear before he steps in front of the treadmill I'm running on. "Hell, watch him too," he says, and his words piss me off more than they should.

"She's an adult now. You know that, right, old man?" I slow my speed, bringing the machine down until I'm at a steady jog instead of an all-out sprint. I ran my ten miles, so now I can cool down before hitting the shower.

"Since when have I ever given a fuck about her age?" He doesn't wait for my reply, not that I had one. "Watch your sister, Dom. That's an order. And if she leaves with him, I want to know immediately."

"Don't worry, Dad, I'll be the first to rat my little sister out. I always am." *Because God knows Ren wouldn't,* I think to myself. He'd let her elope with that bastard if she ever tried to. We all know Sienna still has a crush on De Salvo. She proved that when she wouldn't let me take him to interrogate like I did her college buddy, Calvin Ross.

I enjoyed every second I was on top of that fucker, beating the snot out of him. And although he passed every question I threw at him, and every question my father demanded an answer to, there was something I instantly didn't like about him.

My sister thinks his brother-in-law needed money, or wanted money, and thought he could play both sides. Levi had an in with Vin working for us, so with Vin paying him to help him with jobs, he took that to Frankie Romano and told the rat he could bring back information to use against us.

I don't know if I buy that, but Vin swore up and down he didn't know Levi was working with Romano, that he was only trying to help his sister with money problems by giving her husband a side job. It's plausible, of course, I have to admit that. His sister doesn't have a job and her very dead husband did everything he could not to work. They lived in a house that was paid for and once owned by Vin's deceased mother. Still, you need money for utilities and food—and in Levi's case, cocaine. His coke problem wasn't a secret. He'd been known to drop his pants if it scored him some blow.

Still, something in my gut doesn't sit right when it comes to Sienna's friend Vin, but for now, the shit for brains is nursing cuts and bruises and a broken nose. He was lucky, all things considered, and he won't get another job from my father; that bridge has been burned.

"I should hope so, Dom. And believe me when I say I wish I didn't have to put the responsibility of your brother and sister's safety on you." His brows turn inward, his breath coming out in huff through his nose.

They are my responsibility. Though, I don't tell him that. They've been my responsibility for nearly twenty-four years.

Lifting my hand to the machine, I jab the decreasing speed button with my finger, bringing the treadmill to a walkable pace.

"I'm going to grab a bite to eat, then I plan to head home," he tells me as I pluck my smartphone out of one of the cup holders.

"Don't worry too much about Si. I've got her. You know that." I hold up my phone, angling it so it recognizes my face. Once open, I tap my finger over the application that tracks everything and everyone of value to me.

It's public knowledge among us that we all know each other's whereabouts at all times. My siblings know mine, the same as I theirs, and our father knows where all three of us are. But my tracking abilities of the people that mean more to me than my own life go a bit deeper, and that's something Ren and Sienna aren't in the know about. My old man, on the other hand, does know the lengths I go to make sure everyone in our family remains breathing.

Looking at the screen, I see Sienna is exactly where I know her to be. I can also see her through the gym window on the other side of the street. She and the kid are in a booth and De Salvo is sliding in across from her now.

Ren, on the other hand, is exactly where he shouldn't be—but I keep my trap closed about that. I may divulge a lot to my father, but there is still a great deal I don't for everyone's sake.

Little sister doesn't know her bestie the way she thinks she does. If she knew where Ren spends a large amount of his time, she'd flip her goddamn shit.

Si spent so much of her youth pretending to be docile and shy that she does everything in her power to prove she is anything but. Tame my sister is not. And although she was quite the little actress back in her school days, even she couldn't hide her feelings for a certain boy that grew up to be known as The Beast.

In a boxing ring I couldn't take Matteo De Salvo. Hell, I probably wouldn't make it five rounds. On the street, however, that motherfucker would be dead before he got one swing.

Ren is different, though. He harbors a secret; a sinful desire that would create the biggest war our world has ever seen if it got out. So, yeah, my siblings are my responsibility, and Sienna's little crush is the least of my problems.

"I worry about all my kids, Domenico, every second of everyday. When you have some of your own, you'll understand that."

"Night, Dad," I say, not acknowledging his comment. Kids aren't on my list of life goals. Neither is a wife, for that matter.

"Son." He nods his head before turning away, leaving me as I press the stop button on the machine.

Grabbing my shit, I head for the shower, but not before glancing back in my sister's direction. Why she had to go and fall for De Salvo, I have no idea. Why my brother had to fall for his forbidden fruit I don't understand either. Both of them are set up for heartbreak, and that is something I never want to partake in.

Not today.

Not tomorrow.

Not next fucking year either.

I lost love once and it'll be a cold day in hell before I allow another woman to break me. Not in this lifetime.

CHAPTER 13

SIENNA

My eyes wander from where Brooklyn is seated across from me in a booth to several feet behind her as Sasha Nikolayev enters, my gaze following her until her long bare legs stop at the counter in front of the register. Her blonde hair is pulled back into a high ponytail, the strands slick and a shade darker, telling me her hair must be damp like she just took a shower. Her pink running shorts barely poke out from underneath the sleeveless hoodie she's wearing. It's black and oversized for her slender frame, the arm openings so large you can see her pink sports bra and most of her inked flesh down to her hip.

The same teenager that took my order steps up to her, asking what she'd like to order this evening. It's still early, not even six o'clock, and I usually wouldn't eat dinner until later in the night, but Brooklyn was complaining about being hungry, so I offered, not believing the words as they fell out of my mouth. Brooklyn's excited expression warmed my chest, and then pizza sounded like the best idea I'd had in a long time.

But now that the Russian whore has graced us with her presence, the small appetite I'd mustered up is gone.

I can't help myself as I listen to her order. She's always had a loud mouth. Though both her parents are Russian, Sasha doesn't have the same accent being born and raised in the States her whole life. She sounds like a New Yorker like the rest of us.

"I called in a large Hawaiian Sea on sourdough." The cashier nods, but her request catches me off guard, my head tilting to the side. That's my twin's favorite pizza, which is every bit as disgusting as it sounds. Not only does it have pineapple on it, but it also has anchovies—neither of which go together. Even the thought of anchovies has me gagging and my barely-there appetite is gone in a flash.

Pizza should be savory, not fishy and sweet. Pineapples destroy everything that a pizza should be.

"Here's your order, Si," Kevin, the owner, says as he places the pizza pie down in front of us and I watch in fascination as Brooklyn's eyes grow in size and her lips curve up on both sides. "One large, half pepperoni and half pepperoni and Italian sausage. You both enjoy."

"Thanks, Kev," I reply, glancing up and forcing my lips to give him a warm smile.

As I'm plating Brooklyn the slice she requested, my gaze catches sight of Matteo as he jogs across the street, heading our way. The plain white T-shirt he's wearing hugs his biceps, and it must be windy outside, because I can see the indentions of his abdominal muscles through the window. His black basketball shorts hang to his knees, but when my eyes continue downward, I can't control the laugh that breaks free.

"What's funny?" Brooklyn asks. Her hands reach forward, taking the plate from me.

"Your dad," I tell her, my eyes still on Matteo's as he steps inside the pizza joint.

"My daddy is hilarious. Is your daddy funny? He doesn't seem very funny at all," she remarks, scrunching up her nose, her eyes on the slice in front of her instead of me.

Matteo looks right, scanning the booths on the other side.

"Funny isn't a term I'd used to describe him," I admit to her, at least, not anymore. We used to have funny moments—him and my brothers—back before my mother was killed. I caught him making her laugh all the time. "But he used to be," I whisper.

Matteo's head swivels, his eyes stopping when they connect with mine. For a few seconds, I'm caught in a stare and can't look away—neither does he. Matteo is the first to break the connection when a couple from behind him tries to enter, but his large frame is blocking the entrance. He mumbles something to them, but his words are inaudible.

Brooklyn takes a huge bite, getting pizza sauce on both corners of her mouth.

"Pizza just arrived if you want some," I offer, looking up as he stops next to his daughter's side of the booth. "We have plenty." Matteo eyes the pizza and then Brooklyn, as if he isn't sure he wants to join us. Perhaps he thought she'd be done eating and he could bail. "Or not," I say, feigning disinterest as I pick up my tall glass of ice water, the condensation coating my palm as I bring it to my lips, my eyes back on Brooklyn.

The pizza sauce now covers even more of her face, but she doesn't seem to be fazed by it. Her head turns up to her dad. "We got our favorite. Eat with us, Daddy."

Bending down, he slides into the booth, scooting his kid over to the other end. She reaches for her plate and Matteo pushes her kid-sized drink with a lid and straw closer to her food.

"I was supposed to have you over to your moms"—he flicks his wrist, glancing at his watch—"five minutes ago." A sigh slips from his lips, then Matteo's gaze snaps to mine as he pulls a slice of pizza off the stand. "We're already late. What's another half an hour going to make a difference?" He tears into the slice, taking damn near half of it into his mouth, and for some reason, the creeper that I am when it comes to him, I can't take my eyes off his mouth. Like Brooklyn, remnants of the pizza sauce gathers on his lower lip. "See something you want to taste?"

Forcing my eyes up, I meet the sexiest eyes I've ever seen staring at me like I've been caught doing something I wasn't supposed to be doing. "Nope," I comment.

"Liar." A smirk forms on his full lips and I see he licked the sauce from them. *Bummer*. He was right. I'd love a little taste, but that isn't something I'll admit to *him* of all people.

I don't respond. Instead, I reach across the table and pick up a slice of my pepperoni. It's rare that I indulge in greasy food, but when I do, I enjoy the very best. The inside of my mouth salivates at the anticipation.

"Just pepperoni?" he asks but doesn't wait for a response. "How boring."

"I don't like Italian sausage." I take a normal size bite and moan, my eyes closing of their own accord.

"What do you have against Italian sausage?" When I open my eyelids, it's not me that's eyeing a mouth this time. Matteo's dark stare looks hungry for something *other* than pizza.

"It has fennel seeds in it. I hate fennel," I answer honestly, and then take another bite. I haven't eaten today. I didn't realize just how hungry I was until that first bite. With my dad not talking to me, the thought of food was unappealing.

"What's fennel?" Brooklyn asks.

I'm about to answer her when someone steps up next to our booth. Her voice alone makes the muscles in my shoulders tense. "Hey, De Salvo, what's kickin'? Saw your fight a few months back," she adds.

A few months back? I repeat in my head. Matteo's last fight was seven months ago. I know, because I was there. What the fuck is this bitch going on about?

"Hey, what's up?" Sasha switches the pizza box to her other hip and then proceeds to lean down, giving Matteo a hug like they're pals. She's a whore, so she either wants in his pants or she's already been in them. That sends a cold ripple down my spine.

I will massacre this fucking bitch if it's the latter, maybe even if it's the former.

"Just grabbing dinner." She stands back to her full five-feet-nine height, her eyes solely focused on him with an easygoing smile attached to her ugly face. Okay, Sasha isn't exactly bad looking, but I'll never admit that out loud. She has straight, blonde hair that looks sleek and magazine perfect even in a ponytail, not to mention a set of the lightest blue eyes that seem to pull yours to hers like the goddamn siren she is.

"Well, can't you grab it and go?" I question as I lean back against the worn vinyl and cross my arms, my voice louder than I intended.

"Wasn't addressing you." She arches an eyebrow in challenge, her eyes finally cutting to mine.

"Private party of three." I motion between Matteo, Brooklyn, and me. "Mosey on to somewhere else."

"You're always a delight, Sienna." She sneers at me, before turning back to Matteo. "Didn't figure you for a man that hangs out with uptight bitches, De Salvo. Speaking of . . . How's Kennedy?"

"In case you can't take a hint," Brooklyn looks up as she pulls a second slice of pizza from the tray, "she wants you to leave, lady."

My sour mood just perked up a few notches.

"Brooklyn!" Matteo scolds. I scowl at him, but his whole body twists toward his kid. "That was rude."

"She was rude to Si. I don't see you getting on to her," she sasses, and my lips curve up. This little girl has *cojones*. I like her. She's a little pistol.

"I'm out," Sasha says. She turns, stepping toward the door, and as she walks away, she throws a final comment over her shoulder. "Tell Kennedy I said hello."

Bitch.

That's okay. I got something coming her way not long from now anyway.

As much as I love training, I don't have any aspirations to fight professionally. I reserve my abilities to beat the crap out of my brothers and to make sure I can defend myself should I be placed in a position to do so. I love my job and plan to remain working for the family businesses. If it hadn't been for the opportunity to get Sasha Nikolayev in a kickboxing match, I wouldn't have accepted the challenge. She wants this just as bad as I do, and is likely the one that threw my name out there.

"So," Matteo tilts his head, "neither princess likes each other." He smirks and huffs out a laugh.

Sasha's father, Mischa Nikolayev, is the head of the largest

Russian criminal organization in the U.S. As much as Matteo's little jab hit its mark, he's not wrong in referring to her as a princess. But where I accept my family's lifestyle, Sasha does not. She refuses to be part of that family and does everything in her power not to be associated with them.

"Do you have a boyfriend?" Brooklyn asks. I'm so caught off guard that I halt the slice of pizza midair, my eyes cutting to where she sits beside her dad. Her elbows are on the table and her chin is resting comfortably in her palm, her big brown eyes on me. Guess she's had her fill; though sauce is still gathered in the corners of her mouth. For some reason, it's cute on her.

"Do you have a boyfriend?" I repeat her question, only it's redirected at her now.

"She's five," Matteo answers like it's the dumbest thing anyone could ask.

"Of course, I do," she says, her head bobbing up and down.

"Excuse me?" Matteo's head whips around, his body swiveling in the same direction, facing Brooklyn. "You do not have a boyfriend. You're nowhere even close to being old enough for a boyfriend."

"Daddy," she draws out, her tone bored. It makes me fall into a fit of giggles. Matteo only makes it worse when he scowls at me.

"What are you going to do, go find a five-year-old and threaten him if he doesn't stay away from your daughter?" I ask, still half laughing.

"Oh, Damon is six. He's going to first grade next year," she chimes. The look on Matteo's face is priceless, and it's the highlight of my evening. I can't contain the laugh that erupts from my lips, and the scowl I witness after only produces more cackles from my side of the table.

The drive to Kennedy's apartment isn't far from the gym I sometimes go to, nor my townhouse, for that matter. The only reason I live in this part of Long Island is because it's one of the only decent areas that Kennedy can afford to rent, so when I allow her time with our daughter, it's easier to live close to each other.

Besides, if anything were to happen, I'm as close to Brooklyn as possible without having to live within breathing distance to her mother. To say I can't stand my ex is an understatement, and the only reason I even consider her an ex is because after she came to me pregnant, I tried to give a real relationship a go. It didn't last long. The woman only cares about herself and who's able to line her pockets with cash or pour liquor down her throat.

I have full custody of our daughter; something Kennedy gladly relinquished when she realized Brooklyn wasn't going to get her a ring put on her finger and how hard raising a baby really was. She wasn't cut out for motherhood, but Brooklyn loves her, so I do my best to make sure my daughter gets to see her mom.

"Sienna was jealous when that girl was talking to you, Daddy." Her statement brings me out of my negative thoughts where her mother is concerned. For a minute, there was a time where I regretted sticking my dick in that bitch, but then I held my daughter for the first time and realized what unconditional love felt like.

I snap my eyes up, capturing her stare in the rearview mirror. "How do you know what jealousy means?"

"Momma told me. So, I know that's what Sienna was. Momma says that's how I act when another girl talks to my boyfriend." Her nose crunches up like she has a bad taste in her mouth.

"You don't have a boyfriend," I hiss as I put my eyes back on the road. "Thanks, Kennedy, for filling our kid's head with nonsense," I mumble under my breath.

"Yes, I do." Her voice comes out like a taunt as I pull into an empty parking space in front of Kennedy's apartment building, then, shutting off the engine, I shove the gear stick into park.

A text message dings on my phone, but I don't grab it from the center console where it's sitting in one of the empty cup holders. Instead, I look at Brooklyn through the rearview mirror again and say, "Unbuckle, kiddo. Grab your bag before you get out too."

She'll only be here for a day or two at the most, so there wasn't a need to pack much of her stuff. She has clothes at her mom's, but she still likes to sleep with the same plush tiger she's had since she was one.

Kennedy lives in an apartment complex that was renovated three years ago. Her dumbass signed a lease before laying eyes on the condo, but by doing so, she got in before the prices doubled.

The complex isn't aesthetically pleasing with its weathered brick exterior, but the inside is updated and on the nicer side. You have to have a six-digit code to enter the lobby of the building outside of normal business hours, and to enter the residential areas of floors two through eight you need to have a key to the elevator or stairwell. I may not live here, but I made Brooklyn's mom supply me with a key in order to allow our daughter to come over.

I'm not a complete asshole; though Kennedy would probably disagree. I gave Brooklyn's mother a key to my townhouse as well, since our daughter mostly stays with me. Since I don't have a wife or a girlfriend and no plans of either in the foreseeable future, it's not a big deal. Kennedy knows not to show up out of the blue without a phone call or a text. She sticks to those rules, and as long as I don't feel my kid is in danger, I do the same.

"Can I enter the code, Daddy?"

"Sure, baby girl. Go for it." Like every kid, Brooklyn loves buttons. The little shit even tries to get me to let her enter the code when we checkout at the store, but I'm not dumb enough to give another person the code to my debit card.

It's well past six in the evening, so when we walk through the lobby to the elevators, there is no one at the front desk to greet us.

"Key, Daddy," she demands, flipping her palm up as she stops in front of the metal doors. Dropping my set in her hand, I wait, giving her time to find the correct one. Within a minute, we're walking off the elevator and onto the third floor. Brooklyn races the length of the hallway until she stops at the last door on the left–her home away from home.

She has to knock three times before her mother greets us. When the door finally opens, Kennedy is wearing a soft pink silk robe open with a matching nightgown that barely stops below the apex of her thighs. At twenty-four, she isn't a bad sight to look at, though I lost interest in her before I graduated high school. She still keeps her natural dirty-blonde hair bleached platinum, but now it stops at the nape of her neck instead of hanging in long strands down her back. In all honesty, this look suits her better. It brings out the bitch she doesn't hide.

"Hey, Matty." She grins as she leans her hip against the doorframe.

I stopped telling her not to call me that long ago. It doesn't do any good. She just ignores my requests, so now I do the same. I act like it doesn't faze me, when in reality, it's like nails on a motherfucking chalkboard.

When she doesn't acknowledge our daughter standing in front of her, I cock an eyebrow. I earn an eye roll before she finally looks down.

"Can I go play on my iPad?" Brooklyn asks.

"Sure, baby girl. Go for it. It's in your room."

Brooklyn tilts her head back, looking up at me. "Bye, Daddy. Love you."

"Love you more," I tell her, meaning it down to the core of my existence.

I continue standing in the doorway until Brooklyn is out of earshot, then I turn my attention to her mother and cross my arms. "Limit her screen time, please."

"Why?" Kennedy's nose scrunches up and she gives me a look like she didn't understand the words I said.

"Because she doesn't need to be on that damn thing all night, or all day for that matter." Given the chance, Brooklyn will stay on her iPad for hours. I've caught her sneaking out of her bedroom at my house several times, trying to take it to her room to play on it when she's supposed to be sleeping. Like every kid, myself included when I was younger, she thinks she's slick, but she isn't.

"When did you turn into such a party pooper?"

"When you popped out my kid and suddenly I had responsibilities." I give her a pointed look. "You know, the same ones you have but choose to ignore."

"I take care of her just fine, Matteo. When she's with me, it's my say what she does and for how long."

"An hour to an hour and a half tops," I say, ignoring the garbage that fell out of her thin lips.

"If you want to monitor her time then maybe you should stay."

"Maybe you should learn to be a parent," I counter. She does this every time I bring Brooklyn over without fail. I don't know if she does it because she's hoping one of these days I'll give in or if she's simply fucking with me. Either way, I'm not going to bite. The last place I care to be is in Kennedy's presence. If we didn't share a child together, I would have ditched her a long time ago.

"I parent just fine. If you'd hang around more often, Matty, you'd actually see that."

"Says the mother who can't handle her five-year-old more than a day or two at a time." I hold up my hand, stopping her comeback when she goes to open her mouth. "I'm not having this argument with you again. I'm out. I'll pick her up tomorrow evening at five."

When she doesn't reply or interject asking for more than one day, I pivot and walk back to the elevator. Once I'm back inside my Lexus, I pick up my phone before starting the vehicle, seeing a text message from one of my friends—another boxer that I've known for a few years.

Thomas: Wanna hit up a club tonight?

Me: Sure. When and where?

Thomas: Eleven at Club Rouge. But . . . if you want to come out early, I'm about to walk in Headliners now.

I'm not even surprised. Headliners is an upscale titty bar that's rumored to show more than just skin. With my rigorous training schedule and having Brooklyn most nights, I haven't seen the inside of a club in over a year. I couldn't tell you the last time I've been to a strip joint.

Me: Club Rouge it is. I'll meet you there, bro.

I still have time to get in another workout, so I might as well head to my house. I prefer working out in the home gym I have inside my garage anyway. I only go to a brick and mortar gym when I'm training another boxer or traveling.

This could be fun. I need a night of letting loose, having a few drinks, and maybe getting laid. A club is just what I need to unwind.

CHAPTER 15
SIENNA

Walking to the bar, I jerk my head up, gaining the bartender's attention. By the time I step up to the counter a tall glass filled with bubbly liquid is pushed my way with a straw already bobbing between the ice cubes.

"Thanks, Jeff," I bite out as his dark green eyes slip in a slow descent, stopping at my chest. I didn't go for a modest look tonight. The girls are on full display, amplified by the corset-style bodysuit I have on underneath my form fitting, strapless red dress.

Clasping my fingers around the drink, I pick it up off the bar and then turn, putting my back against the sleek lacquer bar top. Jeff isn't bad to look at per se, but he's never held my interest in that way. Then again, very few do.

After scanning the dance floor, my gaze flicks over to where my brothers are seated with one of Dom's martial arts buddies. Domenico and Rick seem to be in a light mood, but Ren looks antsy, like this is the last place he wants to be. Even though Dom looks like he's in a relaxed state, I know that's just an illusion. He never lets his guard down. He's always in parent mode when Ren and I are present, and he's far worse when it comes to Lorenzo and me—sometimes, maybe even more so than our dad. Even though both of us are capable of taking care of ourselves, he makes it his role to watch us more closely than what is necessary.

Suddenly not in the mood to walk over to either of my brothers, I scan the floor on the top level, my eyes landing on Vin almost instantly. His head is tipped back, and that's when I notice he's talking to another person standing next to his table that's pushed against the iron half-wall.

Those interested in a more relaxed, laid back atmosphere often congregate on the second level versus the first where the music is loud and the dancing is nonstop until last call.

Matteo pulls out the chair across from Vin and then proceeds to sit down with a glass tumbler in his hand. There isn't a smile on his face, and Vin is sporting a pinched look, so I can take a guess that Matteo is likely asking him about last Friday and what happened.

I'm curious myself, but for different reasons. I know what happened to Vin that night; well, mostly. I know while my father was doing the dirty work—handling Levi—Dom was likely making Vin spill his fucking guts.

Why *did* Vin bring his brother-in-law in or try to? He's always told me the guy is a piece of shit and wishes his sister would grow up and find a real man. No scenario I conjure up makes sense. Something feels off about the whole thing, but what?

"You know," a familiar voice says, and I have to force the smile not to form on my lips, "your gut instinct is usually right. You ever thought about listening to it, Sienna?"

Rolling my head to the right, my dark eyes land on eyes so light blue that at first glance, Krishna Nikolayev looks like an angel with his pure eyes and golden locks. He's seated, but from many past encounters at his full height of six-foot-six, he towers over me. Tonight, with his ass on a stool, I'm eye to eye with a man that looks more like a god than Mischa Nikolayev's second-in-command.

"How would you know what my gut is saying?" I ask instead of giving him an answer.

He swivels on the barstool, angling his body to face the side of mine. Lifting his right foot off the floor, he plants it onto the metal footrest attached to the stool. I don't have to peek down to know the front of my body is partially blocked against the bar by how far his knee juts out. He smirks thinking he's trapped me exactly where he wants me.

Bringing my flavored sparkling water to my mouth, I wrap my lips around the straw, sucking the liquid slowly as I wait for his answer.

His stare flicks away from mine, glancing to the floor above where I was looking moments ago. Following his eyes, mine stop back on where I spotted Vin and Matteo.

"The day you dropped that mask you wore for so long, you burned that motherfucker," he says, his warm breath fanning my face. When he doesn't say more, I turn my head back to him. "In other words, you're transparent."

"Yeah?" A dry laugh slips from behind my lips. Turning, I sit my empty glass on the bar, finished with it. "What's my transparency saying, Krishna?" I pronounce his name in the best Russian accent I can muster. When his eyes dip to my lips, I know the effect hit its mark.

Krishna stands, squeezing his large frame between me and the stool behind him. “At the moment, it says you’re playing with fire.” He steps closer, pressing himself against my hip bone. When I don’t react to the hardening muscle between his legs, he smirks, as if expecting it. Lowering his head, his nose tickles the shell of my ear. “I’m not like your brothers, Sienna. There is no honor to be found in my bones; no respect, and certainly no mercy. The only reason I’ve never fucked you is because no pussy is worth starting World War III over—not even yours.” His face moves away from me, but his crotch remains fused to the side of my body.

“How would you know? You’ve never had it.” I lean my head back, arching an eyebrow up at him.

“No bitch is worth that much trouble.” His eyes leave mine for the briefest of moments, and I know he glanced over in my brother’s direction.

“Says you.”

“I know it’s not,” he throws back.

“You going to explain what you mean or not?” I ask, bored with this conversation.

Stepping away from me, he plants his ass back down on the barstool. He’s silent for at least half a minute, his eyes boring into mine, searching for something, I presume. Finally, he breaks our locked gaze, jutting his head to the side and up. I glance in the direction he’s requested, my gaze once again landing on Vin, Matteo’s presence ignored.

“You were wondering if he should’ve been fish food too, like that other fuck.”

“I have no idea what you’re talking about,” I say in a steady voice. I won’t allow him to ruffle my feathers if that’s what he’s trying to do.

"Right . . ." Krishna nods as a smile ghosts his lips. "But then your family differs from mine in that way. We wouldn't have simply beat him to within an inch of his life; though,"—Krishna glances up to the floor above us briefly, then his eyes come back to mine, only this time they're colder, harder than before—"from the looks of it, your brothers didn't do much of a job if he's walking and talking and drinking less than a week later."

"Maybe my family doesn't believe in someone paying for the sins of a man they're related to," I remark.

"Everyone is a sinner, Si. Even you—as innocent as you portray yourself as—have a dark need to fulfill."

"What . . ." I pause, because there's a laugh on the tip of my tongue. Inhaling, I finish my thought. "What gives you the impression that I'm innocent?" I turn to face him. "Does anything about this seem innocent to you?" I point to my attire.

"Just because you enjoy inflicting pain on another person doesn't mean there isn't a part of you that's still innocent. If there wasn't, you wouldn't be able to get my dick hard." He smirks, and for the first time tonight, his eyes dip, gazing upon my pushed-up cleavage. "As for your clothing choice, well, that just intrigues me more."

Suddenly Krishna's body language and facial expression changes. It hardens into the cold-blooded killer he's rumored to be. "I'm not the only man you intrigue."

His eyes veer up, but I don't follow his gaze. *Is he talking about Matteo?*

"He watches you, and you're oblivious to it. He's been doing it for a long time. I don't even think your brothers or your dad realize it."

"Realize what?" I'm dumbfounded. What he's saying isn't

making any sense. "Who?" I ask.

Krishna is silent for a long beat and his penetrating stare only makes my mouth dry. I finished my drink, but some of the ice should have melted enough to wet my lips. When I grab the glass and bring the straw to my lips, I discover Jeff replenished me with a full beverage. I suck the contents down.

Finally, Krishna sighs, as if deciding whether or not to answer my questions.

"They spared his life because he's your friend, but that's the thing, Sienna. I don't believe he is your friend at all. He doesn't look at you like a guy that simply wants to get into a girl's pants, or even a guy interested in taking a girl out on a date."

"Like you take girls out on dates," I cut in.

"I don't, but that's not the point."

"Then what is your point?"

His eyes leave mine, snapping over my head to look behind me. It's not long before his stare is back on me, but this time the ice inside them has thawed—only by a hair, but it's still more emotion than he usually shows.

Pulling his cell out of his pocket, his head looks down and my gaze follows his, landing on a text message that he's thumbing out so quickly I don't have a chance to read what it said; only that it was to Domenico.

Interesting.

"My point is . . . I have a feeling he's biding his time for something. That something being you."

"I've already shut that down," I tell him. "He knows I'm not interested." And I'm not. Not in the least.

"Just because you were never interested in his bitch-boy ass doesn't mean he stopped being interested in you." He says that like it should be obvious, but it's not, and I think he's wrong. At least about Vin wanting me in the way he is suggesting. Men—Italian men anyway—have too much pride to set themselves up for a second round of rejection. It's not happening, not in this lifetime anyway.

"What did you text my brother?" I ask, changing the subject.

"Not to put a bullet through my head and to control your twin when I kiss you."

"And what makes you think Dom is going to let you put your hands on me?" My brothers would flip their shit; not about *a* guy touching me, but they would about *this* guy in particular putting his hands on me.

"Because I'm proving a point to him the same as I am you." There's a heartbeat of silence, but before I can come up with anything to say, he continues, "And I told him to trust me."

"Why would Dom trust you?" He cocks an eyebrow, silently telling me that was by far the dumbest question to leave my mouth.

"You know why." He steps forward, but his glacier eyes once again peek over my head. Krishna doesn't need approval from anyone except his father, and even that's questionable. *Damn Russians*. Except, that's exactly what I see in his stare that's obviously seeking out my older brother from another part of the club.

I don't exactly know the *why* like he inferred I do. I have my suspicions, though, but that is all they are—suspicions, a sibling sixth sense so to speak.

Krishna's eyes land back on mine and then they flick down to my lips. "If you weren't his fucking sister . . ." His breath fans across my face, his voice low and seductive, making me want to squirm. It takes every ounce of control not to move, giving myself away. "I'd fuck every ounce of innocence out of you, right here, right fucking now, and in front of everyone in this goddamn place, Si."

I suck in a breath. I wasn't expecting those words to exit his sinful mouth, though it's not like he hasn't said similar things over the years.

Trying to play off his affect on me, I tip my lips up, but I glance away needing a second away from the seriousness in his eyes.

"Still with that innocence mumbo jumbo." I roll my eyes, but he grabs my chin in a firm hold between his fingers, forcing me to look back up at him.

"Domenico and I really are a lot alike, sweetheart. Like I said before, if you weren't so pure, you never would have caught my interest in the first place." His fingers tug on my chin, pulling me closer to him ever so slowly. His digits are complete opposite of his eyes. His skin is warm.

"Gross. Please do not compare me to the virgins you and Dom love to deflower." I let out a breath. "Besides, innocent girls don't want to do the things I want to do."

"Just because the sight of blood turns you on the same as it does us, Sienna, doesn't mean you're like us. The damage you inflict heals. We, on the other hand . . ." His words hang in the air, pissing me off. I know he's likely to have taken a life before, but he's insinuating that Dom has too, and that doesn't settle well with me. I'm not naive. I know Dom is capable of doing that if he had to, and maybe he has, but he's never admitted that to me. I already deal with Ren's secretive shit, I shouldn't have to from Domenico too when I'm a goddamn open book to them.

He tugs a little more, pulling me out of my thoughts, and my heels lift off the ground, allowing him to move me where he wants me. "I'm going to kiss you now, but before you close those stunningly dark eyes, I want you to look up there at that so-called *friend* of yours. Look hard, because if you look close enough, the eyes never lie. People are never as clever as they think they are."

"What makes you so sure I'm going to close my eyes?"

Krishna's tongue juts out between his lips. He's so close to my mouth that the tip touches my lips, wetting them. My lips part, and as if on reflex, I suck in a breath. My eyes lower, finding the corner of one side of his mouth curved up.

"Because you're not going to be able to hold them open, baby." He leans in the rest of the way, and before his lips touch mine, his head tilts to the side, giving me the perfect view to the second level. I see exactly what Krishna wanted me to see, but I can't analyze it, because the moment our lips touch, my eyes glide to someone else.

Matteo.

He's staring at us, at me. Our gazes lock. Krishna was wrong, so wrong. I can't even force them to close, which is exactly what I want to do at this very moment. Looking at Matteo feels right. It's always felt right, which is why I could never stop myself from staring at him. I knew it came off creepy and weird, but there's a pull that won't allow me to look away, just like now.

However, the lips connected with mine, and the tongue making love with my own feels wrong. For the life of me, I don't understand why. It's not like Matteo has ever been anything more than an acquaintance, if even that. I should be enjoying the kiss; this sensual kiss. Krishna is good with his mouth. He's skilled. But I'm not enjoying it. It's more of an indifference, and maybe it has nothing to do with the man my eyes are locked with or the murderous expression marring his beautiful face. Maybe it has more to do with Domenico, or that Krishna himself is probably picturing said brother in his mind right now instead of me.

It's not that men haven't been interested in me. It's that the men I'm interested in have never been interested in me. I have no doubt that Krishna, or even Matteo, would sleep with me given the chance. I've felt them both grow hard against me, but that's all it would be—just meaningless sex.

And therein lies my problem; one of them, at least. I'm not like most twenty-three-year-olds. I don't want to bang every Tom, Dick, and Harry that presses his erection against my thigh.

I'm peculiar. So picky that it annoys the hell out of me.

"I had a third point to make too." My eyes snap to his at the sound of his voice, and that's when I realize he's no longer kissing me. Instead, Krishna's thumb runs back and forth across my lips. "Did De Salvo watch me eat out this hot mouth?"

What? Why would he ask that?

His eyes dilate and his lips spread slowly. The expression on Krishna's face is positively sinful. "Good," he says with a nod, acknowledging whatever my eyes are telling him.

"What point were you making with Matteo?" I finally ask when my brain isn't putting two and two together like apparently it should be.

"That you're not on his menu." I scowl, and Krishna yanks my chest flush with his, my feet lifting off the ground. He plants a quick kiss to my lips and then I'm placed back down. "He doesn't deserve you. Hell, no man does. You're too good; too strong for even the champ himself. He's a fucking douche for never seeing you until now."

"*I'm too good for him,*" I mock. "That phrase doesn't make any sense no matter the context. No one is too good, nor not good enough for someone else, Krishna. It's the same as life. It's neither fair nor unfair. Life is just life. Humans are just human. If we want something, we say or show we want it, and if we're able, we take it. If they want us in return, then great. If not, it is what it is."

"Then why haven't you taken him? Huh?" His eyebrow arches, demanding an answer. Instead of giving him one, I cross my arms over my chest and purse my lips. "And there's my final point."

My jaw hardens into granite. If this dress wasn't so damn tight and restricting, I'd ram my knee between his legs.

"I'm not scared, nor do I . . ." I inhale as rage courses through every cell in my body. "Care whatever fucking point is in your stupid fucking head that you're attempting to make."

"Oh, my point hit its mark perfectly, baby." He smirks down at me, then lifts his glass from the bar, bringing it to his lips slowly, his eyes never leaving mine, not even when he tips the amber liquid to his lips, downing the remainder.

"You're just trying to bait me."

"No *trying* to it. You're already hooked on the line and now all you have to do is go prove me wrong. Go flaunt this hot, sexy little body in front of De Salvo. Watch him salivate and fall to his knees in front of you. Simple as that."

My nose scrunches up, but not because the thought grosses me out. It doesn't. Quite the opposite actually, but I don't want Matteo for a quick, wham bam thank you ma'am. I want him—all of him—and I want . . . *forever*. And therein lies my biggest problem: I want him but he doesn't want me. At least not in terms of forever.

And if I can't have *that* then I don't want a slice of the pie at all. I'm an all or nothing kind of girl. I won't bend or change my ways, not even for Matteo De Salvo, the hottest man to ever grace my fantasies.

Fantasies I've been having far longer than is likely considered normal.

"No, thank you. I'll pass."

"Fine. Stay the scared, weak little bitch I always knew you were deep down." I mentally shout, fuck it. To hell with the material of this dress. If it rips to shreds right here in front of a club full of people, so be it. It'll be worth all the eyes and cameras that no doubt will snap candid shots. Kneeing Krishna in the balls so hard he pukes will be all the satisfaction I need.

I go to do just that, but apparently my facial expression must give me away. He's ready for the move, and the next thing I feel is the palm of his hand on my bare knee before he shoves my leg back to the ground.

"If you don't want to play with De Salvo, whatever, but at least go up there and see for yourself what your boy's real agenda is. You may be a scared little girl at times, but you're no dumb bitch."

"I saw what you wanted. You made that point. Satisfied?" I ask, my voice coming out like a hiss. How I didn't realize Vin was still interested in me that way, I don't know. He never touches me inappropriately. There are never any lingering looks that I can recall, but it's not like I really paid any attention either, so could I have missed it? Then again, this isn't my problem. So what if Vin likes me more than just a friend? I don't share the same interest in him, so it's never going to happen, and if he remains interested, then that's on him.

Krishna sighs, shaking his head as if everything he's attempted to show me in the last ten minutes has been for nothing.

"What do you—" I start to demand, but I'm cut off at the sound of Domenico's seething tone.

"You need to go the fuck home, Sienna."

I whip my head around, finding my brother's impressive frame standing in front of both Krishna and me, his arms crossed over his powerful chest. His eyes roam from mine to Krishna's and then settle back on me, his dark eyes blazing.

"Last I checked, I don't call you Dad, so fuck off, Dom. I don't have to do what you say."

"I can call him if you'd like. I'm sure he'd be thrilled to know his daughter had her tongue down the enemy's throat. You're what, daughter of the fucking year with that?"

"Jealous much?" I spit daggers back in my brother's direction.

"Careful, little sister. I'll make every inch of you match the color of that fucking dress if you keep running that mouth. Red is your color, after all," he sneers down at me, anger coating his face.

"Would you two stop getting my dick hard before I have to find some random cunt to unload my shit into? Jesus fucking Christ." Krishna turns his back to us, facing the bar. Lifting his right arm, he signals the bartender for another drink.

"You're gross," I tell him to the side of his face.

"I'm a lot of things, Sienna." A slow smile drags up his face. "You're welcome to jump on my train and find out just what things I can be."

"Enough!" Dom breathes, forcing a hard exhale out of his mouth as he combs his fingers through his black hair.

"I'll pass on that too." I wrinkle my nose at Krishna before twisting to face my brother. "I'll get out of your hair, but don't order me around again, Dom."

Before I step around him, he reaches up, snagging my upper arm in a vice-like grip, his hard eyes pulling my attention to his. "If Vin has any ill intent toward you or our family, I'll shove my

Glock so far down his throat he'll choke to death before the bullet kills him. Are we clear?"

Dom's eyes bore into mine and I know he means every word. "If that's the case, I'll do it for you," I reply, my voice calm for someone who's never taken a life or contemplated taking one before. But I know, without a doubt, if I had to for my family, I would do just that.

"Never." He shakes his head, and his fingers loosen from around my bicep, his eyes warming. "That's my job. My duty. My responsibility." Then Dom's eyes harden once again when he flicks his gaze to Krishna. "Just like ripping apart anyone that touches my sister without my approval."

Krishna's eyes do a slow sweep from Domenico's face, down and back up again, a chuckle tumbling out of his throat when their eyes meet. "I've already been turned down by one pussy tonight." Krishna's eyes flick to mine and then back to my brother's. "Not looking for more . . . pussy that is."

"You boys have fun." I pat my brother on the shoulder as I slide my arm from his grasp. "That's my que to leave."

Slipping around them, I glance back up to the second level of the club. Matteo and Vin are still sitting across from each other, but both are looking straight at me. Their facial expressions damn near mirroring one another's, though there's one thing that Krishna said that rings true–I'm not dumb. I may not have noticed Vin's interest, but now that it's on my radar, I'm planning on finding out if he deserves the second chance he was gifted, or if I need to dirty my manicured hands.

With that thought, I head toward the stairs.

CHAPTER 16
MATTEO

Rage isn't an emotion I feel often. I like to think I'm a fairly easygoing guy. If I thought about it, I bet I could count on one hand how many times I've been so mad that I could feel my body heating from the inside out. As a boxer, no opponent, referee, or commentator, not even a fan has ever gotten under my skin like that did. I talk shit like most athletes in my profession, but I don't let anyone get to me. I may change into a beast for the duration of a match, but rage is the furthest thing from my mind when I step into the ring, or even when I'm getting my face and body pounded by another boxer.

But that's exactly what I felt when Sienna and I locked eyes as I watched Krishna Nikolayev shove his slithering tongue down her delicate throat. It's dumb as fuck to feel this way. I know this, yet I want to wring her goddamn neck for allowing that shit to happen. Krishna, on the other hand, I want to knock the fuck out for touching her. Watching him paw at her only moments ago has me feeling ways I don't want to feel.

She isn't mine. Sure, I want to fuck her, but I don't want her as my girlfriend. I have two ladies in my life—my daughter and mother—and they are plenty. I've never had the desire for a big family. I was an only child. I turned out fine, and Brooklyn will too.

So why do I feel this pull toward Sienna all of a sudden?

Could it be something lingering from when I'd catch her watching me all through school? Or perhaps she just piques my interest now that she doesn't come across as a scared little mouse. Whatever it is, it isn't going to get out of my system until I stick my dick in her and fuck it out.

It's a solid plan; though it still doesn't explain the shitty mood that settled deep inside me when I couldn't peel my eyes away from her. Them. *I wonder if that Russian prick knows she had her eyes on me the entire time they were swapping spit?*

That thought has the corner of my lips tipping up the slightest bit. I didn't know she was here when I walked in. I'd seen her brothers, but it never crossed my mind that she might be here too. Hell, it's been less than a week since I found out she was related to one of the most feared families on the East coast. Funny how the Nikolayev's are right up there with the Caputo's in reputation.

If I didn't know the Caputo's and the Nikolayev's were sworn enemies from at least three generations ago, I'd question if Sienna and Krishna were together. There was nothing about their interaction that was smooth. They aren't lovers; that I'd bet money on. I'd bet my next fucking fight on that shit.

When I spotted Vin lounging on the second level of Club Rouge, I made my way up here thinking he'd give me some insight on exactly what went down at Raymond's last Friday. He's the reason I spotted Sienna in the first place. After I sat down, I didn't beat around the bush. I asked him where the Caputo brothers took him and about his brother-in-law's current whereabouts, but he never got around to answering me. I doubt he even heard the question.

Wondering what had his attention and why he'd gone from relaxed to seething in zero point three seconds, I turned my head and glanced over the balcony, my eyes locking with Sienna's instantaneously.

So, in other news, I'm also not the only man that's hard up for the little mafia princess. Vin's got it bad for her too, and that's a realization that pissed me off even more. Two realizations actually. One, he wants to fuck her, and the other I'm actually bothered that he wants in her pants. There's possession in his eyes, and something about that ticks me off. Sienna doesn't strike me as a woman to be owned. She's her own person. She's rough and tough, and I like that about her.

What I don't like is this motherfucker right here thinking she's up for grabs or Nikolayev thinking he can lock lips with her anytime he wants to. I'm on the verge of telling Vin he doesn't have a shot in hell with Sienna Caputo when a tingling sensation runs down the length of my spine. She's behind me. Vin confirms it when his eyes look over my shoulder, his jaw locked.

Well-manicured hands with nails that match the tight red dress she's wearing land palms down on top of the table—between Vin and I—so hard our drinks slide. Not acknowledging my presence, her brown eyes collide with the man across from me. Anger rolls off her body in waves that I wouldn't want to be on the receiving end of Sienna's murderous stare.

"Care to explain?" She doesn't elaborate, only cocks an

eyebrow. When Vin doesn't open his mouth, she continues. "Let's start with why you haven't bothered to call with an explanation, Vin?"

His eyes cut to the lower level of the club before he finally speaks. I wonder if he was looking for her brothers. "This isn't the time nor the place for that conversation, Si."

"Not even a thank you for saving your ass?"

"Like I said," he grits through clenched teeth, his brows lifted.

Her lips purse before she straightens her posture and then takes a step back. She looks down at where I'm seated. "Aren't you going to offer a lady a seat?"

"If by seat, you're referring to the one I'm occupying, and by lady you're referring to yourself, then by all means"—I slide my chair backward without standing—"have a seat, baby," I offer, a smile that I'm certain comes off cocky spreads across my face, but from the gleam she's trying to mask, I know I haven't offended her.

"Such a gentleman you are," she coos.

I'm really not, but I don't tell her that. The only time I attempt being anything that resembles gentlemanly is when I'm in the presence of my mother and that's because she has no qualms about taking a wooden spoon to any limb on my body or chewing me out if I give her a reason to.

I think Sienna is turning around to continue her conversation with Vin when she surprises me and plants her plump ass on my lap. I'm so caught off guard that I sit frozen when she twists around to face Vin.

"So, you were saying?"

"I wasn't saying anything. But since you want to hear something, how about this. There are plenty of vacant chairs at other tables. You don't have to sit on top of Matteo. Especially since you were just sucking face with that Russian scumbag," he seethes.

"To be Russian you have to be born in Russia. I would have thought you knew that, Vin. I bet even Matteo knows that." She turns her head, looking over her shoulder, and fuck me, she is even hotter at this angle. Makes me think of . . . "You knew that, right?"

"Of course," I agree, having forgotten what she said at the thought of fucking her from behind clouding my mind. If I'm not careful I'm going to get hard with her on my lap. Then again, maybe that's not such a bad thing. She's felt it before, and why beat around the bush? I might as well lay all my cards on the table, letting her know exactly what I want to do with her.

"See." She faces away from me again but leans back until her back is only inches from my chest. My right hand moves up, cupping her hip and I lean forward meeting her the rest of the way and grab my drink with my free hand. "Besides, I can suck whatever I want with whomever I damn well please. It's no business of yours. Even Matteo here if I want to."

"You can suck anything on me you want, baby," I inform her. Mainly because I want Vin to understand that she isn't his and won't ever be. "In fact, you can even suck my drink down if you want."

"Aw, that's sweet." There is sarcasm in her tone. "But I'm not a big drinker."

My brows furrow, remembering the bartender from Raymond's bringing her a drink last week. "Funny. I clearly recall you downing at least two shots worth of whiskey only a few nights ago."

"True. I can't argue with you there, but I was stressed . . . and pissed." I feel her chest expand, pulling in a deep breath. "Someone that was supposed to be my friend had betrayed my family and I thought he was going to be fish food."

"I didn't betray no-goddamn-body."

Sienna shoots forward, but I don't release my hold from her hip bone. "Keep your voice down," she bites out.

"You're one to fucking talk," Vin says, his eyes going over her shoulder to me and then flash back. "You shouldn't be saying shit in front of him."

"That's my call, not yours. I want to know why Levi was photographed with Rico Romano. A rat, Vin. Was he planning something against my family, or anyone else's? And lastly, I want to know if you knew that your sister's husband—who lives in your house, let's not forget that piece of information—was involved with him."

"The answer you're so hard up for is, I don't know a damn thing about Levi and Rico's relationship or what they were up to, if anything. Levi wasn't that bright, so I can't see him being up to much." Vin tosses the remainder of his drink back, and after placing the glass back on the table, he stands. "What I won't do is sit here and watch you wiggle your ass on another man. I've seen all I can handle for one night. And just so you know, your father ordered me to stay away from you. That's why I haven't called or texted you."

With that, he leaves us remaining at the table, Sienna still in my lap, sans any wiggling. "He's a buzzkill," I remark.

"Yeah, but he was right. I shouldn't have said any of that in front of you." She sighs. "But when I get mad, I run my mouth."

"Well," I begin, lifting my hand up, cupping her cheek, and

then I run my thumb across her bottom lip. Her skin is like velvet with no trace of lipstick or gloss. I don't need to give that too much thought, not wanting to remember Krishna's lips against them. "If you need help keeping it closed, I got something you can wrap these soft lips around."

"Do you now?" she asks, but I can tell it's a rhetorical question. "Doubt that's something you would have offered back in high school."

"Probably not, but since we aren't in high school anymore it's irrelevant, don't you think? That's long past us."

"Not really. You seem to think I'm a different person than I was back then." She shakes her head. "I'm not. I'm still the same, just in different packaging."

"And it's nice packaging." I laugh as she rolls her eyes. "Real nice packaging, baby."

"Like I've told you before, I'm not your baby. I'm done here. Have a nice rest of the night, and *do* forget what you heard me say to Vin."

She goes to stand, but I wrap my arm around her waist, squeezing her to my front as I lean up, placing my lips to her ear. "Where are you running off to?"

Her breath hitches and she licks her lips. "Not running," she tells me, her voice masked with a calmness I know she doesn't possess, though she is a good little actress, I'll give her that. "I'm done, so I'm going to find someone to dance with. The only thing at a club to do is drink or dance, and since I don't drink when I'm at a club, I want to dance."

"Then you shall dance." I smirk at her. "With me."

Tapping her hip, I signal for her to stand, which she does, but doesn't step away to give me room to stand. Instead, she eyes me with a question I can't quite decipher. I don't want to analyze it, so I grab her hips and push her backward as I stand. Not letting go, I seal her front flush with mine. "Whatever you want tonight, take it from me."

Instead of waiting for a response, I release her hips and slide my hand into hers, leading her to the stairs. She's wrong. She's a completely different woman than the girl I knew during our school days.

Unless, of course, the girl I thought I knew wasn't who I assumed she was. If that's the case, what did I miss? And how? Guess there is only one way to find out. Get to know the woman she is now. Which I intend to do—sooner rather than later is preferred.

CHAPTER 17
DOMENICO

"Fuck," I bark out in irritation.

I don't need this shit tonight. I wanted one night where I don't have to be in charge. It's Ren's fucking fault for telling our sister where we were headed. She shows up and Krishna's fucking ass decided to play his mind games. Granted, he made his point, and now my suspicion of Calvin Ross not being who Sienna thinks he is, is looking more and more on point. I'm rarely wrong about people, and from the day I met Vin I knew something was off with him. He definitely wants my sister. And yes, I'm an asshole of a big brother. I'm slightly overbearing when it comes to protecting my siblings, even though there is only one year between us in age. Still, they are mine, and when it comes to Sienna, I'm not going to allow just any fucker to touch her. Should someone worthy of her time step forward, I wouldn't have a problem letting my strings loosen with her.

"What?" Lorenzo calls out without looking up from the third

glass he's drank in the last half an hour, which means he's going to be another one of my problems for the night to deal with.

Why didn't I leave them both at home?

"Your goddamn twin. That's what." I jerk my head toward the dance floor. "De Salvo might as well be humping her out there." I should walk out there and rip that bastard's hands right off her, but on one hand, Matteo touching her doesn't get under my skin the same way Vin's eyes on her did, or when Krishna had his tongue down my sister's throat while eye-fucking me from across the bar. On the other hand, my father has made it clear to all his children that Matteo De Salvo isn't to touch his daughter in any way. Tony Caputo doesn't like the boxing champ, and it has nothing to do with his former relationship with Matteo's uncle. Everyone knows Si has had a thing for Matteo since we were kids and De Salvo never paid her a bit of attention. If she wasn't good enough for him then, she isn't going to be good enough for him now, and I don't plan on letting my sister be another notch on his bedpost.

"Lay off her," Ren bites out. "Let her get her rocks off if she wants. Hell, she needs to get that fucker out of her system. Maybe fucking him will do that."

"Wish she'd rub that fine ass on me."

Ren and I both look to my right. "Do you want to bleed tonight?" I arch an eyebrow as I look down at Rick from where my ass is perched on the arm of the chair he's slouched back in, a tumbler of whiskey in his hand.

"Did I say that out loud?" He smirks, not really caring if I answer him.

"She wants in *his* pants. There's a difference. She doesn't want to fuck you," Ren chimes in before I do.

"How do you know? Maybe we should ask her," he smarts off.

"Maybe you should shut the fuck up before I shut you up—permanently." I blow air out of my mouth, showing my frustration. "I gotta call Dad."

"Why?" Ren asks. "Can't you just let her be for tonight?"

"There are cameras everywhere, Lorenzo. If I don't call him when he can clearly see that I see her with De Salvo, he'll have my ass. And just because the two of you get away with shit, doesn't mean I do." I stand, pull my cell out from the inside of my right jean pocket, and then I walk toward the bar where the music isn't as loud. "Fuck my life."

Dad picks up on the second ring, as he always does when it's one of his kids calling him. "Hello."

"Si and Matteo are talking," I tell him, cutting to the chase.

"Just talking?" he inquires, his voice sounding almost bored.

I turn my head, looking back to where I saw them last. The music has changed, the song faster and even more upbeat than the last. *Jesus.* She's basically riding his fucking leg. "More or less," I answer.

"Don't give me that shit, Dom. You're beating around the bush. What is your sister doing?"

"They're dancing. Together," I add.

"Okay."

"Okay?" I repeat, slowly, as if questioning the word I clearly heard. His "okay" was far too calm for a man that doesn't want his daughter around a certain man.

"If she tries to leave with him, you can intervene. Otherwise, let your sister make her own mistakes. Hell, give De Salvo some rope. Maybe he'll hang himself with it, or maybe he won't, 'cause we'll see, won't we?"

"Sure, old man. If that's what you think is best."

"It's rope, Dom. You give a little. Some things you give more of it on, but you don't let the end of the rope go."

"Got it," I say. "Wrap it around his fucking neck should I feel the need to."

"Son, I got Sienna from my end. Go decompress for the night. You need it after this week."

"I'm fine, Dad," I assure him.

"Of course, you are. You're a Caputo. But still, everyone needs a night off, so take it. Let the twins handle their own shit and you handle yours. Goodnight, Son," he says, right before the call ends.

You don't have to tell me twice. I don't even eye my sister before I pocket my cell and head toward the door. I drove, but being as my father owns this bar, my car will be safely parked in the small parking garage next to the nightclub. I've had enough responsibility to last me a lifetime. A good fucking time isn't going to be had here tonight, but it's still early, and a strip joint sounds like the type of relaxation I deserve. So, to Headliner's it is, where tits are plentiful.

"You don't strike me as the type that gets drunk often." Matteo's face is flushed, his cheeks stained with a rose shade and perspiration runs down his temples. I'm sure my face mirrors his, minus the diluted buzz he was getting from the alcohol.

"Depends. I'm not usually," he informs me. "Never when I have Brooklyn, and even when I don't have her, anything could happen, and if I can't get to her, then what good of a father am I? The few times I do drink is when my parents have her and I'm not training for a fight."

"So, which is it tonight?" He switched to water when we came to the dance floor an hour ago. I've drank my weight in aqua tonight, so I'm surprised I haven't had to ditch him for the bathroom.

"I'm not training." He shakes his head. "I will be after this weekend, but I'm not in training mode this week. Brooklyn is at her mom's." His chest expands, and then he lets out a powerful sigh that fans my face. "I'm never relaxed when she isn't with me or my parents."

"You don't trust Kennedy with her own daughter?" Her name comes out like a sour taste in my mouth, but I don't bother to mask my dislike for his ex.

"Fuck no! That bitch is the last person I trust with my kid. But Brooklyn loves her mother and I want my daughter to be happy, so, I relent and let Kennedy have time with her." His jaw locks and the evidence of his disdain is all over his face.

"Does that mean you have sole custody of her?" I inquire.

"It does. I know it seems odd, me being her dad when usually it's the mother that gets full custody, or both parents have joint."

"Not really." My head shakes, disagreeing with him. "I was raised by my dad, and if you're the better parent then she should be with you."

"Yeah, but your mom di—" He catches himself before the word is fully out of his mouth. "Shit. I'm sorry. That was—"

"It's fine, Matteo." I interject, cutting him off. "She did die. That's a fact. You aren't hurting my feelings by stating what's reality."

"Yeah, but . . ." he trails off as the song changes and I turn in his arm, facing away from him with my back against his chest and my butt against his jean-clad crotch.

"I didn't find it insensitive, so relax."

I press against him more when he doesn't comment back. I like the way it feels being fused together with Matteo. He's solid everywhere that's touching me, and his body towers over me, sort of like there's a wall of protection at my back and it's there for me alone.

Being the daughter of a man that's simply feared for the

reputation his last name holds, I've never felt unprotected. With my dad and brothers it's suffocating at times. This feels different, and part of me is afraid that it's not real. That I'm making it more than what it is in reality. My insecurities send a shiver up my spine and it takes all the force I can muster not to pull away from him.

"Why are you trembling?" he whispers to the outside of my ear.

I shrug, giving in to the need to retreat and pull away from him. "No reason."

Matteo tightens his hold around my waist, before spinning me to face him. He tugs me in closer, my stomach meeting the front of his pants. "There is a reason. You just don't want to tell me."

"I should go find Ren and go home." His eyes bore down into mine and it's too much.

"Ren left half an hour after Dom did. Tell me," he demands.

"Krishna is prob—"

"Fuck Nikolayev. You aren't going anywhere with him or near him. Now tell me what I want to know."

I look away, surveying the club to confirm my brothers aren't here. Irritation flicks across Matteo's face as if he thinks I'm searching for Krishna instead of Dom and Ren. I hadn't realized either had left. Ren disappears often so I'm used to that, but Dom doesn't. He always tells me when he's leaving and offers me a ride. I guess he's pissed at me over what Krishna did earlier. Oh well, he'll get over it.

Matteo's warm fingers touch my chin, applying the slightest bit of pressure, before turning my face to gaze back up at him. When our brown eyes lock, his silent demand is coaxing me to answer. Being tired from dancing, I relent. Slowly raising my eyes, I stop when they land on his and give Matteo an honest answer.

"You make me nervous. You always have."

CHAPTER 19
MATTEO

Her words come out as a whisper; almost too low to hear over the beat of the music, as if she was hoping I'd missed what she said.

You make me nervous. You always have.

Those words silently replay as I continue eyeing her, wondering if it's a good kind of nervous or a bad. I don't want to scare her, and I don't get the feeling that I do. She went toe to toe with me only a couple of days ago. Someone that was afraid of me wouldn't have done so with the ease and confidence I saw in her.

"If that's the case, why didn't you say something already?" I joke. "We could have gotten out of here and been back at my place working out all the ways I make you a nervous wreck, baby." I tug her closer. "A couple of hours from now I'll have you completely relaxed."

"God, you're full of yourself." Her nose scrunches in disgust at the same time she tries to pull away from me. "And do not put words in my mouth, Matteo."

Not releasing her, I smirk. "I'm not that full of myself, but you could certainly be stuffed with me."

"That's a hard pass."

She twists away, barely making any effort to get out of my grip. Pulling her back to my front, I lean into her, bringing my mouth to brush against her ear over her black, silky locks. "You can pretend you don't want me, but I know you do, and I want you too, Si. It's that simple. What's the point in prolonging the inevitable?"

Turning her head to look back up at me, she arches an eyebrow. "Did you learn nothing from my father showing up at your place Sunday morning? If memory serves me correctly, and it does, he had a loaded weapon pressed against your forehead, threatening your life. A repeat of that is only going to end with him pulling the trigger this time."

"You handled your dad well and I remained unscathed. Besides, you're an adult, aren't you?"

She doesn't answer my question, but a yawn creeps up her throat. Closing her eyes, she brings her hand up, cupping her mouth until it passes. I release her, giving her room to breathe.

"It's nearing one in the morning and I'm up by four most mornings, so that I can get an hour and half of mat time in with my trainer. If I don't get a few hours of sleep, he's going to kick my ass in the literal sense. The only place I'm going is home, to my bed, alone."

"Then at least let me drive you."

"I drove. My car is in the parking garage."

"Yeah, mine is too." I sigh, blowing out a breath and fanning Sienna with warm air. The top of her arms breakout with goose bumps. "Your eye lids have been at half-mast for a while. Let me drive you?" I ask again, all joking and wanting to fuck her aside. I do want to make sure she gets home safely.

"Fine," she relents. "But if my father is home and doesn't take too kindly to your generosity, don't say I didn't warn you."

"I'll take my chances with the boss."

"Then you must be a complete dumbass."

Without replying, *I know I am*, I lace my fingers with hers and pull her from the nightclub as my phone buzzes in my pocket. I don't bother checking it, not caring that I'd made plans to meet up with one of my buddies tonight instead of escorting a girl home where she apparently still lives at her father's rather than her own place like most adults.

CHAPTER 20
SIENNA

I didn't need an escort. Sure, I'm as tired as he remarked earlier, and I did almost doze off in his SUV at least once on the ride to my house, but leaving my car parked in the city is going to be more of a hassle than it's worth. There is no way I'm getting past Daddy without an interrogation, and in a few hours when I need a ride to the gym, he's going to crawl my ass for taking my car to the city in the first place.

He hates it when I go into the city alone. It's okay if I'm with Dom or Ren, but God forbid I drive myself. So yeah, I'm sure this isn't going to go over well.

"You didn't have to walk me to the door, you know." I stop and turn around to face Matteo.

"What kind of gentleman would I be if I didn't?" One corner of his mouth curves up in a half smile, or maybe it's an arrogant smirk. I'm too exhausted to decipher.

"Are you?" I ask instead.

"Am I what?"

"A gentleman."

He takes a long stride forward, stopping only inches away from the toes of my heel-covered feet. "Answer my question and I'll answer yours, Sienna."

"You haven't asked one." He did and I haven't forgotten it, but I choose to play dumb despite the fact that his blue eyes are calling me on my bullshit.

"Tell me what it is about me that makes you nervous. You don't look nervous right now."

Looks can be deceiving, I think to myself, but instead of telling him that, I say, "You don't know enough about me to make that judgment, De Salvo."

"Then let me get to know you better."

"Why?"

"Why not?" he counters, and I roll my eyes. "It's a legit question. I'm not being funny or an asshole. I do want to get to know you. The *you* I apparently didn't see when we were kids." His admission only serves to grate on my nerves. Crossing my arms, I tap the pad of my foot and stare at him. "I'm not leaving until you throw me a bone."

Dropping my arms, I step forward, entering his personal space. Matteo holds his spot. He doesn't back away at my advancement. "You make me feel like I need to put on a jacket and then zip the jacket all the way up to my neck. There. I threw you a bone. You can leave now." I hold his stare, waiting for him to pivot and leave.

He does neither.

"So, I make you feel vulnerable or insecure or both?"

"I don't know. I haven't really given it much thought." I'm lying. I've analyzed the shit out of it, and that's exactly the way he makes me feel. And I hate it. I hate it so much that I want to punch him in the face for it.

The corners of his mouth tip up, spreading into a slow, satisfied smile. He leans forward but I pull away from him.

"If you kiss me, I'm going to send you to your knees in a world of pain."

"Why are you fighting this so hard?" He blows out a breath, stepping back, giving me breathing room. "You know, you might legally be an adult, but you haven't grown up. If you were grown, you'd be able to admit you like me and that you want to be in my bed just as much as I want you in my bed."

"I can admit anything I damn well want, should I want to admit it." I step forward, shoving my finger into the center of his rock-hard chest. "You're hot, Matteo. I can admit you're attractive. That doesn't mean I want you, and it doesn't mean you're my type. Maybe you're reading this wrong and it's just you that wants me. But newsflash, champ, I have no desire to be another notch on your bedpost."

"Now who's the one making assumptions? You can't fault me for thinking you were this angelic good girl and then turn around and assume I just want in your pants without giving me a chance first." He arches an eyebrow. "Dinner tomorrow night?"

"No."

"Friday night?"

"No."

"Saturday night then?" Before I can repeat my last answer, he continues, not allowing me to speak. "That's my date night with my daughter, but I'm sure she'd be fine if you crashed it. You can even pick the venue."

At the mention of his kid, my chest tightens, and I think I

actually want to say yes. I'm so appalled at that revelation that I shout, "No, Matteo! No. No. And no."

"So, I need Daddy's permission then?" He nods as if answering his own question. "Okay, then. Invite me in. Is the Boss even still awake or is the old man asleep by now?"

"You really have a death wish, don't you?"

"No. I just want to take you out on a date, Sienna. And if I have to ask Tony Caputo for permission, I'm man enough to do that. Being the adult that I am . . ."

"I manage a multi-million-dollar enterprise. I'm an adult, Matteo. Just because I still live under my father's roof doesn't change that."

The nerve of him. I'll never go on a date with him now. He doesn't get to insult me and then wine and dine me. That's not how you treat a woman. My mom may have died when I was young, but I remember how my father spoke to her, respected her, cherished her. *No one will ever live up to my dad.* That's one of my problems with men. Daddy set the bar too high. It's unreachable.

Before I realize what's happening, Matteo's lips are on my cheek, delivering the softest kiss I've ever felt. It sends fire down my neck, and I'm frozen to the spot I'm standing in on the porch.

"Until our date . . . Goodnight, baby."

I finally blink, regaining my bearings and watch as Matteo strides to his SUV, not even giving me a backward glance.

Our date? Not happening. Not in this lifetime anyway. Besides, Daddy will never allow it. That much I can count on.

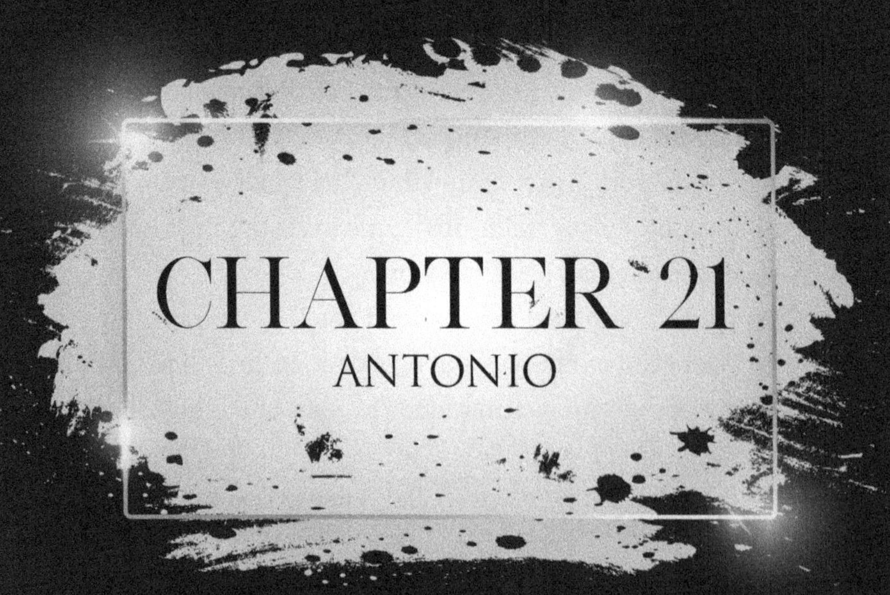

CHAPTER 21
ANTONIO

The thing about being in my position, you have to be on guard every minute of every day. I have allies and I have enemies. Friends are few and far between. When my wife was murdered, I knew in the pit of my stomach it was done by someone close, but eighteen years later, I still don't know who.

The day I watched my wife's coffin be lowered six feet into the ground, I vowed I would find out who was responsible, and when I do, they'll beg me to send them to Hell before I'm finished with them.

The tragedy of her death taught me to pay attention to everything around me: scenery, body language, conversations. I have to be able to recognize the monsters that lurk in the shadows. The everyday thug perched against a brick wall on a street corner, smoking a joint and waiting out his time to mug a passerby. The street punk trying to offload mommy's prescription meds for a couple of bucks.

I've practically made a profession out of spotting the people that go unnoticed every day, so when I whiz by a shitty apartment building in a rundown, almost dilapidated part of Queens, I know instantly who the girl sitting on a set of brick steps is.

My tires screech, burning rubber as my body lurches forward, only held back by the strap preventing me from slamming into the steering wheel. Out of reflex, my right arm flies out, connecting with my son's chest to prevent him from getting hurt, even though he too is already secured by a seatbelt.

"Jesus, Dad. What the fuck?" Domenico's voice rushes out in shock. It's mere seconds for my son—my most trusted associate—to take in my expression and then act on it, preparing for the worst.

Dom's seatbelt releases, and before I can blink, he pulls his Glock from the inside of his suit jacket, all while his eyes are looking three hundred and sixty degrees around the vehicle, searching for the threat. "Put the weapon away, Domenico." I order, putting the car in park in the middle of the road. Unbuckling, I open the driver's side door and climb out of my Maserati. I turn upon its closure, looking over the roof at the rundown apartment building as I button my suit jacket.

The passenger side door opens as I stare at the child that caught my attention, her elbows on her knees with her chin resting in her palms.

"If there isn't a threat then why did you brake so goddamn hard?" Dom asks, eyeing me over the roof of the car. "Why'd you stop here?" he continues.

I nod my head in the girl's direction and answer his question. He'll either recognize her, or he won't. Either way, this is something Domenico needs to learn if he's going to step into my shoes one of these days; not that it's what I want for him, but at the same time, I know it's inevitable.

Walking to the rear of my car, I round the vehicle and step toward the curb, stalking to where she's remained seated in the same spot, oblivious to the dangers around her.

If that dumbass is responsible for his little girl being in this neighborhood, I swear to God it'll be the last mistake he ever makes. Prostitution, drug deals, fucking drive-bys are a daily occurrence around here. This is no place for any kid—girl or boy, young or even ones in their teens.

I stop at the bottom of the stairs. Seconds of silence pass before her blue eyes glance up. "What are you doing out here alone?" I ask as Dom stops next to me.

She's on the second to the last step from the top of the concrete stairs but still has to tilt her head back to meet my eyes. "Waiting," she whispers.

"Waiting for who?" My question comes out harsher than I meant for it to.

"Mommy," she replies. I hate to admit it, but relief floods my body, relaxing my shoulders at her admission.

The champ will live another day.

"And where is your mother, Brooklyn?"

"In there." She turns, looking over her shoulder at the closed door. It's a four-story building, so 'in there' could be any of at least fifty or more doors.

"Do you know which apartment number?" She shakes her head. "Do you know what floor?"

"Second. She told me to just play outside and she wouldn't be long, but it's been a long time and there's nothing to do out here."

I start to open my mouth to tell Dom to escort the girl to my car, but before the order is out, he steps to the stairs, taking them two at a time, and then disappears inside the apartment building. When there is dirty work—blood spilling that must be handled—I prefer to stain my own hands. My children were never supposed to be involved in that manner. I made a vow to my firstborn, the first words uttered out of my mouth upon a nurse placing him in my arms that I would change my family and the families of those who answer to me. I would change the world for the better. I wouldn't allow my children to follow in our family's past mistakes. I wouldn't let them spill the blood of the innocent or taint their own flesh with the greed of my father's generation and his father and so on.

Things were supposed to be different for my wife and children. I've tried to keep them innocent for as long as I can, but everything I set out to accomplish on the day Domenico was born hasn't happened yet. That hope, that dream, seems to dwindle more and more as each year passes.

I sigh out a long breath as I stare down at the brown-haired little girl. She reminds me of Sienna when she was that age. There's spunk in this kid. I saw it last weekend when she tripped me, and for whatever reason, that little act of bravery and defiance earned her a spot inside of my chest that I thought was already filled to the brim with my late wife's memory and my lively three kids.

"Come here, Brooklyn." I open my arms and bend downward. She scrambles to her feet and is down the steps in seconds. Gathering her in my arms, I place her on my hip. "We're going to teach your father a lesson on who he leaves his daughter in the care of."

A lesson I'm sure he's not going to react well to.

But it's one he's better off learning now, from me, rather than later with a much different outcome. Anyone could have come along and taken this child, and no one would be the wiser, which is exactly what I'm doing, but with me, Matteo will get his daughter back.

A shudder runs down my spine, making me grip Brooklyn tighter at the mere thought that anyone else could have seen her sitting alone with no parent in sight. Being a father, those *what if* questions have haunted me for over twenty-five years. I still imagine worst-case scenarios all the time, even though my three children are adults.

"Where is your mom's car?" I ask the girl. There's a parking lot on the other side of the street across from the apartment building, and I'm guessing that's where the tenants park; although, the lot is sparse, lacking many vehicles.

"Some man left in it," she answers.

Fucking figures, I silently think, shaking my head. I was going to retrieve the booster seat so that Brooklyn is properly secured in my car, but that's not happening. Guess Dom will just have to sit in the back with her.

Reaching into the pocket of my trousers, I grab my key fob and then press the unlock button, before reaching for the backdoor on the driver's side, pulling it open. "What's your name, Mister?"

"It's Tony," I say, ducking inside and setting her gently on the leather seat. "But you can call me Grandpa, sweetheart." I offer a warm smile, hoping to put her at ease, but then realize there's no need. She isn't scared or searching for her mother at all. If anything, she's excited that I'm taking her away from this place.

That's another thing I'm going to have to have a chat about with Matteo. She should be kicking and screaming at the top of her lungs right now, but she isn't. She's perfectly content allowing a stranger to kidnap her, and *that's* unacceptable.

"Why are you so pissy today? Huh?" I drop my phone on my lap and roll my head left, eyeing the side of Ren's face as he drives. "You look like shit. You haven't shown up for any training session this week and I know you haven't gotten home before three in the morning this whole month. What's up, Ren?"

"You ever thought about minding your own business?" He glances at me, taking his eyes off the road to drive his point home. *He doesn't want to talk*. Well, too bad. It's high time for him to spill his guts. He's hiding something. I know he is. He's the secretive one out of the three of us. I may have been good at playing plain Jane, but I only did it at the demand of my father after our mother was killed. Ren has been secretive for as far back as I can remember. Domenico and I get enjoyment out of making him tell us things.

"All I do is mind my own business. It just so happens that you are one of my businesses, brother." He's my twin. Everything he does is on a need-to-know basis with me.

"Lay off, Si." This is where he and Dom differ. Domenico is harsh and barks out orders. Lorenzo is more laid back, though today he is far from relaxed. Something is bothering him. He's angry, but he looks like he's brooding. Only Dom and I know him well enough to tell the difference.

"Not until you come clean and tell me what's going on with you. Who are you mad at, for starters?"

"Maybe school is getting to me. We all have our bad days. Today is mine."

"School isn't getting to you, you little liar. You just don't want to tell me. Why is that? What are you hiding that you can't tell your best friend, Ren?" I cross my arms, staring at the side of his face. "I tell you everything." My tone comes out accusing, which is exactly how I feel. I'm just not sure what I'm accusing him of.

"You ever think that maybe you tell me too much? Being as I'm your *brother*."

"Don't pull that B.S. We shared a womb. There is no such thing as TMI between us. Now tell me what it is that's bothering you, or who is bothering you, and I'll kick their ass for you."

"You know, you're bound to meet your match one of these days. Someone besides Dom and me is going to whoop your ass." He doesn't look at me. He just continues to stare out the windshield as he pulls through the open gate at the entrance of our neighborhood.

"Until then . . ." I nod, sounding cocky, but I know he's right. I'm not the badass I try to portray. I know there are stronger, more skilled fighters than me. Plenty more in fact. I'm way down the list on badassery.

"Yeah, well, just make sure I'm there so I can witness it."

"Oh, bite me," I bark back. Crossing my arms over my chest, I look forward, pursing my lips. I don't know what's crawled up Ren's ass, but I'm not going to take the brunt of his anger. I got next to zero sleep this morning after I got home. Instead of canceling with my trainer, I still managed to get to the gym, where I knew what would happen; I got my butt kicked and I still have the aches and bruises to show for it. I'm tired. I'm not up for dealing with my brother's problems. "I simply wanted to know what, or who, is keeping you from your normal training routine. You've always preferred to get it in before the gym is crawling with people."

"No. You do. I just drag my ass with you because that's what time you want to train with Caesar. Then I go back in the late afternoon or evenings so I can get a real workout in when I'm actually awake and functioning like a human."

"No one ever said you had to go to the gym with me at five every morning. If you don't like it, then sleep."

"Dad doesn't like you going there alone. He'd beat my ass if Dom wasn't going in my place."

"Are you for real right now?" Before the question exits my mouth, I know the answer. Of course, Tony Caputo would make sure one of my brothers escorts me like I need a fucking babysitter and can't take care of myself. "Fucking Dad!" I seethe.

When are the men in my life going to realize I can handle my own damn self perfectly fine? I'm more than capable of handling me. What the fuck do I have to do to prove that to them?

"There is nothing to prove, Si." Lorenzo sighs after doing his twin mind reading thing as he pulls into the driveway, parking his Range Rover behind Dom's SUV. "He's always going to keep a tighter leash on you. He's not going to chance what happened to Mo—"

I reach for the door handle, bolting out of the vehicle before Ren finishes his statement. I'm not our mother. I don't need to be handled with special care. It's why Dad put us in self-defense and martial arts classes. He wanted us to be prepared for anything and anyone.

Slamming the door, I head toward the front of the house, not waiting on my brother. His door closes soon after. It only takes a few seconds before I feel his presence behind me. "It is what it is, Si. Just accept it."

I don't respond. His comment only further pisses me off, but I don't get the chance to reply with a snarky comeback. Squealing tires coming to a stop halt my movement before I reach for the front door. Turning, I watch Matteo throw the driver's side door open, before exiting his Lexus.

"Didn't you see enough of him last night?" Ren blows out a breath, fanning my hair, before opening the front door of our house. "Get rid of him before Dad finds out he's here."

I follow my brother, but stop inside the doorway, planning to do just that. Matteo doesn't take no for an answer well. I'm not going out with him. Sure, I want to, and he was right, I am attracted to him, but I knew that was obvious years ago. Why should I make it easy for him now?

"You're wasting your time if you're here to ask me out again." I brace my elbow against the doorframe, placing my other hand on my hip. As Matteo jogs up the steps, I realize he's seething. He's pissed.

He doesn't slow his stride as he nears me, and I'm about to step backward when he snags my bicep in his hand, squeezing his fingers around my bare skin. Pushing me inside my house, he wears a murderous expression. "Where is Brooklyn?!"

CHAPTER 23
MATTEO

She stumbles, but I place my free hand on her hip to steady her. Sienna tries to snatch her arm from my grasp, but her attempt to get free is futile. I have her, and she isn't getting away from me unless I allow it.

A cold, sharp blade of metal presses against my throat before Si opens her mouth. "I suggest you take your hands off my sister before I make you choke on your own fucking blood." Ren's breath is hot next to my ear. I don't blink or acknowledge his presence or even the knife biting into my skin.

"Why would I have any idea where your kid is, Matteo?" Sienna lashes back, her cheeks flushing with anger. Until right now, I've enjoyed witnessing the fury in her dark eyes and the fire that's housed inside her irises ready to be released on a moment's notice. Part of me finds it cute, sexy even, but all I care about right this minute is finding my daughter and pulling her into my arms where I know she is safe. I'll go through *anyone* I have to, even the beauty standing before me, her brothers and her father included.

"If you don't heed my brother's suggestion, it's not your blood you're going to be choking on. You'll be dead before one drop leaks from your skull." The barrel of Dom's gun jams into my temple.

"Where. Is. My—"

"Your daughter is in the boss's office. She's fine, but I can't promise the same thing about you if you don't take your hands off my sister," Dom issues a threat, his voice deep, lethal.

"What's Brooklyn doing in Dad's office?" Sienna's anger settles into confusion. Her eyes leave mine to peer at her eldest brother. *She didn't know Brooklyn was here.* That revelation soothes something inside me. My grip on her loosens, my vision finally expanding to more than just her face, and it's now I realize how tight my fingers were wrapped around her arms.

"That's between De Salvo and the boss. Stay out of it," he tells her.

My hands fall away from her, dropping to my sides. I see the red marks I left on her, and on the inside I cringe, not believing I'm the one who caused them, but I school my features, not prepared to show any of them something they can perceive as a weakness. Sienna's brows furrow like she can see the inner turmoil raging inside me.

"My daughter," I bite out through clenched teeth. Domenico retracts the weapon, and suddenly I'm able to breathe again. It's impossible to mask the relief my chest visibly shows.

"Come on, big guy." She reaches forward, tugging the material of my T-shirt. "I'll take you to my dad." When I don't move, her gaze snaps to her twin. "Back off, Ren."

He didn't remove his blade when Dom removed the barrel of this gun from my head. Instead, the metal digs deeper into my skin, and it takes every ounce of willpower I have not to turn on him. I can take Ren. I'm even certain I could remove his knife from my throat without getting nicked, but I won't be quicker than a bullet should Dom decide to pull the trigger. I have my daughter to think about, so I stand stock still, my eyes remaining locked with the mafia princess's.

"Make a habit of hurting my sister and I'll do the same to someone you love, De Salvo. Only my marks won't fade away as if they never happened. My marks scar." He steps back, pulling the knife with him. The sting of the blade slicing through my skin burns. The pain is minimal. I'm used to pain, to my flesh splitting. I'm not looking into a mirror, but I doubt the cut is deep.

Sienna's gaze falls to where blood leaks from the wound. Her eyes flash the same as they did when I watched Ren do this to her last week. She has a fascination with violence, making me wonder what all she's been subjected to growing up, and what she is still subjected to.

I need to get my kid the fuck out of here.

I always thought my mom overreacted when I'd hear stories about how she only agreed to marry my dad if he walked away from his family, if he left the Mafia behind. Not that he was deep in it. His oldest brother became the head of the De Salvo family when my grandfather was killed. My dad once told me that seeing his father lying in an alley, shot to death was a defining moment in his life. He didn't want to be part of that world, so when my mom gave him an ultimatum, he welcomed it. He embraced it and never looked back.

I'm starting to understand my mom's side of it. I don't want this life for my daughter either.

Turning her back to me, she tugs my shirt once more,

beckoning me to follow.

Tony's office isn't far. From the foyer, we bypass the stairs and then their enormous living room to head down a corridor, before Sienna turns left, now walking down a dimly lit hallway. Giggles I could recognize in a crowd of hundreds hit my eardrums, propelling me to step around Si, quickening my pace until I reach Tony's open doorway. Brooklyn's back is to me. She is sitting cross legged on his desk, her long, straight, dark hair covering the T-shirt I know damn well I dropped her off in at Kennedy's last night.

Tony's eyes snap up, connecting with mine. His easygoing smile instantly hardens, making me question if he was actually wearing one at all.

"Brooklyn Martina, come here," I order, my eyes never leaving the man that should not be in possession of my little girl.

Twisting the top half of her body, she eyes me. "Daddy," she squeals. Her legs untangle and then she pushes off the desk, landing on her feet, before running toward me.

When she nears, I bend, grabbing her under the arms and lifting Brooklyn into my embrace. Once she is secured and my blood starts pumping again, my anger returns.

I'm about to lash out when Brooklyn stuns me into silence. "Oh, Daddy, I've had the best day ever with Papa Tony. Can I come back tomorrow?"

Papa what? Did she just call him Papa fucking Tony? The most feared man in all of New York?

"You're welcome to come back anytime you like." Tony leans back, crossing his arms over his chest.

"What's going on?" Sienna ducks between the entryway and my side, squeezing inside the office to stand a few inches past me. “Why is Matteo’s daughter here?” She straightens her spine, standing tall, and crosses her arms to match her father’s.

“I’d like the answer to that as well,” I tell him.

“Princess, why don’t you take Brooklyn to do whatever it is five-year-old’s like to do. I’d like to have a talk with De Salvo.”

“Why?” she questions, her eyebrows furrowed.

Tony stands. Leaning over his desk, he places both hands palm down. “Let me rephrase. Take the kid and shut the door on the way out.”

His tone leaves no room for argument, but either that didn’t register with Si or she isn’t fazed by it, because she takes a confident step toward him. “Not until you answer my first question. Why is she here?”

“Are you the girl’s mother?”

“What?!” Sienna drops her arms, then shakes her confused head. “You know I’m not, but what does that have to do with answering my question, Dad?”

“Your question is irrelevant just like this conversation. Why Brooklyn is here doesn’t concern you. If Matteo decides to fill you in then so be it, but I’m not. Leave, Sienna. You’re trying my patience and it’s at its max for today. Capisce?”

Sienna balls her fists and grits her teeth. She wants to argue but doesn’t. “Fine. Let’s go, Brooklyn. We aren’t wanted with the big boys.” Si leaves, and my daughter squirms out of my arms, following, confusion and worry on her little face too. I need answers from Tony, and until I get them, I’m not leaving this office.

Sienna doesn’t shut the door, obviously being the brat she is, so I do it and then turn back to face him, crossing my arms over my broad chest. “What is my kid doing here?”

"Have a seat," he orders, dodging my question or refusing me an answer; I don't know which.

"I'm not doing a damn thing until you tell me why you kidnapped my daughter. And don't you dare give me that, I'm the fucking Don, do what I say shit. You crossed a line with me when I found out my kid was here and not where she was supposed to be. Why the fuck do you have her?! Where's Kennedy?" I yell, my anger growing with every word coming out of my mouth.

"I don't really care for the Don, mobster reference, De Salvo, so don't give me that shit, but I am who I am, and you are in *my* house. You will show me some respect, and if you want answers you'll sit the fuck down so we can have a chat about the type of woman you shoot your shit into and make babies with. Now, take a fucking seat before I tire of this and put you six feet under and keep your kid. Frankly, I like her more than I do you."

"Stay the hell away from my daughter." Stepping toward him, I do as he says and sit in the chair in front of him. He mirrors my move, sitting back down in his leather chair. "I did what you said, now talk."

He arches an eyebrow, as if shocked by my own order. The old man probably isn't used to someone not bowing down to his every demand. I'm smart enough to recognize that it's dumb to talk to a man capable of murdering me and then covering it up, but he isn't the only one that's been pushed to his limit today.

So, have I.

"How about we start with how you knew where to find Brooklyn. I didn't order anyone to inform you, and Sienna didn't know. Only Domenico and I knew she was here. Does the necklace she's wearing have GPS installed?"

"Of course, it does. So does the watch she sometimes wears."

If Tony is surprised, he doesn't show it. Brooklyn isn't always with me, so to put my mind at ease and not constantly worry, I make sure she is wearing something that will show me her whereabouts at any given moment. I know it's not rational. I know that if someone were to take her, they can remove any device. Still, it gives me peace of mind.

"Well, then perhaps I won't put a bullet in your head after all."

CHAPTER 24
SIENNA

I carry Brooklyn on my hip into the kitchen where I find Domenico unwrapping a Tootsie Pop and shoving it into his mouth. He eyes us but says nothing. Brooklyn squirms, so I set her on the floor.

Dom motions with his fingers, telling Brooklyn to come to him. Concern isn't etched on my face, but my interest is piqued. Picking Matteo's daughter up, my brother places her gently down on the granite top of the island in the center of the kitchen just left of the sink.

"There are three things you and I need to clear up," Dom informs Brooklyn as I watch them interact like she's a problem he deems to fix. "And if you agree to do as I say, I'll give you one of these." He pulls a wrapped Tootsie Pop from his pocket. I'm sure he has at least several since he's come in the kitchen and restocked his pockets.

"I love candy," she chimes, her already big eyes expanding at the sight of the lollipop Dom is waving in front of her.

"Of course, you do. That's why this is going to be an easy arrangement."

"What's an arrangement?" she asks him.

"The things you're about to agree to." Brooklyn starts to ask another question, but Dom continues, not giving her a chance to speak. "One, you are not to refer to me as pretty ever again." I raise an eyebrow, wondering where this is going, but neither are paying me any attention. "Two, if you ever hear anyone else refer to me as pretty, you're going to punch them in the mouth. Has your dad taught you how to throw a proper punch?"

Brooklyn shakes her head but remains silent when Dom purses his lips as if her answer doesn't satisfy him. If Dom ever has kids, they're going to come out of the womb knowing how to fight. I feel sorry for the woman my brother marries, if he does end up marrying a girl that is. She can't be weak to handle him.

Dom glances in my direction finally. "You need to correct De Salvo's lack of parenting."

"Who are you to say he lacks something in that department? Not like you have one yourself. Besides, Dad didn't put us in martial arts until we were older than she is now."

"And Dad learned the error of his ways." That's the extent of Dom bringing up anything to do with our mother's death. It's not a subject he likes to discuss. I know he helps Dad in his continued search for Mom's killer, but neither talk about it. Turning his attention back on Brooklyn, he says, "If she won't do it, you come tell me, and I'll show you how to knock some punk kid to the ground. Would you like that?"

"Yes!" She exclaims, nodding her head in rapid succession. "I really, really would, but Daddy says I can't hit other kids."

"We won't discuss what your Daddy is. On to number three. From here on out, I'm the scariest person you have and will ever meet. Agreed?"

"You're so not scary." She shakes her head, disagreeing with him. The look on her face is so comical I have to bring my hand to my mouth and clamp my teeth down over my lips to keep from laughing. "Why would you want me to think you're scary?"

"Because I am scary. And you should be scared."

"Nah." She continues her head shake. "You're still too pretty to be scary."

"You just broke rule number one. Do I need to start over?"

"Brooklyn is right," I chime, smirking at my brother. "You're way too pretty to ever be scary." I'm lying, but I can't help myself. In some ways, Dom is scarier than our father. With Dad, I'm scared of disappointing him or getting in trouble. At twenty-three, I still get in trouble and Dad still reprimands me all the time. Adulthood didn't change that. He can't ground me, but he can sure lay into me, or give me the silent treatment like he did recently, though I wish he'd just ground me instead.

Domenico has a darkness that our father lacks. Dom learned his ruthlessness from our father, but he's more wicked than Dad will ever be. I'm not scared of my brother. I know he wouldn't maliciously hurt me. We beat the crap out of each other a lot. Dom makes me a better fighter than my personal trainer does.

With Dom, I'm scared how far he can be pushed to protect those he loves the most. If Dad or Dom ever find out who killed Mom, I'm more afraid of what Dom will do to that person than I am of what Dad would do. Dad would kill the person, sure, but he wouldn't drag it out. He wouldn't torture the bastard, whereas Dom would.

"Careful, sister, or I might be inclined to show the kid just how scary I can be and teach you a lesson in the process."

"You kicking my butt will have to wait. I have a nail appointment in an hour and I'm taking the kid with me." I turn my attention to Matteo's daughter. "Hop down. We're leaving."

"Yay!" she cheers.

"Did you not see how De Salvo reacted when he showed up? I don't think taking his daughter is the smartest thing you could do. Don't make me trigger happy," he orders, his playful demeanor vanishing, hardening to Dom's normal self.

"Keep all weapons holstered where Matteo is concerned," I issue an equally firm demand. "Dad told me to take the kid. I'm leaving, so I'm taking her with me. Matteo obviously knew how to find her. I'm sure he's just as capable of finding her when she's with me in town. Let's go, Brooklyn."

"At least take De Salvo's shit. Dad wasn't happy he had to bring her home without a proper kiddie seat she's supposed to be strapped in."

"Fine," I agree. Matteo jumped out of his Lexus so fast he left the driver's side door open anyway. Keys are probably still inside, unless it's an ignition with a start button, then I'm screwed, but I'm sure I can figure out how to transfer her kid seat to my car. "Come on, kid."

When we get out to Matteo's SUV, Brooklyn climbs in through the driver's seat and then over into the back like that's how she gets in all the time. Matteo's vehicle is a button ignition, but I find his set of keys in one of the cup holders. It's stupid to leave anything of value in your car, even in an upscale neighborhood like this one, which is gated, but the gates are usually open until dark. Open or not, it wouldn't keep criminals out if they were determined to get inside, but being who my father is, the thug would be even stupider to steal anything on Dad's property.

"Ever had a mani-pedi?" I ask, looking at Brooklyn through the rearview mirror as she buckles herself.

"No. Been with my nana, though."

"Want one?" She nods, a grin forming on her lips. "Then you shall have one." And with that, I shoot my father a quick text letting him know I left with Matteo's daughter and his SUV, then I start the vehicle seemingly excited to be hanging out with this kid again. I have no idea why taking her to the nail salon seemed like a brilliant idea when I left Daddy's office, but for some strange reason, I like her. I might even like her more than I like her father, and as much as I hate to admit it to myself, I have it worse for Matteo now than I did as a teenager.

He's too hot and cocky for his own good. Apparently, much to my irritation, that's still my type.

WHEN I WALK INTO THE POLISH BAR, I stop at the check-in counter to sign in, seeing every waiting chair full and every station except one filled with a body. There is even a woman and a couple of teenagers standing around waiting for their turn.

This is why I always make an appointment, and why I usually come during the work-week at lunchtime to avoid the crowd. I once came when I didn't have an appointment and I'll never make that mistake again. I waited almost three hours just to get seated for a pedicure.

Never. Again.

It's not even a small nail salon. For every station there is a technician on duty. The only time a station goes unused is if someone calls out and the owner can't get anyone else to fill the spot.

"Hey, Si. You ready?"

"Yeah. But . . ." I glance from Manny down to Brooklyn. "Is there any way you can fit in an extra tonight?" I smile, but it's more of a plea. With this many people here, he's liable to shoot me for asking.

"I'd do damn near anything for you, but that isn't one of them. We're swamped this evening. I've been turning down clients without appointments for the last hour." He peeks down at Brooklyn and I can see he wants to tell me yes. Not because he's afraid of me or what my father might do if he denies my request. He knows who I am. I've been getting my nails and toes done here since I was about the same age as Brooklyn, maybe younger.

He was stuck here hanging around because his mom had to work and couldn't afford childcare. We don't run in the same circles. I didn't go to school with him and he didn't attend my brothers' private school either.

Hang is the reason Manny doesn't treat me with kid gloves or bow down to my every request. Manny's mom is fearless, and she made sure Manny didn't grow up being afraid of someone based on a certain reputation.

She's of Vietnamese descent. Her parents came over when Manny's grandmother was pregnant with one of his uncles. Whereas his mom was born and raised in America, but fully Vietnamese, Manny is only half Asian. His mom married a black guy she fell in love with during college. Manny's mom is barely five-feet in a pair of heels and his dad is at least six-feet barefoot. They're cute together, and I still see them from time to time.

Hang may be petite, but she doesn't take orders from anyone. She gives the orders in her household, and her basketball-player-sized husband is perfectly fine with that. Hang was never fazed anytime my dad brought me in here. The only time I've ever seen her feathers ruffled was when Daddy had to leave me here to handle business and he had my grandfather swing by to pick me up.

You'd have thought the air had changed the second the door chimed and he walked in. It was unnerving to see Hang flinch, but at the time I got it. That's often how I felt anytime I was in his presence too. As a kid, the old man scared the crap out of me. As an adult, I've grown used to him and simply don't like his old school way of thinking or business sense.

"I get it," I tell him. "I knew it was going to be a slim chance the moment I walked in. Let Brooklyn take my place and I'll reschedule for next week."

"That we can do." His lips part, spreading into a toothy grin that shows his perfect white teeth. Manny is pretty to look at. He has the creamiest warm-colored skin and curly hair that he keeps braided in rows close to his scalp. He isn't as tall as his dad, but he and I are usually eye level unless I walk in wearing a pair of heels. "What color polish are we doing?" he asks me.

"It's her choice." Tipping my eyes to where she is seated on my hip, I point to the back of the shop. "See that wall in the back? Every color of nail polish imaginable is back there and you can choose any one you like."

"I want pink to match my new outfit."

"A girl after my own heart," I swoon, teasing her.

I got a text from the assistant manager of the gym informing me that the new fightgear I ordered had come in when I was leaving my house with Brooklyn. Wanting to be the first to see the new fight attire, I made a small detour. I changed out of my dress and heels and into a newly designed gym branded tank top, sports bra, and a pair of the newest line of Muay Thai shorts. My tank is white with the gym logo in black across my chest and the shorts are mostly black material with the word FIGHT written in all caps, in white, at a slant on the right side and the company name across my butt in black outlined in white.

Not only did the adult sized clothing come in, but so did the youth. Brooklyn picked out a white tank top with a pink logo and a pair of matching pink, glossy shorts to go with them. I also outfitted her in a pair of six-ounce boxing gloves for kids and shin guards, both in pink and white to complete her little badass look she has going on. The gloves she took off, but the rest she's still wearing.

Even though Matteo's daughter looks more like her mother than I care to confess, I have to admit she looks adorable decked out in clothes I helped design.

"Look at the top shelf," Manny tells us as I start to tote Brooklyn to the nail polish wall. "There's a pearl pink that would go perfectly with the girl's digs."

Manny graduated with a business degree the same as me, only a year earlier. He runs his mom's slew of nail salons all throughout New York City and Long Island now that his parents have retired in the Hamptons. Manny's folks struggled for a long time with only one shop, this one, until my dad approached Hang and offered to help her open a second location, then a third, and kept on until reaching ten salons. All of which are highly sought-after and successful nail shops. They're always busy, hence the reason I schedule appointments.

I don't know what made Daddy make the offer. He doesn't profit from any of the shops like he does all his other investments. I never asked, but I guess my father just wanted to help out a good-hearted couple trying to achieve the American dream.

Once Brooklyn's fingernails are painted the color Manny suggested, the nail tech moves us to an open chair to do her toes. When I place Brooklyn down, I notice the person in the next seat over, on the other side of Brooklyn, with her head tipped down, staring at her smartphone while another technician is filing the heel of her left foot.

None other than Sasha Nikolayev, my archenemy and the pro kickboxer that I'm fighting in July. "Well," I draw out, eyeing her with disdain about the same time her arctic blue eyes snap up to mine.

The technician says to me, "You want to take these off so I can do the bottom of her feet?" She points to the shin guards Brooklyn wanted to put on her bare feet and legs before we left the gym.

"No!" Brooklyn whines, her voice stern for a five-year old. Turning her head up, she looks at me. "I don't want them off. I love them."

"Let her wear them. She's still so young she probably has baby-like feet. We can just do her toes."

"I'm not a baby!" she argues, copping an attitude.

"I didn't call you a baby. I said baby feet, as in soft feet. It's a good thing; a compliment."

Her eyes narrow. I can see the accusation in her eyes and the snarky remark wanting to burst out of her mouth. She must decide against saying anything, because her lips remain sealed.

Good choice, kid. I think in my head.

CHAPTER 25
MATTEO

When Tony explained where he found Brooklyn and his reason for taking my daughter, I came unglued. That piece of shit bitch was getting high while our daughter was left alone in one of the most dangerous neighborhoods in the city.

Only one other time in my life have I wanted to wrap my hands around a woman's throat and drain the life right out of her. Both times that woman was Kennedy. Both times were because she endangered our daughter. The first time I thought it, I was ashamed the image ever graced my mind. But now . . .

Now I'm more determined than ever to make sure she never sees *my* daughter again. Brooklyn isn't Kennedy's; not anymore. She put herself above *my* daughter's safety. That stops today. She will never get close enough to see her again, and if she does, it'll be over my cold dead body.

I never thought Antonio Caputo would earn my respect, but

on some level he did, and after today, I owe him. He assured me I didn't, but that's bullshit. I'm indebted to him. I just don't know how I'm going to repay him, because it sure as shit isn't going to be by staying away from his daughter—that's for damn sure.

After I calmed down, my phone started blowing up with calls and text messages from Kennedy's mother, but knowing I didn't have the willpower to deal with her without calling her daughter every dirty word in the English dictionary, I put the device on silent and shoved it back into the front pocket of my jeans.

Before I left Tony's house half an hour ago, I found out his daughter helped herself to my daughter and decided to take her into town. Did the Boss tell me their location? No, he did not. Just mumbled something about keeping track of my own kid from now on and told me to get the fuck out of his house.

Not only did Sienna take off with my daughter, but she stole my Lexus too. After everything that's happened in the last couple of hours, the mafia princess cruising town with Brooklyn in my SUV is the least of the things boiling my blood.

I'm assuming Kennedy is in the hospital somewhere recovering, seeing as Domenico called in an anonymous tip about a woman that overdosed before they left with Brooklyn. I don't know what her current condition is or her whereabouts. The last place I need to be is in reaching distance to the goddamn mother of my child. In the emotional state I'm in right now, I'm liable to kill her if the drugs didn't do it, and since I plan on keeping the Boss's daughter tonight to unleash all this pent-up frustration, I ordered an Uber to the small strip mall the GPS tracker showed Brooklyn to be at.

"Here you go." I hand two twenty-dollar bills to the old man, letting him keep the extra ten bucks as a tip, then exit his Honda

Civic and glance at each sign. The only two shops open just after seven tonight are a nail salon and a tanning salon.

I decide on the nail shop and make my way inside. I stop and scan each patron. The place is slam full of women, dudes, and a couple of teenagers. When I finally spot Brooklyn in the far back, I'm not prepared for the way my chest constricts at the sight before me.

Brooklyn isn't dressed in the same dirty clothes I saw her in when I arrived at Tony's house earlier. Sienna has turned my little girl into a miniature version of herself, and something about that makes my lips curve up.

My daughter's long, brunette hair is braided down the side facing me, starting tightly at the top of her scalp and ending two inches from the end of her hair. Sienna is standing on the opposite side with her hands behind Brooklyn's head, her mouth moving—talking to someone—but I can't hear what she's saying. My guess is she's braiding the other side of my daughter's hair judging by her stance and focus.

No one besides my mom or me messes with Brooklyn's hair, though I do take her to the hair salon every few months. It's only to keep her wavy locks trimmed to hang near the end of her back. She likes it long and so do I. It's a bitch to get untangled, but my daughter is too adorable with it long for me to cut it short.

She looks happy based on that giant smile gracing her beautiful face. In ways it pains me that Kennedy can't put a grin on our daughter's beautiful face the same as Sienna seems to do so easily.

It doesn't go unnoticed that I feel my dark mood making a turn for the light, and that has everything to do with the woman giving Brooklyn the attention Kennedy should be willing and able to give but never has.

As if sensing someone watching her, Sienna's movements still, then her head snaps up from its downward position, her eyes locking with mine. Now that I'm somewhat calm, I refuse to let my ex pull me back down the murderous road I felt two hours ago. I still haven't figured out what's so different about Sienna from all those years ago except her appearance. *Was I really that shallow?* Of course, I was. I was a stupid teenager after one thing: easy pussy.

Nothing about Sienna screams easy. Then again, nothing I've ever truly enjoyed and loved has been easy to obtain. It's taken years of mental discipline and training my mind and body to get to the level I am today, to get my body to the size I am. Doing that on top of being a single father has had many rough moments. There have been times I've wanted to call it quits and find a job where I was guaranteed a paycheck, but I'm no quitter; especially when I want something, and right now, I want Sienna Caputo.

I want her bad.

And I aim to get her.

If I'm honest with myself, I don't think I'm going to be satisfied with only one night.

CHAPTER 26
SIENNA

Are you the girl's mother?

Your question is irrelevant just like this conversation. Why Brooklyn is here doesn't concern you. If Matteo decides to fill you in then so be it, but I'm not. Leave, Sienna. You're trying my patience and it's at its max for today.

Capisce?

I could go the rest of my life without hearing the word capisce. I hate when he treats me like I'm a fucking child. It pisses me off.

"You're hurting me," she complains for the third time, pulling me away from my recollection in my dad's office.

"I have to pull your hair tight or the braid will fall out." Her hair is long and fine. The strands will likely loosen and unravel on their own without a gallon of hair spray being used to secure her hair in place. "You're the one that wanted to look the part of a little badass, so hold still."

"I said I wanted to look like you, not a badass."

"Language," I scold. "Looking like me is looking like a badass."

"Hmph," comes from the chair next to Brooklyn, but I ignore her the same as I've done since realizing she was here twenty minutes ago. "You might want a new idol if you're going for the badass look. Sienna isn't exactly up to par in that department."

Sasha loves to goad people. It's her specialty—one I stopped playing into three years ago. She's Krishna's little sister, and like Ren and me, they could pass for twins. They look a lot alike except for the height. Sasha isn't short, but she isn't tall either. She's two inches shorter than my five-feet-eight height. I'm fit, toned, and muscular, but she's in the gym more than I am. It pains me to admit it, but I'm softer than she is. We're in the same weight class or we wouldn't be able to compete against each other. She just happens to be slimmer, more toned, and more muscular than I am, and I secretly hate that about her.

Well, it's not exactly a secret. I've never liked her, and the feeling is mutual. Like Brooklyn's mother, Sasha is an attention seeker. She's perhaps worse than Kennedy in that category. She purposely made herself the black sheep in her family. She doesn't get along with her dad and makes sure the world knows it.

She also had the privilege of attending the same private school my brothers did, and I've held that against her for a very long time. We're the same age, so she was in the same graduating class as Ren. Sasha has always had a thing for my brother. He denies it and brushes it off like she doesn't, but she does. I've seen her watch him enough times to recognize it. It's the same way I used to look at Matteo.

She isn't good enough for Ren. She'll never be good enough for my brother. Luckily, he doesn't hold the same interest in her as she does him, so there isn't anything to worry about; not that there would be even if he did. It's like Krishna said . . . it would cause World War III, mafia style.

The Caputos and the Nikolayevs have been at odds since my great-grandfather ran things. They both wanted the same territory in New York back in the 1930s or '40s. My grandfather inherited the "family business" upon his father's untimely death at the hands of reigning Pakhan of the American-Russian mob back then.

There is a lot of bad blood between our families. It's one thing for my father to go legit while maintaining his stronghold on a criminal empire. It would be another to allow his kids to fraternize with a Nikolayev.

Brooklyn's head swivels and I almost lose my grip on her strands. "She is so a badass," Brooklyn sasses.

"Ughh," I breathe through clenched teeth as I pull on her braid. Placing my hand on top of her head, I position her to face forward. "Stop moving your head and do not talk to strangers."

Disobeying me, she looks up. "She isn't a stranger. Her and my mom are friends."

"Wouldn't go that far," Sasha quips, still staring down at her phone while moving both thumbs across the screen like she's typing.

"But you told my daddy to tell my mom hey."

Pausing, Sasha looks to Brooklyn, then to me, and then back to Brooklyn. "That was only to piss Sienna off. And it worked as planned. It's too easy to get under her skin."

"If you keep talking, it's not only my skin you're going to get under. It's going to be my body and all my limbs coming at you," I chime, but my tone lacks any real punch. I'm not in the mood to bicker back and forth with Sasha. We have plenty of that coming up the closer we get to our upcoming match.

"My daddy said you two are going to fight soon." Brooklyn tries to turn her head again, but I grip her neck, making her keep her head straight. *So, Matteo knows about my upcoming kickboxing fight*. Interesting.

"Yep." Sasha pops the word out of her mouth. "I'm finally going to show Sienna just how much of a crappy fighter she really is."

"Good luck with that," I tell her, flashing a fake smile.

"Well, I'm betting on my daddy's girlfriend," Brooklyn says, matter of fact, and with a little bit of a snarky attitude, mind you. Even though I tug on the end of her braid for lying, I want to fist bump her for her snarky little mouth.

"Who's my girlfriend?" My head snaps up, seeing Matteo stop next to the nail tech as she's applying the last swipe of topcoat on Brooklyn's pinky toe.

"Sienna," she singsongs as she answers her dad.

"No, I'm not," I correct the little hellion, tugging her braid as I twist the ponytail holder around the end of her strand to hold the braid in place.

"How much are we betting?" Matteo asks.

"Don't humor her," I chastise, dropping my hands from Brooklyn's hair and planting them on my hips.

"Might want to place your money on the fighter that's actually going to win," Sasha interjects.

"Nah. My kid is right. I have to bet my money on the girlfriend I just acquired. Can't be starting our relationship off on the wrong foot by betting against her." He laughs. I don't. Sasha rolls her eyes but doesn't comment back. This is probably the one and only time her gesture is fitting, but I refrain from copying her. "Are you two done here?" Matteo asks, looking at me, his laughter gone, but a smile remains on his handsome face.

"Just need to pay." Grabbing my purse, I pull out my wallet, retrieving the credit card inside and start to hand it to the nail tech.

"I'll get it," Matteo says, but I ignore him, handing my Visa over. The technician stands from her crouched position, taking my card and pivoting to walk toward the receptionist's desk. "I said I'd get it," Matteo repeats.

"No one asked you." Pulling out his keys, I hold them out to him. He takes them and then bends forward, picking up his daughter.

"Do you like my new clothes, Daddy? What about my nails? Aren't they pretty?" Brooklyn fires off.

"Prettiest nails and toes I've ever seen. My favorite color too. You do that for me, Irongirl?"

"Pink is my favorite color too, Daddy. Duh."

"You're in a far different mood than you were earlier," I comment, walking past him to checkout and sign the receipt so that I can get my credit card back.

"Oh, no, baby. I'm way past murderous right now. I've moved on to manic level." Tossing my head over my shoulder, I cock an eyebrow in his direction. "Pay. Let's get out of here. I'll tell you about it when little ears aren't in hearing range. Deal?"

I nod, but otherwise don't say anything. Matteo is here and he looks unharmed, but he's also the heavyweight boxing champ of the world, so I wasn't worried for *his* safety. Should I have been concerned for my father's? When I left, Dom and Ren were home. No way would Matteo have gotten a hand on my dad without coming away marked himself, or dead at the hands of one of my siblings.

So, what was it that my father told Matteo but didn't want me to know unless Matteo chose to tell me himself? Guess the only way to find out is to go with him.

Curiosity is too much of a bitch sometimes.

CHAPTER 27
MATTEO

I brought us to my place. I didn't ask Sienna, nor did she object when I pulled in the driveway, or when I parked, or when I turned off the ignition. I got out of the SUV, pulled Brooklyn from the backseat, and waited until Sienna followed me inside.

She was quiet during the ride here; more like the old Sienna from high school than the version I've become used to in the last few weeks. I have to admit, I don't like the silent, timid side. I prefer the loud, mouthy, takes-no-shit woman I now know her to be.

I cooked us dinner. Nothing fancy or complicated. I had steaks in the fridge I'd planned on grilling anyway, along with a hefty salad. She and Brooklyn split the second steak. For a small child, my daughter eats well. She doesn't whine or fuss about what is placed in front of her. I likely have my mother to thank for that. She doesn't cater to my daughter's every want, and since I turned out fine, I follow suit and try to parent the way I was raised.

After dinner, Sienna mentioned that she was going to ask Ren to come get her, but Brooklyn begged her to stay long enough to watch a movie. None of us watched any part of the movie, though it was playing in the background. Brooklyn asked Si to teach her how to braid, so Sienna did, and I couldn't take my eyes off them. Sienna let Brooklyn braid her hair and my daughter attempted to make Sienna's braids match her own, but it didn't turn out that way. One side she did okay, the braid is a braid, but the strands are loose. She couldn't get the other side to do right, so she ended up leaving that side down.

That was the last thing I remember until I heard someone bang their fist on my front door, jarring me awake. I must have dozed off on the other end of the couch. When I look around, the television is still on but the movie that was playing isn't the same one that's on now. Sitting up, I glance down from me, seeing Si and Brooklyn snuggled together and fast asleep. I don't get the chance to process what my eyes are witnessing for the incessant pounding that continues, successfully irritating the fuck out of me. And after today, I have a short fucking fuse.

I make my way to the stairs and then jog down them. After I unlock the door, I pull it open to find Kennedy on my doorstep looking worse for wear. Her blonde hair is stringy and tangled in sections like the wind blew it all over the place. She's in a pair of green scrubs and a white T-shirt.

"I've called you repeatedly for hours. So has my mom," she says, her voice accusing, like I've done her wrong or put her out in some way.

"And I see you didn't take the hint. I don't want to talk to you, Kennedy. I don't even want to see you right now, maybe ever."

"Matty, I've had a bad day; a real bad day, and I need sleep."

She takes a step forward, but so do I, blocking the entryway and crossing my arms. "What the hell?"

"You have some nerve showing your face here of all places," I seethe, yelling at her. Clenching my teeth, I ball my fists, squeezing them as tight as I can, feeling my joints pop.

"Why are you being this way? I tell you I've had it rough and you don't even care? You don't even want to know what happened to me? Matty . . ." she whines. But then she pokes her lips out and I almost lose it.

I drop my arms and start to take a step. "Let me tell you something, you piece of—"

"Whoa, big guy." Sienna grabs my shirt, tugging the material, before squeezing between me and the doorframe, stepping onto my small stoop. She places her palm on my chest, and instantly, it deflates. I exhale. "Let's bring our voices down to a level that isn't going to wake little ears. Okay?"

Brooklyn is a sound sleeper. Nothing or no one is going to wake her, certainly not my voice. When she's asleep, she's dead to the world until morning.

"Who the hell are you?" Kennedy snarls, her lip curling in disgust.

Sienna swings her head from me to look over her shoulder at my ex. "Someone who is going to give you another scar to match the one I gave you above your right eyebrow if you don't watch yourself," Sienna remarks.

Wait a minute.

Kennedy does have a scar. It's faint, but it's there, and she got it our senior year of high school. She told me her heel broke on her shoe and she stumbled into the metal latch on a locker.

Si is responsible for that? How did I not know?

"Oh, my god." Snapping her attention to me, her mouth hangs open. "What the fuck is this weird bitch doing here, Matteo?"

Sienna pivots, facing away from me, but I wrap my arm around her waist, snagging her backward against my chest before she bolts toward Kennedy. "Easy, bad princess," I whisper close to her ear. "No need to waste your time on her."

"Matteo!" Kennedy huffs. "What is she doing here?" Kennedy plants her hands on her hips, staring long and hard at Sienna. "If you think for a second, you have a chance with him, you're delusional. He's mine. He's always been mine and always will be."

"You're the one that's delusional if that's what you think. We've been over for a long time, Kennedy."

"We have a daughter together."

Fire shoots through my veins at the mention of Brooklyn, putting my feet in motion. I step forward, pushing Sienna along with me, but she juts out both arms, bracing them against the doorframe on both sides, halting us. For someone small, she's strong as fuck. Any other time I'd take a second and admire that, but right now, I want to wrap my hands around my daughter's mother's throat.

Sienna must sense that and is intent on stopping me. "At what point today, or tonight, did you remember you have a kid? Where do you suppose Brooklyn is right now?"

"With you, obviously." She sighs, shaking her head. "Matty, please tell her to leave and let me come in. I'm tir—"

"I'm not the one leaving," Sienna remarks, cutting Kennedy off. The confidence laced in her words soothes me somehow, but the sight of Brooklyn's mother only fuels the fire burning inside me.

"You're damn right my daughter is with me, which is exactly

where she belongs. No thanks to you. While you were laid up in the hospital, did you ever once ask if she was okay?"

"Wait a minute. You knew I was in the ER and you didn't come check on me?"

"Are you kidding me right now? You placed Brooklyn in danger today and that broke my last straw with you." My head swings from side to side. "I'm not letting you anywhere near her again. And if you don't have a reason to see Brooklyn, you certainly don't have a reason to see me, or show up at my house or any of my fights."

"What are you talking about? Of course, I do. I belong here."

"Leave, Kennedy. Get off my patio. Get away from my house. Get away from me. Now," I warn, my tone darker than I've ever heard myself.

"Matteo," she exasperates.

Yanking Sienna inside, I slam the door and then flip the lock before I put her on the floor.

"You ready to tell me what happened today?"

"You couldn't figure it out after all that?"

"I have a guess, but why don't you paint the picture for me."

"Let's go upstairs." I grab her hand, interlocking my fingers with hers and tug her up the carpeted stairs, back to the living room. Brooklyn is still sound asleep, lying on her stomach on the couch.

Dropping Sienna's hand, I trek to the couch and gently pick my daughter up, pulling her to my chest and embracing her small body. She's my world, and a number of bad things could have hurt her today. That thought alone makes me feel murderous. I'd do anything to ensure my daughter's safety. If that wasn't clear before today, it is now. I'd walk through Hell for her. I'd take on the devil himself and come out the champ if I had to save my baby girl.

Once I have Brooklyn tucked under the covers in her bedroom, I walk out, closing the door behind me. Sienna is still standing in the same spot she stopped when I let go of her hand. Not going to lie, when our fingers were connected it felt right, and when I released her, my palm itched to have her flesh back with mine.

"What are you doing?" I ask when she snatches her cell phone from where she plugged it into the charger on the table next to the stairs.

"I'm going to ask Ren to come get me."

"No, you're not." I step toward her and pluck the phone from her hand. "You asked me a question and I plan on answering, but I'm tired, so we're going to talk in bed. Let's go."

"I don't think so, big guy." She extends her arm, demanding her phone back without words.

Glancing down, I press the button on the side of the phone with my thumb to brighten the screen. "It's almost two in the morning. No sense in making your brother come get you. I'll take you home in the morning."

"Do I need to remind you of what happened the last time I fell asleep here?"

"No. My memory works just fine." A yawn escapes my lips. "Baby, I don't scare easily. Besides, if you really want to know, then you have to stay to find out."

Pivoting, I walk away from her still clutching her phone in my hand. I set it on the nightstand next to the side of the bed I normally sleep on and then pull my T-shirt over my head, tossing the shirt in the direction of my closet.

Sienna appears in the doorway, her body language suddenly

shy, and hesitant. It makes me wonder if I'm pushing her too far too fast. I've never had to work this hard for pussy before, but then I've also never wanted to make an effort before.

"Just talking and then sleeping," I clarify, in case she thinks I'm expecting more. I definitely want more, but I've already come to realize she isn't the type of girl to fall into a man's bed after the first date. Maybe not even the second or third. I'm going to have to get more persuasive if she drags this out. "Oh, come on, it's not like I'm the first man you've ever slept in the same bed with."

I drop my eyes to the floor and kick off my tennis shoes. When I look back up, she steps in my bedroom, still silent, still reluctant.

"Leave the sweats on," she says when I place my hands at the waistband of my pants.

"Sure." I hold my hands up in surrender. It's not unusual for me to sleep in my sweatpants or gym shorts. Every now and again Brooklyn will sneak in my room in the middle of the night and crawl in my bed. For that reason, I always sleep clothed when she's home.

Pulling the covers back, I slide between the dark gray sheets. Sienna stares at me the entire time she is taking off her shoes and then a beat after that. The uncertainty in her dark eyes makes me want to reassure her that I'll stay on my side, but honestly, I can't fathom not touching her if she decides to crawl in my bed with me.

Her expression changes, morphing into what I'm starting to think is part mask, part show, or a combination of the real woman behind it. A coy smile spreads across her face as she pulls back the covers and slips under the sheet. She's still wearing her tank top and shorts and whatever else is under them, but I can't fault her for remaining clothed when she ordered me to keep my pants on.

"There's no shame in admitting you want the same thing I do," I tell her. "Neither of us know whether this is something just for now or something else that I won't bother to put a label on at this point."

"Way to make a woman swoon, De Salvo. You're really selling this," she states sarcastically as she inches closer to me. Lying back and laying her head down on the pillow, she turns toward me, her dark eyes curious. "Why are you suddenly interested in me?"

"Who said it was suddenly?" I counter, not wanting to admit the truth.

"Before two weeks ago, I was just some girl you graduated high school with. You probably didn't even remember my name. That is *if* you knew it to begin with. It's not like you noticed I existed back then. You never looked twice at me."

There's sorrow reflecting back at me; perhaps even a bit of anger, though her tone is even. Had I not been watching her closely I might not have even recognized it. Besides, her accusation isn't true. I looked at her. I looked at her more than I care to admit. "I noticed you."

Her eyes roll and then she scowls at me. "No, you didn't. Don't start this out with a lie, Matteo." Lifting her head and coming up on her right elbow, she points back and forth between us with her left hand. "That's going to end this before it even begins."

"It's not a lie," I vow. "Back then I didn't understand it. I told myself you weren't my type. But I did notice, and maybe if you hadn't been pretending to be some little goody-two-shoes then I wouldn't have stayed away from you."

"Now you're blaming me?" A sardonic laugh filters past her lips.

"Well . . . kind of is your fault, babe."

"Subject change," she singsongs. "Why did Dad have Brooklyn at the house today? And exactly how did Kennedy put her in danger like you claimed?"

The anger I felt when I opened my front door, seeing my ex standing on the patio like some washed-up drug addict returns full force. My jaw locks and my skin burns as my muscles coil.

Sienna reaches out, her palm pressing into my chest. "Relax." Her tone is soft, like a melody, but it hits my eardrums like a command that my body seems to obey. My shoulders drop and air expels from my lungs. "If you don't want to tell me it's fine."

It's not fine. That thought throws me for a loop. I've never felt the need to explain myself or anything that happens in my life to anyone other than my parents. Being an only child, I'm sure I was somewhat isolated compared to the way siblings are with each other. I didn't have to share my toys—or my thoughts.

She goes to retract her hand, but my reflexes are quick. I grasp her palm, stopping her, and then flatten her hand back out on my chest. I like the way it feels when she touches me and I'm not ready to lose that just yet.

"Your dad was driving down a street in a not so pleasant area. He saw Brooklyn as he was passing by an apartment building." My fist curls from where it rests at my side as I'm propped up on my other side facing Sienna, her palm still firmly planted in the center of my chest. I don't understand how her touch soothes me so much, but it does, just like her being here with me in my bed. We aren't even naked, yet I enjoy the ease of conversation, even if the topic is Sienna's dad and my daughter.

I fill her in on as much as Tony told me. I don't believe for a minute he told me everything, but that doesn't matter. Kennedy had our daughter in a part of Brooklyn, New York—the very city my daughter is named after—she never should have been in. Don't get me wrong, I love Long Island. Hell, I even love New York City. This is my home, but like any place in the world, there are bad parts mixed in with good places. My daughter is still a kid and I plan on keeping as much of her innocence intact for as long as possible. There are things no kid needs to bear witness to, and things that go on in that small part of the city is one of them.

"I don't like Kennedy, I never have, but I didn't take her for a heroin addict."

"She isn't," I deadpan. "At least, I'm pretty sure she doesn't do the hard stuff. She smokes pot, and has since junior high. She drinks too much and doesn't have a responsible bone in her body, but she's never, to my knowledge, crossed *that* line."

My stare penetrates hers as silence envelops us both, swirling around us like a cloak. After a long beat, she's the first to move as she cocks an eyebrow, her assumption pouring out of her brown eyes before her pretty lips part. "Something you're not saying, Matteo?"

"Not something I'm not saying, Si. Something you're already thinking," I accuse.

"Daddy wouldn't have touched her. And he certainly wouldn't have shot her up with heroin, or any other drug for that matter." Her breath coats my face like molten lava as the tips of her fingers slowly move across my bare chest, her nails sinking into my skin like claws.

This is the woman I witnessed at Raymond's a few weeks ago. She's lethal when it comes to protecting her family; that's easy to pick up on. If this conversation was about anything other than what it is, I'd smile and feel a sense of pride in how strong she comes off. I can't deny that watching this side of her turns me on. Hell, if I'm honest, every side of her turns me on.

"Someone shot her up with heroin. Someone caused her to overdose." I take a breath. "I'm not searching for any excuse for her. I simply don't believe Kennedy did it herself."

I said those exact words to Tony. He didn't refute my claim, nor did he admit to being her catalyst either. What he did say didn't really make any sense to me. Still doesn't, and I've repeated them over and over since they left his lips.

The woman you choose to be the mother of your children, your partner, and the only person you can truly trust in life other than yourself should be the most careful and thought-out decision you ever make, Matteo. Choosing wrong will leave you with life-long consequences.

It was on the tip of my tongue to ask him if he chose wrong, if that was why his wife is dead. Something told me that would be the wrong question to ask the Boss.

"If she OD'd on heroin, then the heroin was already in the apartment she was in, Matteo. She may not have been partaking in it, but it was there and so was she, and she had your daughter in that environment by choice. What does that say about her as a mother?"

"She's a shitty mother. I've known this for five years. That doesn't make it okay for your father to shove needles in a woman's arm to try and kill her."

"My dad didn't do that," she snaps back. "That's something Dom would do, not Daddy. My father would never lay a hand on any woman in a negative or harmful way," she reiterates.

"Funny. What do you call what he did to you last weekend?"

"A lesson. But I'm also his daughter and a Caputo. There is a difference. He wasn't beating on me. He wasn't abusing me. He didn't do anything a coach or an opponent wouldn't have done in the same circumstance. Tony Caputo never took a belt or used any other object to spank *his* kids. He taught us lessons in other ways—some verbal, some physical. But he was never abusive, and you better bet your ass he never took us to a drug den either." Her torso lifts until she towers over me, and I have to look up to see her eyes. They're heated, and she's pissed. "If Dom did do what you're suggesting, then I'd applaud him. The world would be better without her existence. Brooklyn would be better off without her."

When she finishes, her breathing is labored like she ran a marathon, but no remorse resides behind her eyes. She meant every word. I can't fault her for them. If I did, I'd have to fault myself too. It's not like I haven't wished Brooklyn had any other mother in the world rather than the one she does.

Sienna snatches her hand from my chest as if my skin burned her—that I find fault with. I'm not ready for her to stop touching me. Not by a long shot.

She turns away from me and starts to scoot her ass out of the bed, but I snag her around the waist and pull her against my chest. "Where do you think you're running off to?"

"I'm leaving," she bites out, and I can't control the smile that spreads across my face.

Throwing my heavy leg around her, I tighten my grip. "No, you're not, baby. You're staying right here with me."

"Stop calling me 'baby.' It's annoying." She huffs out an exaggerated breath that seemingly dissipates my sour mood, making me bark out a laugh.

"I forgot. You prefer *bad* princess."

"Let me go, Matteo." She pushes down on my forearm but there's no power behind her action. She may be a lot smaller than I am, but I've gone toe to toe with her. Maybe not in a real spar, but enough she can handle herself, and if she really wanted me off her, she'd find a way to get out of my hold.

"No. I think I'm going to keep you."

"I'm not a toy."

"You're right, you're not. You're so much more. And I don't want you to leave. Stay. I'll take you home in the morning." I inhale the scent coming from her hair. I can't place it, but it smells fruity. I like it. "Maybe," I add.

"What if I really want to leave now?"

"If you really do want to go, I'll wake Brooklyn and I'll take you home. But I don't believe for a second that's what you want to do."

"What I want to do is beat Kennedy's ass. You're lucky you hadn't told me earlier tonight. I would have laid that bitch out." There's something in her voice, beyond her anger, that warms me. It pissed Sienna off when she learned where Kennedy took Brooklyn. She cares about my daughter, and that does something. It affects me in a way I'm not sure I understand. Or maybe I refuse to recognize the feeling it gives me.

"I'd have let you, babe."

She pivots her head, looking over her shoulder, her eyebrow raised in challenge. "Let me?" *God, I fucking like this girl.* "Learn this now, Matteo. No one—and I do mean no one—*allows* me to do anything. I make my own choices. The only person that owns me is me."

If she only knew how much of a turn-on that bold attitude of hers is . . .

"I'm going to enjoy having you for a girlfriend." I laugh, easing up my hold around her waist. "Let's go to sleep before I try to fuck you."

"I'm not your girlfriend."

"We'll talk about that tomorrow."

"Tomorrow won't change that fact, Matteo."

"We'll see. Good night, Si."

CHAPTER 28
SIENNA

Voices penetrate my eardrum, pulling me from slumber. It's a good kind of sleep too. Cozy. Warm. Like being wrapped up in the warmest blanket. I could stay here forever and be content.

I'm half lying on my side and front with something solid and heavy pressed against my back. The bulkiness isn't uncomfortable; far from it actually. It's welcoming, with an air of protection that isn't like anything I've ever felt. And that's strange considering I'm not only Antonio Caputo's daughter, but the youngest amongst my brothers. Lorenzo may only have a few minutes on me, but there's a pecking order in my family—which puts me last.

"Where's your dad?" A woman's voice registers, causing my eyes to flutter. It's a warm sound, yet the authority in her tone doesn't go unnoticed, even in my semi-awake realm.

"They're still asleep." Brooklyn's sweet, sassy rasp warms my insides. I've yet to figure out what it is about the kid that I like so much. Maybe I see myself in her. Otherwise, what could it be?

"They?" the woman draws out, irritation palpable.

"Daddy has a girlfriend, Nana." The excitement in Matteo's daughter's voice almost makes me wish her statement were true.

Hold up. Where the hell am I?

"Fuck." Matteo's curse is whispered so close to my ear that I feel his hot breath coat the back of my head. "Mom's here."

The events of last night filter back through, replaying in rapid succession. I'm suddenly baffled as to why I agreed to spend the night. As soon as that thought exits, I realize that warm, cozy blanket is Matteo's body wrapped around me, and my eyes pop open as I suck in air.

I'm in bed with my childhood crush.

Was I drinking last night? No. Not one drop. Can't blame it on being inebriated. Not that I ever get that way to begin with, so . . .

Pushing his arms off me, I scramble out of bed, half falling down before I bounce up. His chuckle from behind me does nothing to settle my nerves. "Forget where you were, babe?"

"I'm not your babe. You keep forgetting that." My stare is steady as I bend down, grabbing my tennis shoes from where I kicked them off last night. I'm still wearing the fight attire I changed into at the gym yesterday before Brooklyn and I went to the nail salon. The way Matteo's eyes are appraising my body is doing things to me that I don't need right now—or ever where he is concerned.

My cell phone chimes with an incoming text message, so I grab it from the nightstand and pivot, leaving Matteo's bedroom. *I should not have stayed here last night.*

What the hell was I thinking? I wasn't, or maybe I was and wanted to be in his bed way more than I should. I know he just wants what isn't being freely offered, and there is no way I'm going to be another notch on his bedpost. *Fuck that.* I have too much pride to allow that to happen. I'm a Caputo, after all.

Glancing at my phone as I head down the hallway, I see the message is from Dom.

Dom: I'm waiting at the curb, little sister. Let's go.

Before I can open the message and reply, another message comes through.

Dom: Don't make me come inside.

Great. Now I get to deal with daddy number two. Sometimes Dom is worse than our dad when it comes to me.

I need to grab my bag that has my dress and heels in it from when I changed yesterday, but I'm pretty sure I left it in Matteo's SUV last night. With my tennis shoes in hand, I pad into the living room, coming to a stop when I see Brooklyn with a middle-aged woman standing next to the couch she is bouncing on.

"Sienna!" she screams when she sees me. The kid is still dressed in the same outfit I changed her into, including the shin guards. My lips curve up, seeing her hop off the couch, running to me. As she nears, my eyes go to the other woman in the room—Matteo's mom. I remember her from time to time when she would come up to the school whenever he would get into trouble. I used to work in the principal's office back in high school. It was one of my electives from tenth grade through senior year.

Mrs. De Salvo places her hands on her hips, watching me closely. It takes seconds, but I swear the way her motherly eyes penetrate mine, our stare-off lasts ages. Recognition flashes and I know that she knows who I am—or rather whose daughter I am.

"Hey, kiddo," I greet Brooklyn. Personal space doesn't seem to be in this kid's vocabulary. Just like that night at my mom's restaurant, she launches herself at me and I have to release my shoes, letting them drop to the floor in order to reach out and catch her.

"Are you going to spend the day with Daddy and me?" Her breath fans my face, and the smell of chocolate sweetness wafts through my nose, making me wonder just how long she's been awake and what all she got into while Matteo and me were asleep. *Sneaky little kid this one is.*

"I can't," I admit, and before she can interject, I glance over her head to Matteo's mom. "Hey. I'm Sienna."

"I know who you are." Her tone is harsh. Nothing like the voice she used with her granddaughter only moments ago. *Ouch.* This lady hates me before she even knows me. Not that I'm not used to that type of reaction. It goes with being a Caputo. I'm used to it, but I have to admit, this one stings more than usual.

"Hey, Mom," Matteo says from behind me. "Morning, Daughter."

"Mornin', Daddy." Brooklyn giggles as if Matteo made a funny face. When she wrinkles her little nose, I have to bite the inside of my cheek to keep from laughing with her.

"You got into the Cocoa Puff's, didn't you?" Matteo asks, and Brooklyn's head bobs, her smile expanding, not the least bit worried. Not that Matteo sounds irritated. The opposite really. He sounds rested and happy and something about that makes me feel warm inside. Too warm. I've got to get out of here. Matteo's hand squeezes my hip in a silent greeting. "I don't remember you telling me you were coming, Ma."

"I didn't know I needed a reason or an invite to visit my son and granddaughter." Her dark eyes are still boring into me like an accusation. If I don't get out of here, I'm bound to open my mouth, and then she's really not going to like me.

Loosening my grip on Brooklyn, I let her slide down my front until her feet touch the floor. After letting her go, I squat, picking up my shoes, then proceed to stuff my feet into them without socks. I lost my socks sometime during the night between Matteo's sheets.

"I never said you did," Matteo replies. "If you're going to be here a while, I need to run Sienna home. Can I leave Brooklyn with you?"

"No need, big guy. My ride's outside waiting on me."

"Who?" There's an edge to his tone. One in which I can't decipher.

Turning to face him, I wave my phone in his direction, but it's snatched from my grip. He's lightning fast; something I should already know considering who he is, and I do, but I didn't expect him to take the device from me—again. *Dick.*

His eyes scan the messages that I'd just opened, but then his fingers are moving across the screen, a slow smile spreading his lips out.

"What did you just do?" I accuse, knowing he did something I'm not going to like.

"Text myself so I could get your number." His eyes pop up, locking on mine as he holds out my phone for me to take.

"You could have asked."

"Would you have told me?" He cocks a knowing eyebrow as he crosses his arms over his thick chest.

"No."

"There you go. Had to go a different route." That smile of his should not be doing what it's doing to my belly, but hell if I can't make this feeling stop. What I can do is mask my expression. For some reason that's harder to do with him than it is others. "I'll text you later with the time I'm going to pick you up for our date."

It's on the tip of my tongue to spout back that he's the last man I'd go on a date with, but I don't since we have an audience. Instead, without another word, I turn away from him and make my way to the stairs that lead to his front door.

I can always tell him to go jump off a bridge when and if that text ever comes through.

Domenico's black Range Rover is parked on the curb, just like his message said. The vehicle is running, and I can see my brother's head downcast, most likely working from his smartphone. Dom may appear distracted, but he has eyes in the back of his head; that I'm convinced of. There is no doubt in my mind that he knew the moment I opened Matteo's front door and stepped out of his house.

Walking down the driveway, the chill of the morning air coats my bare legs and arms, making me wish I had the lightweight jacket I keep in my gym bag just for mornings like this. The sun is already out, and by late morning it'll be a lot warmer. May in New York is the best time of the year. It's not humid yet, like it is in the summer, and the temperatures aren't too hot.

The doors unlock as I reach for the handle. Once inside, I drop my cell phone between my legs and pull the seatbelt across my body, buckling myself in.

"Morning," I greet my brother.

Setting his cell phone down, he rolls his head in my direction, giving me a once-over. Dom has a stare that's penetrating—and not in a good way. It's accusing without saying the accusation.

"If you have something to say, then spit it out," I order, frustrated. It's too early on a Saturday morning to be getting my panties in a wad.

"Couldn't you have tried to comb that rat's nest you have sitting on your head? You look thoroughly fucked, little sister." His eyes narrow and his jaw hardens.

"Mind your own, Dom."

"I do. Every fucking day." His hard, dark eyes are still on me. "Do I need to go in there?"

"I'm good. Is this mine?" I grab the disposable coffee cup in the rear cupholder. Dom always places his drinks in the one closer to the dashboard.

He nods, confirming what I already knew was true. Anytime Dom picks me up he always has my favorite coffee drink waiting. He's a good brother. Overbearing and an asshole, but I wouldn't trade him for anyone else—ever. "I need to know if you slept with De Salvo. Or have at any point slept with him."

"The term TMI went over your head, didn't it?"

"Knowledge is—"

"Power," I finish for him. "Blah, blah, blah. Can we leave now?"

"I'm not Dad, Si. I don't care who you fuck, though you could do better than him. I just need to know in case issues arise from it."

"Issues?" A humorless laugh falls from my lips. "You and Lorenzo screw whoever the hell you want. No 'issue' ever comes about from either of your sexcapades." I roll my eyes. Double fucking standards. I should be used to it in our family, but I'm not.

"You're right. I do fuck who I want, but I don't think Ren does."

"He's not a virgin, Dom." *Because who's a goddamn virgin at twenty-three*. "And yeah, Ren does get it on the regular."

"I didn't say he didn't. What I meant is that I don't think he fucks multiple women. He's seeing the same one he's been seeing for a while now."

"You know who he's dating?" My anger flares, roaring up at a rapid pace. "Not even I know that."

Lorenzo is secretive. I may be the *bad princess* as Matteo likes to refer to me as, but Ren is the dark prince. It's the only thing I despise my twin for. It's petty, but he isn't supposed to keep things from me.

"No," Dom admits. "I don't know her identity, but I know he's a one-woman type of man."

"And you aren't?" His eyes flash the first sight of light since I slid in the passenger seat a minute ago. "Right. You like your promiscuous ways."

"I like my sanity. Women have the ability to ruin men."

My brother has a lovely view of the opposite sex. I don't bother to set him straight. I wouldn't be able to change his mind. Dad wasn't the only one affected by mom's death. We all were, but Dad and Dom never recovered. Sometimes I think Dom loved her as much as Dad did—just in a different way. He placed Mom on a pedestal just like Dad.

No woman will ever compare to her, just as no man will ever compare to my father. We were lucky to witness true, unconditional love between our parents, and I think that high of a standard ruined Dom for any potential relationship. He will never risk falling in love. He's too afraid of suffering the same fate our father did.

In an effort to change the subject, I ask, "So where are we headed?"

Dom glances at me from head to toe again. "That the new line?"

"Arrived yesterday," I tell him.

"Michael said you outfitted the girl and yourself. Looks good by the way. I like the look of the bold colors this time over the pastel color from last year."

"Me too," I agree. "And her name is Brooklyn."

"I lined up a meeting with Niccolò Bianchini," he continues, ignoring my correction. "He's only in the city today, so we're headed to have brunch."

"Merchandising is my area."

"Yeah, well, you've been too busy with an overrated boxer and his kid. It came up, so I arranged a meeting that likely wouldn't have happened otherwise."

Niccolò Bianchini owns a conglomerate of corporations; one being a chain of MMA gyms spanning from Florida and throughout Texas. I've been trying to nail down a meeting with him for nearly a year. How my brother managed to do it piques my interest, but his comment about Matteo gets under my skin.

"Matteo has been undefeated for almost two years. I wouldn't call that overrated."

"Boxing is dead. Has been for years. Your boy should think about stepping into the octagon. Then we'd really know what he's made of." Putting the gear stick in drive, Domenico pulls away from the curb. "There's a change of clothes in the back. You'll need to change and get ready in the car. We don't have time to stop by the house. We're heading to the city now."

"It's a quarter past seven, Dom. Are we eating breakfast with Bianchini?" Normally, I'd still be asleep. Saturday is the one day a week I allow myself to sleep in. Surprisingly, I'm not the least bit tired. Probably due to the fact that I got the best night's rest that I can remember. *Why did it have to be with Matteo?* I mentally whine. On one side, the schoolgirl in me is thrilled, but the responsible adult, not so much.

When it comes to Matteo, it won't amount to anything real. I'm a challenge for him, that's all. I'm not the woman he takes home to Mom. In fact, I'm willing to put money on him getting a tongue lashing at this very moment by his mother on account of me walking out of his bedroom. The look on her face told me everything I needed to know, and I'm the last woman on earth she wants her son and granddaughter around.

"Hop in the back and change," Dom says, his voice laced with irritation. "Breakfast, brunch, it doesn't matter what you call it, we're doing it now. We can't let him leave the city without sealing a deal with him."

Unbuckling, I twist in the passenger seat, giving him a *I hate you right now* death glare as I climb into the back of his SUV. Plopping down in the middle, I survey what Dom brought. There's a black garment bag hanging in front of the window. On the floor, I see my favorite pair of pumps—the only comfortable pair I own—along with the ones I refer to as Satan's heels. They're black six-inch heels with a red bottom, and I swear Lucifer himself designed them. I only wear them when I'm going for sex appeal and know I won't be standing for long periods of time, like to dinner, so why Domenico brought these I haven't a clue.

Opening the garment bag, I pull the material of the clothes out. My crisp, white, show my girls-on-display shirt is staring me in the face. Behind it is my red pant suit, followed by a black cocktail dress that I recently bought and haven't worn yet.

I glance at Dom in the rearview mirror, but his eyes are focused on the road. “Are you trying to pimp me out?” I deadpan. The power suit and the *I'm gonna fuck you tonight* shoes is making me question my brother's motives. I'd believe this behavior from Ren, but never Domenico. He's the protective one. Not that Lorenzo isn't, but he's my twin soul. We've always been one and the same. He wants me to have fun, and he knows that I'm capable of defending myself. Dom will forever see me as his baby sister needing protection from her knight.

“I didn't pack your shit. Dad did. I just swung by the house and grabbed it when I told him about the meeting.” Dom doesn't glance in the mirror. “I was perfectly happy doing this solo. Dad was the one that insisted I take you.”

“Hello,” I say louder than necessary. “Again, my department.”

This time he does look at me through the rearview mirror, his facial features hardening. “The three of us are in this together. We're equal partners. If I can get us the meeting when you couldn't, then it is what it is. Be happy. Don't pitch a hissy fit over something petty, little sister.” His eyes cut back to the road. “What the hell did Dad pack anyway?”

“An outfit that clearly says, *no need to buy the cow when the milk is free*,” I singsong in a sarcastic tone.

“He's old, Sienna. Give the man a break. He probably just snagged the first thing he saw in your closet.”

“Grandpa is old. Dad? Not so much.” At least not in my eyes. The man could take on both my brothers and me in a match at the same time and beat all of us. That I'm certain of. He didn't even break out in a sweat when he kicked my ass the other week.

Besides, he didn't gain his reputation by being thought of as old. Most people won't even look him in the eye, and Dom can't be *that* eager to step into Dad's shoes this soon, can he?

"We don't have time to stop by the house. Can you make it work?"

"Yeah," I tell him. "There's another one, but it's basically a prelude to the fuck me dress."

Dom sighs heavily. "I'd say it was your twin fucking with you, but he didn't come home last night either."

"Where's Ren?" I ask as I yank the unprofessional white blouse from its hanger. Glancing in the mirror, I see Dom's eyes are on the road, so I pull my tank over my head.

"Getting his dick wet, I would imagine. At least he better be. I've about had it with his brooding, mopey shit." I slide my arms through the material and start buttoning it from top to bottom.

"He can fuck, but I can't?" My lips purse and my eyes narrow at the back of his head.

"You can," he says in an all too calm voice, and then his dark eyes cut to the rearview mirror, his expression deadly. "So long as you're okay with me breaking the motherfucker's neck."

"Sexist ass," I chime. Dom shrugs, but flicks his eyes back to the road.

"Only with you, little sister. Only with you."

Pulling the red dress pants from the hanger, I slip my shorts off, tossing them to the floor, and then pull on the pants. I'll do the jacket when we arrive or I'll start sweating.

"So, do you have a plan, or did you get a read on Bianchini? Do you think he's interested in selling our fightgear in his gyms?" My travel makeup case is sitting on the seat next to me, but having already put on my clothes I know I'll get shit on me if I try to doll myself up, so I open the bag and grab mascara and a tube of lipstick.

"That's your area," my brother responds. "Didn't you just

say this not five minutes ago? I figured getting the meeting and escorting you there would be enough on my part."

"Now you're just being a dick."

"Maybe if you'd been in your own bed instead of me having to pull you out of De Salvo's, then I'd be in a better mood. You fuck him?"

"Again, none of your business." What is it with him and Dad? Do they really think that because I'm a girl I'm supposed to keep my V-card until I'm married like the Italian tradition the Mafia is known to expect from the women in the family? Grandpa, sure. If it were up to him, I would have been married to a made man and pregnant with a bambino at the age of nineteen instead of college bound.

Of all the things the criminal organization of the Italian people could honor, it's a woman's virtue until her wedding night. It's laughable really, and I find it hard to believe my father waited to have sex with my mother until they were married, so he can't expect the same thing from me.

Besides, it's the twenty-first fucking century. It shouldn't be as hard as it is for a twenty-three-year-old to get laid—but it so fucking is.

CHAPTER 29
MATTEO

After I hear the click of the door shutting, I turn to face my mother, only to find her pale blue eyes narrowing in my direction. She's either seconds away from blowing up, giving me an earful, or simply finding the nearest object and beating my ass with it—in the literal sense.

"Irongirl," I call out to get my daughter's attention. "Why don't you go to the bathroom and clean up your chocolate-covered face."

"Sure, Daddy."

She bounces up and down on her toes before sprinting down the hall and out of earshot as my stare remains locked with my mom's. After a long stretch of silence, I inhale and then release a sigh. Before I can speak, my mother beats me to it. "Have you taken so many blows to the head that you've lost all the sense I taught you?"

"Stop being dramatic, Ma." Stepping forward, I walk the short distance to the kitchen and pull out a bottle of water from the fridge. Normally, I'd be rushing to my coffee maker, needing a steaming cup of Joe to wake me up, but this morning it isn't needed. I haven't slept a full night since Brooklyn was born. I always wake up during the night to check on her, and it usually takes me going another solid hour on the heavy bag to get back to sleep before I'm dragging my body back out of bed only a few short hours later.

Was it because I had a warm body in bed with me?

The click of her sandals against the hardwood floor clues me in that my mother followed me, so I turn around to face her as I uncap the plastic bottle, taking a swig of cold aqua.

"You call me dramatic when it's you that has a criminal in your home?"

"Does she have a rap sheet that you somehow know about?" I ask, my brows furrowing. "Has she done something illegal that you're privy to, Ma?" I love this woman. I've always respected her above anyone else. She's the best mother anyone could be gifted, but she's taken this too far.

"She's connected. She's one of them, Matteo, and if you think for a second that you won't get caught up in their life—"

"Jeez." I cut her off before she continues. "I'm not planning to marry her. I just want to date her." My words taste sour on my tongue, but they aren't untrue. I do want to date her, or fuck her, or I don't know, find out what it is about her that I can't get out of my head. To figure out why, even as a teenager, there was something intriguing about her.

"Her father is the boss. Not a capo. Not a made man or soldier, not even an associate of theirs. He's the boss, Matt. The one with all the power. Did I keep you so far away from your father's family that you know nothing about the mob?"

"I know who Tony is, Ma."

"He's a Caputo. He's the worst of the worst kind of man, Matteo. He's a murderer. He's a criminal. And he's untouchable. That in itself should make you turn and walk in the other direction when you see him. That should make you not want your daughter—my granddaughter—anywhere near anyone in that family or connected to them. What were you thinking getting mixed up with that girl?"

"First," I bite out, surprising myself with the tone I'm giving the woman that gave birth to me. "Her name is Sienna. Secondly," I say, forcing my tone to ease up. "I'm not mixed up with anything. I'm simply taking Sienna out on a date tonight. You know, to see how things go and to see if we hit it off." I already know we're gonna hit it off. The chemistry between us is off the charts. She's bold and sassy and she's a turn-on like no woman before.

"You don't *simply* do anything with the Boss's daughter. Thinking that shows your stupidity." She breathes in, pulling in a lungful of air before blowing her breath out in frustration. "I worked so hard to keep you away from *that* life. Why would you willingly go after the one woman every man with any common sense should stay the hell away from? Why would you do this to me, Matteo?"

"Ma, I'm not doing anything to you. You're taking all of this way too serious. You're searching for a reason to not like her when you don't even know Sienna." She did the same thing with Kennedy. It was instant dislike, a fact she didn't try to hide in front of my ex.

"I don't need to know her, Son. And maybe she isn't a bad person, though growing up in that life, I find that hard to believe.

But she was born into the wrong family; that is something I cannot help. You, on the other hand, need to cancel whatever date you were planning and distance yourself now before it's too late."

"I'm not canceling our date. I like her. Brooklyn likes her too, and,"—I can't help the smile that forms on my lips—"Sienna is good with her. She's great with her, in fact."

"I can't believe the words that are coming out of your mouth right now, or the fact that you let my granddaughter around anyone connected to the Mafia."

"My uncle is Giovanni De Salvo. We're already connected to the mob, or did you forget he is Dad's brother?"

"And he's in prison. That's what happens to people in the mob, Matteo. It's either prison or death. That is not the life I want for you. It's certainly not the life I want for Brooklyn. She is the person you need to think about right now and put first, not yourself."

"The life I give my daughter and the life I choose for myself is mine and mine alone. Maybe Sienna will be part of that, or maybe she won't, but I won't know that until I see where this thing between her and me is going."

"I'll never accept her, Matteo. Ever." Her vow slams into my chest like a hammer, and all I can do is sigh, hoping like hell I'm not given an ultimatum like my father was. I can tell her right now I won't stop going after Sienna. I'm going to see it through; if anything just to see what's there, because there is something, and I don't think it's just the drive to get into her pants.

"Then I guess you've said your piece."

One thing about my mother is that no one can change her mind except her. She'll either come around or she won't. I guess asking her to watch Brooklyn for a couple of hours is out of the question.

"WHERE ARE WE TAKING SIENNA ON OUR date, Daddy?" Brooklyn asks from her booster seat in the back of my Lexus as I pull into Tony Caputo's driveway, stopping and parking behind a black, Mercedes G Class. *Fuck, these people have money.*

I don't consider myself rich. I make a decent living doing fights a few times a year and my house is paid for, so I don't have jack shit to complain about. I know there are a lot of people more well off than me, but there are even more that don't have it as easy as I do.

"The Flamingo." I'd texted Sienna around noon, telling her I'd pick her up at eight. She replied, telling me to *eat shit and die*. I didn't figure a follow-up to that was needed since I gave her a time to be ready. Her car is parked in front of the closed garage, so at least that's a sign she's here.

"That don't sound like pizza, Daddy."

"Because it's not. It's fancy food," I inform her. I figured when I dressed her in a dress and shoes that she typically wears to Mass with my parents she would have caught on that we were going to a nice restaurant, but then she is five, and her idea of nice is pizza.

"But she likes pizza, Daddy, like me."

"I'm sure she likes fine dining too, Daughter. Besides, you look pretty in the new dress Nana bought you last week. Don't you like your dress?"

"I lovvvvve my dress, Daddy," she draws out, her blue eyes big and round, sparkling through the rearview mirror. The sight of my daughter makes my heart swell. I'd do anything to keep a smile on this girl's face.

"Well, let's grab Si so that I can take the two prettiest girls out to dinner."

After pulling her out of her booster seat, I close the door and place her on the pavement. She doesn't walk beside me. Instead, she takes off for the front door. By the time I step up the stairs to the expansive porch, the front door is opening.

Tony's eyes cast down to Brooklyn, before glancing over her head to look at me, his expression blank and unreadable.

"Figured you'd have a housekeeper to answer your door," I say.

"My housekeeper cleans my house. She isn't responsible for kicking the varmints off my property. What do you want, De Salvo? It's late. Doesn't your kid have a bedtime?"

Flicking my wrist up to view the time, I cut my eyes back to Tony as he crosses his arms. "It's five 'til eight. And my kid's bedtime is my business, not yours."

Before I can continue, Brooklyn chimes in. "We're taking Si to a fancy dinner."

"Jesus Christ," he says on a sigh. "What is wrong with your generation? Do you not know proper dating etiquette?" He places his hands on his hips, his eyes going from me to Brooklyn and then back to me, a scowl on his face. "I've heard of *take your kid to work day* but *take your kid on date night* . . . really, De Salvo? That's how your mother raised you?"

My jaw locks as my anger flares. Forcing my teeth to stay together so that I don't pop off takes more willpower than it should. After a long beat with Tony and I locked in a stare down, I realize he's not going to be the first to speak, so I shove my hands into the pockets of my black slacks.

"Not that it's any of your business, but I don't have a babysitter on retainer. My daughter goes where I go unless she's with my parents or her mother, and the latter is out of the question at this time."

"I should hope so, considering," he growls, leaving the rest of his thought open for interpretation. His dark eyes flare with fire and disgust, allowing me to see just what he thinks of my daughter's mother. My own mirrors his, but I'm not about to tell him that, especially in front of Brooklyn. Besides, I have my own thoughts as to what took place at Kennedy's supposed heroin overdose. *I doubt she was the one that administered the needle in her arm.* Question is, was it Antonio Caputo or someone else?

"Can I just get Sienna and leave now?" I request, leaving his remark unanswered. "I don't want to be late for the reservation at the restaurant."

"Too bad," he utters, his expression changing to amusement, and perhaps even triumph. "You're an hour too late from her departure for her *other* date."

"What other date? I'm her date," I declare, my spine straightening.

"Apparently not, De Salvo. She left with someone else."

"What the—" I stop myself before I yell a curse word in front of Brooklyn. Once again, my teeth smash together to keep my mouth from spewing words that would likely get me shot. She fucking knew I was coming to get her, and yet still went on a date with someone else?

"I told you, Daddy, we should have taken her for pizza. Not some fancy place like you told me," Brooklyn chimes in, shaking her head like she's little miss know-it-all.

"Where?" I request, my words lethal.

Smirking, Tony cuts his eyes down to Brooklyn, before squatting down to her level. "Do you like cake, sweetheart?"

"I love cake. Who doesn't love cake?"

"There is a really sweet lady in the kitchen. Why don't you head in there and tell her I said to cut you a very big slice. Would you like that?"

What the hell is he doing? I don't have time for this shit, nor do I plan to stay here any longer than I have to, but my daughter apparently doesn't see this, as her head bobs, no words coming out of her mouth.

Tony pulls her inside, lightly pushing her in the direction of what I assume is his kitchen. Brooklyn takes off running.

"Where is Sienna?"

"Why, Matteo? Are you going to storm into the restaurant and drag her out? If that's your plan, do you really imagine my daughter not putting up a fight?" He laughs, but I don't see the same humor he does. "And how is that going to even work when you have Brooklyn in tow? Think you can wrangle two women at the same time?"

It sounds dumb as fuck the way he puts it, but that's exactly what I want to do: pick her up, sling her over my shoulder, and tote her sexy ass out.

"I'll tell you what," he says. "Leave the kid here and I'm willing to tell you where my daughter is."

"Why are you so quick to tell me, and no, I'm not leaving Brooklyn."

"You are leaving Brooklyn, because I'm offering and I said so, and because Sienna is at one of my restaurants, which means I have access to see how this plays out. I have no doubt the guy is going to see you and piss his pants if he recognizes you. Si, on the other hand . . ." Another laugh bubbles from his lips. "She'll go toe to toe with you in a heartbeat, and well, it's thrilling every time she kicks some schmuck's ass."

"Just tell me the damn name of the place already and then send my daughter out here."

"I've already told you she is staying here. If you're going to smash Sienna's date, then you're going to do it like a man. Bringing your five-year-old isn't going to have the desired effect, De Salvo." He licks his lips, eyeing me from the entryway. Tony is slightly one to two inches shorter than I am, but with the added inches from the threshold it feels like he towers over me. I don't like it.

Looking past him, I gaze into his home. All the lights are on and it's bright. I can't see the kitchen or even the great room from where I stand. He has one of those grand foyers that opens up to two sets of staircases that go up to the same level on the second floor. I can't see my daughter and I can't hear her, but for whatever reason, I'm not worried that she's in his house. For the life of me I don't know why that is. I may not know all the details of this family, but I've heard enough throughout the years to know their business isn't of the legal sort.

"If you're going to tell me you don't trust me with your daughter, Matteo, then I'm going to tell you I don't trust you with mine, and you can fuck off." His brow over his right eye arches in challenge.

"That wasn't what I was going to say, Tony." He told me the other day in his office I could call him by his nickname rather than Antonio or Mr. Caputo, or even Boss, thank God, because I don't know if I could have done the latter. "Are you going to tell me where Sienna is?"

"Constantino's."

"Do you have restaurants that aren't Italian?"

"I'm not even going to answer that dumb-as-fuck question. Are you going to remain standing on my porch until she returns or are you planning to go after her?"

"I'm surprised you're letting me."

"It's not my balls. Besides, I'm more interested in seeing what kind of man you really are and if you have the potential to live up to your last name."

"I think I've proven that more times than not every single time I step into a boxing ring, Tony."

"I'm not talking about your father's legacy as a boxer. You've surpassed him and I'm sure he's very proud of you for that. I'm speaking about the weight the De Salvo name carries. The reputation your uncle gained as a De Salvo."

"I barely remember my Uncle Giovanni. Can I leave now?" Tony nods, and I turn, only making it one step.

"Matteo," he calls out. The edge of darkness in his tone stops me, and my eyes dart to his deep brown ones. "There's one thing you need to understand if you're going down this road with my daughter."

"I break her heart. You break my legs. That goes without saying. I understand, Tony."

"You break Sienna's heart, it won't be me that you have to worry about. My daughter will cut your balls off—unless one of my two sons get to you before she does."

"Then what is it you want me to understand? I have a date to break up, so please, enlighten me."

"Careful, De Salvo," he bites out. The look of a father who is seconds from smacking his son in the back of the head for saying something dumb crosses his features. I recognize it, because still to this day, it's a look I often get from my old man. From Antonio it should seem weird, but for whatever reason, it doesn't. "*Omertà*," he finally says, sending a chill straight down my spine, something no one has ever managed to produce from me.

"What about it?" I ask.

"It's a real thing. I need to know that you know what it means."

"A promise. An understanding," I reply.

"An understanding, yes, but it's more than a promise. It's an oath. One I take very seriously. One that you cannot break and walk away from."

I'm silent; one, because I'm in uncharted waters and I don't know what I'm expected to say, and two, because my mother's words come back to me, making me question if I should be standing here to begin with. *He's the worst of the worst kind of man, Matteo. He's a murderer.*

"This is where you reassure me that you are not only serious about my daughter, but also that you will not under any circumstances speak to anyone in law enforcement about anything, Matteo."

"I am serious about your daughter, Tony." I pause, eyeing him without cowering to his powerful stare. "But I'm also not willing to get involved in anything illegal or criminal; therefore, I have nothing to tell anyone in any form of law enforcement. Happy?"

"Wrong answer." He shakes his head.

I'd laugh, but with the expression he's giving me, he really would pull a gun and shoot me. "I said what you wanted to hear, so what's the problem?"

"No, you did not say what I wanted to hear. What you said tells me that you do not have the first clue what it means to date my daughter. You don't know what it means to involve yourself in her life or what it entails to bring your own daughter into my family. You don't even know your own family."

"Then I guess I'm still waiting for you to enlighten me on the ways of *Cosa Nostra*."

"Smart boy knows big words," he mocks. "Been brushing up on mafia terminology, I see." He doesn't wait for a response. "To date my daughter means you put her life before yours. You protect her at all cost. If you'd die for your kid, then you'll die for mine too. It means that if you are going to be associated with my family in any form, you do not talk to cops, or local or federal agents. If they stop you—and they will—the only words out of your mouth are 'I want a lawyer' or 'I have no comment' and you walk away if you are not under arrest. If you're friends with anyone in law enforcement now, you disassociate with them immediately. That's what it means, and that's what I expect or there will be consequences. Am I clear?"

"Crystal," I bark, but not because that's what I want to respond with, but it is the only thing I'm sure of that won't get me killed.

"I hope so, because Matteo, you don't want to be the subject of my consequences. Now beat it before I call my daughter and warn her that you're coming to ruin her night."

I walk away without another word. Hell, it can't only be pussy I'm after if I'm willing to leave my daughter in the hands of a mob boss. The thought of Sienna on a date with someone else boils my blood and makes my head run away with crazy thoughts. I've never felt this way about another woman.

This can only end in one of two ways: a hot, scorching flame that never goes out or a bloody fucking disaster.

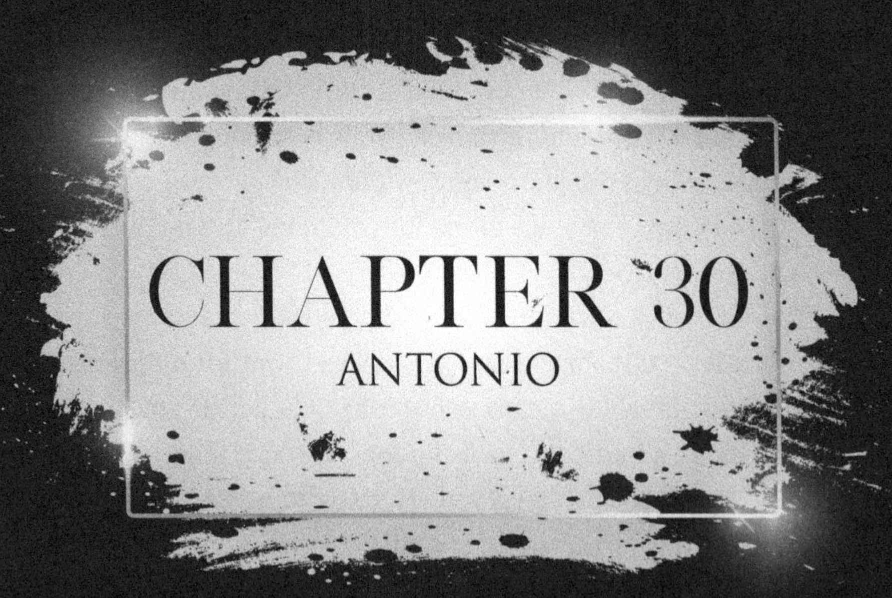

I close the door after watching Matteo pull out of my driveway. I really do hope he's not a disappointment. I would hate to end his life. He has a lot to prove to me if he has any hopes of actually dating my daughter. Taking her to dinner isn't going to get him anywhere with me.

"He has the capability of being a true De Salvo."

Irritation grates on my nerves as my furious eyes cut to the man dressed similar to me, wearing a dark suit and tie with a glass of Blanton's Single Barrel clasped in his right hand. It's the same whiskey I was enjoying until Matteo interrupted my night, though I was waiting on him to do exactly what he did, so perhaps there is hope for him yet.

"You were supposed to wait in the basement until LeAnna and my sons have left for the night. What wasn't clear about that?"

"I wanted to see him. I want to see the girl too."

"No. Now make yourself scarce," I order, walking toward him.

"Stop reminding me why I hate you."

"You never hated me, Tony. You just wanted to shoot me."

"And I regret every day that I did not do just that."

"Yes, that was an error on your part. It would have prevented so much bad blood."

"I have to go check on the kid. Go back down to the gym. I'll text you when you're allowed to come play with the adults, G."

"Fuck you, T."

Walking away, I make my way into the kitchen where I find Domenico perched on a stool at the island counter with Matteo's daughter sitting with her legs crossed on top of the granite, the massive three tier cake in front of her. Like a heathen, she has a fork in her hand and she's eating the cake from the platter instead of a plate like she should be doing.

"Where's LeAnna?"

Dom's brown eyes snap to mine, a mischievous smirk settling on his face. It's better than the scowl he typically wears. In this moment, he looks his youthful twenty-five years instead of the dangerous underboss I turned him into. On one hand I'm proud that he's strong enough to handle what I'll eventually lay at his feet, but at the same time, it tears at my soul. I never wanted this for him or his siblings. I promised my wife. I made a vow that they wouldn't become me. She's in the ground because I failed her, and I'm failing my children the same way.

"Left ten minutes ago."

"So, this is your doing?" I stop on the other side of the counter in front of the sink, pointing to Brooklyn. Not only is her face covered in chocolate and strawberry icing with crumbs, but she also has it all over her dress and on the countertop.

"She told me that you said to give her cake. As instructed,

she's eating cake, right?"

"Are you going out tonight?" I probe.

"Not unless you need me to. I'm going to take a shower and then crash. I'm exhausted."

"Good." I nod, staring at him. "You get to watch Brooklyn for the night."

"Yeah, I'll pass on that. Why is she here . . . again? I thought you returned her."

"That's not any of your concern. Just go clean her up and keep her upstairs. Turn on a movie or something in Sienna's room, but make sure you stay with her. I don't need a child to go tumbling down the stairs because you're closed off in a different room, Domenico."

"Where's the girl's father?"

"Daddy went to get Si," Brooklyn mumbles through a mouthful of cake. There are sizable chunks scooped out on both sides. The cake arrived this afternoon for the twin's birthday celebration tomorrow. Sienna's favorite is strawberry with strawberry icing and Ren's is chocolate on chocolate. I used to get two separate cakes, but over the last five years I've had the baker make one where there is chocolate on one side and strawberry on the other. "They're going on a date," she proceeds to say.

Dom's resident scowl returns. "You already sent her on a date tonight. What's going on?"

"Your sister is my concern not yours. Now I've given you an order and I expect you to take care of it. Can you do that, please?"

"Not if De Salvo thinks he's going to get with my sister. I kept my mouth shut the other week when you told me not to interfere, I'm not doing that again. You keep the kid. I'm going to get my sister. He's already knocked up one chick, I'm not letting him do that to Si."

"No," I bite out, displeased that he thinks he can give me an order. "I run this family the way I see fit, so you will stay out of it, and you will take Brooklyn and give her a bath and you will stay upstairs for the rest of tonight unless I call for you otherwise."

He huffs, but doesn't backtalk me. Instead, he grabs the girl, pulling her gently from the counter, and places her on the floor. "Go that way, kid." He urges her out of the kitchen. "I hope you know how to bathe yourself. I'm not doing it for you."

Brooklyn looks over her shoulder, an attitude already plastered on her cute face. "I'm a big girl, not a baby." Then she stomps out of the kitchen, reminding me of Sienna when she was that age.

Rounding the island, I grab Dom by the elbow, halting him. Lowering my voice, I ask, "Had she actually OD'd when you found her?"

"The bitch was high—oblivious to the world around her. What does it matter if I helped her over the edge or not?"

"She's a woman, Domenico," I reprimand my eldest child. "You know more than anyone else I take a hard line against harming women."

"She put her daughter's life in danger. You have a line of steel against hurting kids." He shrugs like his excuse should satisfy me as he pulls his arm loose from my grip. "Had it been someone else, someone with *other* intentions that drove by and noticed a five-year-old girl sitting on those steps alone, her mom nowhere in sight, things could have played out differently. The only thing I did wrong was call nine-one-one. I shot enough heroin in her veins that she wouldn't have woken up without paramedics injecting her with Narcan."

"If anything, Dom, that was the one call you did right."

"If you expect me to be *you* one day, then I have to get my hands dirty, Dad. It's the way this life is. You're just pissed I handled it and not you."

He's not wrong. I am pissed for that exact reason, but not that reason alone. I never wanted his hands stained the way mine are.

Not waiting for me to continue scolding him for his actions, he heads out of the kitchen and I follow, checking my watch for the time. As irritation flares at the time, the chime of the doorbell can be heard in every room in my house.

"Who the fuck is here now?" Dom barks out.

"Handle the child. I've got the door, Son," I say to the back of his head.

"Domino," Brooklyn calls out and we both look to the top of the landing, finding her with her fingers wrapped around the railing on the second floor. The kids' bedrooms and three extra guest bedrooms are on that floor, while my master suite is on the first.

"If you can't say Domenico, then say, Dom, but do not call me Domino again, girl," my son calls up. His irritation from our conversation has vanished and there is light back in his eyes. If Matteo's daughter has that affect on him, then I may just keep De Salvo around even if Sienna doesn't like it.

Instead of going up the stairs after her, he heads to the front door.

"I said I've got our guest. You have a duty to do."

"You are not answering the door. There is no telling who could be on the other side that is here to harm—" He stops in his tracks and it's obvious he recognizes the figure through the glass on both sides of the door. "What's Nikolayev doing here?" Dom questions, turning to face me. Being my second-in-command, he's usually privy to every part of my business. *Except this.* Which is why I wasn't expecting him to be here when Mischa arrived.

Mischa Nikolayev is the head of the Russian crime organization in the United States. Whereas I only run a slice of the Italian Mafia, every syndicate in this country goes through Mischa. Like I'm the Boss, or the Don, he's referred to as the Pakhan in his circle.

"Nothing you need to be concerned with. Mischa and I have business to handle that's only between him and I."

"Everything our family is involved with, everything you're involved with, includes me too."

"Only when I say it does."

"What are you keeping from me, Dad?"

"Nothing of importance at the moment. Stop worrying, and for the love of God, do as I have instructed and take care of the little girl that's waiting on you."

"That's all the more reason to worry, Boss," he states, addressing me in a term that I despise coming out of any of my three children's mouths. "You don't want me involved. Why? What do you really have cooking?"

"Upstairs, now," I order in a low tone he knows not to cross. He may be twenty-five, and he may be his own man, but he will always be my son, and I will always expect my rules to be followed over his own just as I expect from his siblings. In this house, in this family, it is my way and my way alone. There are no second options, no alternatives.

The bell chimes again while Dom grinds his teeth back and forth. Finally, his eyes leave mine and he takes the stairs two at a time. When he reaches the top, he scoops Brooklyn in his arms, pulling a giggle from her lips. Once they've disappeared down the hall that leads to Domenico's bedroom, I walk to the door.

"You're late," I say.

"Flight was delayed. Get over it, Caputo," Mischa tosses back at me. He isn't afraid of me like most. He doesn't succumb to my orders the way I prefer. He and I have that in common being the boss of our people. For a long time, I didn't like him. Hell, we're not exactly friends, but we have a common idea of sorts, which is the only reason I allowed him to enter my home.

"My office." I raise my arm, gesturing for him to enter. "You know where it is. We have things to discuss," I say, closing the door. Before I follow, I pull out my cell phone from the pocket of my slacks and send a message to my other guest, telling him he's allowed to come up now.

Things are starting to unfold the way we planned, I just have to make sure each piece fits the way I want them to.

Coming out of one message, I tap into another, sending Sienna a message to check in on her.

Me: Is Bianchini behaving himself?

His trip to the city couldn't have come at a better time. I killed two birds with one stone. I gained a business deal and I thoroughly pissed off my soon to be son-in-law. That is, if he doesn't disappoint me again.

Sienna's reply is almost immediate as I make my way down the hall that leads to the master suite, the basement entrance to my gym, and my home office.

Princess: No business deal is worth subjecting me to this amount of boredom, Daddy.

Me: Baby girl, I've already closed that deal.

I'll have to watch the camera footage later. The look on her face right now is going to be priceless. I pocket my phone even though several more text notifications come through.

"Gentleman," I say, walking in my office and closing the door behind me, "let's get down to business."

CHAPTER 31
SIENNA

I read my father's text message again, and I'm still thoroughly confused, so I read it once more. *He's already closed the deal.* I thought that was the reason I'm here, wining and dining this meathead. In all fairness, he's not exactly a meathead. Nico is intelligent. I realized that early on in our conversation at brunch talking shop.

It's more the fact that he comes off too fake Italian for me. Before today, I didn't even know that was a thing outside the movies. Maybe he's watched too much of *The Godfather* or *The Sopranos*. I don't know, but whatever it is, it's a complete turn off. Maybe I'm being judgmental. He is from Italy, or spent time over there, I'm not sure which. Maybe New York Italians are just a different breed than the rest.

But that doesn't explain what the hell I'm doing here. I fire off several text messages to my father.

Me: Come again?

Me: What the fuck, Dad????

Me: Hello!!!

I set my phone down, face up in case he decides to reply. Looking at my dinner guest, I lean back and eye him. He smiles over the forkful of charcoal roasted salmon that he just shoved into his mouth.

"Did you sign a business contract with my father when you met privately with him earlier today?"

Swallowing, he places his fork on the table and gulps down a drink of his red wine. Finally, his head bobs, and then he replies, "Yes, of course. Did he not tell you?"

"No, he did not. And since he's not here, care to tell me why we're eating together if the deal has been made official with your signature?"

If this motherfucker comes back and tells me this is supposed to be a motherfucking date, I may strangle him before going home and strangling my father too.

"Tony," he says, his accent thicker than earlier today. "He asked me what I thought of you, so I spoke the truth. I told him you are not only a very smart woman, but beautiful too; the most beautiful girl I've seen." He places his palm over his heart, and I have to swallow to avoid vomiting the little bit of my dinner that I did eat. "He said I should let you take us out to dinner and celebrate our companies doing business together. So, here we are in this fancy restaurant, eating a delicious meal and enjoying one another's company."

"His name is Antonio or Mr. Caputo—I don't really care which you use—but since we're in business, I expect you to address him respectably." I'm full of shit. Dad probably told the guy to call him Tony, but I'm pissed that I'm here instead of out with Matteo. Not that I'd planned on going with him, but it would have been amusing to answer the door in my pj's. "Are you expecting anything more once the meal is finished? Any happy ending to this night?"

"He's not getting a goddamn thing from you. That I can assure you."

My attention snaps up to Matteo pulling out the chair to my right and proceeding to plop his ass down.

"I'm sorry, can we help you?" Nico asks, confusion marring his face.

"Yes, actually," Matteo states. "You can vacate the seat you're sitting in next to *my* date, and then you can leave." He leans forward, steepling his palms together with his elbows on the table, eyeing Nico.

"Your date?" Nico starts to laugh. "I'm pretty sure—"

"Let me stop you right there. If you don't leave right now, tonight isn't going to end well for you. I'm not in a friendly mood, seeing as I'm finding another man with my woman."

"I thought you said you weren't seeing anyone. Isn't that what you told me on the way here." Nico turns to face me, expecting an answer, but I'm bored with him and pissed off at my father, so I cross my arms over my chest.

"It's complicated and doesn't concern you," Matteo says.

"Maybe it doesn't concern you either, Matteo," I chime in.

"Matteo," Nico echoes his name, only slower.

"Baby, everything about you concerns me. And finding you here with him isn't going to end well for you either. You're going to pay for this bullshit."

Nico's eyes grow wide with recognition. "You're Matteo De Salvo, aren't you?"

"Good. You know who I am, and I'm sure you now realize what I'm capable of." There's a pause where no one is saying a word. “Yet you’re still sitting in the chair I told you to vacate. Are you trying to push me further than I already am? Trust me, you won’t like the results. Leave.”

“I don’t think–”

“I don’t care what you think. Leave before I cause a scene and ruin the night of everyone in here–especially yours. I don’t know you and you don’t want to know me. Am I making myself clear?”

Nico pushes his chair back and stands. Looking down at me, he says, “Sienna, it was a pleasure doing business with you, but I’m going to head back to Miami where physical harm isn’t within arm’s reach. You have a good night.”

Matteo and I stare at one another as Nico leaves, succumbing to Matteo’s demands. I don’t know how long our gaze stays locked; could have been seconds or minutes, but the moment ends when the waitress chimes in. “Did the other gentleman leave?”

There’s worry in her tone like she’s scared she isn’t going to be paid. I’m sure she isn’t used to the woman paying very often, but when I go to retrieve my wallet from my purse, Matteo whips out a credit card, handing it to her. “I got it covered, sweetheart.”

“Thank . . . you,” she says, pulling the plastic from his fingers and leaving us.

“Are you done eating or do you want to finish that?” Matteo asks, his head nodding at my plate.

“I’m done.” The meal was good, but the company wasn’t with whom I wanted to share the evening with, and that fact irritates me.

“Good.” Reaching in front of me, Matteo grabs my plate and places it down in front of him. “I’m starving. I’m supposed to be eating right now, but my date ditched me.” He scoops creamy pasta onto the fork and then shovels it in his mouth as he eyes me, the fire returning in his stare.

I grab my glass of water, taking a sip. The ice has all but melted, leaving a few cubes, but it's still cold enough that it cools down my dry throat.

"You have anything to say for yourself?"

"You're hot when you're angry." I didn't really want that to come out of my mouth, but it's the truth, so I didn't stop the words. His scowl and the heat in his stare dissipate, being replaced with the cocky smirk I've come to be familiar with.

When his phone rings he pulls it out of his pocket, glances at the caller and then silences it, before placing it on the table and returns to polishing off my dinner. It's not even a minute later before it's ringing again, but Matteo does the same thing, silencing it without answering. "Food too important not to answer?"

"I'm on a date with you. It would be rude of me to answer. Besides, I don't recognize the number and it's not one I have saved in my contacts, so the person must not matter that much," he tells me at the same time my phone rings. Looking at the screen, I pick it up, answering it when I see it's my dad.

"I'm so mad at you," I tell him instead of greeting him.

"Hand the phone to Matteo," he demands, ignoring my comment.

"How do you even know he's here? Are you spying on me, or did your new business associate call and tattle?"

I'm pissed off over the contract being signed without my involvement, and he needs to know this. "Put De Salvo on the damn phone already. I'm not dealing with your attitude tonight."

"It's for you." I hold out my arm, shoving the phone in Matteo's direction. Did my father tell him where I was? He had to have, otherwise how would Matteo have known where to find me?

Fuck this shit.

Taking her phone, I raise it to my ear, watching Sienna's anger flare.

"Is my daughter okay?" I ask, knowing it's Tony based on Sienna's interaction with the caller.

"Do kids today not know proper phone etiquette? Brooklyn is fine. I filled her belly with cake and ice cream and soda. She's bouncing off the walls and ready for you."

Sienna stands, her chair sliding back like she's about to bolt when I clasp my left hand around her wrist. "I'm on a date, so you'll have to deal with that shit. Besides, Brooklyn hates soda," I tell him, calling him out on his bullshit.

The waitress appears, sliding the pad with the check and my card on the table. She takes one look at the situation and quickly leaves. Holding Sienna with one hand as she attempts to yank free, I lift my shoulder to keep her phone in place as I write out the tip and sign the receipt.

"You didn't disappoint me, Matteo. I'm calling to let you know that you can proceed with this fucked-up date of yours, but have my daughter home by midnight or this time I will pull the trigger. And De Salvo, I have a lot of money riding on your fight in a few short weeks, so if you make me put a round in you then it will be multiple bullets."

"Got it. Have the bad princess home before curfew or you'll pump me full of lead. Anything else?" Sienna yanks on her arm again, but this time I release her, and she almost falls backward. Standing, I grab her by the waist to steady her, but she snatches her phone from my ear and twists out of my hold.

"Time's up, Dad. Goodnight," she barks, walking away from me. I follow but keep enough distance between us until we reach the elevator.

She stops in front of the metal doors, her purse hanging from one shoulder with her arms wrapped around herself and her hands sliding up and down her bare arms. That dress she's wearing barely covers anything, so I'm guessing she's cold. After pressing the round button to bring the elevator car to us, I remove my suit jacket and place it over her shoulders as I pull her purse from her arm so that she can slide them inside.

"Thanks," she says, her voice soft with no anger lingering. The door slides open, and I wait for her to enter before following. Once in and the doors close, I hand her purse back.

"You barely touched your food. Are you hungry?"

"Yes," she admits, and a ping of regret hits me.

"Why did you let me eat all of your dinner? Was it not what you wanted, or is there another reason you didn't eat, Si?"

"What does it matter? Just take me home." The elevator stops at the bottom, and as soon as the doors open, she scurries out.

“I’m parked in the middle on the right,” I say, instructing her to head toward my Lexus. Pulling out my keys, I press the unlock button, seeing the taillights come to life in the fully lit parking garage. There are multiple restaurants in this building, and all of them must be busy tonight. There isn’t an open parking spot in sight.

When Sienna turns, making her way to the passenger side, I detour, following her. She goes to pull the door open, but I slam my palm against the upper panel, closing the few inches she had opened. She quickly pivots to face me, annoyance crossing her features as she folds her arms over her chest.

“Why didn’t you eat?” I ask again. “Be honest.”

“*He* wasn’t who I wanted to eat with. Happy?”

“Immensely.” Grabbing her by the neck, I pull her forward until my lips smash together with hers, shocking her. She gasps, parting her lips, and I take full advantage, deepening our kiss as I back her against the metal of the car door, my front pressing to hers. Forcing my mouth an inch away, I say, “I meant what I said. I’m going to punish you for the shit you pulled tonight. Now tell me I can touch you.”

“You’re already touching me.”

Snatching her purse from her, I slam the massive thing on the hood of my SUV, then I fuse my body back against hers and move my free hand down to the hem of her tight dress, fisting the material.

“Let me kiss you.”

“You just did. You didn’t ask the first time. Why ask now?”

“Baby,” I call, gliding my hand from her throat to cup her chin, then I proceed to slide my thumb back and forth across her pouty, swollen lips. “I like these lips a lot, and I do want more than my tongue inside this hot mouth, but that's not the lips I'm asking to touch. Grant me permission, Sienna." My words come out as a demand, but we both know it's a plea. I'm begging her to let me touch more than her exposed flesh.

I want her.

I need her.

Her breath hitches, coming out in pants as her chest rises, her cleavage becoming more pronounced with every inhale of air. Finally, she nods, answering my prayers. Not wasting a second, I yank her dress up to her waist and pull her black panties down her thighs.

"Matteo," Sienna's voice rushes out. "We're in public." She's wearing my large sports jacket, so even if someone saw us, they wouldn't see much of her. They won't see what I see.

"I don't give a fuck where we are. I need you right now, right here. Yes or no? But let me be clear. If I take you, you're mine. That means no one else touches you with their mouth or takes you on dates except me, and no one enters your body but me while we're seeing each other." I eye her hard, making sure the full effect hits the mark. "This is not a line you cross with me. You use another man to make me jealous, he's going to get hurt. Badly. Hospital, ICU fucking bad. Do you hear me, baby?"

Looking to the side and then back to me, she nods her head, and I drop to my knees, the concrete biting hard. "Matteo, your pants are gonna—" I part her thighs and the moment my tongue touches her, I'm lost. "Oh, God."

I clamp one hand under her thigh, lifting her leg, while my other hand tightens around her calf so that her ankle doesn't buckle in the high-as-fuck heels she's wearing. I lick. I suck. I even bite, marking her as mine.

Sienna's fingers pull and tug on my hair. She claws my scalp and the side of my face, but I don't care. I want to punish her. She deserves to be punished for what she did to me, but now that feels wrong. I want to make her come undone. I want to drive her as crazy as she drives me. I want to be the one that makes her soar and then catch her on the free fall down.

"Ah. Ahh. Ahhh." Her breaths increase as she pants like a cat in heat.

I dive my tongue inside her pussy, fucking her good. Her juices drip into my mouth, and I swear I've never tasted anything this good before in my life. Pulling out, I flatten my tongue, running it upward until I'm at her clit. I swirl around the hardened nub a few times before I pull her clitoris through my teeth and suck until she's grinding into me, trying to fuck my face as I eat her out.

Sienna has no idea how hard I am or that I could easily come in my pants when she orgasms on my tongue. Her nails dig in and she pulls my head forward. I feel her coming just before she unleashes a scream of pleasure that could be heard in a mile radius.

Slowing my rhythm, I push her thighs farther apart and lap at her entrance, wanting every drop of cum her body released—because this too is all mine and only mine.

Looking up, her head is leaning back against the window and she is more beautiful than I've ever seen her. This sight makes me want things with her I never imagined I'd find.

I place her lifted leg on the ground, pull up her panties, and right her dress. Then I stand, running my hand from her center, over her dress, and up over her covered breasts until my hand is wrapped around her throat once more, applying the slightest amount of pressure. Her eyes are heavy, hazy. Leaning forward,

I savor her lips this time, kissing her softly without the frenzied need from before.

The need to fuck her is present now more than ever, but I want her in my bed, not up against my SUV in a dirty parking garage. Seeing as I have to have her home, that's not going to happen tonight. If Tony didn't have my daughter, I might have been willing to risk life threatening circumstances to get inside of her.

"Come on, baby." It takes effort to pull away from her. "Let's get you in the vehicle. I need to feed you before I take you home to Daddy."

In her blissful state, she doesn't come back at me with a snide comment. Instead, she lets me glide her inside. Once I grab her purse, I go to the other side and get in next to her.

After I'm back over the bridge and headed in the direction of her house, I swing by Mario's to grab her a slice of pizza for the road. By the time we got there, she was roused up and decided we were getting two large pies to go instead.

After half an hour wait for them to be made we're back on the road with the savory smelling pizzas on the backseat. I'm pushing it on the time, but I'm not going to let her go hungry.

When we're a few minutes from reaching her house, Sienna grabs the stapled papers I tossed on my dashboard two days ago. It's a renewal contract with my manager that I was supposed to sign last month and never got around to it.

"Nosy much?" I say when she starts reading it.

She doesn't answer, and every few seconds I glance over, seeing her brows pinched together. She flips the first page and continues reading in silence. There are at least ten pages to it, but it's the same contract that I've signed for the last three years, only a few amendments.

Turning into her long driveway, I park, shutting off the vehicle, but before I can wrench the door open, she finally pipes up. "You aren't seriously considering signing this agreement, are you?"

"Of course, I am. Why else would I have it? It's nothing, Si. It's my contract with my manager. That's it."

"No. This is stupidity if you put your name on it, Matteo," she says, my name coming out in a way that could give my mother's scowling a run for her money. "Tell me this is not what you've been paying him. He doesn't seriously get forty percent from every fight you win and twenty if you lose, does he?"

"Hell no," I say. "I told you it's just—"

"He's fucking you is what this is, Matteo," she interrupts.

"You don't know what you're talking about." The second the sentence is out of my mouth I realize I'm the one that's fucked up. Anger flares behind her brown eyes. Instead of bitching me out, she flings her door open and exits the SUV as if she's on a mission, her legs power walking.

Getting out, I grab the two boxes from the backseat and jog to catch up. I'm taking the steps two at a time by the time she is walking through the front door.

"Daddy," Sienna barks out, marching toward him. Shoving the papers against his chest, she says, "Tell him he's a dumb fuck if he signs this bullshit."

Whipping around, she steps to me, snatches the boxes of pizza from my hands, and stalks up the stairs, disappearing down the hallway on the left.

"Do you think I could have that back?" Tony glances up, but no words leave his mouth. Flipping the pages, the same as Sienna did, he reads in silence. "How about you just tell me where Brooklyn is and we'll get out of your house."

It's not like I can't print another copy. The email is still sitting in my inbox from when Jimmy sent it to me a week ago since I never dropped by his office to sign it.

"You are a dumb fuck." Tony's arm lifts, the pages waving in his hand. "And this disappoints me, Matteo." He proceeds in ripping the pages in half and then tears them up further. "You aren't signing this shit."

"Okay." I nod my head like I'm agreeing with him even though we both know I don't give two shits what he just did. "My kid."

"She's asleep. Leave her that way. Now take your dumb ass to my office so that I can explain how your now ex-manager was planning to rip you off. I'm guessing Sienna tried to do that and you wouldn't listen—also, dumb as fuck on your part." When I don't move, his spine straightens, irritation and anger forming right in front of me. "Now, Matteo, before I go find this motherfucker and the night ends with him on the way to the mortuary."

"Fucking hell, you people." I shake my head as I follow his command, when really, all I want to do is grab my kid and hightail it out of here.

Jimmy wouldn't screw me. He doesn't have the balls.

CHAPTER 33

SIENNA

He's the stupidest fuck I've ever met. *You don't know what you're talking about*, he said to me. I wanted to punch him in the face. I should have punched him in the face. At least then I'd feel some satisfaction from the whole ordeal. He's the one that doesn't know what he's talking about, but did he even hear me out? No.

Asshole.

I'm about to fling my bedroom door open when I notice it's ajar, which is something I never do. So instead of barreling inside, I push the white interior door open, peeking inside. My bed is the first thing you see when coming into my room, so it's Brooklyn that I notice first. She's in the middle of my bed, lying on her stomach with her golden locks covering her face, sleeping. Suddenly my sour mood diminishes and the corners of my mouth tip up in a smile.

Matteo may suck but his kid is cool.

Tiptoeing inside, I place the pizza boxes down on my dresser, then I pull my heels from my feet and walk them to my closet. Once inside, I grab my comfy pajama pants, a black racerback tank, sports bra, and a pair of black panties, toting them with me to my bathroom.

My shower was quick. I didn't savor the heat and wasn't in there long enough to steam up the mirror. I'm not in the mood to bask in a long hot shower. I didn't even wash my hair because I don't want to take the time to dry it. I snagged a clip that was laying on the counter and pulled my tresses high on my head.

After I'm dressed, I walk barefoot back into my room, picking up the boxes, and just before I exit, I look over my shoulder, checking on Brooklyn once more. I'm guessing Matteo is still talking to my dad since she's zonked out in the same position as five minutes ago.

Leaving my room, I pad across the hall, opening Ren's room without knocking. None of us ask permission to enter each other's bedrooms. My brothers know the same as I do, if we don't want each other or anyone else to come in, we lock the door. That's common sense for it's not a good time and walking in will likely make someone uncomfortable. It's an unspoken rule, and because the door is locked, no one can break that rule.

When I see my twin isn't in his room or even his bathroom, that leaves one more place to check—Domenico's room, which is where I better find him. If he chose to go out tonight and not come home before midnight, I'll be pissed and hurt. This is our night, and we've always stayed up well past midnight to ring in our birthday together—the three of us and Daddy too.

But Ren has been off for months, maybe even closer to a year. I don't know what's going on with him and I hate that he won't talk to me. I'm sick of him telling me nothing is the matter when I know he's lying. I try not to push him. I want him to confide in me like I'd confide in him if something were the matter.

Dom's bedroom is at the other end of the hallway on the second story. We all used to be on the same end of the house, but when Dom entered high school, suddenly he wanted more privacy; something I still haven't forgiven him for. It's not that I'm a clingy sister, but they are both my best friends and I want them close.

Looking down to the foyer as I pass the landing, it's lit up bright but there is no one in sight, and I don't hear voices. I guess Daddy and Matteo are holed up in his office with Daddy giving him the verbal lashing he deserves. At least my father trusts my knowledge and abilities, and at the end of the day, that's what matters the most, though it irks me that Matteo doesn't and wouldn't even hear me out.

His loss.

When I get to Dom's room, his door is also ajar, so I push it open and walk in. Domenico is on his bed on the side he usually sleeps on, leaned against his headboard with two pillows and his laptop on his lap. He's wearing black rimmed glasses, so he's already taken his contacts out for the night. This is a version that very few people see. In spectacles, Dom doesn't look the part of the mean and scary underboss that he is during the day. This is the geeky version of my older brother.

Ren, on the other hand, is lying on the opposite side of Dom with about two feet between them on the king-size bed. He's on top of the covers whereas Dom is underneath his charcoal comforter. Domenico has a high upholstered headboard bed. It's similar to mine, but three feet higher.

Lorenzo's dark gaze flicks up to mine and I'm relieved to find him here.

"I brought food?" I lift the boxes, before placing them down on Dom's dresser.

Not waiting for an invite, I step to the foot of the bed and then crawl up the middle, plopping down on my back between them. There's a movie playing but the volume is relatively low for it to draw my attention. Looking to my right, I see a face mixed with anxiety and disgust. Ren hates horror movies more than I do, which is why Dom forces us to watch them when we come hang out in his room.

Scooting closer to Domenico, I peek over his shoulder, eyeing the screen on his laptop. It's mostly black with a lot of white text that makes no sense to me, which means Dom is likely doing something he shouldn't be. "Whatcha doing, big bro?"

"Hacking the police commissioner's finances," is his immediate response, no hesitation or thought to hide his wrongdoings.

"Why does Dad care about New York's police commish?"

"Probably doesn't." Dom clicks away, typing some type of code, I presume. This kind of thing used to interest Ren, but it makes me want to close my eyes and go to sleep. My twin's attention span as a teenager has never matched Domenico's, so after a few months, Ren moved onto something else—girls.

"Careful," I warn. "The boss doesn't like it when he isn't in the loop on everything."

"Good thing there's no one to rat me out," he comments, a hint of a knowing grin graces his tan features. I'm the least one of us that would tattle on either of my brothers. It would have to be a life or death situation for me to run to Daddy.

Turning, I move my back against Dom's bicep to face Ren.

"You look like you're about to bolt from the room."

Peeking at the television, I see why. The scene on the screen has me itching to look away. I turned at the worst moment. It's Johnny Depp's bloody death scene from *Nightmare on Elm Street*.

"Oh, look, it's the best part of the movie." The bed shakes with Dom's silent chuckle as blood shoots from the hole in the bed up to the ceiling. It's gross. It's freaky. I could go the rest of my life without watching horror movies. "You can shut it off, Ren," my brother says, giving away what time it is.

"It's after midnight?" I ask, my voice squealing with excitement, the movie already forgotten.

"Twelve-oh-three," he responds, the corners of his lips trying hard not to tip up.

Ren jumps from the bed and I scramble to follow. He beats me to the stairs, jogging down. He's wearing socks, so his feet slide, making him off balance and giving me the advantage to slip in front of him.

Entering the kitchen, I see our birthday cake on the island, a good-sized chunk already missing. "Hey!" I shout. "Who got into our cake?"

"Probably your boyfriend's kid," Ren grumbles, annoyance laced in his tone. Grabbing forks from the drawer, he hands one to me and then comes around to my side of the island, perching a foot on the stool leg instead of sitting like I am.

Daddy has a different layout done each year to make our cake different, but it's still basically the same: chocolate on one side for Ren and strawberry on the other for me.

I don't waste time or wait for my brother. I dig in, stabbing through the icing and cake. My mouth pops with flavor when the icing lands on my tongue. It's delicious. Never a disappointment. As I'm scooping up another bite, Dom sets the pizza boxes on the counter to my left, lifting a piece out, then he rounds to the other side, standing across from Ren and me. It's a large, wide slice, but Dom gobbles it up within seconds.

"Hungry?" I ask between bites.

"Starving. Thanks for bringing dinner." He jerks his chin, silently asking for another slice. Without placing my fork down, I lean over, rummaging my hand inside the white box. After I hand it across the island, I go after another forkful of cake even though the smell of greasy goodness is calling to me. "Was the douchebag respectful?" Dom asks, a bite in his words that tells me if I say anything to make him think otherwise, Bianchini will be paid a not-so-friendly visit by not only one of my brothers but both of them.

"He was a lame-ass pussy that ran away before I made him piss his pants." The satisfaction in Matteo's inflated facts has me rolling my eyes. His ego is stupid too.

"Why are you still here?" I question. I figured he would have grabbed Brooklyn and taken off the second Daddy dismissed him from his office. He must have graduated high school on his looks, because his intelligence couldn't have gotten him a diploma.

When he doesn't answer, I look over my shoulder to see him staring at the three of us, his expression blank, or guarded, I'm not sure which.

Daddy enters the kitchen, stopping to take in the scene. After clucking his tongue, his dark eyes snap to Dom's. "You're letting them act like heathens too?"

"Not my kids." Dom shakes his head. "Besides, you let them do whatever the fuck they want on their birthday."

Matteo stops next to me, but I act like he isn't there even though I can see him lift the pizza box from my peripheral vision. "You didn't tell me it was your birthday," he mentions, his words more of an accusation than casual observation.

Glancing at the clock on the microwave, I say, "It wasn't until twelve minutes ago."

"I see," he says, and in the next second he's standing behind me, plucking the fork from my fingers. The pointed part of the pizza lines up with my lips next. "Eat."

"She's not a child, she can feed herself," Dom grunts. "Don't you have your own kid to take home? I'm sure it's way past an acceptable bedtime."

"She's asl—" Pizza is shoved into my mouth, stopping my words that were an attempt to defend Matteo. Why I felt the need to defend him is beyond me. Snatching the slice from Matteo's hand, I rip a piece off with my teeth. I'm too irritated with his actions to enjoy it. But that doesn't stop me from chewing and swallowing it, or taking another bite, filling my belly.

Dad walks over, stopping next to me. "Move," he orders Matteo, who steps away. Looking up, my father has a rare smile on his face. It's not a full-on smile, but it's the best one he gives us when he's happy. "Happy birthday, princess." He leans in, kissing my forehead, before moving to my right, telling Ren the same and pulling him into a hug as my twin continues shoving chocolate cake into his trap.

"Thanks, Dad," Ren says when he pulls away and walks to the opposite side of the island to stand beside Dom.

"Thanks, Daddy," I tell him. "Best cake yet."

"Agreed," Ren chimes in.

"Why are you still here, De Salvo?" Dom's voice is cold. I'm not at all surprised by his dislike of Matteo. Domenico knew about my crush when I was a kid. He hated that I went to a separate school more than Ren did and I've yet to understand that. I mean, I get that he didn't like it. We all should have went to the same school, not me at a separate one.

"Brooklyn's already sleeping. He isn't going to wake her, so he's going to have to sleep in Si's room or one of the guest rooms, or hell, the fucking couch for all I care," Dad declares, and my eyes go wide with shock.

"Like hell is he sleeping in my sister's bed," Dom pipes up.

"Who says I even want to stay? I have my own bed in my own house as does *my* daughter," Matteo says.

"This is my house," Daddy declares. "Which is where said daughter is sleeping and I've already said what's going to happen. My house. My law. You'd do well to abide by that, Matteo."

"What the fuck, Dad?" Dom asks.

"Jesus, Domenico. Sienna and Lorenzo always sleep in your room the night of their birthday. It's been that way since they were toddlers. Why would tonight be any different?" Daddy pauses, and I keep my mouth shut, but when Dom does as well, Daddy says, "That was a question, Son. I expect an answer."

"He shouldn't be here at all is my point. I don't want him around my sister."

"Too late for that," Matteo says. "Already been on a date with her. My daughter even considers her my girlfriend. It's practically a done deal."

"Tonight was not a date," I correct Matteo.

"You're right, it wasn't. Last night after we shared a meal, and you fell into my bed. *That* was our first date."

"You motherfucker!" Dom yells.

"God, you really are dumb," I mumble.

"Silence! All of you," Dad yells equally as loud as Dom. "Everyone go to bed. You're all acting like petulant teenagers instead of the adults you are, and it's pissing me off."

"What did I do?" Ren questions. "I'm just sitting here eating my cake. I haven't even gotten to the pizza yet. Why am I getting punished?"

"Why did I have kids?" Dad blows out a huff of air. My comeback is on the tip of my tongue, but he speaks before I muster the courage. "Lorenzo, finish eating, but make it quick. The rest of you get out of my sight. I don't want to see you until breakfast."

Taking my marching orders, I turn on the stool and hop off. Grabbing Matteo by his elbow, I yank as hard as I can, requesting for him to come with me.

"Sienna," my dad calls, his voice like ice. I stop and look over my shoulder. "Do not let me catch you where you should not be. Understood?"

"Never, Daddy," I say, smiling innocently. It only makes him narrow his eyes, and I laugh. "Yes, sir. I promise. I'm the trustworthy kid, remember?" I glance at my brothers, smirking, and then I grab Matteo's hand, lacing our fingers for show and pull him out of the kitchen.

Tonight is going to be the longest night of my life, and I doubt I'll catch one minute of shut eye with him down the hall. I wasn't lying to my father. I wouldn't do that in his house without his blessing, and hell would freeze over before I ever got that.

Tonight is going to suck. Happy birthday to me.

"Slow down," Matteo calls out.

"Shut up, stupid," I reply, with venom in my tone.

CHAPTER 34

MATTEO

Waking up to my five-year-old screaming and jumping on Sienna's bed was not how I planned to start today. Usually, I get in a two-mile run and then I'm in my garage gym for four, sometimes five hours. I have a big match coming up in less than six weeks. It's the first one this year. This is when I put most of my time and energy in getting prepared to face off against my opponent—not taking a day off to walk around Coney Island, eating trash food.

But do I give a fuck about any of that right now? No, I do not. After learning today is Sienna's birthday, I spent hours lying in bed next to my sleeping daughter, thinking of something fun and meaningful that the three of us could do. I didn't even recognize myself in the bathroom mirror when I swiped some of Si's mouthwash from her bathroom this morning.

We did a couple of rides in Luna Park, making my daughter happy. She's never been here, and I've been wanting to bring her for a while now, I just hadn't taken the time and figured it might be something Si would enjoy too. I have no doubt she's been here multiple times, being as it's a staple in New York. My parents used to bring me here every summer, even if it was to the beach to play in the sand.

We're walking along the boardwalk, heading to the end of the pier. It's my favorite part of coming to the Southside of Brooklyn. Not to mention we're near Brighton Beach, where the food market is second best to my mother's authentic Italian cooking. She'd disown me to know I love Russian cuisine nearly as much as my own heritage.

"Why did I agree to come again?" Sienna asks, lacking any of the annoyance her question was supposed to pose.

"Because Brooklyn asked you to. If I'd asked, you would have told me to eff off."

She turns to face me, walking backward so that we don't stop on the crowded pier. "You shouldn't use your sweet daughter like that."

"It's one of the perks of having one, so yes, I most certainly should have and will definitely do it again," I admit.

"Come here, kid," Sienna calls out to Brooklyn. Holding her arms out, she flicks her fingers on both hands, motioning for my daughter to come to her. Once she's in reaching distance, Sienna scoops her up and hugs Brooklyn to her side, securing her on her hip. "We're taking a selfie."

My daughter squeals, pulling a smile not only from Sienna's lips but mine as well. There's a recurring feeling I get when I watch the two of them together. My chest tightens, but not in a bad way, and it's getting harder to not give meaning to what their interaction with one another does to my heart.

What if I'd paid more attention to Sienna back in high school? What if I'd even attempted to talk to her or gotten to know her? What if Kennedy hadn't been the girl I knocked up . . .

Too many *what ifs* have been surfacing lately. I'm questioning far too much, but not only that, I'm picturing futures I never dreamed of before.

"Put your phone away," I tell Sienna as I dig into my cargo shorts and pull out mine.

"I got this, but thanks." She gives me a tight smile, then proceeds to squeeze Brooklyn to her as she angles her cell out in front.

Instead of arguing with her, I step forward and pluck her phone from her hand, pocketing it, and then offer the same tight smile she flashed me. Pulling up the camera app, I turn my phone sideways and hold it out in front. "Don't let my daughter fall."

"What about, *I've got this*, wasn't clear, De Salvo?"

"Can we take the picture now?" Brooklyn interjects.

Smirking, I glance at my daughter. "Of course, now smile you two."

Sienna doesn't give me anymore shit, and finally, her lips curve up and part into a stunning, happy look on her beautiful, olive-tinted face. I snap two shots of them.

"Now, hold that pose." Stalking over to stand on Sienna's side, opposite of Brooklyn, I wrap my free arm around them both and hold my phone higher up and away from us, snapping a couple more shots. She must be humoring me, because I swear the smile on the screen is genuine. It must be for my daughter.

Stepping away, I go ahead and text Sienna a copy of all the pictures since it was her idea. "Can I have my phone back now?"

I peek over my shoulder. Brooklyn is still fused to her hip and

Sienna is holding her hand out, waiting. Pulling her phone out of my pocket, I give it back. She didn't give me crap, so I'm not going to deny her what she's requesting.

While I'm still holding my phone, I shoot my dad a text, asking for a favor.

Me: Will you and Mom keep Brooklyn tonight?"

His reply is almost immediate. The old man must have been on it. He's been addicted to some tennis game app. It irritates my mom that he's on his phone more often than not.

Dad: You really have to ask? Bring me my grandbaby.

Dad: And whatever you did to piss off my wife, fix it. I'm tired of your mother biting my head off every time I say a goddamn word.

"Are you ladies ready to head back or do you want to stay down here longer?"

"I wanna go to the beach, Daddy," Brooklyn says.

"Baby, I'm not wearing the right shoes for sand. But I'm taking you to Nana and Pops' soon. I bet if you want to go out on the water tomorrow, they would take you." I suggest, knowing she loves getting to go out on their boat. Since the weather is warm, it's the perfect time for Dad to do some fishing.

"Yes!" she chirps as Sienna puts her back on the ground.

Me: She's going to have to get over whatever bullshit she has against the Caputos.

Dad: I'm not touching that subject. You're a grown man. You'll make whatever choices you feel are right, but being on the outs with your mom is unacceptable. Fix it.

Like it's that fucking simple. He could be the voice of reason here, but by his text, he's not going to get involved at all.

“Why are you scowling?” Sienna questions.

“I don’t scowl.” I shake my head. “My mother is upset with me and my dad is likely getting beat up over it.” She gives me a strange look, so I clarify. “Not literally. With her mouth is what I mean.”

Dad: What time will you be here?

Me: At Coney Island, but we’re wrapping it up, so probably by four.

Sienna and Brooklyn start to head back, and I follow, still holding my phone, waiting for Dad’s next message to come through.

“Is she mad at you or is your mom mad that I was at your house the other morning?” Si asks. She’s holding Brooklyn’s hand, swinging them back and forth. More warmth coats my chest over their simple ease with one another. Brooklyn has never been around another woman in my life outside my mother and Kennedy. I didn’t know how something like this would go over with her. I never imagined it would be this easy either.

“Doesn’t matter. She’ll get over it, and when she gets to know you, she’ll feel different.”

“Doubtful,” she says.

Dad: Since you’re so close to Brighton Beach . . .

Me: I’m sure bringing you Russian food is going to do a world of good for making Mom happy.

Me: I’ll get it, but if you get caught, don’t rat me out to save your own ass.

Dad: Never.

Dad: You’re a good son.

Dad’s love for Russian dumplings is not something that makes my mother happy. In fact, it’s possibly the one and only thing she loathes about her husband. Dad's former boxing coach's wife was from Russia and introduced them to him years ago.

"I need to make one stop before we leave," I announce, catching up to my girls. *My girls?* Where did that thought come from? I haven't even slept with Sienna; well, not in the sense that I want to sleep with her, and until then, I can't really consider her my anything. Brooklyn may think Si is my girlfriend, but she hasn't actually consented to that yet.

Tonight, I plan to change that.

We walked from the Boardwalk over into the Russian community of Brighton Beach. There is one restaurant my father loves above all others he's experienced, and being as they're always packed, I called his order in on the trek over so we wouldn't have to wait.

As much as I've loved spending time with Sienna and Brooklyn together—and I have, more than I anticipated—I want alone time with Si. I need alone time with her. More than anything, I want to see exactly where this thing with her is going. My mind is on a constant loop at all hours of the day and night, Sienna taking up the majority of that time. I'm intrigued by her, but it's more than that. I want to be in her space at all times, whether it's holding her, teasing her, or sparring with her. I still can't get that time with her in the gym out of my head. I've never faced off with a female, not even playing around.

I know my strength and I'd never willingly hurt a woman, yet I find myself craving for her to be my opponent. That's insane, but something tells me she can hold her own. She knocked me on my ass and that floored me. I don't think I've ever been more surprised in my life, not even when Kennedy told me she was pregnant just before our high school graduation, and that has been the shock of a lifetime.

"Why are we heading into enemy territory?" Sienna asks, caution in her tone, and that pauses my stride. *Enemy territory?* What the hell is that supposed to mean? Are there people here that don't like her? Perhaps it's her last name. Is this the type of thing I have to question now when I'm with her?

She stops a few steps in front of me, turning to stare back. There is a beat of silence, and then her eyes widen like realization dawns. "You have no clue about our heritage, do you?"

I arch an eyebrow, not opening my mouth. I don't like it when someone looks at me like I'm stupid, and though it's on the tip of my tongue, it's better to keep that to myself. "Gang wars back in the day. Italians and Russians aren't exactly on friendly terms here in the U.S. The only ethnic groups we dislike more than the Russians are the Irish, and the one we despise more than them are the Albanians, but that's more recent than the decades stacked on top of decades of bloody history we have with the Russian and Irish communities."

"Can't you people just get along?"

Jesus, I do not understand hatred at all.

"You people?" she spits. "Matteo, you're either one of us or you're not. There is no in between." She sighs. "Dad was right. You were sheltered."

"Ever think maybe you should have been too?"

Maybe Mom is right. Maybe I don't belong in their world. That thought feels wrong and I have no idea why. It's like I'm battling my moral compass. I know the things the Caputos have done and likely still do to a large extent are wrong, yet, I want inside Sienna's world. I want to *be* her world.

But why?

Wrong is wrong.

Murder and crime are illegal.

Two wrongs will never make a right.

I know all of these things. They are things my parents taught me. They are things I truly believe, and they are things that her life is full of. I still can't walk away. I don't want to walk away. I want to see all of this through.

Even the thought of not ever seeing Sienna again feels like a weight so heavy my chest could cave in. I've had men that mirror my own power hit me square in the chest, punch me in the face and every inch of my body, yet the thought of Sienna not being in my life, even for a split second, hurts more than any amount of physical or emotional pain I've ever felt.

"I was to an extent," she responds, successfully jerking me from the internal war going on in my head. "I have seen things no kid ever should, but my parents, my dad, did everything within his power to keep a lot from my brothers and me. He even agreed with my mom to send me to a different school than Ren and Dom because I was the girl in the family, and they didn't want anyone to know I existed. Not because they didn't love me, and not because they cherished me more than my brothers. My mother grew up in a different time. To her, I imagine being female meant being the weak one, and she thought if I were away, even from my brothers, that I would grow up and want a different life."

"Yet you ended up square in the middle. Tony says you're practically in charge of the entire family," I admit, telling her part of my conversation with her father from last night.

"Daddy is full of shit." She laughs, and her face and eyes

lighting up. Brooklyn giggles, obviously hearing the curse word. I can't bring myself to call Si on that slip up in front of my daughter. "I do manage our family to an extent. I'm in charge of finance and marketing on certain businesses. But, Matteo, I am not *the boss*. And yes, I am square in the middle, which is exactly where I want to be. I've always wanted to be a part of this life, and not because of the stereotypical crap, you know? Though there is a lot of truth to it. It's because I believe in my father's vision."

"Which is what exactly?" I find myself asking, too curious not to inquire.

"Not something that's for your ears." Her voice suddenly becomes serious; harder like that first night I saw her again in Raymond's bar when she waltzed in and turned my world sideways. I hadn't seen that side of Si again until right now. Her spine straightens, and I swear she grows an inch taller, looking every bit of what her last name represents.

"My feet hurt," Brooklyn whines. "Can we go to Nana and Pops' now?"

"Come here," I call out.

"I got her," Sienna chimes, bending and scooping my daughter into her arms before I reach her.

My eyes collide with Sienna's when she looks at me, and I know she sees the silent questions blooming in my head.

"I like you, Matteo." Her voice is softer once more. "I like you more than I should, and more than I thought I would if I ever saw you again. Maybe I never stopped liking you and that's my problem, but the thing is, you aren't one of us." My brows furrow. "By one of us," she continues, "I don't mean my family's circle of . . . people connected. I mean my dad, my brothers, and me. That circle. Our inner circle. There are things I cannot and will not tell anyone outside of that circle."

"Don't you have a grandfather that used to be the . . . you know?" The boss is what I didn't say.

Her face scrunches up with irritation, followed by what I've come to recognize as anger. *She doesn't like him.* "Fuck that old coot," she snarls.

"Bad Si!" Brooklyn yells, drawing a wince out of Sienna, likely from the volume of my daughter's voice so close to her ear.

"Shit." Another, more intense wince rolls off her. "Crap. I'm sorry," she says, her head whipping around to my daughter. Disappointment in herself mars Sienna's facial expression, and I hate that look on her. "Please never repeat that word. Okay?"

Brooklyn purses her little lips and narrows her eyes. "Consequences," she tries to say, but it comes out mumbled. It's what I tell her when she does something worthy of punishment, and for some reason, it makes me laugh.

"Yeah, of course, whatever you want," Sienna rushes out.

"Don't tell that girl, *whatever you want*. She's cunning. She'll have you doing God knows what." I'm not mad at all, though I hate when the f-bomb is dropped in front of my daughter. I've done it a couple of times, but I do try to refrain from cursing when Brooklyn is around, though I know I can't shelter her from life. "Brooklyn, she isn't used to curbing her grown-up words. Give Si a break, yeah?"

That, 'you're a dumb shit' look that Sienna graced me with minutes ago is the same expression staring back at me from my daughter. It makes me want to pinch and tickle them both at the same time. Shaking my head, I step forward, grasping Sienna's face gently with my hands, and then I dip, leaning down and kissing her lips chastely. "If she doesn't want to cut you a break,

I will, babe."

"I really am sorry," Si repeats.

"Pay up." Brooklyn flips her palm face up, waiting for one of us to place a dollar in her hand.

Stepping back, I chuckle as I pull out my wallet. Snagging a bill from the money slot, I slap it in her hand as I slip my wallet back in my pocket. "That should cover the rest of the year. Deal?"

"Matteo!" Sienna eyes the hundred-dollar bill and then her stunned eyes flick to mine. "How much do you think I cuss?"

"Enough to pay my kid off." I lift both brows, daring her to argue. Her lips thin out, but they don't open. Glancing at Brooklyn, I restate my question, "So, we have a deal?"

Her eyes are big and round, but finally, her head bobs and her loose, brown curls bounce. "Good. Let's grab Pops' food and get going."

We turn and I start to stride past them when I notice Sienna is suddenly standing like a statue. Following her gaze, it lands on a couple across the street, a ways down the block. The guy's back is facing us, but the woman is visible with her sleek, blonde hair and colorful works of art displayed on her arms giving her away. *Sasha Nikolayev.*

"You two don't like each other, do you?" I know Si has an upcoming kickboxing match against her, but not all fighters that face off are enemies. Most of us genuinely like and respect each other.

I recall weeks ago when Sasha walked in Mario's Pizza joint that the two seemed at odds, but I didn't really question it. Is it because the woman is Russian-American? Sienna said moments ago this is enemy territory. Do they really dislike one another because of some stupid gang history, or are these people still at some war that I know nothing about?

"Ren," she says in a whisper. Looking Sasha's way once more, I notice the guy has turned and that's when I see Lorenzo Caputo. "What's he doing with her?"

"Um . . . maybe they're friends?" If I had to guess, he's probably fucking her, but I don't verbalize that thought. Something tells me it wouldn't go over well.

"Over my dead body," she comes back with. "He'd never." Her tone is adamant.

"Not too long ago, I recall those lips of yours, which are now my lips," I remind her, "being fused with Sasha's brother's. So, what's this enemy stuff you were going on about? You didn't act like he was *the enemy* then," I grumble, getting slightly angry over that memory.

"That was different." She rolls her eyes then glances back in her twin's direction. We both watch as they stride farther away from us. They aren't holding hands, just walking side by side. For all I know, they are actually just friends even if Sienna looks disgusted by the thought.

"It's not, but I don't want to continue this discussion. Come on," I tell her, and then step in front of them. "Let's grab the food and get out of here."

That motherfucker better not put his lips or his anything on her again. I may be laid back for the most part, but when I view something as mine, I'm selfish, and that *thing* in this case is *her*. She belongs to me now, even if it's only for a short time, so that split second pissed me off beyond comprehension when I pictured her kissing someone else.

I don't understand why I want her as bad and deeply as I do.

CHAPTER 35
SIENNA

Matteo's parents live in a gated community one city over from my father's house. When we arrived to drop Brooklyn off and the meal he picked up for his dad, I elected to stay in the vehicle. Matteo wasn't happy, but he didn't argue, which took me by surprise. I'm certain he's a momma's boy, so the fact that she doesn't like me isn't sitting well with him. He thinks if I'm around her then her opinion of me and my family will change. Maybe because it's my birthday he'd rather save that battle for a different day.

That's the thing about being a Caputo that I understand—we aren't liked by many. By most we're feared, which I hate to an extent. I don't like our family's reputation, but it's not something that will change overnight. I wasn't lying when I told Matteo I believe in my father's vision; one in which changes the way the American Mafia is viewed.

Mafia.

I hate that term. Not that Mafioso or Cosa Nostra are much better, but those are the real terms derived from the Sicilian organized criminals that came to America to extend their reach. My great-grandfather was part of that unit of immigrants who helped establish the original five families that ran anything from racketeering, smuggling dope, weapons, and I suspect women, to armed robbery, murder, prostitution, and the list goes on. It'll twist your guts at how crude and cruel those men were.

My dad's father grew up among the old school generation of men, believing and thriving on the same ideology. Rafe Caputo was molded to follow in his father's footsteps and to continue his stronghold over the largest city in the United States. Still to this day, my grandfather only cares about power and getting off on the fear of others. He's often nostalgic over the olden days. His way of thinking and doing business is archaic, and to this day, he still believes his way—the way things were done in the past—is the only way.

Essentially, that old coot was a follower. He didn't have a vision; he certainly didn't have a passion for change. After grandfather's stroke, my dad stepped up as the Caputo Boss, and that's when the other four bosses began to drop like flies. In his first year, New Jersey's boss disappeared, and still, twenty-eight years later, no one knows what happened to him. Two years after that, Philly's boss committed suicide. That evil fuck was known for making his victims appear to have killed themselves.

How ironic.

A month before my mother's murder, the Boston Boss dismembered his entire unit, cut tail, and moved out to the Pacific North West. It was rumored that the Feds were close to nailing him, but if that were the case, moving to the other side of the country wouldn't have prevented them from arresting and putting him on trial, so . . .

Then Mom's life was taken. A week after her funeral, the fourth boss—the one that ran factions in Ontario and Montreal—was discovered dead. His beaten body was dumped in the middle of Times Square. It was evident he was tortured, but no one knows for how long. Pictures surfaced showing stab wounds, burns, and bullet holes on various parts of his body, the fatal wound being a shot between his eyes.

After that, Dad spent a lot of his spare time making sure my brothers and me were trained in every form of martial arts. We even had a weapons specialist that taught us how to handle and use different guns. He's the man that taught Dom about knives, and then my twin and me. Dom was never interested in them like Ren. Domenico's weapon of choice has always been a handgun since the very first time he gripped one in his hand. I can still remember his face when he pulled the trigger. His eyes sparkled like I'd never seen before. Something inside of him changed that day, and only God knows if that was a good change or a bad one.

"What the fuck is she doing here?" Matteo's hot anger snaps me from my thoughts, my eyes searching in the direction he's eyeballing where I notice the car parked in his driveway.

"Who?" I ask when he pulls alongside the flashy, red BMW.

"Kennedy," he seethes through clenched teeth with so much venom that the initial jealousy I felt at hearing her name ebbs off a little, but not enough to extinguish my immediate anger and hatred.

"She's *in* your house?" I question. "How would she have gotten in?" She isn't in her car, so that is the only logical place she could be. Did she break in? That bitch is too dumb to pull something like that off.

"She has a key," he says, and I detect a hint of hesitation like he didn't want to admit that to me. Sparks ignite along my arms, the green-eyed monster inside raging.

"Fuck that," I spit. Pulling on the door handle, I push it open with so much force I might have bent metal, but I don't particularly care at the moment.

"Si," he calls out, his voice seemingly tired as I storm around the front of his SUV.

I don't wait for him to let me in his house. I jog up the couple of steps to his small stoop and then I push his front door open, glad to find it unlocked. Racing up the stairs, I halt when I see a rail thin body lying on his couch with her legs crossed and propped against the back of the cushions.

"Leave before I toss your nasty ass down the stairs," I order in a voice I reserve for rare occasions. It's my 'don't fuck with me' tone that's unmistakable. Matteo stops behind me, his warmth coating the fire roaring inside of me. I cross my arms, still looking at the trash on Matteo's couch.

Her back snaps up and her legs swing to the floor. "I have more of a right to be here than you ever will. He's mine. He's always been mine and he'll always be mine, Minnie, so it's you that needs to leave."

"Minnie?" I don't even know why I'm inquiring about this. It's not like I didn't hear Matteo refer to me as Minnie Mouse when we were younger. I'd just somehow forgotten that term until now.

"That's what he used to call you," she informs me.

"Get out, Kennedy," Matteo says from behind me, his breath blowing my hair on one side. "You know you are not welcome here. And just so we're clear, again, I was never your anything.

The only thing you'll ever be is the cunt that birthed my kid. Now get out."

"Matty," she whines, turning on what I'm guessing must be her version of a puppy dog look, but it doesn't hit the intended mark. "You don't mean that."

Tired of this shit, I stomp forward until I'm towering above her. Grasping her neck between my fingers, I spit words in her face. "Call him that again and I'll shove your teeth down your goddamn throat. Understand?" Shoving her back, I say, "Now get the fuck out before I make good on my promise of rolling you down the stairs."

Seeing a set of keys laying on the coffee table, I snatch them up and toss them to Matteo. "Remove your key from that ring." I eye him with every ounce of seriousness I have in my body. If he doesn't do it, this thing between us is done.

Over.

Finished.

And it'll never happen again.

I relay all those thoughts through my silence. Finally, he nods, and does what I've commanded of him.

"Matteo, no." Kennedy stands, and I step around her, going to stand behind the couch to keep myself from laying another hand on her. Dashing toward him, she says, "Where is *our* daughter?"

"That's none of your business. You lost that right, and I'll never give it back. Now get out before I let Sienna do exactly what she's itching to do to you."

Grabbing her remaining keys, she stabs her finger in the center of Matteo's chest. "We are not finished. We'll never be over, Matteo. Ever. Just like all the others, she's a short-term fix. You'll come back to me. You know you will and so do I."

Her eyes slide to mine and her lip curls into a snarl. She believes her vow, that's obvious, proving just how dumb this bitch really is. Turning, she pads down the stairs. I remain silent until the door closes.

"Take me home," I request.

"No," he tells me. "You are not leaving here pissed at me, and I'll be damned if that bitch ruins the night I had planned for us."

"Matteo, I'm not asking again. Either do it or I'll call one of my brothers. In fact, that's a better option anyway."

I go to pull my phone from the pocket of my romper when it's snatched from my grip. "Apparently, you did not comprehend that no meant you aren't leaving here tonight."

"Try to fucking stop me," I snap at him. "You don't understand. I have to leave. I'm mad as hell. I'm angry to the point I want to hit something right now. I *need* to hit something!" I yell.

"There's a heavy bag in the garage. Have at it. Take out every ounce of pissiness you have on it, babe."

"This," I point to the center of my chest, "isn't pissiness. It's not PMS or whatever else you're thinking in that thick skull of yours. I need to fight, Matteo. I need to hit someone. Make someone bleed." I don't know how to convey to him that I have to get what I'm feeling out of me. This is where Ren and I differ. I don't keep anything bottled up. I need release.

"I'm not going to hit you, Si. Not for real. Not—"

"Exactly," I interrupt. "But Ren and Dom will. They know how to deal with me, and they won't hold back. They can handle the type of shit I need."

His nostrils flare. "I'm sorry, but did you just tell me I can't handle *my woman*? Is that what I heard, Sienna?" Reaching out, his fingers snatch the material at the top of my romper, where the three big buttons lined my chest, and yanks me inches from his face. Snarling, he says, "You ever think maybe it's not fighting you need? Getting fucked hard and fast might work better. Because that," he spits, "I will give you. Right here, right now."

My mouth falls open and a gasp escapes, no words following. Not waiting for my tongue to catch up to my brain, he releases my clothes, only to plant his hands on my hips. The next thing I know, I'm hauled over his shoulder, and then Matteo stomps down his hallway until he reaches the master bedroom. Once in the room, I'm thrown for a loop when he tosses me on the bed, literally, my butt and back meeting the soft material of the comforter.

At some point in the tussle, my sandals are removed from my feet. Whether he placed them or they fell, I don't know. When I get my senses back in check, I glance up, seeing him reach behind his neck. Grabbing the collar of his shirt, he pulls it up and off his body. His bare chest and tanned abs stare back at me, mocking me, but I lick my dry lips, wanting this.

"Get that green shit off," he orders. Matteo goes for his belt and the button on his shorts next. "If I have to do it myself, you won't be able to wear that garment again. Unless you want it in the trash when I'm done ripping it off, baby, I'd be undressing right now if I were you. Once I have the condom on, it's game on."

I sit up and go for the buttons on my front. Once they're pulled apart, I slide the strings down my arms and work the ensemble past my hips until I can kick it to the floor.

"Come here," he says, motioning a come hither with his index and middle fingers. Twisting, I get up on my knees and move to the edge of the bed where he's standing.

Matteo eyes my strapless black bra, then his gaze lowers to my matching bikini panties, staring between my legs. After a long beat, those mesmerizing irises roam back up, landing on my lips, before returning to my own eyes. He runs his knuckles tenderly over my cheek in a way that eventually lands his hand on the back of my neck, where he snatches a fistful of hair, jerking my head back. His lips and teeth smash against mine in one brutal motion.

He may not be fighting me, punching or kicking me, but this is a battle–one in which he currently has the upper hand. He's winning. And easily so.

Pushing on his chest, I pull my head back. "Rubber up. Now," I direct, attempting to swipe some of his control. He half grins, a small dimple appearing on one side of his face.

"Lose the other shit too," he says, his eyes never leaving me as he reaches to the nightstand on the right side of the bed. Pulling the drawer out, he grabs a condom, and by the time my bra and panties are off so are the rest of his clothes. My eyes follow from his lips down his bare chest, continuing on a path that leads me to a patch of trim dark hair, and then finally, his . . .

Matteo grabs his cock in one hand, and with the other, he rolls on the condom. I swallow, and I feel my eyelids expanding, my short moment of bravery vanishing at the sight of his dick. It's not the first I've seen, but the size isn't anything I've ever seen in person or on TV, or maybe I have and didn't realize the true magnitude of girth. Matteo not only has thickness but length too.

"As long as I've waited to view those spectacular tits–and they are better than I imagined–get on all fours, Sienna." There is zero amount of playfulness in his tone. This isn't the fun side of Matteo. This is the boxer. And maybe he won't fight me in the same sense I'm used to, but that doesn't mean he can't give me a different fight. This Matteo is *my* boxer.

Doing as he instructed, I roll over and come to my knees, only to be gripped by the waist and hauled back until I slam into his chest. He palms and squeezes one of my breasts while his other hand is wrapped around my lower half, pulling my ass cheeks to his body and rubbing himself against me.

"Have you ever been fucked so hard it knocks you out?" he whispers against my ear, before releasing a sinister low rumble of a laugh. "That's what I plan on doing, baby."

Oh, God. I don't know if I'm prepared for that much of an impact. I think I would have been better off in an actual match, facing off with *The Beast* bringing all his strength and stamina.

He pushes me away and I land on my hands. Gripping my hips in a bruising fashion, he pulls my ass back against him again, grinding himself against me. It feels incredible and unlike anything I've ever experienced, because well, technically . . .

Feeling his hand behind me, he positions the tip of his cock at my entrance, and that's when my body tenses, going rigid. It wasn't on purpose. It was an automatic reaction that I couldn't control.

"Si?" He says my name slow, like a question. Even he felt my muscles coil and that makes him pause his pursuit.

"There's probably something I should tell you," I admit, my voice sounding unsure, unsteady, and certainly unlike me. I should have told him before we got into this position, but how the hell does one start that conversation?

"Then hurry the fuck up, baby. My dick is going to explode if I don't shove it inside you."

Yeah, that's the exact problem my body is currently fighting. My opening is clenched together so tight I'm not sure I can relax enough to let this happen. I hate to admit it, but I don't want my first time to be hard and fast. Does that make me a girl? Maybe.

But do I care, is the question.

I've fought so long and so hard that everyone thinks I'm as tough as the show I put on. It's not always a show. I can be hard when I need to be, but there's a soft side too. I just refuse to show it most of the time. Pretending to be weak and mousy is something I vowed I'd never do again.

"Sienna." My name comes out both like a warning and a plea—an urgent plea at that.

"I've never actually done it."

That stills him, and his arms come off me like I have a disease, making me regret the admission. I should have kept my damn mouth shut. He's going to shut me down all because I'm not ready to be fucked the way he wants. I want this. I want it bad, but I want it nice and slow for my first time.

It's not like I'm proud to still be carrying my V-card—I hate it.

"Are you telling me you're a . . . virgin?"

"Yep." The "p" sound pops from my lips as I nod my head. I push back, coming to sit on my heels.

"You're twenty-four." It's just like him to state the obvious. It takes longer than it should for me to muster up courage, but finally, I turn my head, looking back at him over my shoulder.

"I know, Matteo!" I shout, my anger snapping and my breath rushing past my teeth and out of my mouth. He scoots closer, his chest meeting my back and my body trembles against his solid frame. "If that means you don't want to have sex with me then let me the fuck go."

"If you think I'm going to stop just because you've never had dick, then let me set that shit straight. I'm not," he whispers against the shell of my ear as he squeezes my hip. "Knowing you're a virgin makes me want you even more." He lightly smacks my right butt cheek. "Turn over, baby."

There's an order in his tone, but it's soft, not hard. I slide my knees down the smooth sheet and then roll to my back. When I look up, Matteo's dark blue eyes are on mine and there's so much heat behind his stare that it knocks me sideways. I can't decipher the look. He looks slightly . . . possessed.

"I can ram my dick inside this sweet-as-sin pussy and fuck the anger out of you another day." I glance down to see his hand on his cock, his fingers rolling the condom off. I'm confused, and my brows scrunch together when I flick my eyes back to his. *He said he wasn't stopping, so why is he . . .* "It's your first time. I'm fucking you right."

And that means without a condom? I mentally question.

My thought must be written on my face, because he laughs, and it's the sexiest and cutest damn thing I've ever witnessed, but I don't get him. "You're confusing me."

The bed dips on one side when he plants his knee on the bed, and then again when he does the same on the other side. Crawling over me and between my thighs, he hovers above, staring into my eyes. He presses one hand into the bed next to my head, and with the other he cups the back of my neck, fusing his lips with mine in the gentlest, most passionate kiss I've ever experienced.

His eyes remain open, and so do mine. This kiss is more exciting than when my brothers and me would sneak down in the middle of the night while Dad was asleep and open our biggest Christmas present, only to re-tape them and pretend to be surprised on Christmas morning.

Matteo's lips on mine, our tongues intertwining, is more exhilarating than winning my first amateur kickboxing fight years ago. There is passion and something more behind the swipe of his tongue and the scrape of his teeth.

Pulling away but remaining close, his gaze penetrates mine with a force I've never felt. "You remember me telling you that while we're together you're mine and no one else's?"

"Yeah," I say, breathless. A crease forms between my eyes, wondering where this is going and why it needs to be repeated. I'd never cheat on someone, and the same better go for him too.

"You can scratch the *while we're together* part." Thinking back, I try to recall his exact words. I somewhat remember them, but he had me all hot and bothered like he does now, so it's not easy to concentrate. "From this moment forward, you are mine, Sienna Caputo," he vows. "Not just while we're together, but forever. None of that until one of us takes our last breath bullshit either. Forever means you are mine until the end of time, and you know what, even past that. Mine means mine, Si."

"What about you?" I stammer, my legs starting to shake in a way that I can't control. His lips tilt, and in the next second, my opening is breached, and he enters me faster than lightning and harder than a category five hurricane hitting land. Pain rips through me, and it's nothing like any punch that I've taken to the gut before, or even my head. Matteo doesn't move. He's still, like a statue.

"You own me: every breath, every beat of my heart, and every ounce of blood in my body. I am yours forever too, even if you decide I'm not."

The pain seems to dissipate more and more with every word that leaves his mouth, but another kind of ache replaces the fire; a need I know only Matteo can fill.

Reaching up, I grip the back of his neck, lowering his head so that we touch but we aren't kissing. "That's not words you'll ever hear from my lips, Matteo. Now, please," I plead.

Clamping down on my lower lip, Matteo sucks and bites at the same time, his body moving in and out of me in a glorious, yet infuriating and agonizing rhythm. It's torture and pleasure tangled together, both fighting to take over and both remaining as equals.

I throw my head back, a pant rushing out of my throat. Matteo's teeth scrape along my neck as he continues pulling out and diving back inside me. He bites me, hard and I squeeze him from the inside, my walls claiming ownership of not only the part inside of me but also the man as a whole.

My man. My Matteo De Salvo. My forever.

Time is lost with each thrust of his hips as his cock stretches me, filling me, taking the one thing no other man has ever come close to taking—my virginity.

I haven't a clue if he's made love to me for minutes or hours. My nails dig into the skin wrapped around his biceps. "Oh, my God, I can't . . ." His voice trails and that's when I'm coated with warmth from this inside. His load shoots inside of me and something happens.

My body convulses. It's violent and raw, and a magnitude of pleasure flows through me, ripping through my lungs and past my throat. I've given myself plenty of orgasms over the years, but I've never felt it in every limb, every muscle.

"Jesus Christ, you're milking the ever loving fuck out of my dick." Matteo's body falters, half-collapsing on top of me, but he presses one hand to the mattress, trying not to let his full weight pin me to the bed. His forehead drops next to mine, his breath hitting my neck and shoulder with every pant that leaves his mouth.

"Matteo," I whisper, my voice airy as the full realization of what we just did comes to me. "There's probably one other thing you should know."

"Yeah?"

"I'm not on birth control."

He's silent; we both are, then I feel his lips stretch, tipping up on both sides. In the next heartbeat, he lifts himself off me, pulling out as his body rises, and that smile I thought I felt is a full-on grin, shocking me.

Glancing down, his eyes stop between my thighs. "You know, the sight of my cum dripping out of that slice of Heaven between your legs has to be the hottest thing I've ever seen."

"I should probably go pee and clean up," I tell him, not knowing what else to say or how I should be reading the strange look on his handsome face.

"Oh, baby, we'll shower, just not anytime soon. Now spread your legs so I can clean you up and make you come again. Give me a few. I'm going to come inside you again before this night is out."

His head disappears between my thighs and a gasp rushes from my mouth when his tongue meets my sensitive flesh. I'm positive it's only seconds before I'm coming for the second time tonight.

Why doesn't the thought of Matteo shooting his seed in me scare me? He already has a daughter. Does he want another? Do I want a kid?

God, I hope my father doesn't kill him. I'm pretty sure I'm in love, and if that's the case, Matteo isn't the only one fucked–so am I.

Daddy is going to kill us both.

CHAPTER 36
MATTEO

I shouldn't have fucked her as many times as I did. Hell, I'm not convinced I can even call what we did fucking. It was . . . different. It was more than sex. More than two bodies coming together to reach a much-needed release. It was a lot more of one thing in particular; a thing that has a name, but one I've never spoken or thought of when it came to a woman I've been with.

It's not that I'm afraid to say those three little words. I'm not. I've never felt this fiercely for someone until now, so when I do say them for the first time they'll have a lasting meaning. She'll feel my confession all the way down to the marrow in her bones.

Propped up on my elbow and lying on my side, I watch Sienna while she sleeps, taking in every visible inch. She's on her stomach, her face turned my way with her hair half covering her profile. Her back expands and collapses as she breathes.

My daughter is the only person before Sienna that I've watched sleep, and like Brooklyn, she's now part of me too. One I plan on keeping.

I don't know what was going through my mind when I removed the condom. Learning she'd never been with another man must have short circuited my brain. My dick got harder. I wanted inside of her and I didn't want any barriers. I still don't, and as crazy as it sounds, coming inside her doesn't scare the piss out of me like it should. In fact, it has the opposite effect. If I wasn't forcing myself not to turn her over right this minute and wake her, I'd do it again. I will do it again.

My condom wearing days are over. As far as I'm concerned, the rest of the box can go in the trash. She's mine. I'm hers. There is nothing and no one that will stand between us—I won't allow it. If she does get pregnant—and at the rate we're going, it won't be long before that happens—then so be it.

Vibration from my phone pulls me from my thoughts. Leaning over Sienna, I snatch it from the nightstand.

Tony: Anything happens to her, I have a bullet with your name on it.

Me: I'll have her home tomorrow.

Tony: I should just shoot you and call it a day.

Me: Or you can, not.

Tony: Be in my office at 9AM sharp. You're late, I shoot you. You're early, I shoot you. Capisce?

I send him a thumbs up emoji to piss the motherfucker off. I follow it with the smiley face wearing a shit eating grin.

"Matteo," Sienna whispers. Her head lifts from the pillow, her eyes hooded in her sleepy state.

"Go back to sleep, baby," I tell her, as I lean over once more, putting my phone back in its original spot.

"Why aren't you asleep?"

"I'm about to be," I reply. "Are you good? Do you need anything?"

We took a shower a couple of hours ago. That's when we went into round three. I still haven't taken her hard, and I'm not sure I will until I know I won't hurt her.

"No. I'm okay."

"You sure?" I question. "If you need me to get you back to sleep, I'm more than happy to oblige."

"My vagina has closed shop for the night," she informs me, making my stomach clench as a chuckle falls from my lips.

Falling to my back, I say, "Come here, Si. Come sleep against me."

Not waiting for her to scoot closer, I reach for her and tug her warm, naked body until her chest is draped against half of mine. It's seconds before her breathing evens out and I know she's fallen back into a deep slumber. I follow within minutes, enjoying the feel of her skin against mine and knowing this is exactly how I want her every night, and how I want to wake each morning.

I SHOW UP AT EXACTLY NINE O'CLOCK, knocking on Tony's home office door—after I did his daughter, of course. Once while she was standing at the sink in the bathroom brushing her teeth, and then again on the bed after I made her come with my tongue. Luckily, I'd already brushed my own teeth before Sienna used my toothbrush, so I opted to leave the taste of her in my mouth, on my lips.

Licking said lips, I close my eyes, remembering her spread out on the bed, my head between her thick, muscular thighs.

Who knew pussy could taste that good? If I keep on this train of thought, her dad is going to open the door to find more than he was anticipating.

She's upstairs now changing. Apparently, I made her late for work. If I have my way, I'll be making her late for work every day, and I'm okay with that.

I'm about to knock again when the door finally opens, Tony appearing in front of me, dressed neck to feet in black. I'm starting to think his entire wardrobe is all black. It's as though he's permanently dressed to attend a funeral.

"You can show up on time, but you can't return a man's daughter after a date he didn't sanction?" He crosses his arms over his broad shoulders, taking up most of the space in the doorway.

"She got a curfew I don't know about?" I arch an eyebrow. She's an adult. How the fuck does she deal with this shit? A better question would be, why is she still living in Daddy's house, but that would go for not only Sienna, but her brothers too.

"Just get the fuck in here, Matteo." He takes a step back into his office. Turning his back to me, he strides behind his desk but doesn't sit. He stands, waiting for me to enter.

"Why am I here other than for you to threaten to shoot me? Again," I add as I step over the threshold. He doesn't answer, so I close the door and then take a seat in front of him on the other side, not waiting for instructions. If he was going to shoot me, he'd have done it the morning he put a gun to my head.

The last time I was in here the lights were bright, but now it's dim like I'd imagine it might be if he were working late into the evening instead of first thing in the morning. His desk is cluttered. I get the feeling that's not common. Everything I've observed previously tells me Tony likes everything neat and orderly.

There are cards lying haphazard. There's a lighter and switchblade that looks . . . expensive. It's matte black with the blade pointed in my direction. A bottle of rubbing alcohol sits atop what I'm guessing is a hand towel. There's even gauze and a roll of bandage tape laying out in front of him.

"Do you know anything about the rite of becoming a Man of Honor?" Tony inquires, finally lowering to his chair.

There is something in his deep tone that makes my body go rigid, yet I can't pinpoint what. He's at ease behind a big, mahogany desk, his posture is comfortable with the air of power that's always around him, so what's different?

"No," I answer, never having heard that term outside of the name of a movie, though I doubt that's where this conversation is headed. I'm also pretty sure I'm not going to like the path he's leading me down.

"It's usually a title bestowed upon someone connected or associated with one of *the* families," he explains. "It's often referred to as a made man. Someone who graduates in a way from a soldier, so to speak."

A chill runs down the length of my spine, the temperature in the room seemingly dropping degrees at a rapid pace. *Why is he telling me this, showing me these things? He doesn't expect . . .*

"Membership has been closed since I took the reins thirty years ago; at least within the Caputo family, that is. Do you know why that is, Matteo?" He leans back, his chair rocking, and the squeaky sound echoes off of the walls.

"No. But I guess you're going to get to that point."

"There are only three living people that I fully trust in this world. Three," he repeats. "I'm sure you can take a guess as to who they are."

Sienna. Lorenzo. Domenico. His children would be my guess. But surely there are others in his family. He has a father, though Si obviously doesn't like the former boss. Aren't there more members of his family? I have a large extended family on my mother's side. We've never been close to my dad's side, for reasons my parents will never fully divulge aside from, *we don't associate with the mob*.

"Your kids," I state, though I still wonder about his friends, or associates, I believe the term is in his line of work.

"Smart man. And yes, my children would be the right guess."

"What about other members of your family? Friends even?" I'm not sure why I want to know the answer. I should be running out of his office, out of his house, away from *his* family. But I'm not itching to leave—not one bit. I've always had a thirst to learn about my father's family, to know them, to know about the Mafia's way of life and if the movies and books depicted them with some form of accuracy. I suspect there is some truth mixed in with the fiction.

"Similar to the way your parents kept you away from Pete's family, mine distanced themselves from my mother's side of the family before I was born. And like me, my father was an only child. He severed ties with Sicily years before I took over. As far as friends go," he continues, "I have them. I keep the list short, but even they aren't family. Family are the only people you should ever trust. Everyone else will either shove a loaded gun down your throat or stab you in the back given the chance."

"So why are you telling me this?"

"You've recently entered Sienna's life. You're rapidly becoming a fixture." The way he says the last word is as though it's a sour taste on his tongue.

"Back," I say.

"Pardon?"

"You mean, back in her life."

"You might want to rethink that statement. The first go-round doesn't count. If it did, I'd have to kill you on principle. You snubbed my daughter from what I recall."

"I didn't know her then." My head shakes on reflex. "I mean, I knew her, but we didn't converse. We weren't in the same circle." Even to myself, my words sound like an excuse. Knowing her the way I do now, part of me wishes I could go back in time, but then another part doesn't want that at all. If I'd gotten together with Sienna back then, noticed her in the way I do now, then Brooklyn wouldn't have been born, and well, all I can say is that I am glad things happened the way they did. My daughter is my greatest accomplishment. The fact that I created her is a feeling like no other.

"Even you know that's a sorry excuse, but it's one I'll overlook as long as it won't be repeated behavior." There's a heartbeat of a pause where our gazes come to an understanding. Tony is showing me that when it comes to Sienna, he is not a forgiving man, and I wouldn't expect him to be. I'd be the same with my little girl too. "The point to all of this, Matteo, is that if you are going to remain in my daughter's life, if I'm going to trust you with her, then I have to trust you completely. For me to do that, you have to be one of us. You have to be part of *the* family. My family. A Caputo."

"Don't you think it's a little soon for wedding bells?" That question tastes tart on my tongue. Mainly because it's a lie. I basically told her I was going to marry her last night without saying the words outright. I told her she was mine for eternity and me hers. That was the truth last night and it remains the truth now.

"Don't jump ahead of yourself, De Salvo. I said I was considering bringing you into the family, not making you one of my kids. You have to stop being such a disappointment for me to give over my daughter." He arches an eyebrow high on his forehead.

Irritation, and possibly more than a notion of anger crosses my features. The top of Tony's lip twitches with amusement, making my teeth grind together. *Give her over?* Wonder what he'd think if I declared she was already mine and I'm not in the habit of requesting returns.

"You going to tell me what all this bullshit on your desk is? I do have places to be and stuff to do." My nostrils flare as I pull in air, and I lock my jaw so my mouth doesn't continue making me sound like a disrespectful prick.

"This *shit* is what I was getting at, dumbass." Tony's lips thin before he leans forward. Snatching the blade, he eyes me, his expression hard. "This is the rite—the way you earn my trust. This is the way you enter my family without being married into it."

"And exactly what the hell do you expect me to do? Repeat some words after you and that's supposed to automatically make you trust me? Seems . . . dumb."

"Seems . . . dumb that my daughter wants anything to do with you, but do you see me giving her shit for it?"

I purse my lips.

"Now, where was I? Yes, the fucking rite. Pay attention, De Salvo, I don't like repeating myself." He grabs a mug from the right of his computer screen on his desk and brings it to his lips, taking a sip of what I'm guessing is coffee. After he places the cup back on a coaster, he continues, the blade still in his left hand. "This would have been easier if you actually knew about your own family, been raised as one of us, but there is no use fretting over spilt milk. In the old days, to be inducted as a made man, or as others called it, a Man of Honor or Man of Respect, one first has to be an Italian or of Italian descent."

His eyes roam up and down, an annoyed look marring his face like he wants to question my heritage. "You have the first requirement, though it's not like I actually care. The way I see it, this is my way, so if I want to bring someone in that wasn't born with Italian blood running through their veins, I will. Might be a better option for Si if you ask me."

"Tony," I bite out as I lean forward. "She's mine. Let's get that clear right now. I don't give a fuck about this little display. Stop beating around the bush and tell me what the hell you want me to do. You have a knife, so if you want to cut me, or stab me, just do it. Get it over with. Because I'm not going anywhere, and it'll be over my dead body before she goes out with another man that isn't me."

"As I was saying," he starts, ignoring my rant and pissing me off. "Italian or not doesn't matter to me. Your loyalty does. Your loyalty means everything, Matteo. This is an initiation, a baptism of sorts. It's usually a ceremony, but that bullshit means nothing. You do this here and now. You recite the oath, as well as one other small detail. You become one of my own. You become part of *my* family. You are one of us for life. Even if Sienna kicks you to the curb there is no leaving *the family*, Matteo. It's a commitment for life. Unlike marriage, there is no clause in the contract where divorce is an option. The only way out is death."

"Just tell me what you want me to say and do," I deadpan, wanting this over and still ticked off at the image he shoved in my head of Sienna with someone else. Seeing her with that guy two nights ago comes rushing back, and I could go the rest of my life without picturing that.

"You state the code of silence, I slice a cut across your hand, and you seal the deal by dripping your blood on a card before you burn it. At that point, it's done. You'll be a full-fledged member of the Caputo family. So, tell me, Matteo, are you willing to go to that length to continue seeing Sienna?"

"What's the script?" I say without hesitation. He pisses me off further when he doesn't say anything or make one move to hand me anything. "Today, Tony. Let's get on with this. You want me to prove my loyalty, well, tell me the words to say."

Finally, he sits back and then he pulls open a drawer under his desk. After pulling out a small card, he hands it over to me. "Read it."

When I reach for the card and pull, he doesn't let it go. Instead, there is a beat of silence before he says, "You better mean every word. Don't do this because she's your current flavor of the month. My daughter isn't a piece of ass. Ever treat her as such and I will put a bullet between your eyes and not feel one ounce of regret. We clear?"

"Got it." I yank the card from his grip. Once I scan over the paragraph, taking in the words and mulling them over, I speak them, stating words that encompass loyalty and always honoring *the* family in life and even in death. Once the last sentence is out of my mouth, I stretch my arm across his desk, palm facing upward. "Slice away, Boss."

I watch as the blade inches closer to my flesh, and I realize there is no fear, nothing inside me screaming for me to bolt. Only the feeling of resolve settling within my gut.

When the knife is within a centimeter of my hand, Tony

suddenly retracts the blade, placing it back down in its original spot on this desk.

"You can go."

"Wait. What?" I stand abruptly. "What the fuck?"

"It was a test, Matteo. I wanted to see if you'd actually do it. Be happy. You passed. You live another day."

"A fucking test," I seethe. "Are you kidding me right now?"

He glances up, his body still at ease even though my anger is rolling off me in waves.

"Leave." His voice is low but lethal, leaving no room for argument.

"Whatever, this was bullshit anyway. And so we're clear, Sienna is staying at my house again tonight."

I step around the chair and turn away from him when he says, "No, she isn't. She missed a session with her trainer that she'll have to make up after work."

I stop and glance over my shoulder. "She stays with me. She's mine, Tony, and that is something I will fight you on. Don't push me."

"Dinner is at seven. Don't be late."

Without arguing further, I turn, storming out of his office. *A test?* What bullshit. Oh, he's Mister Tough Guy. The Boss. I should have knocked his fucking teeth out. I ought to turn around and do just that, but I won't. I'm not *that* stupid. He just better be glad I don't actually have a death wish, or I would have shown him exactly why I'm called *The Beast* in the ring.

Thank God Brooklyn is at my parents and I don't have to pick her up until later. The need to hit something—to pulverize something—is too high, and not something I want her to witness. It's why she's never seen me fight. It's why I'm not sure if I'll ever want her to see one of my matches.

I don't feel different.

Looking in the mirror, I can't spot any difference in my appearance. I don't even ache between my legs. Shouldn't I at least be sore? Even a little . . .

I heard—or should I say read—that when you lose your virginity your muscles feel overworked. It's rare that I have time to read anything these days, but back in my high school and college days I'd often read well into the morning hours, devouring hundreds of books a year. And I have no shame over the types of books I enjoy; mostly romance, some mystery, and the occasional supernatural or paranormal, none of them lacking detailed intimate scenes.

So why do I feel like I was lied to in all of those books? Granted, fiction is just that; it's exaggerated or embellished truths, made-up stories, but I also thought those parts were believable.

Maybe Matteo fits me *that* well, like he was meant to be the one to take my virginity. I don't normally have cliché thoughts, but . . .

Of course, it's not like I don't overwork or overuse every muscle in my body on a regular basis either. Speaking of working out, if I continue missing training sessions with Caesar, I'm going to get my ass handed to me in a couple of weeks when I face off with Sasha.

When her coach and manager reached out to my personal trainer six months ago, putting the bug in my ear, I grabbed at the chance. Why the thought never occurred to me I don't know. Sasha and I have never liked each other, so to be able to go toe to toe without causing a war between our families was the perfect opportunity.

There was a time when I was a teenager that I thought about becoming a professional kickboxer for a hot minute. For me, it's fun and more of a mental release than something I want to do for money. Besides, my love for my family and wanting to take a more active role won out, so I focused on business and finance in college.

Sasha, on the other hand, focused on training—both on a mat and on a pole. *Fucking slut that she is.* And yes, she's actually a better fighter than I am. I'll never admit that out loud, but I'm not stupid or in denial either. Even if I lose, it'll be worth it to make her bleed.

The sound of a bang followed by my bathroom mirror rattling brings me out of my thoughts. *What in the hell?* Something would have had to slam rather forceful to make fixtures move.

I'm dressed, I just need to grab my purse from my bed and then I'm ready to head to the warehouse in Jersey. Once I'm down the stairs, I see Matteo through the glass windows, flooring it in reverse from our driveway.

What did Daddy do now?

The asshole could have said bye. Fucking douche.

Setting my purse on the accent table in the foyer, I pivot and make my trek to Dad's office. When I peek inside, he is standing in front of his desk, his head cast down, fiddling with items.

"You threaten to shoot Matteo again?" I ask from where my shoulder is braced against the doorframe, my arms crossed.

"Get in here and sit your ass down," he orders, glancing up at me, his dark gaze a mixture of something I can't decipher. I'm not sure if he's pissed at Matteo or me or both or someone else entirely.

I comply, walking in, but I stop behind one of the chairs in front of his desk and place my hands on the backrest.

"I hope you're smart enough to learn from his first mistake by making him wrap his shit up," he tosses out, anger laced in his tone. *He did not just say that!* My eyes round and the heat in my cheeks send a wave of dizziness throughout me. "You get pregnant before you're supposed to, Sienna, and I will follow through with my threats. Do not force my hand. The winnings from his fights make up a quarter of my income. I'd hate to take him out of the game, but I will if he disrespects my daughter. Are we fucking clear?"

My mouth drops. I'm stunned speechless, but that doesn't stop my own temper from flaring. "Don't refer to Brooklyn as a mistake, Dad." I steel my spine and cross my arms, standing four inches taller wearing my peep toe heels.

I'm not sure why his reference to Brooklyn being a mistake was what sparked my outburst rather than my dad calling out the fact that he knows I'm having sex with Matteo. When I found out he was having a baby with Kennedy, I was crushed. I don't think

I'd ever cried so hard in my life. But now that I've gotten to know Brooklyn, I don't hate the idea of her existence.

"Can we not have this discussion, please? Seriously. I'm not talking about *that* with you."

"If you can't talk about it, then you aren't old enough or mature enough to be doing it in the first place. My point is—"

"Wait a minute," I interject as I eye the items on his desk and in his hand. "What is all that? Is that . . ." My voice trails. No. It can't be. Is that why Matteo stormed out? "Daddy, what did you do?"

"I tested him."

"Tested him?" I repeat my father's words, tasting the bitterness on my tongue. "Dad, that is not a test. That's . . . that is the real deal. Even I know that. I-I don't even know what to say. Did you freak him out?"

He must have. I'm freaked out right now looking at the remnants of something I thought my father did away with.

Why did he do this?

What could he possibly expect of Matteo?

"The man that marries you and the women that marry your brothers will prove their commitment, honor, and loyalty to this family, to my family, before I give my blessing, Sienna."

"You expect—"

"Silence, daughter. I'm not finished." He drops what he's holding in his hand. "I bulldozed my way to the top so that I would have enough power that no one would be foolish enough to cross me. Fear alone is not enough. And trust is not something I hand out."

"Dad, I understand that's earned but . . . this?"

"Is our way of life," he says pointedly. "There are things I can change and will, but this," he fans his hand across his desk, "isn't one of them. This is something even I believe in. Vows and oaths carry meaning."

His office is dimly lit, and his skin is tan like mine, but even so, I can see the heat marring his cheeks, telling me his emotions are on edge. It's a rare glimpse he's allowing for reasons I'm not sure. Maybe he's trying to show me rather than simply telling me why he feels this is important.

"De Salvo passed, in case you were wondering."

"Fucking great, Dad. So, he's a full-fledged member of the mob now?" I spit, my tone etched in sarcasm and disrespect; something until this moment I never would have believed would fall from my lips in front of my dad, or even behind his back.

"Betrayal will not be tolerated, but neither will disrespect. Do you hear me?"

A chill slithers down my spine, and as if on reflex, I take a step back and then another. Dad's brows furrow, and a line forms between them. "Sienna?" he questions, his voice full of caution all of a sudden.

"No." I shake my head back and forth in rapid cessation. *He wouldn't do that*. "No," I repeat, my feet retreating again.

"Princess, why are you looking at me like that?" He steps around his desk, but stops at the corner.

"You wouldn't," I say, but it's more of an internal argument with myself, not with him. He wouldn't do that.

He loved her.

"Wouldn't do what?" His voice is a command, and I see worry etched in his dark eyes. Eyes that until those words came out of his mouth have always been my sanctuary. He's my daddy. My rock. My biggest supporter, and until recently, the only man I ever wanted to make proud. "Sienna, you're looking at me like I'm the Devil himself."

"Are you?" falls from my lips without thought. *He's not. He can't be.* Not Tony Caputo. Not my father.

Long strides eat up the space between us until he's in front of me, and my back connects against the bookshelves that line one of his walls. "I'm a lot of things, Sienna. Not all of them are good, but not all are bad either. And there is not one thing I would do to *ever* make my daughter, or my sons, think of me as such." He closes the rest of the gap between us and grabs my elbow before I bolt. "Sienna . . ."

That voice, both powerful and soft at the same time is etched with more worry than I've heard from him before. "You need to tell me whatever it is you think I've done. And you need to tell me right now." I can see he's losing patience, but he's trying hard to rein his temper in—for me.

"You said . . ." I gasp. I can't even repeat the words. Words I've forgotten until now. How did I forget them? When did I forget them?

"I said what?" he prompts, and then his eyes narrow. They're trained on me, but he isn't looking at me. He's thinking back to what he said and then he's uttering that dreaded phrase once again. I start to shake uncontrollably. "Is that what I said that made you . . . freak out?"

I nod. Words won't leave my throat.

"Why?" He grabs my other arm, running his palms up and down both of my arms in a soothing, fatherly gesture. I want to step out of his grasp, yet at the same time, I want to step into his arms and pretend I didn't hear *those* words.

I swallow, and then my breathing becomes labored. That stops him, but only for a second. His right arm lifts, and the next thing I know my chin is caught firmly between his fingers. "Why would those words inflict fear in your eyes? I can't recall ever saying them until now. I'm not even sure why I did. I hate those words. I despised them every time they fell from his mouth."

"Who?" I ask, finding my words again.

"Not until you tell me where you heard them and why I'm scaring my own daughter." He lifts my chin and I have no choice but to look him in his dark storm-filled eyes. "Princess, you are the last person on this earth that I'd ever scare or hurt. Tell me," he urges.

"M-Mom," I choke out.

"Ari," he says, her nickname coming out as he exhales. "What about your mother?"

"When you found me in my closet, after she was . . ." I can't say the words out loud. I've never been able to say killed or murdered outside of my thoughts. "When it happened, I wasn't in my room."

"Where were you?" His grip on my elbow hardens.

"In the kitchen cabinet, below the sink."

"Sienna." My name comes out of his mouth like a breath of air. Like sadness over the thought of what I must have heard or saw. "Why didn't you tell me?"

"Before she made me get in there, she told me that no matter what I heard, never to repeat it. So, I didn't. I-I didn't even remember them until now."

"But you heard those words?" His voice comes out murderous, and his fingers tighten around my chin. I don't think he even realizes the amount of pressure he's applying with both his hands. There's going to be bruises, but in this moment, I don't even care. I need to know that my dad did *not* kill my mother.

I close my eyes and nod my head.

"Tell me everything, Sienna, and don't leave anything out." The venom in his voice matches the darkness I see when I open my eyelids.

"Tell me you didn't kill mom. Please, Dad," I plead. "Say you didn't do it!" I holler.

His fingers loosen and they roam to the back of my head where he cups my neck in another firm grip. His other hand comes up and he keeps my head tilted back to look up at him. "There are no words that can even begin to explain how much I loved that woman. I worshiped the fucking ground that she walked on. And I have never once stopped searching for the person who took her from me, from us." He pauses, taking in a deep breath. "No, I didn't kill, Ariana. I didn't kill my wife, Sienna." His voice booms, making my ears ring.

My back sinks against the shelves, relief flowing back into my body. *I knew he wouldn't have done that.* His confirmation soaks in like oxygen, ridding me of the hurt and betrayal his words sprang.

It takes me longer than it should to remember what he said a minute ago. *Why would those words inflict fear into your eyes, Sienna? I can't recall ever saying them until now. I'm not even sure why I did. I hate those words. I despised them every time they fell from his mouth.*

My eyes snap to his. "You know who did it?"

"Tell me the rest," he demands, not answering me.

"It was silent for a few seconds after mom put me in the cabinet, then I heard footsteps on the tiled floor. They had to be expensive shoes from the sound of it. I didn't know that then. I just had that thought actually." I take a breath, pulling in air through my mouth. "Mom asked why he was there, and when he spoke I knew it was a man. Something about his voice shook me. I didn't like it. It was harsh, mean. He said something that I didn't hear. I remember my ears ringing back then, and I had to put my hands over them. But then he said something about Mom changing someone. Ruining everything he'd worked hard to build. And then . . ." I trail out, my tongue refusing to say those words.

His head tilts back, resting on his shoulders. "That motherfucker," he seethes.

"Dad," I call out, my voice loud to get his attention. "Who killed Mom?"

His head falls forward, eyes distraught and filled with so much hatred that I'm not sure I'm looking into the eyes of my dad. "My father," he finally says, and shock grabs ahold of me.

"What?" I breathe the words out, fanning his face with my breath. "Wh-why?"

"I . . ." His eyes close, his jaw locking in place as a war brews deep within my father's bones. My grandfather killed my mother. Dad's own father killed his wife.

Is that why I've never liked him? Did my subconscious recognize that he was the one who took Mom's life? Why did it take until now to remember what happened? Dad asked me for weeks if I heard or saw anything and I always said no. I drew a blank every time I tried to recall that night. I didn't even remember being placed inside the cabinet until a few minutes ago.

"How could I forget?" My voice is weak. "Dad, I'm sor—"

"You do not have one thing to be sorry for, Si. Nothing was your fault. You were a kid who experienced something horrific. If anyone should be sorry, it's me for failing to protect my wife and child." He pulls me against his chest and my body sags, mental exhaustion overwhelming me. His lips graze my forehead, lingering until he wraps his arms around me, holding me to his chest.

My eyes sting but tears don't fall. I don't know what that says about me. I'm not a crier; never have been. Maybe it's because I was raised by a strong man, but even when I was younger and Mom was alive, it was rare for me to cry.

"I'm sorry, baby girl." He pulls back and I have to snap my gaze up to see his. "But you can't tell your brothers, Si."

"What?" My shock is evident in my voice, because I am. "Why? They need to know."

"They do," he agrees. "And they will, I assure you. But not before I handle this myself."

"What are you going to do?"

"You know what I'm going to do. You might not know exactly, but you know the end result."

He's going to kill his father.

Tony will finally avenge the death of his wife, even if it's the last thing he does. Even I know that. I've always known that. Anger courses through me like rapid fire, burning through my body. "If you aren't going to tell Dom and Ren, then let me help."

"No," he barks, and then turns away from me, heading back to his desk and taking his comfort with him. My arms are cold despite the warmth in the house.

"Dad," I bite out just as harshly. "I can help."

"I said, no, Sienna." He whips around, his eyes flaming. "You are never going to go down that road. Neither will Ren. I hate that I have to involve Dom in some of the things I do. None of you were supposed to be touched by the shit I do."

"But we're family. We're your kids. And Dad . . ." I sigh,

stepping toward him. "We can handle whatever it is you need us to shoulder."

He meets me halfway and he wraps his hands back around my shoulders, squeezing. "I know you're tough, kiddo. You're strong, and I'm so proud of the woman you've become. But this life, the way of the *Cosa Nostra,* is not and will never be something I want for you. I made a vow to myself on the day Domenico was born. I will change this life, this family, for my children. I'll never steer away from that." He tightens his grip. "You cannot tell your brothers, not even Matteo. Is that clear?"

I'm silent. I don't know what to tell him. I don't hide secrets from my brothers. And Matteo and I aren't that far into our relationship. It's so brand-new I don't even think there's a term for whatever we are. Sure, it's been a fairly quick and fast-paced love affair, but I know deep within my core that it's real for the both of us.

How can I keep something this big from the man I've been in love with since I was a kid? I'm not delusional. I heard what he said last night, and I do believe he meant it, but that doesn't mean I'm expecting him to profess his undying love for me anytime soon.

"If Dom finds out before I execute my plan, he will jump the gun and go after my father himself. He won't be able to hold back, Sienna. You know your brother."

I do know him. I know both of them. Ren is dark, but he holds things in better than Dom. Domenico's emotions, though he hides them well, are wicked when he sets his sights on something. But he has a reckless streak too. And when he finds out who killed our mom . . . I don't even want to fathom the destruction, the hell he is going to rain down on our grandfather.

"When it comes to the people Domenico loves, he doesn't think straight. His judgement is clouded. If I'd been thinking with a clear head after your mother was killed, maybe I would have put it together that my own father murdered my wife because I decided to take this family, my family, in a different direction than he wanted. Because I wouldn't step back down."

I look my father in the eyes, promising him before the words leave my lips. "I'll stay quiet, but will you at least tell me what you are planning?"

He shakes his head, and I know he won't give an inch—not on this.

Pulling me forward, he places a warm kiss on my forehead. "I love you, Princess, but I need you to leave. I have too much hate coursing through me and I don't want you to see it." He pulls back, but he doesn't release my shoulders. "I don't know what I'm going to do yet. I need a solid plan and I won't have one tonight. I may not even have one tomorrow, but once I do, you better believe I will avenge my wife's death. She's the mother of my children, my best friend. That's a promise, daughter."

With those last words he steps away from me. Turning his back, he walks out, leaving me in his office, alone with my thoughts, my fears. How the hell am I supposed to keep this from my brothers, let alone Matteo? At least he doesn't know me like Dom and Ren, so I have that going for me. Ren is AWOL so much lately that I can skirt around him, but Domenico? He'll see right through me.

I'm fucked. Which means we're all fucked.

Maybe I should just handle Raffaele Caputo myself. The monster killed my mother, he deserves to die. I can't put that responsibility on either of my brothers, and Matteo? If Dad didn't already make him run for the hills with all that mob ritual BS, this certainly would. Besides, I couldn't take that from my Dad even if I wanted to. If it were me and someone gunned down the love of my life, I'd want to be the one to drain the life from their body too.

Work will have to wait. There is too much tension and confusion and hate building inside that I need to expel it all. But I can't call either of my brothers. I'll cave and spill everything, so instead, I go in search of my phone and send a text to my personal trainer, begging him to fit me in his schedule now instead of later this evening like I'd originally asked when I blew him off this morning.

One thing is for sure, Grandfather's time is limited. His card has just been pulled; I only wish it were me throwing the punches, squeezing the life from his eyes.

Caesar's response comes quicker than I expected. He can fit me in if I come now, so that's what I'll do, already grabbing my purse and heading for my car. I keep gym clothes in my trunk, so there is no need to change.

Instead, I speed, getting to the gym in record time.

CHAPTER 38
MATTEO

After my meeting with Tony, I threw myself into training harder than I typically do to get my mind off his *test*. That was a week ago today and I still haven't been back to his house or seen him since. I'm still just as mad over the situation as I was when I stormed out of his house.

I got out of dinner because at the last minute he canceled. The only reason I'd planned to go over there in the first place was to get my girl. I meant what I told him. Sienna was staying with me. For all I cared, he could get the fuck over his issue. She's a grown woman. She can sleep in my bed and stay through the night if she damn well pleases—and she has. Si has been with me every night since I pushed through her virginity.

Tony hasn't shown up or threatened to shoot me again, so maybe I really did pass his fucked-up, bizarre test of loyalty and trust. He has texted me each night, asking if his daughter was here. That's been our only mode of contact, and I didn't lie. I told him she was here with me.

Something tells me he already knew she was at my house, but I didn't question him or ask Sienna if her father tracks her whereabouts through her phone. I wouldn't put that past him, seeing as he knew where she was the first night she stayed over when she fell asleep in Brooklyn's bed, and then again the next night she slept over when all we did was sleep.

Can't say that's happened again. Sienna's appetite for my dick is almost as insatiable as mine is for her pussy. We go at it for hours. I've never met someone whose stamina matches mine in and out of the bed, but hers does. She's been joining me in my home gym for a few hours after her early morning training sessions with Caesar. The woman has more strength and willpower than I'd given her credit for weeks ago.

Had you asked me if I thought she'd win a kickboxing match against Sasha Nikolayev a couple of weeks ago, I would have said no. Now, I'm not so sure. It's usually not good for a fighter to overtrain, but the effect it has on most is not the same as it has on Si. Every day, something she did the day previous only improves, whether that's her stance, her footwork, or her throws. She's got a mean elbow, and I almost pity that loser that was on the receiving end of it the night she walked into Raymond's.

Placing bets on fights has always been more lucrative than a boxer or any fighter winning the actual match. I'm even considering putting my money on Si. I'm typically not a betting man; I don't get off on it. For me, there is no adrenaline rush that gambling ignites like it does in others.

"Fuck," I draw out as pleasure flows through me at the feel of Sienna's walls convulsing around me. "You ride my dick so good."

She throws her head back, our eyes disconnecting. Her top

teeth sink into her bottom lip as Sienna's orgasm crests and she tries to suppress the moan I know is struggling to leave her throat, all so that Brooklyn doesn't wake up. I've told her over and over there is no amount of screaming she could do that would wake my daughter from a deep slumber, but she doesn't believe me.

I buck my hips to jolt her, and my efforts work. Her lip slips loose, and a gasp escapes her mouth. She's been moody, sad even; at least I think that's the way she's been feeling since she showed up last week, the night dinner was canceled at her father's.

Once her pussy slows its milking mission, I lift my back, coming up onto my elbows, then my palms. "Woman, I know how to make you scream."

Placing my hand on her lower back, I fan out my fingers then I flip our positions, putting Sienna on the bed with me above her.

"Matteo," she pants, and my lips tug on both sides.

Pulling out, I grit my teeth together at the loss of her heat, her tight walls that fit me better than my specially made boxing gloves. Lightly smacking her outer thigh, Si swings her leg around and within seconds, she's on all fours. Grabbing her hips, I slam back inside, a yelp falling from her lips a heartbeat later.

Quickening my pace, I meet her thrust for thrust. She isn't a woman that takes what I have to give. She fucks me just as hard as I fuck her, and I fucking love every second of it. Before Sienna, I got off the quickest and easiest ways at my disposal. Now, I find myself prolonging the pleasure, drawing out every ounce I can muster.

I'm no Boy Scout. I've been banging girls since I was fourteen. Never did I imagine sex could be anything close to this good. She makes every fuck before her dismissible. She makes me question what the hell I was actually doing with my dick, because this . . .

this isn't something I can compare to anything else. And I'll be damned if I ever let this go. Someone would have to pry her from my cold, dead hands.

This woman is mine—for now and for always.

Letting go, the rippled current takes me over and I ride the wave of ecstasy, coming inside her like I've done every time since learning she was a virgin. That piece of knowledge was better than any surprise Christmas present I've ever unwrapped. There's no amount of lottery I could ever win that will top the gift she gave me.

There's a part of me that knows I shouldn't be reckless with her, but every time the thought of using a condom with her crosses my mind, it's quickly squashed. By the angel on my shoulder or the devil, I don't know. Either way, wearing one feels wrong. With Sienna, there should be no barriers; not during sex and definitely not with our feelings.

If she were to ask me to suit-up, I would, no questions asked. But she hasn't and every time that realization hits home it makes me wonder if she's as frenzied and crazy as I am, or if her feelings are in line with mine—no barriers.

Falling forward, I push her flat against the bed with me lying on her back. I brace myself with my hands pressing into the mattress so that my full weight isn't on her; even though I have no doubt that she could handle it.

My sweat mingles with hers as I continue pressing my body against her. I don't want to pull out of her despite my dick softening. It'll fall out any second if I don't get up. But getting up means she's going to leave me, even if it's only for a few hours, and I'm not ready to be without her.

Leaning down, I graze her glistening shoulder with my lips,

kissing her, thanking her, or hell, I'm not even sure what I'm trying to convey. After a long beat, I push off and out of Sienna and fall to my back, my head landing on the pillow that she's been sleeping on.

Turning around, she plants a chaste kiss upon my lips, and without words she crawls off the bed, her feet padding into the bathroom where she closes the door. While she's cleaning herself up, I keep lying in her spot, my mind going ninety miles an hour, thinking about everything and nothing at the same time.

Is she going to come back again tonight?

Do I want her to? Fuck yeah, I do.

My mom still doesn't want to formally be introduced to her. I haven't the first clue how to get my mother to bend. You'd think she would be ecstatic that Kennedy can't sink her claws into me anymore. That's been a worry for her since Brooklyn was born. She thought with a baby that Kennedy would wear me down and the need to be present in my daughter's life full time would win out. But with the shitty mother Kennedy turned out to be, that was never an issue.

Then there is Sienna's father; her family. There wasn't any hesitation on my part. I would have gone through with Tony's ritual, his weird fucking mafia seance with the religious cards. I had to Google that shit. Turns out, it's legit.

Si and I briefly talked about it. She brushed it off like Tony was fucking with me, but the thing is, I don't think he was. Not even a little bit. I think he was one hundred percent serious and I surprised him with my willingness to go through with it. I threw him for a loop. He wasn't expecting compliance.

If I'm honest with myself, I shocked myself too.

The bathroom door opening jars my thoughts and pulls

my eyes to where Si is walking out. She's dressed in her typical workout attire and it makes my chest deflate a little, disappointed that she isn't going to get back in bed and sleep for another few hours. I never thought I'd enjoy bed company this much, but I do. I look forward to it more than fucking and lovemaking, and we do a lot of both.

"Do you have to go so early?" My question comes out grumpy but I couldn't care less. The fact is, I want her in my bed next to me while I sleep. I want to snuggle my junk against her ass. It's *his* safe place. *He* enjoys it just as much as I do.

"I have too much work to complete today, which is why I have to get my sessions done before work. I hate training at night, and if I can avoid it, I will. I've spent too much time here with you, only going into the office half-days. I have to stop or Dad's going to notice shit isn't getting done."

"I hear ya, but I don't like you driving on the road this hour of the morning. Anything could happen and no one would be the wiser." That thought has plagued me the last two mornings. I don't know why last week was different, but something about her leaving yesterday didn't sit right with me and neither does today. It's nearing four o'clock. It isn't even daylight for another two hours.

"Matteo." The way my name rolls off her tongue has to be one of the sexiest things I've ever heard. "You do realize I'm capable of handling myself, right?"

"I know you can. But that doesn't mean I have to like or be okay with knowing you're off alone when very few people are on the road."

"Exactly. It's safer this time of the morning." She says it matter of fact like she believes that down to her bones.

"Maybe in some ways, but not in others."

"Just give me a kiss so I can get out of here before I'm late." I comply by reaching up and guiding her lips to meet mine when she leans over the bed. Pulling away she says, "Besides, Ren will be there by the time I arrive."

"He was supposed to be there yesterday morning too, but the fucker wasn't," I remind her, my irritation at the fact that her twin has blown her off every time he was supposed to meet her at the gym. Disappointment mars Sienna's facial expression, furthering my growing dislike for her brother.

"I know. But he promised last night when we texted that he'd be there this morning. Ren doesn't break his promises, at least not to me. He'll show. You'll see."

"If he doesn't, I'm going to kick his ass."

She laughs, but I'm dead serious. If I find out he's a no-show again, his ass is mine. I don't give a shit if his father is *the Boss* of a Mafia organization that may or may not be connected to criminal activity.

"Text me after you drop Brooklyn off at preschool, okay?" she asks, backing away from me. "Maybe we can grab a late lunch after your training."

"Training won't be the same without my new manager," I holler as I roll away from her and pull the covers over my torso.

"I'm not your manager," she singsongs at a low tone. "Not happening, De Salvo."

I already anticipate a legal battle on my hands after my fight in four weeks. There is no doubt in my mind that Tony put the fear of God into Jimmy Lightheart, but when I win, and pull in the amount I do, he's going to expect a piece of the pie. Tony told me he'd deal with the legal shit and to just make sure I win, but until now, I hadn't thought of the fact that my former manager had almost fucked me over. My dumbass knew better than to trust him, but he talked a good game. He'd been my manager from the beginning. I had blind faith in him, and if Sienna had not been nosy, I would have lost my ass.

The motherfucker is lucky she caught it before I signed on the dotted line. The thing is, when I step into a ring, I go in beast mode. It's how I got that nickname. My opponent does not stand a chance. It's like my mind flips and the only thing I'm focused on is winning. Had Jimmy fucked me over, I would have lost my shit on him, and I'm not sure I would have been able to control myself enough not to cause permanent damage.

After forty-five minutes of tossing and turning, my thoughts not shutting off and a strange feeling filling my gut, I pull myself out of bed and head to my home gym. It's where Si should be instead of across town. She could have worked out with me or she could have told her trainer to come here. I'm not sure why she thinks Caesar is more qualified than me. I can help her prepare for her match with Sasha better than anyone can.

And tonight, I'm going to tell her just that. I'm not trying to take money out of Caesar's wallet, and if that's the case, I'll pay him whatever amount to make sure I'm the one prepping her and no one else.

It's early, and I feel like shit. I know hitting the heavy bag is the only thing that's going to get my head straight without her here, so that is where I head.

CHAPTER 39
ANTONIO

I haven't gotten a full night's sleep in over eighteen years. At this point, I'm not sure if I remember if I was able to sleep through the night when Ari was alive. I do know that sleeping next to my wife was the only moment of pure peace I've ever felt.

We married when I was nineteen and she was only a week past her seventeenth birthday. She was still in high school, but that didn't stop me from claiming her. I knew from the minute we met that she would be mine no matter what it took to ensure that would happen.

I would have changed. I could have done a nine to five desk job. I could have done hard labor. In hindsight, that's exactly what I should have chosen, even if it meant running from my father.

Arianna never asked me to get out of this life. Like me, she thought I could change it; make it different for our children. She wanted me to legitimize my income, so that's what I set out to do.

I knew from a young age that when you are born into certain

families then there are things that are expected when a boy becomes a man. You will rarely hear the term *Mafia* come out of my mouth, but that doesn't mean I don't know and understand that's exactly what my family is and has always been part of for my entire life and longer. In the old country, as my father refers to Italy, the Sicilian Mafia is called *Cosa Nostra*, meaning *our thing*.

Before Ari, I thrived as a full-fledged member of my Italian-American mob family. My father started me out as a soldier from a young age. I became a made man upon my seventeenth birthday, and within six months I was a caporegime, a captain, running my own crew. At the time it was the happiest days of my life. I thought I was a real badass. I thought I was invincible.

Looking back now, it disgusts me. I was a stupid kid following ideals I didn't really understand. It was cool to be the son of one of the five bosses. My father ran New York City like he was the President of the United States. For a time, he was untouchable, and I wanted to be him.

Then I fell in love.

I was taught to find a respectable woman to marry and bear my children—but never fall in love. My father had a different woman on his arm every night of the week, and none of them were ever my mother.

I thought I hid my feelings for Ari quite well from Rafe Caputo, and I suppose I did for a time, but mainly because he never expected me to bend a knee to a woman, to anyone. He thought he did a damn good job raising me into the man he expected me to become; a man like him.

There was even a time when my father was proud of the choice of wife I'd made. She was pure—until she wasn't. She was docile, but unbeknownst to him, it was only in front of him or other men I was associated with. Submissive was never in Arianna D'Angelo's vocabulary, and that was exactly what drew me to her.

She was my fire. She burned brighter than the goddamn sun on the hottest day. And I've missed her every fucking second that she's been gone. There is no one that will ever compare to her, and no woman has warmed my bed since. I had the best, and it's not in me to settle for anything less than my wife. God willing, I'll have her back in my arms one day. It just won't be today.

I can't leave this earth until I've paved an honorable path for my children. The problem is, like their mother, they are my greatest weakness, and also my greatest success, but still a weakness, nonetheless. I'm not a strong enough man to hide my emotions when it comes to any of them. I love my kids more than anything on this earth or beyond it. I'd do anything for my children. I'd die for them without hesitation.

Pulling in a long breath of air, I hold it in for several heartbeats then it releases on a shudder. Turning my head, I eye my alarm clock like it's an enemy.

4:44

Sixteen minutes until I need to be in my home gym working my tired old body like I'm still twenty-eight instead of forty-eight. I sit up, not having to toss the covers off. I never sleep under them, only on top. That's just another one of my many weaknesses. I haven't been able to crawl under sheets since the night before my wife's murder.

Standing, I pad to my closet, pull out a black T-shirt, and pull it over my torso where the hem falls just below the top of my sweatpants. As I'm pulling on my sneakers, I can't shake the feeling in my gut. I've avoided my children for the past week, but I can't keep that up much longer.

There is so much hate in my chest that I don't want them to see me like this. It's taken every ounce of willpower I have not to gut my father like the fish meat he is. He's another person I can't avoid either. If I do, his paranoia will get the best of him and he'll start to question what I'm up to.

He's not a stupid man, which is why I have to play my part smarter than him, staying two steps ahead. He will die at my hands, but I can't walk in his house guns blazing no matter how much I want to do just that.

For taking Ari from me, he will suffer pain like no man before him has ever experienced. For her, his death will not be quick.

The sound of my phone ringing pulls me from my morbid thoughts.

"Who the fuck is calling this early?"

Snatching it from my nightstand, I don't eye the caller ID. Instead, in a tone that leaves no impression that I'm happy to be answering my phone before the sun is up, I say, "This better be good."

"Tony, it's Caesar." A chill rolls down my spine. His voice alone has alarms firing off. "Sienna's hurt. Someone tried . . ." his voice trails off and my balance falters. My arm juts out, my palm gripping the corner of my nightstand the only reason I don't go to the ground.

"What?" I demand, my voice coming much stronger than reality. "Someone tried to do what?"

"Hurt her, rape her, take her, I don't fucking know. And she won't let me call an ambulance."

"I'm on my way," I tell him, racing from my bedroom. "And Caesar, if she needs to go to the hospital, get her to a goddamn hospital."

I pocket my phone into my sweats not even hitting the button to disconnect the call. "Domenico!" I yell as loud as my vocals will boom, knowing he's home, knowing the sound of my voice will alert him to the fact that something is wrong.

My hands are already shaking. I know there is not a chance I can drive in my current state, but I have to get to my baby girl. I can't lose her too. I won't. If someone thinks they can take her from me, they chose the wrong man's daughter to fuck with.

My vision hazes and I see red.

"Jesus Christ, Dad," Dom yells, his feet stomping as he flies down the stairs. "What the fuck?"

"Someone is going to die today. Let's go," I order, and with those words I yank on the door to the front of my house like I'm trying to rip it from the hinges. No motherfucker is safe from my wrath today.

The funny thing is, or maybe the not so funny, is that I'm not even worried about my own injuries. My lip and jaw hurts from being backhanded. That alone makes my blood boil so hot it feels like my insides are cooking. Whoever did this to me will pay. He will pay with every fiber in his body after I'm finished with him.

My ribs on the lower left side of my body hurt the worst. I'm sure they are at minimum bruised. I doubt they're broke, but what the hell do I know, I'm not a doctor, I just refuse to go get them checked out.

My ass is even sore, and my ankles are skinned up from being dragged across asphalt. My scalp hurts from where that motherfucker snatched me by the ponytail. My clothes are a mess; what's left of them anyway. There are rips in every direction I look, so I'm basically avoiding anything downward—and mirrors. I haven't even checked out the damage to my face yet.

But no, it's not me I'm the least bit worried for. It's Ren.

I've never seen Dad or even Dom in the state both are in. The glower marring both of their faces have been in place since they showed up to get me an hour ago. I argued with Dad for over thirty minutes because he was adamant about taking me to the hospital to get checked out.

He isn't thinking clearly, though. At least Domenico agreed with me. Going to the hospital but not calling the cops? Yeah, that wouldn't be wise. Not when I know Dad is out for more than just blood.

He has enough on his plate after learning the truth behind Mom's . . .

I used to be able to let the thought of what happened to her pass through my mind, but for the past week I can't seem to even do that. I force my mind to stop *that* word from forming.

This incident was the last thing Dad needed to deal with. Had I not been in such a daze, I wouldn't have let Caesar call my father. I would have had him call Ren instead. If I'd done that, my twin wouldn't be in the world of trouble he's going to walk into any minute.

If I knew where my phone was, I could have warned him. It had been in my hand when I was jumped from behind, so for all I know it's still in the parking lot or worse, ran over and smashed to pieces.

Fuck . . . I haven't even called Matteo and we're supposed to meet for lunch.

"Dad," I call out, my voice sounding like a frog croaking, which makes no sense. I didn't scream or wail, so what the hell? Dad's haunted gaze snaps to mine, making me cringe. There is so much pain behind his eyes that I falter, not asking the question I originally intended to ask.

"What, Sienna?" His tone is harsh, but not in a way that he's angry with me, because he's not. His emotions are fried. In reality, he's worse off than I am. If I thought walking over and giving him a hug would fix the expression he has trained on me, then I'd fight through the pain to do just that.

"Can I borrow your phone? I don't know where mine is," I finally voice.

"So, you can give your brother a heads-up?" His head shakes. "Fuck that."

"Daddy," I whine, and even to my own ears I sound like a child. Glancing to where Domenico is seated, his laptop on his knees, I say, "Dom, help me out here."

Pursing his lips, his gaze goes from his screen to mine and I see a second of indecision behind his brown eyes. "Sorry. Ren deserves more than the ass chewing he's going to get from Dad and you know it. I may beat the shit out of him myself."

"This is not Ren's fault. Stop blam—" The sound of the alarm system chimes, signaling that a door opened, stopping my argument, and my stomach clenches tight with dread. It's the longest ten seconds of my life before the figures come into view, though with the breath I was holding, it could have been less.

"Took you long enough," Dad barks in irritation as I sigh with relief that it's Matteo and not Lorenzo.

Matteo's hands go into the pockets of his black slacks and he stops at the entrance to the living room. He's wearing a dress shirt with the sleeves rolled to his elbows. My brows pinch together, and I'm confused by his attire. It's still early; so early that most of the east coast probably hasn't even made it to work yet.

So why is Matteo here? And why is he somewhat dressed up

when I know he was going to get in his workout before lunch?

"We having a family meeting?" Matteo jokes, a smirk set firm on his luscious lips.

"If we were, you wouldn't be here," Dom chimes in, his head never lifting from the laptop he's back on doing God knows what. If I had to guess, he's searching the gym cameras and the ones of the surrounding businesses for the man that tried to grab me.

"Wasn't talking to you, *brother*," Matteo says to Dom.

Matteo surprised me last week. I thought for sure he was going to run for the hills after Dad's little display of a tradition that goes back longer than I know. My brothers and I went through a form of it after we turned eighteen, but other than us, he's never done it to anyone else to my knowledge. And not in the way he relayed it to Matteo either.

What Dad performed with Matteo was closer to the real deal of becoming what's known as a made man in the world of the American-Italian Mafia. From my understanding, there are other boss's that still perform the rite of passage from a soldier to someone higher in rank. No one below the consigliere, the third highest ranking position, can perform the ritual.

"Cut the shit, De Salvo," Dad says, his patience waning. "And from now on, bring my kid home or I'm going to come take yours and see how you like it. *Capisce*?"

"From my recollection, you've done that already," Matteo deadpans, the amusement from his features gone in an instant.

"I'm not a kid, Dad. Jesus," I wince, closing my eyes and gritting my teeth.

In the length of three heartbeats that it takes the sharpness of the pain to pass, my lashes lift to find Matteo crouching in front of my chair. "What the fuck happened?" Matteo's breath fans my face, his ocean-blue eyes wide.

"It's nothing. Don't—"

"Don't you dare try to brush this under the rug, Sienna," Dad seethes. "It's far from nothing. And when I find out who did this to you, I'm going to drain the life from that motherfucker so goddamn slow. Do you hear me? That's a promise."

I meet Matteo's eyes, seeing his pupils dilate. "Someone . . . did this?" His chest expands and then deflates in such a slow pattern that if you didn't know his ring habits like I do you'd think he was taking this news calmly. He's far from calm; a hurricane brewing is a more apt description. It's exactly what he does when he climbs the steps before stepping between the ropes to face an opponent. "When?"

I don't get the chance to answer the question that's directed at me. Dad decides to interject. "When she arrived at the gym a few hours ago."

"Hours ago?" Matteo repeats. Swiveling his body to look at my dad, his fists clenched together. "Why the fuck didn't you tell me my girlfriend was jumped fucking hours ago, Tony?"

My dad clicks his tongue. "We'll talk about that girlfriend term later, De Salvo. I told you to get your ass over here, didn't I?"

"We won't." Matteo's head shakes. "That's a done deal. And had you told me Si was hurt I wouldn't have dragged my ass, motherfucker."

"Watch your fucking mouth with me. This is my house. This is my daughter. You will show me respect."

"Would you two stop?" I force out, my tone telling them I'm not listening to their shit anymore. I'm sick of Dad and Matteo's constant pissing contests. It was hot at first, someone standing up to Tony Caputo like I've never seen before, but now I'm over it.

"Holy fuck. What the hell happened to your face?" My eyes widen and my head whips to the side at the sound of my twin's voice. In all the bickering, I didn't hear the front door open. "Did Dom finally drag your ass home?" A laugh leaves Ren's lips and I know he's fucked before Matteo moves.

Pushing to a stand, Matteo turns to face Ren. "Where the fuck were you?"

"Last I checked, I'm not your business."

Wrong thing to say, brother, I voice to myself as Matteo vanishes from in front of me quicker than I've ever seen someone move before. Dad lunges for Matteo as Dom tosses his laptop aside, but neither are quick enough. Instead of rounding the other couch opposite of the one Dom was occupying, Matteo steps onto the cushion and is over the top in record time, standing chest to chest with Lorenzo.

"Where the fuck were you?" Matteo yells this time around. When he shoves Ren backward my brother loses his balance and goes to the ground, Matteo on top of him in a blink of the eye. "You were supposed to meet her this morning."

"Get the fuck off me, you prick."

"Matteo," I call out, "Get off him."

"You weren't fucking there, were you?" Matteo accuses.

Dad rounds the couch first and bends, grabbing Matteo under the arms, attempting to yank him back, but doesn't succeed. Matteo's solid frame doesn't budge.

"Let him go, Matteo," Dad says as Dom grips him on the other side. They both pull but Matteo doesn't release Ren.

"Matteo," I try again, but no one hears me over their struggle.

Ren's going to get knocked out if I don't do something. *Fuck my life right now*. I can't believe I'm going to do this . . .

Unwrapping my arms from around me, I plant both on each side of the cushioned arms of the chair I'm occupying and push myself into a standing position. The movement hurts but I clench my teeth. When I see they are all still scrapping on the floor, I blow out a breath of air as I shake my head, annoyed. Then I fall to my knees.

"Matteo," I cry out, hoping the damsel in distress act pays off. A ripple of pain latches onto my side, and for a second I regret the decision until I look up and Matteo is on his knees in front of me.

"Baby . . ." His palm goes to the side of my face that doesn't ache, cupping my cheek in a gentle gesture of affection. *It worked.* My lips spread a hair in triumph. "Are you . . . Wait." He pulls back, his brows furrowing. "Was that . . . Did you fake that fall?"

"Next time I call you or tell you to stop, do it."

"I can't believe you just faked that shit." Matteo sits back. His hand drops from my face, and with the comfort gone my body aches resurface, causing me to cringe.

"The pain is real if that's any consolation," I tell him. Glancing up, I see my father straightening his T-shirt. It dawns on me what he's wearing. On a rare occasion, Christmas usually, I might see my dad dressed down. I'm surprised he hasn't gone to change his clothes yet.

"Where else are you hurt?" Matteo asks, his brows pinched together.

"Someone want to tell me what the fuck this is about?" Ren's voice booms from where he's finally standing in his original spot in the entrance way.

"Motherf—" I snatch Matteo by his bicep, pulling with half my strength as pain tears through me from my sudden movement. When his eyes cut to mine, I shake my head.

"Someone tried to grab your sister when she stepped out of her car this morning," Dad informs him.

"Grabbed?" Matteo whispers. "As in someone tried to kidnap her?"

"What?" Ren's voice turns serious, panicked almost.

"We're not sure, but from what she told us, that's what it sounded like," Dom fumes. He walks behind Matteo as I push myself up to sit back in the same spot I was seated in before, same as Dom does, pulling his laptop back over onto his thighs.

"He was probably just looking to get lucky, you guys. Why would anyone want to kidnap me?" I toss out, but even as the words exit my mouth, something in my gut tells me that's exactly what the man was doing.

Something about him just . . .

Hell, I don't know. My head hurts and I'd rather be showering right now than sitting front and center continuing the interrogation that started when Dad and Dom showed up. I've only seen my dad visibly shake one other time, and that's when he found me hiding in my closet after what happened to Mom. When he toted me to Dom's Range Rover, he not only placed me in the back but got in with me, his limbs vibrating the entire ride home. He didn't let me go until he sat me in the comfy chair I'm occupying now.

Standing, Matteo takes one step and stops in front of my chair, looking down. "I want to know exactly what happened, Si."

"I don't know. I got out of my car, and as soon as the door was closed I saw a shadow through the window and the next thing I knew the guy's arm was around my waist. Then I was lifted off the ground and he was moving us away from my car, in the opposite direction of the gym." I take a breath and then continue, relaying the events of earlier this morning the best I can remember. "I was struggling to get his arm loose, but he said something like *You belong to me,* but my ears were ringing so maybe I didn't hear him right. I threw my head back, connecting it with his face, and that's when he dropped me, but he recovered quicker than me. He snatched my hair by my ponytail and started dragging me. I fucking panicked, okay?" My voice rises as my fist balls, and I slam it down on the arm of the chair, mad at myself, at the way I handled the situation. The vibration sends a jolt of pain through me, but I clamp my teeth together to stop myself from crying out.

Glancing up, Matteo is still looming over me, arms crossed over his chest, waiting for more details. With an exaggerated huff, I continue. "I finally got my footing on the ground and used my hands around his wrist to come to a semi-stand. That's when it hit me, and I remembered something Dom taught me a few years ago." I glance at my brother and his attention is focused on me. "Remember when you made me practice letting you yank me around by my hair for like a week and I thought you just wanted to torture me?" A real laugh bubbles out of my throat for the first time in hours. "Well, I was able to turn myself and kick him. Not that it did much; he still had ahold of my ponytail and was able to kick me back. I swear to God the bastard was wearing steel toe boots."

I splay my fingers out and wrap my hand back around my ribs. The pain is bearable when I'm still or I move slowly. "Anyway, that's about when I heard Caesar call my name. That must have scared the bastard and he took off."

"Si," Ren calls out, his voice laced with so much regret it hurts my ears to hear him sound like that.

"What did he look like?" Matteo inquires. "Did you see his face?"

"No, he was wearing a mask," I repeat the same thing I told Dad and Dom in the car ride home. *Only there is something about that statement that hasn't sat right with me since the first time I said it.*

"You know who it was, don't you?"

Matteo's question catches me off guard and I snap my shocked eyes to his. "What?" I ask, sounding dumbfounded. *Why would he question that?*

"Do you?" my father demands, my eyes flicking up to where he stands next to the fireplace. "Why haven't you told us?"

His assumption that Matteo's question is true ticks me off. "No," I say with all the authority I can summon. "I mean, there was something about him that felt familiar, but I can't put my finger on it. Dad, if I knew I would have told you when you picked me up."

"Si?" Ren's voice cracks, but I hear the silent question in that one word. *Is this my fault?* When I glance over, the pain on his face matches the pain I feel all over.

"The question is where the hell were you, Lorenzo?" The fire in my father's voice makes me shudder. Daddy can be cold. He can be hard as steel, but this is unlike anything I've witnessed before. He's angry at my twin, which is exactly why I played it off like I wasn't hurt as badly as I'm coming to realize I might be.

There was a time I may have been in worse shape. I did amateur kickboxing fights throughout my high school and college years. The only difference is that I wore headgear and was never caught unprepared.

I should have been able to take that bastard to the ground.

"I'm taking you to the hospital," Matteo says. "Lift your arms?"

"I'm not going to the hospital," I argue, turning away and

twisting my body to face Dom instead of Matteo. That small amount of movement causes me to tighten where my palm is holding pressure to one area of my ribs on my left side.

He grasps my chin between his fingers in a gentle but firm grip, forcing my gaze to his don't-fuck-with-me posture. He can kiss right the fuck off for all I care. No one is making me do anything I don't want to do myself.

"You are going even if I have to throw you over my shoulder, but I don't want to cause you any more pain or hurt you any more than you already are. Stand up or raise your arms and I'll lift you. Baby, you're going. I don't want to hear an argument."

"Go," Dad orders, backing Matteo and pissing me off.

"You need to back out of your fight with Sasha next month," Ren says from where he has taken a seat on the couch Matteo leapt over. "You can't fight—"

"Like hell I will," I throw at him as I look over my shoulder, stunned that he would even suggest such a thing.

"You didn't stand a chance in perfect shape," he says like it was a forgone conclusion that she was going to win. "Now, after this . . . No, Si. Forfeit the match."

"Are you kidding me right now?" I kick my legs off the chair, swiveling to face Ren despite the ache protesting my jerky movement.

"Way to be in your sister's corner," Matteo says, disgust laced in his tone.

"Butt the fuck out," Ren barks. "Why the hell are you even here, De Salvo. You aren't—"

"He's right," Dad cuts in. "Where the hell is your loyalty, Lorenzo? Because it sure doesn't sound like it's with your sister, with your family. Maybe it's time you take a long, hard look in the mirror. Because if you aren't one hundred percent with us, for us," Dad does an air circle with his finger, "then you're against this family and that does not work. Your name is your goddamn oath, so until you understand that get the fuck out of my sight."

"Daddy!" I yell.

"Shut it, Sienna. Get your ass up and do what Matteo says," he orders, and my jaw drops to the floor, too stunned to backtalk him like I normally would. "All of you will fucking learn that I run this family. I say what goes and what does not. And all of you will follow my orders from here on out or there will be consequences none of you want."

With that speech—words from the boss, not Dad—he walks out of the room, leaving at least three of us in silence. When I look to my left, I find Dom with a dark brow arched. "What the fuck are you all waiting for? Do what he ordered. Now."

Sienna fought me tooth and nail about taking her to the emergency room, claiming her injuries weren't severe enough to need that level of care. Being in the line of work I'm in, I know enough medical personnel that I was able to get a sports medicine doctor to order an X-ray at the clinic he works at part-time when he's not on retainer for sporting events.

Turns out, Si's ribs were minimally bruised, and she only had a split lip and swelling from getting slapped. She had a few scrapes where her bare skin was exposed between where her Capri leggings stopped and her shoes covered her feet. All her injuries were superficial, and I was relieved when the doctor delivered the news.

The large patch of black and blue skin on her left side looked worse than anything else. Being a boxer, I know surface area is usually like that, and oftentimes, there is little to no internal damage, but I had to be sure.

Still, seeing her like I did put shit into perspective. Had she gotten marred up due to a fair fight, I know I wouldn't have reacted the way I did. I would have joked alongside her. Someone maliciously set out to hurt her, or worse, nab her? That doesn't sit well with me in the least, even weeks later after her injuries have all healed like they never happened in the first place.

Sienna doesn't want to talk about what happened, so trying to find out if her Dad made good on his promise to end the scumbag's life is like trying to pry open a safe with a screwdriver. She's embarrassed, and I know that's the reason she wants to put the whole thing behind her. She doesn't have any reason to feel that way, but there is no convincing her otherwise.

Tony has let us both train and workout in his personal home gym instead of going to the one he owns or even going to my house. Other than trips to get more clothes for Brooklyn and me, I haven't slept in my bed since the morning of Sienna's attack. Every night after being inside of her, I've fallen asleep with my head on one of her pillows and my body wrapped firmly around Sienna while my daughter sleeps in a room down the hall across from Domenico's bedroom.

If Tony knows I've been occupying Sienna's bed as much as her body, he hasn't said anything. Perhaps the whole ordeal gave him perspective too and he's just glad she's back to sleeping under his roof instead of mine. Not gonna lie, I like it better here than in my cramped space.

At some point in the last month the room across from Dom was painted hot pink with an accent wall in white. I don't think I've ever seen my daughter's eyes grow so big in my life. Now she thinks it's her room and not the guest bedroom that she's staying in while we're at Tony's. After I win my fight later tonight, those winnings will be going toward a hefty down payment on a bigger house closer to Sienna's father's place. It'll even be closer to my parents, so it's a win-win as far as I'm concerned. Plus, if I have my way, Sienna will be moving in with me.

"What the hell am I doing here, Matteo?" The sound of Tony's voice pulls me from my thoughts and I look over my shoulder to see him standing a few feet inside the jewelry store, his hands shoved into the pockets of his black dress pants, his suit jacket open.

"Papa Tony," Brooklyn squeals from her perch on the glass jewelry display case. Lifting her arms, she squirms to the edge, so I put her on the floor where she runs in Tony's direction. She's in his arms and on his hip in the next blink of an eye as I turn to face him.

Brooklyn has spent more time with him in the last week than she has stayed with my parents. In that time, I've come to find out he's been teaching her the basics of Jiu Jitsu. After what happened to Si, I don't have a problem with it like I would have before, since he never bothered to ask my permission in the first place.

"Hey, tiger." He smiles at her as he squeezes her to his side, then his eyes flip to mine and his stare hardens. "I have places to be, so spit it out."

Reaching in my pocket, I pull out the black velvet box and present it to him. With his free hand he swipes it, flipping open the top. He's silent as he eyes the diamond for longer than necessary, his expression unreadable. Finally, the box snaps shut and his dark brown eyes flick to mine. "You have something you want to ask me?"

"No," I deadpan. "Whether you give me your blessing or not, I'm still going through with it. I'm giving you a heads-up out of respect. I'm marrying your daughter," I declare.

"Only if she says yes, De Salvo." He passes the ring box back to me and I pocket it.

"Does that mean I have your blessing?"

"You just told me you didn't need it, so why even ask?" He hands Brooklyn back over to me and I keep her attached to my hip instead of putting her down. "Let's just see what her answer is. Even if she does agree to a proposal you'll likely screw up, that doesn't mean I'll let her walk down the aisle."

"I could elope with her, you know."

"And make your child fatherless? I think not. I hope you're smart enough to know what I'd do goes without saying." His eyes flick to Brooklyn's and then back to mine, his brow lifted. "You've wasted enough of my time. I'll see you later tonight. And make sure you win. I lose money on you and you can kiss my daughter goodbye."

He turns to leave when I say, "Hey, Tony," as the glass door pushes open a few inches to the outside. Stopping, he waits. "If I do join *the family,* I want to know what happened to the person that did *that* to her last month," I tell him, cautious of the words I use in front of Brooklyn.

"I'll only say this once, Matteo. Before you join my family, be damn certain this is the life you want for not only yourself, but your daughter too, and even your parents if you plan on continuing your relationship with them. Don't ask my daughter what you plan to ask if there is even a shred of doubt in that thick skull of yours. Do you hear me?"

"I was certain when I presented my hand to you and I'm still certain now. My mind will not change."

"I hope for your sake, for Sienna's, and for hers too"—he juts his chin in Brooklyn's direction—"that's true, because there really is only one way out, Matteo."

He pushes through the door, leaving me standing in the same spot, my decision set in stone. I may not know exactly what I'm getting myself into, but I know I love Sienna and I want to spend the rest of my life with her. To achieve that, I'll do whatever is needed.

"Daddy," Brooklyn says.

"Yeah?"

"Can I go see Momma?"

Fuck me. Not this again. She keeps asking and I keep telling her no. She hasn't seen Kennedy in weeks, maybe even months. I'm not sure at this point.

"We talked about this, sweetheart, and I know you don't understand but your mother put you in danger. I don't trust her with you alone." I don't trust her period, but that's more than Brooklyn can comprehend. She hasn't even started kindergarten yet. She's still a little kid and is a long way from understanding the situation with her mom.

"But I miss her, Daddy. Can't I just see her for a few minutes? That's all. Please."

God, I'm going to fucking regret this. Even knowing I'm going against my better judgement, I have a hard time telling my daughter no over and over. It's not that I want to keep her from her mother; I just wish she had a better one.

Pulling out my phone, I call my ex—the last person on earth I want to speak to. Sienna is going to fucking murder my ass, and rightfully so.

Please don't answer.

"Matty," she chirps.

Fuck.

I RELINQUISHED AND ALLOWED BROOKLYN TO STAY with her mom for five hours. If I didn't have Sienna's fight to watch and then have to get to the city for my own, I would have gone back to pick her up myself. Instead, Kennedy is supposed to drop her off at my parents' house for my mom to watch until tomorrow morning.

Dad wanted to see Sienna's match too, so he came with me to the Muay Thai-Kickboxing Tournament being held in a casino hotel in Long Island.

On one hand, it fucking sucks that we both have our events on the same night. I can't kick back, have a few beers, and watch my girl fight in a relaxed state. Instead, I'm in a rush to see hers over so that I can congratulate her and then hightail my ass to where my fight is taking place an hour away in Manhattan. Luckily, my match is still hours from now, so I have plenty of time to get there.

Sasha isn't ranked high in the kickboxing world, so she isn't the headliner. Their match is third on the fight card for the night. It's rumored that Sasha wants to move over into MMA where the money is better, which could be a smart move for her if she's serious about going pro.

Otherwise, I hear she's a decent stripper, so there's always that for her if this doesn't pan out. Not that I'm knocking that. People should do what they enjoy regardless of what anyone else thinks. Everyone's business is their own, so in that respect, I don't judge.

"That your girl?" Dad leans over, pointing to the woman dressed in white silky shorts rimmed in crimson and a matching sports bra. Pure white against her tan skin is breathtaking. I saw her fifteen minutes ago and I had to leave her dressing room before I fucked her. I was turned on from the sight alone.

"Yeah, Pop, that's Sienna." He hasn't formally met her yet. I'd planned to rectify that earlier, but with a hard-on that wasn't happening. I still plan to introduce them after her fight, provided she doesn't get too fucked up during the match.

I haven't told either of my parents that I'm going to ask her to marry me before the night is over with. Hell, I'm not even sure whether I'm going to do it before my fight or after. I tried to think of a romantic way to ask, but everything I've thought of so far seems cheesy or cliché, and that's the last thing I want her proposal to be remembered as.

"She got potential to go pro?"

"Potential? Sure, but she doesn't want that." That much I do know. Sienna loves finance and business. I hate that bullshit, but that's why I do what I love and she does her thing.

"Then why is she out there?"

"So she can kick the other chick's ass." Saying it out loud makes me chuckle, but when I look to my left, Lorenzo is scowling at me. Dom, on the other hand, has a smirk on his face.

"She's gonna need to bring a whole hell of a lot more than she's packing if she's going to knock my sister out."

The sound of Krishna's voice pulls my eyes over my left shoulder to the row behind us where Sasha's older brother is seated directly behind Domenico, his eyes on his phone and not on the ring in front of us. "Why are you even over here, Nikolayev? Can't you sit somewhere else?"

Every time I see him, all I remember is his lips on Sienna, and I want to knock him through a wall like I did the night he sucked her face off in front of a club full of people, her brothers included. I thought for sure Dom was going to do the job for me, but he didn't so much as lay a hand on the prick that night.

"I sit where I want. If you got a problem with that, Punchy, then man up and do something about it. Otherwise, shut the fuck up."

"The last thing you want is to be on the receiving end of my fist. Unless you're dumb enough to think you can take me."

"You keep believing that, Punchy. Any time you want to tie up with me just say the word."

"Motherfucker," I start, but Dom interjects.

"Cut the shit, K. I'd like to see my sister beat the fuck out of yours too."

"She's going to need more than luck on her side for that to happen, but you keep dreaming, Caputo." Krishna leans down, whispering something into Domenico's ear, but with the noise around us, I can't hear what is said. By the look on Dom's face, it pissed him off.

"Matteo, you're too smart to let that BS get to you," Dad says, pulling my attention back to the ring where Si and Sasha touch each other's gloves to start the fight.

What Dad doesn't know is that Nikolayev and I won't be even until I ram my fist through the parts of him that touched my woman. Doesn't matter if she wasn't mine at the time, but it sure as hell didn't feel like she *wasn't* mine either. His time will come, likely sooner rather than later.

The first round went by quicker than I anticipated. This isn't a title fight, so there are only three rounds to the match with each round lasting three minutes. Being a pro fight, the typical shin guards and headgear aren't allowed.

At the sound of the bell both girls came in strong throwing punches and kicks to the body. Sienna has improved her footwork since she's been training with me, but even I have to admit, Sasha's stance is better, her form more solid and controlled. Si is able to get in a nice knee to Nikolayev's gut and it pulls a smile to my lips, a feeling of pride forming.

During the second round Sasha got a fuck-ton of kicks in but not many punches to the face. Si, on the other hand, landed an elbow to Nikolayev's jaw and I swear my pride soared to heights I didn't know were possible. It's not the only thing on me that swelled.

Watching women fight, whether in a ring or on the street, has never done anything more than give me a moment of amusement, but watching Sienna . . . fucking hell.

Midway through the third round, Sasha lands a winning head kick to Si's left side, causing her to stumble and go down to the mat. Even before it was called, I knew it was a TKO—a technical knockout.

My neck starts to sweat and my breathing turns labored as my jeans grow tight in the crotch. As Si exits the ring, that's my que to leave. Dad's introduction to his future daughter-in-law will have to wait.

Adrenaline is coursing through my body at such a rapid pace that I still don't feel any of the pain from the fight. Tomorrow will be another story. When I wake up, I know I'll feel every punch and kick my body absorbed, but . . . so will Sasha Nikolayev, and that puts a satisfied smile on my face.

She beat me fair and square; there is no question about that. I'm not even mad that I lost; disappointed, sure, but I'm not angry, nor do I see the point in it. I just wanted to face her and give it my all. I did that and she came out on top.

"You fought good," Dad tells me from behind. "I'm proud of you, princess."

"Thanks, Dad." I glance at him through the bathroom mirror I'm standing in front of in the private suite they loaned me for the duration of the event tonight. It's an open style vanity outside of the closed off shower and toilet. Turning on the water, I wait until it warms and then I splash my face to rid it of the sweat and grime.

grab a quick shower after Dad leaves. I need to hurry so that I can get out of here and get to the city to make Matteo's fight in two and a half hours.

He and his father may have already ducked out so that Matteo can prepare. Hopefully, I'll get to meet his dad later. I don't think I have a chance at winning his mom over in this life, but I'm not giving up on Matteo's dad just yet.

I'm curious as to what Matteo thought of the match. It sucks that I lost, but even I knew it was a long shot. I'd hoped my extreme dislike for the bitch would give me the momentum to knock her out, but in the end, I'm the one that momentarily had her lights shut off—even if only for a split second. It was the second she needed for the fight to be called in her favor.

Even with the loss, it doesn't diminish the pride I feel in the center of my chest. I still accomplished something I couldn't have if we'd gotten into a fist fight outside of the ring or on a mat. This was the only way I could wail on her without causing problems between our families.

"Do you want me to stick around until you're dressed? You can ride with me into the city," Dad offers.

"No. I have my car, so I'm going to drive and will likely stay in the city tonight with Matteo." There will be an after party for sure; probably several. The heavyweight title is on the line tonight, and there is no doubt in my mind that Matteo will be retaining his belt.

"De Salvo," Dad voices, his tone sounding irked, which makes me peek up at him through the mirror after I dry off my face with a hand towel. "Do you love him, Si? I'm not referring to like or infatuated or that goddamn crush you carried for more years than I care to know about. Is this thing with you and him real?"

We've been fucking like two horny rabbits intent on having a litter ever since he relieved me of my virginity, so yes, it's real, but I can't tell my father that. I know Dad is traditional in that sense, and he'd want me married before delivering his grandkids, but I don't want to put the brakes on Matteo and me—nor am I going to.

"Yes, Dad," I start when there's a beep, indicating that the door to the room has unlocked. Dad and I both glance over, and in steps Matteo. A smile tugs at my lips seeing him and I don't try to stop it from forming. I'd hoped he'd sneak up here before leaving, but I didn't expect it. He shouldn't have either. He needs to get to Manhattan. It's going to be a packed venue, so with traffic, he should not chance being late.

Matteo looks at my Dad. "I need to chat with Si."

"Can I not have a minute alone with my daughter that doesn't involve me having to see your face, De Salvo?"

"Can you call that minute over or do it later? I need to talk to her alone. Please," he adds. There is a pinched look on Matteo's face that suddenly has me worried. There is nothing relaxed about his body language.

What's up with him?

"Why are you acting . . ." Dad trails off, then abruptly stands from where he was seated at the foot of the bed. "Goddammit," he curses as he storms past Matteo toward the door. "I should have fucking shot you and been done with it."

"Which time?" Matteo asks, the first hint of amusement peeking out from behind his tone.

My eyes grow big when Dad turns back after opening the door, seeing the gun he keeps tucked in his suit jacket now in his hand and aimed in Matteo's direction. A shot goes off before I can muster a sound. Matteo flinches the same time I do. Without another word, Dad stalks out the door, letting it slam behind him, and then we're left in a moment of silence.

Finally, my eyes trail to the top of the wall where it meets the ceiling, seeing where the bullet penetrated drywall. Thank God it's a wall that faces water and not another room or building that could have been close by.

"He's touchy tonight."

"What the hell was that about?" I find myself asking, confused as ever. Removing the magazine from in front of his pants, I take in the sight of Matteo's erection. "You're hard?"

"Painfully so, and if I don't fuck you right now my dick may actually explode."

"I've heard that before." Leaning my butt against the sink counter, I cross my arms. "Don't you have somewhere pressing to be?"

"The only pressing place I need to be is inside you, and that's exactly where I'm coming—pun intended. Now, lose those shorts and bend that beautiful body of yours over, baby."

"Excuse me?" I ask, planting my hands on my hips.

"I need to fuck you," he declares.

"I just got my ass beat and you want sex?" Is he for real right now? "Matteo, I'm nasty and I need a shower so I can get ready for your fight. You know, the one you should be en route to right now?"

Marching toward me like he's on a mission, he says, "Then we can kill two birds with one stone. I can do you in the shower, baby."

Bypassing me, he opens the door to my right and in the next breath, the shower faucet is turned on and then he reappears in front of me, all six feet, three inches of sexiness in his blue jeans and polo shirt.

Wrapping his hand around my neck, he pulls my head toward him, claiming my lips like a man that's starving and doesn't know when or where his next meal is going to come from. Dropping his hand, he goes for my sports bra, pulling it up between us and forcing our mouths apart. I start to do the same to his shirt, but he beats me to it, pulling it over his head and tossing the white material to the side.

Matteo goes for his belt and jeans next, so I push my shorts and panties down my legs. I had flip flops on when Dad and I came back to my room, but I discarded them as soon as we were inside, knowing I was going to shower.

While Matteo finishes undressing, I step to the shower and get in, wetting myself all over; the steaming water only amplifying the state Matteo's gotten me in with his hungry stare and sinister mouth.

Stepping in behind me, he clamps his hands around my hips and pulls my body against his. My eyes shut, a breath falling from my lips. He bends, kissing my shoulder, then the skin between before he reaches my neck, I relax against him, only to be turned around quicker than the blink of an eye.

"I'm sorry, baby, but this is going to be quick and hard." He grips my thighs behind my legs and lifts me up, my limbs going around his waist and neck.

"I can take whatever you give me, Matteo."

"I know." My back meets the tiled shower wall. "I think you're the only one that can, Sienna."

He drops me enough to maneuver his cock at my entrance, then pushes inside, his eyes on mine the whole time. A gasp escapes my lips at the size that impales me. He's long and thick. I'm not sure I'll ever get used to the first couple of seconds as his length fills me, and I don't want to. Those first few seconds are pure bliss, and almost gives my orgasms a run for their money on the pleasure aspect. "God, there's nothing like this," I admit.

"Like what?" He pulls out, going slow instead of fast like he originally said. Either way, I'm not complaining.

"You. Inside me. It feels . . . Jesus, it feels good."

"I love you, Sienna." His declaration hits me hard, momentarily stunning me. I hadn't expected those words. Sure, he basically promised me forever weeks ago, but I've only ever heard him say *those* words to Brooklyn or when he was on the phone with his mom.

Leaning in, I tilt my head and fuse my lips to his, kissing him like he's giving me the greatest gift in the world—and he has. I don't even know how to describe the way those words make me feel. He's everything I ever wanted, but never believed I'd get to call mine.

Matteo's pace increases and his promise of fast and hard comes forth, him hammering in and out of me with such force that I'm not going to last.

He grunts, and I know he's about to shower my insides with every ounce of him, but that's okay, because my orgasm blooms and my eyes flutter, losing control. My head tips back and a moan rips from my throat as I ride the wave.

When I'm satisfied and spent, I relax my forehead against his and run my hand from his neck up to his cheek. Opening my eyes, I find him watching me. We remain in silence, the only sound the water pelting our bodies.

"I love you too, Matteo," I say, telling him words I've felt longer than I can remember. "I've loved you for a long time."

Releasing my legs, he slips out of me as my feet touch the shower floor. Looking up, I smile at the way his body towers over me.

"You don't have to do it tonight, but maybe tomorrow . . ."

He pauses, and the look on his face has my back straightening.

"Maybe tomorrow what?" I prompt.

"Will you take a pregnancy test?" He stuns me in a way that I don't speak right away. I wasn't expecting him to ask that. "We fuck like we want babies, Si, so if you don't, and you want me to wear a condom, just say so and I will."

"Fuck that," I blurt out.

"Then you're going to get pregnant. You may even be pregnant. I didn't want to ask before the fight. I didn't want to screw that up or make you paranoid, but now, I want to know. I need to know."

"Do you want another kid?" I ask, wondering if he brought up condoms because maybe he doesn't. For all I know, Brooklyn might be the only child he plans to father, but then wouldn't he have worn a condom from the get-go?

"I want you. I want us. And I don't want to prevent anything from coming along on the ride with us. Preventing something from naturally occurring, or stopping it or prolonging it feels wrong."

"I feel the same way," I assure him. Maybe I'm being reckless by not getting married first, but it's not like marrying someone is going to ensure they stay mine for a lifetime, so who cares if we don't do this thing between us the traditional way?

"So, you'll take a test then?"

"If it's important to you, then yes, I'll do it, but I'll be starting my period by the middle or end of next week." I'm not one of the girls that has her cycle down to the exact day, but I usually have an idea of when I'm about to start my cycle. And because it always comes on slow, I'll be two days into my cycle before I even have to use a tampon.

"Thanks." He turns off the faucet and grabs us two towels after stepping out of the shower.

"You need to get out of here before you risk being late," I say, wrapping the towel around me to soak up the water.

"Hurry yourself up and you can ride with Dad and me."

"You go on, babe. It's going to take me twenty to thirty minutes. Besides, I'm not leaving my car here. I won't be far behind." Stepping to me, he kisses me once again and then he pulls away too soon for my liking, my body temperature cooling without him pressed against me.

By the time I soap up, rinse, and then dry off, Matteo is dressed and out the door. I plan to do my makeup before slipping into a pair of tight jeans, a dressy, red sleeveless top, my leather jacket, and black boots, but I need a minute with my thoughts after that spontaneous conversation, so I sit on the bed with the towel wrapped around me.

Am I ready to be a mother?

I'm really not sure, but I'm not scared of the idea of motherhood. I like Matteo's daughter; I have from the first time I met her. She's sassy but sweet. She's cute, and I know I want to help her grow into a strong woman.

I think my mother would have done that for me too. She had her own ideas of how she thought I should grow up or the things I should have been interested in, but something tells me that she would have eventually come around to my individual wants too.

I think motherhood could be fun as much as it is rewarding. Guess we'll find out, since we both agree not to prevent it from happening, and Matteo is right, I could already be expecting.

Maybe I'll make a quick stop at the pharmacy before I head into the city. I've got to hurry, though, if I'm going to make that happen.

Opting for minimal makeup, I was able to finish quicker than I thought, plus I was rushing myself when I usually take my time. Who knows how traffic will be? It's a title match; there are several on the line tonight. I need to get going so I'm not late.

If I hadn't insisted on driving myself tonight, I could have gotten ready in Matteo's dressing room at the venue, but between Dad and Matteo, I haven't had any time to myself. Anytime I've gone anywhere and was going to drive myself, someone suddenly needs a ride—from me.

Like I didn't know what they were really doing.

Dad and Dom still don't know who that guy was, and yeah, I get it. I'm still worried too, but maybe he didn't expect me to fight back. Maybe it was just some sicko looking to get lucky and once he figured out I wasn't going to be easy pickings, he hightailed it out of there and I'll never see him again. Of course, I wish we knew his identity so that nothing like that happens to another woman.

Dad keeps questioning me about what I remember, but it was the same answer every time. He was a couple of inches taller than me with a wide build, like he knows what a weight room is. Other than that, he was covered head to toe in black clothing. I couldn't even tell you his skin or eye color.

With my phone in the back pocket of my jeans, my gym bag full of smelly clothes and my key ring wrapped around my index finger, I push through the glass door, exiting the hotel. I parked my car on the street down from the entrance so that it would be quicker to make an escape than going to the parking garage. I knew I'd be racing against time tonight, and the last thing I want is to miss my boyfriend's fight.

The boyfriend term when referring to Matteo still feels strange, whether rolling off my tongue or saying it in my head. The feeling isn't bad or anything like that; it's blissful, euphoric even, and I'd never admit this out loud, but sometimes I get giddy on the inside thinking about it.

I hit the unlock button on my key fob before pulling the passenger side door open and tossing my gym bag on the floorboard, but when I slam the door closed, I hear my name from somewhere close.

Looking over the roof, I eye the street across from me but only see a few people walking in the direction away from me. The hotel entrance is on the opposite side of the casino, so it's far less busy on this end than the other. The parking garage entrance is even closer to the other side than it is here, but where I'm parked is closer to the freeway.

I don't see anyone.

"Si!" he yells again, and that's when I recognize Vin's voice. My head turns, seeing him a few vehicles down, closer to the wooden steps that lead down to the beach area.

Shoving my keys into the pocket of my jeans, I nod and raise my other hand to wave as I step toward him, passing the rear of my car.

"Hey," I greet. "You catch the fight?"

I haven't spoken to him or seen him since the night at the club. He texted a few times asking to meet up for lunch, but I've been busy and felt after everything that happened with his brother-in-law that it would have been awkward, so I didn't respond, figuring he'd eventually take the hint.

It's not like we were close; though outside of my brothers, he might have been the only real friend I had, even if he was more of the fair-weather type. We never really hung out outside of the college gym we used to frequent. It wasn't until he texted me asking about working for my Dad that we reconnected.

But as soon as his brother-in-law was spotted with someone no one associates with, that was it for me. All ties had to be severed. I'm guessing he hasn't picked up on that. Maybe he wasn't involved with whatever Levi had going on with Rico the Rat, but it's like the saying goes—you're guilty by association.

He's standing perched against a black sedan. It's a Lincoln, I know that much. Cars aren't really an interest to me other than my own, but Dad always made it a point that my brothers and me could recognize most makes should the need arise that we would ever need to recall that information.

"Nah," he says. "You win?" He asks in a nonchalant way, like his question is filler.

I shake my head, stopping in the middle of the sidewalk closer to the car parked behind his, noticing for the first time that his vehicle is parked in the opposite direction than it should be for this side of the street. A cop or parking enforcement officer would issue a ticket for that.

"Then what are you doing out this way?" I ask. Last I knew, he lived in Queens.

"Can we talk?"

"We are talking. And I asked you a question." His size and his build haven't gone unnoticed in the slightest. It never crossed my mind until now that Vin *could* have been that guy the morning I was attacked.

"Si, come on. We were friends. Now you won't answer my texts. Can we grab a drink maybe? Just to talk." Vin and I were *friends* long enough that he knows bars aren't my scene. Unless I'm going out with my brothers to a club, you won't find me in one or a pub.

He's got an agenda. My gut is screaming to back away, but there is something else keeping me rooted to the ground. *But what?* Do I want him to admit it was him, and if so, is that what I want to know? Why and what the hell was he thinking? Or is it something else.

"Spit it the fuck out, Vin. I'm losing my patience and I have somewhere to be. What are you doing here?" I raise my voice, not that it's going to do any good. The street is practically empty.

How is this my luck? This is New York for crying out loud.

"Fine. You want to play it that way, then this is how it's going to go." He reaches for the door handle of the back seat and something about his tone or his body language causes me to take a cautious step backward.

The door flies open, and it isn't until I hear her cry out that I cut my eyes to the inside of the back seat. "Si," she whimpers, eliciting a cold chill that runs down the length of my spine.

Without thought, I say, "Brooklyn, come here."

"I don't think so." When I flick my stare back to him, he pulls a handgun from inside his leather jacket. "Get in the car."

Ignoring the weapon in his hand and that it's aimed at me, I ask, "Why is Matteo's daughter with you?" She was staying with his mother this afternoon and tonight. Fuck. What if something has happened to his mom?

"Doesn't fucking matter at this point. Get in the car, Sienna."

Brooklyn is quick for her small size. She bolts from the opened door and sprints to me. Stepping forward, I scoop her up, placing her on my hip farthest from Vin, farthest from the weapon he's holding.

"You little brat," he seethes. "Both of you get in the goddamn car. Now!"

I squeeze her to my chest with one arm, and with the other that isn't in Vin's line of sight, I ease my phone from my back pocket and slide it between us, praying she takes it.

"You're scaring her."

"I'm going to do a lot more than just scare the little bitch if you don't follow orders."

"Just stop, Vin. Don't do anything stupid," I say.

"If you don't get inside the motherfucking car, the girl's life is going to end real quick, Sienna."

"I hear you, okay? Just give me a second with her." Turning my head, but keeping my eye on Vin, I kiss her temple and whisper, "Call Dom." Then I place her on the ground, making sure she is faced away from Vin. Shoving her, I yell, "Run!" Then I leap in Vin's direction, throwing myself at him and the gun.

I'm not trying to attack or disarm him per se, though if I luck up, I'd be the luckiest bitch in the world tonight. As long as Brooklyn gets away, that's all that matters. Alone and on the streets isn't anywhere close to ideal, but I'd rather chance that and her call my brother than get in the car with Vin and not know what I'm getting us both into.

I know Dom better than most. He's still somewhere close to the casino waiting for me to leave. Ren is probably with him, and as long as Brooklyn is able to call him, he'll see that she gets to safety. She'll be safe when my brothers get to her.

Jesus, I hope she doesn't panic and forget what I told her. It was chaos; I didn't make sure she heard me. Fuck.

"You goddamn bitch!" he yells. Grabbing me by the shoulders, he shoves me into the backseat. Turning away, I try to move quick, pulling my keyring from my pocket and force them between the seat, praying he doesn't see.

Pushing myself up, I chance a peek over my shoulder, seeing the butt of the gun coming at me at lightning speed, then nothing . . .

CHAPTER 43
DOMENICO

"Are we planning on hanging out here all night or going to the city?" Krishna complains to my right while Ren sits on my other side guzzling whiskey down like it's a goddamn jug of milk.

I'm going to have to do something about him sooner rather than later, but what? I don't fucking know. He doesn't need rehab, but he needs something. And that strip club he's in every night isn't helping. Dad should have never let him buy it last year. His time spent there is why our sister was almost raped or snatched or hell, she could have been six feet under the fucking ground right now.

Ren knows he fucked up, but has he fixed his problem? No. If anything, it's gotten worse. At least it's booze and not dope, so there's at least somewhat of a silver lining to the shitstorm that's brewing.

If I thought beating his ass would help, I would have already done that. He can take a beating. It doesn't matter how much you throw at him, he can withstand anything. We're alike in that way, and I used to think that was a good thing. Now I'm not so sure. I'm at a loss when it comes to my baby brother.

"Yeah, we're going to head out as soon as my sister leaves," I say, eyeing the bottle in Ren's fist. Can't you drink from a glass like a normal fucking adult?

"Which will be when?"

I glance in Krishna's direction. He turns to face me, his elbow leaned onto the bar, those goddamn penetrating glacier eyes staring through me. He makes me want to punch him in the face just as much as I want to close my hand around his throat and smash my lips to his.

I don't know why I can't be normal. My sister has been infatuated with the same guy since she was a kid. Ren's obsessed with someone and has been for a while, but no one knows who. He keeps her locked up tight, but then he's always been the secretive one. My father only ever loved one woman. Even in her death, he's still faithful.

It's not that I don't enjoy women. I love pussy. I love to fuck it, eat it, smack it, whip it. Hell, I love to smell that shit. But, for some reason, I like hard just as much as I like soft. Fit women don't do it for me. Whether they're on the thicker side like my sister or the slimmer side like Krishna's, I'm not attracted to them. I like curves, and hair. I like women with long locks and a big ass.

Men, it's the opposite. I like someone that I know can stand toe to toe with me. Someone who can give as hard of a punch as they can take. Someone who gets turned on at the sight of my blood on him.

Maybe I'm just a sexual deviant. But do I care? No.

I don't flaunt it, but I don't hide it either. I'm my own person, and acceptance isn't something I need. I like what I like, and I will not apologize for that to anyone. Ever.

I'm about to pull up Sienna's GPS location when my phone rings, displaying her name and pretty face. Ten minutes ago, she was still in the hotel, but her fight was over an hour ago. She has to be close to leaving if she hasn't already.

"Yes," I answer.

"Domino." Brooklyn's voice catches me off guard. She's answered my sister's phone a couple of times before, but to my knowledge Matteo's daughter wasn't here tonight. She wasn't sitting with us during the match. Hell, she isn't old enough to get in the door, and she wasn't with my Dad or Sienna either, so . . . what's going on?

Her tone has alarm bells ringing, making me itch to reach for the weapon tucked between my jeans and the small of my back. There are metal detectors at the entrance of the casino, but when you're me and know the right people, I don't have to go through them.

"Doll," I say through the phone. Her snuffle is like icy needles piercing my skin. "I'm coming for you, sweetheart."

Grabbing Ren by the elbow, I pull him off the barstool. Krishna will follow, knowing that if I'm alarmed then someone is going to eat a bullet before the night is over.

I'm not a bad man, but I'm far from saintly. I'm certainly not the knight in shining armor my sister likes to think I am. I do what needs to be done. There are far more evil women and men that walk the streets than me, and when I can, I take them out, sending them to Hell where they belong.

"Locate Sienna's phone," I order Ren as we exit one of the

casino lounges.

"What's going on?" Ren demands, instead of pulling his phone out from wherever it's tucked.

"Just do what he says, Ren," Krishna says as I put the phone back to my ear.

"Baby doll, can you tell me where you are?" When no sounds come through I pull the phone away from my head to make sure the call is still connected. Seeing that it is, I place it back. "Brooklyn," I coax. I've never actually said her full name, preferring to call her by a nickname that just came out one day.

"There is sand and it's dark. I'm scared, Domino."

"I'm coming. Just stay where you are. Keep the phone to your ear."

The beach is down the block on the hotel end, so that's the direction I head. *Where the fuck is my sister?* I can't focus on her yet. I just have to find Brooklyn, but I know when I do, I'm not going to react well if Sienna is hurt—or missing.

"Come on," I yell and quicken my pace into a run.

CHAPTER 44
MATTEO

Sometimes you'll find ten to twenty people in a boxer's dressing room before a fight, chilling, shooting the shit, hyping up the fighter. Then, after the match, it's often a madhouse with medical personnel, the press, everyone who was with you before the fight and then some.

I can't work like that. Before a fight I require solitude; that's how I get my head in the game. It's usually me and me alone. I don't need someone telling me I got this match in the bag. Not even my father stays with me until I'm called to the ring. It's why he's sitting front row now, waiting for the main event.

My promoter is standing outside the door, waiting to knock. Usually my manager is too, but since that ended the way it did, it's just Tristen. I joked that Sienna could fill that role, and she can; that I fully believe. Question remains if she wants to. She told me last week when I asked that she'd think about it.

I'm still waiting for her answer, which makes me nervous

about the *other* question I plan to ask her later tonight. No fight I've ever been in has stressed me out like the state I've been in most of the day since leaving the jewelry store.

What if I'm asking too soon? Moving too fast.

Or worse—what if she says no?

I sit on the edge of the leather chair, my elbows resting on my knees, every hope and doubt floating around in my head, causing more anxiety than I think I've ever felt. I would have thought she would have been here by now, so the fact that she isn't is not helping my situation any. I told Tristen when she shows up to let her in. I want her in here with me. I want her walking out to the match by my side.

My cell phone rings from inside my gym bag. I tucked it in the front zipper pocket when I jumped from my SUV after Dad and me arrived. Leaning to my left, I snatch it from the leather couch next to me, pulling the bag to the end of the table in front of me, hoping it's Si telling me she's here.

When I flip the screen to face me, it's an incoming FaceTime call from an unknown number. I press the decline button without a second thought. It wouldn't be the first time that an overzealous fan somehow got my number through a friend of a friend and thought it would be acceptable to call me.

Yeah, not dealing with that shit.

It rings again and I do the same, my annoyance kicking up a notch. On the third back-to-back ring, I accept the call, about to tell the person on the other end of the line to piss the fuck off when the figure on the screen sends fiery heat through me, like a shard of glass digging its way down my spine in a slow torturous rhythm.

Someone yanks her messy curls back in a hard jerk, exposing

her face to the screen, a blade being placed at her throat. Other than the person's black gloved hand and arms concealed in dark clothing, she's the only thing I see. The phone isn't still, like the person holding it is a fumbling idiot. My view of Sienna is making me dizzy, or that could be the realization that slams into my chest.

She isn't here because she isn't coming. Someone has her.

"Throw the fight in the fifth round, De Salvo, or Si will choke to death on her own blood before you step foot out of the ring tonight," a man threatens, his use of her name shortened not going unnoticed. That tells me he knows her on a personal level, but the vice grip around my chest doesn't allow me to analyze it any further.

"Who the hell—" The connection ends as the sound of a fist pounding on the door across from me pulls my gaze away from the black screen.

"Move motherfucker," Tony yells as the door swings open, "before I make you move."

"Someone has Sienna," I tell him, my frame wavering with nausea.

"I know," he admits. "How do you know?" His harsh tone demands an answer.

"I have to throw the fight or he will kill her, and—"

"You aren't throwing the goddamn fight, Matteo."

I stare at him, stunned silent. He can't be serious. This is his daughter's life we're talking about. How can he sound so callous? "You'd sell her down the river to ensure you don't lose money?"

I know he has a lot riding on my fight; him and a hell of a lot of other people, they always do. I'm not the underdog, nor have I ever been. I'm the sure thing, the winning ticket to a lot of cash. "This isn't about money. You think I give a fuck if I lose half a million dollars?" he yells, his eyes widening with rage.

"It sure as fuck sounds like it," I spit back in his face, stepping forward and into his personal space. He may be okay with her life coming to an end tonight, but I'm not. My life started slowly falling into place a couple of months ago when she walked in Raymond's with that don't-fuck-with-me attitude rolling off her in waves that have threatened to drown me ever since.

"It's about you being a man and taking a stand and showing the whole world that no one backs you into a corner, that no one is going to force you to take a knee. You do not bow, Matteo."

"It's a fight, Tony; a stupid fucking fight and one I'm going to throw tonight to save my woman—your daughter."

"My daughter doesn't want a pussy for a man; one that's scared and not thinking with his head. Besides, the second you throw that fight, my daughter, the woman you claim to love, is dead. Then it's all for nothing."

"It's not for nothing if there is a chance that it could save her, no matter the size."

"I'm telling you it won't. We know where she is, or at least we hope we have her location. Dom and Ren are headed there now. You throw that fight and I'll put a bullet in your head to save my daughter the disappointment of finding out you're acting like a bitch right now."

"Goddammit, Tony. Who the fuck has her and why?"

"Doesn't matter. They forfeited their life the moment they grabbed her. If you believe one thing, De Salvo"—my name comes out of his mouth like a lethal weapon—"believe that I will burn the whole goddamn planet to the ground to find my daughter and whoever the fuck took her."

Another fist pounds on the door, this one more forceful than

Tony's.

"Who the hell is that?" I bellow out, needing everything to stop so I can catch my breath. I need tonight to end with Sienna in my arms.

"Krishna, if I had to guess." There is strain in his voice and a snarl on his lip.

"Why is Nikolayev here?" I saw enough of him earlier to last a lifetime.

"He was instructed to bring Brooklyn here."

"Why?" My blood pressure skyrockets as the door pushes open and my eyes snap to find my daughter in the arms of a man I've come to dislike in recent months.

"Daddy," she hollers. Krishna sets her on the floor, and I scoop her in my arms in the blink of an eye.

"What's going on?" I demand. "Iron girl, are you okay?" She's supposed to be with my mom, and I know she'd never come to my fight. It's not her thing. It wasn't when my dad was a boxer, nor was it when I started fighting as a teenager.

"I was scared, Daddy, but Domino found me." She tightens her arms around my neck and I squeeze her back.

"I delivered her," Krishna says, his eyes on me even though he's speaking to Tony. "I'm out."

"Go back up Domenico in case he needs it," Tony commands, ignoring his comment.

"You're not the boss I take orders from."

"No, but I am, so do what you're told." A man that matches Krishna's towering frame steps through the door dressed in a black, tailored suit, his white-gray hair and beard making him standout.

A third gentleman enters behind him, who I assume is Mischa

Nikolayev, Krishna and Sasha's father. He looks to be about the same age as Tony and dressed similar too. There's something about him that makes my head tilt as I scrutinize him from head to toe. It only takes two seconds to realize why. He could pass for my father's twin brother if my dad had one.

The revelation hits me. I'm staring at Giovanni De Salvo. That's impossible. He's behind bars, serving a life sentence for capital murder, yet I know that's exactly who my eyes are connected with.

Without argument, Krishna ducks out of the room, leaving the rest of us here.

"Your mother is fine, Matteo," Tony informs me as if questioning my earlier thought. "Other than that, I don't have time to tell you anything else. Hand Brooklyn to me and get out there and handle your end of this." There is a long beat of silence, all three men staring me down, and the way Tony said my name in that lethal tone of his that leaves no room for dispute. "Matteo?"

"What?" I bark. Kissing my daughter's temple, I pass her to him, trusting him for reasons I don't understand. Brooklyn clamps her small arm around his neck like she did me.

"When the bell rings, you knock his ass out in the first ten seconds of round one."

"I'll make it three," I vow. "Find her, Tony, and bring her back to me alive and in one piece."

The door to my dressing room slams, the metal clanking sending a shiver down my spine as all of them exit. I don't know if I can do this. Gamble with my Sienna's life? I don't doubt that Antonio Caputo will find her and go through anyone to bring her back, but the question is, will he find her in time?

Tony may look at it as being a pussy, as being less of a man for throwing a fight because someone kidnapped my woman, but that means nothing to me. I don't care what anyone thinks of me. If it saves Sienna and meant she wasn't harmed, I'd get on my knees in front of the Devil himself and beg. I'd crawl on my hands and knees in front of the whole world if that's what it takes.

But what if Sienna's father is right? What if I take a fall in the fifth round, lose my fight, my belt, my dignity, and someone slices her throat anyway?

CHAPTER 45

SIENNA

Throw the fight in the fifth round, De Salvo, or Si will choke to death on her own blood before you step foot out of the ring tonight. Vin's words ring in my ears. He smacked a strip of duct tape over my lips before he pulled my half-conscious body from the car, so I couldn't tell him to eat shit, and that Matteo would not go out like that.

The fact is, Vin is a dead man whether I make it out of this dead or alive. He can't leave me as a loose end after tonight is over no matter which choice Matteo makes, and I pray to God he doesn't make the wrong one. He's 9-0 on every title match he's been in. He's still young in his career. He has a long way to go to beat the reigning king of the most wins with no loses to date.

Vin tied my wrists with rope, securing them behind my back. Dumb move considering the jacket I'm wearing. Good thing I never shared that tidbit with him. The only reason I haven't let the knife slide down is because I'm still trying to regain my wits before

I make a move. Doing so too soon could get me killed before I'm able to get away, or before my brothers show up.

Even if Brooklyn wasn't able to call, Dom keeps enough of a tab on me that he would have figured out something was wrong. He's the one person I can count on for ensuring my safety, my perpetual knight in dark armor. I hope he found Brooklyn and that she is safe. I don't have a plan yet, but if I do get unbound, I'm going to slice Vin from limb to limb. He'll wish he'd never heard my name, never met me to begin with.

"Where's my daughter?" My lashes lift, Kennedy standing behind Vin, streaks of mascara mixed with tears dried on her face. "You promised she'd be fine."

"Go do some blow or . . . no, it's H I hear you're into." Vin rips the tape from my lips. It's a good thing I applied a coat of lipstick or a thin layer of skin would have ripped away when he pulled the sticky adhesive from my flesh.

"I am not. That wasn't me. Someone did that to me. It was her fault." She points to me. "If her family had stayed out of my business, that would never have happened. Matteo wouldn't have dropped me like I didn't matter to him anymore."

"Hey, bitch," I call to her. "He wasn't yours even when I wasn't in the picture. You're delusional if you think otherwise."

I know what Dom did—he told me—though I haven't said anything to Matteo. I should have, but how exactly does one go about telling the guy she loves that her brother made his ex overdose on heroin? Never seemed like an appropriate time to bring *that* up.

"He was! You made him take our daughter away from me. But that changed today. He brought her to me. He asked me to watch her. He knows we're supposed to be a family. You were just a fun romp in the sheets. He's mine; he's always been mine."

A growl claws its way out of my throat.

If Matteo did allow Brooklyn to see her mom, to spend time with her, I'm going to knee him between the legs. I don't mouth that thought. No sense in giving her false hope that we aren't in sync—which apparently, we are not, since he failed to inform me of that development. It's not that he had to; Brooklyn isn't my child. I don't get a say when it comes to her in that way, but a heads-up isn't too much to ask either.

Of course, he had a title match; the second one this year to prepare for. When Matteo brought up the subject two days ago, he said Brooklyn was going to stay with his mom and that he and his dad would attend my fight before going into the city for his.

Maybe he forgot to mention it.

Maybe he didn't think it was a big deal.

Maybe I should cut him some slack.

Nah, my knee rammed up so hard he feels the pain coming out of his ears is what he deserves if he made that stupid decision.

"Where is she?" Kennedy demands, pools of tears threatening to spill over her lids.

"Don't know," Vin tells her, nodding in my direction. "That one let her escape."

"Are you crazy?" She turns her heated stare on me, her hands going to her hips, her brows pinched between her forehead. "She's five. You just . . . you . . . she . . ."

"Shut the fuck up, you stupid cunt." Vin turns to face her.

"I second that," I chime in.

"My daughter is missing. Don't tell me to shut up. You have to go find her before Matteo finds—" Vin's fist flies out, nailing her in the face, and her body drops in an unconscious state. *Dumb bitch.*

Even I saw that coming the first time she opened her mouth, her annoying voice hurting my ear drums.

Vin shakes his hand in rapid succession, then squeezes and lets go of his fist a couple of times. “That shut her up.”

“So, is this a thing with you that I never knew about?” I quiz him. “You like to kidnap and beat up on women?”

“If a bitch gets out of line . . .” Lifting an eyebrow, he leaves the statement open for interpretation. It only makes me roll my eyes. I’ve battled bigger, stronger men than him. If he thinks that’s going to scare me into submission, he doesn’t know me in the slightest.

He’s also shit at securing a rope around his intended victims. I’m slowly loosening the cotton braid. It’s too thick for what he used it for. Dumbass should have been smarter. I doubt I’ll even need to use the knife up my sleeve to cut through the material.

“You know you’re not leaving here, right?” he says, as if the thought of killing me disappoints him. “It wasn’t supposed to happen this way. *He* promised you to me. He promised me an *in*.”

“Yeah, and who exactly is *he*? It sounds like you’ve been talking to someone that doesn’t have a say. Let me make something clear.” I lift both sets of brows high on my head. “Not even my father has the power to control who I’m promised to, you dumb fuck.”

“Which is why he isn’t an actual Boss. No man, head of a family, would allow a woman into the ranks of men. He wouldn’t stop profitable businesses either. If he thinks his capos are satisfied with the scraps he tosses them, allows them to do to provide for their own families, he is sadly mistaken.”

“Awww,” I say in a condescending tone. “Are Daddy’s pit bulls upset?”

I’m not surprised by this, though I don’t know why Vin’s

involved, and for that reason alone, I'll keep playing this longer to get more information. At this point, my wrists will slip from the binding easily, and as long as he doesn't walk behind me again, I doubt he'll realize I've been inching them apart.

My father made a comment once that the capos who report to him could eventually start to revolt against him the farther away from criminal activity he took us, them included. He did what law enforcement couldn't or wouldn't do; he took out other bosses, and either you submitted to Antonio Caputo or fled for your life. Every captain that I know chose him as their leader, fearing not only for their life but for the lives of their families too.

"Immensely so," he replies.

"And what business of it is yours? You aren't a made man. You aren't a member of any family that I've been made aware of, so again, why are you sticking your nose where it doesn't belong?"

He has a reason, or at least someone does. Vin is likely just the fall guy if this goes horribly wrong. The question is, who is really running this shit show?

"I have to kill you no matter if De Salvo throws his match or not—the old man ordered it—so I might as well tell you."

"It's the least you could do." I nod my head. "Why don't you start with who this old man is? Is it one of Dad's dogs?" Dumb move if I've hit the nail on the head. Apparently, people didn't learn what happens when my father loses someone he loves. He's a good man in most aspects of life, but you harm one of his own and he'll become the devil himself, unleashing everything dark and deadly that lives in the fiery pits of Hell.

The last boss he took out suffered a long, drawn out, painful death.

"I met him my junior year of high school. I tried to pickpocket his wallet. I mean, he was old as fuck, so it should have been easy. I didn't recognize him, though I should have. He shoved my scrawny ass down an alley, forced me to my knees, and was going to put a bullet in my head. I spit on his Italian leather shoes. I wasn't going to beg him for my life. I guess he liked something about me; offered me a way to pay off my debt he said I now owed him even though I never got a dime."

"Sounds real poetic," I say in a bored tone, not wanting him to think I'm clinging to every word. "And so, 1930s gangster New York."

"You have no idea."

"Enlighten me then. Go on, Vin. Like you said, I'm not going to be breathing for much longer."

"He said I would work for him until I stopped being useful. At first it was nothing big. I pickpocketed strangers, giving all the cash and credit cards to his point man or soldier or whatever the fuck you call them."

"Jesus, you don't even know." I laugh. The Capos run a crew of made men. Made men order the little soldiers around. I don't tell him any of this; it's not for me to run my mouth about.

"Shut the fuck up before I decide to let that pretty little mouth of yours blow my Glock instead of my dick. I'm not done with you yet, Sienna. I still plan on getting what is owed to me."

"Right, because someone promised little ole me all to your big ole self."

Barf.

"I can continue with your ass bent over that table"—he cocks his head in the direction where Kennedy's body landed in a heap of blonde mess—"if it'll shut your mouth up."

"I'm good where I am. Thanks."

"So, anyway, the old man started me in dealing H at nightclubs once I turned twenty-one. By then I was in college, and well, low and behold, we were at the same one together. Funny now that I think about it. He's the one that pushed me to get a degree. Maybe he thought I'd make a better son than the one he's saddled with."

"Nah, that sounds more like he was using you to be on campus. Let me guess, you sold drugs to college kids too."

"Made a lot of cash doing it too. Pulled in more on campus than I ever did at the clubs and bars." He sighs. "About six months into my first semester, he ordered me to get to know this hot little raven-haired beauty with a smart mouth."

"Complimenting a soon to be dead girl, is that even necessary?"

"The moment I saw you I knew I wanted you on my cock, but the old man said I had to wait. Said you might act tough, but that was all on account of who your father is. Said I couldn't tap it unless I married it; something about dumbass Italian traditions or some shit. I'm part Italian; don't go to church or anything, but come on, it's the twenty-first century. Who the hell waits until the wedding night?"

"Probably people who want to, I'm guessing." I hate when stupid SOB's lump everyone in the same bag. If someone wants to fuck, okay, whatever, who cares? If they don't want to then what is the big deal? People today—more so my generation and younger—think that if you still cherish your virtue after graduating high school, then you're some warped freak.

"No man wants a self-righteous bitch in his bed." He pauses, eyeing me hard. "But the more I thought about it, the more I started liking the idea of an untouched piece of ass. Besides, he said I could bang as many whores as I wanted, before and even after being married—that it's expected from men like us."

"You guys sound like real prizes." I was raised by a man that respects his woman, sees her as an equal. Dad never strayed from my mother. Even long after her death, he's never been seen with a woman on his arm. He's never been out on a date with one or brought any home either.

I even told him once that it was okay to have fun, to want a companion. He promptly told me to mind my own fucking business and to never bring the subject up again—so I didn't.

However, what Vin is saying is one of the things television shows got right about men connected to organized crime, at least in the American-Italian communities. Men like to stick their dicks into as many holes as possible, married or not. It's disgusting. Something I'd never put up with either. What Vin fails to realize is that I would not have been marriage material for him or anyone that holds his same logic.

Besides, it's obvious he's nothing more than a follower, a lackey that does another man's bidding. In other words, someone I'd never be attracted to or want to share my life with.

A man steps out on me, he doesn't have to worry about my brothers or even my father getting to him. I'll gut him like a fish and dump his organs and body parts in the ocean.

"It's the way it is, and that isn't something that's going to change, Si."

"Please refrain from calling me that, would ya? Only my friends call me Si, and it's clear we are not friends, nor were we ever friends, seeing as you're telling me you had an agenda and was ordered to get to know me. Question, what exactly does my virginity and me have to do with you? I mean, what was this unnamed man's goal exactly? What was this "in" he promised you?"

"He is going to make me a made man. I am going to sail

through the ranks and eventually take my rightful place directly under him as the Underboss." After a heartbeat of silence, a laugh so hard it literally shakes my limbs bursts past my lips. "Keep laughing, sweetheart. It won't change anything."

"Oh, God." I chuckle some more, before finally gaining control of my throat again. "You do realize that position is already filled and that this old man you speak of isn't the Boss. He can't make that happen. Besides, your last name isn't even Caputo, so I fail to see how you're going to achieve that."

"I was going to marry you," he deadpans, evoking another chuckle. "But Rafe said you're already too involved in things you had no business handling in the first place and that you had to go; that it was the only way to knock your father off his high horse."

"My grandfather is going to take me out?" My humor sobers up at his admission. Why am I even surprised? The man personally saw to it that my mother's heart stopped beating. It's clear he only likes to handle strong women in one fashion; he kills them.

Could he know about my conversation with Dad, about the realization that he was the man that murdered my mother?

Fuck, that could mean Dad's office is bugged, but even thinking that I know it's impossible. Dad had sound interference installed throughout every room of the house. He wanted it to be the one place he could freely talk. It's why certain aspects of his business only take place within the confines of his home office instead of anywhere else.

It could be a coincidence, I reckon. Either way, the house needs to be swept to make sure it's still our safe haven.

"It's time to get this show on the road." His hands go for the belt buckled around his dark pants.

"In your dreams . . ." I say, the warning loud and clear in my tone.

"Whether you're a willing participant, unconscious, or stone-cold dead, I'm getting what's due. I'm fucking you tonight, Sienna. Now, the question is, do you really want to die? You could still get out of this."

"Yeah, and how do I do that?" He's the one that's going to need to figure a way out of the mess he's brought on himself. It's not me that's going to die tonight.

"Run away with me. We could ditch this place and never look back. Get as far away from New York as possible. You just have to agree to be mine."

He really should have tied my ankles to the chair. With the loosened rope in one hand and the hilt of my blade in the other, this is going to be so easy, I don't even see the fun in it.

"That's going to be a hard pass."

"Guess you're choosing the hard way then. I'm going to have that cunt of yours no mat—" I leap out of the chair, my arm swinging around, and I come down hard, stabbing through his jacket, between the meat where his arm connects to his torso. Throwing all my strength into it, I shove the blade as far as it'll go, and then using the handle, I grip his shoulder on the opposite side and ram my knee into his gut.

There is background noise like a metal door being kicked in, but I don't dare look in that direction. I can't allow myself to be distracted now that I'm so close to taking this motherfucker to the ground.

Vin staggers backward, and I try to pull the knife, but it won't come willingly and I have no choice but to release my hold on the handle. Lifting my leg again, I stomp the bottom of my boot into his knee, making him drop to the ground, and cocking my arm back, I send it sailing into his cheek.

"Grab that bitch from the floor and put her in the car." Dom's voice rings through my ears as Vin's gun drops from wherever he had it stored on his person. Before Vin can shake my assault off, I snatch the weapon from the concrete floor and aim it at him as I right myself.

"Sienna, get out of the fucking way," Dom yells from behind me, no doubt his own gun outstretched in his hand.

Fuck that! This asshole was going to rape me and then kill me. Domenico does not get to take this from me. His life is mine to take. The moment I snatched Brooklyn's trembling body off the ground this was going to end with me taking this shit for brain's life.

I pull the trigger. Then I pull it a second time, both rounds nailing him in the chest. A heavy silence falls upon me as I watch his eyes lose their essence, closing with a shock he never fathomed coming.

He underestimated me. Most people do.

"What did you do?" Dom stops behind me, his breath fanning the hair hanging behind my head. "Sienna."

He turns me to face him, snatching the weapon from my palm. Without losing eye contact, he uses the material of his shirt to wipe my prints. "What had to be done," I say, my voice even despite having just killed a man.

After he sets the weapon next to Vin's lifeless body, Dom yanks my knife out, cleaning the blood off on Vin's clothes. Then grabs me by the shoulder, his stare more serious than I've ever seen. "You do not tell anyone about this; not Dad, not Ren, not even Matteo, do you hear me? This stays between us. I'm the one that shot him, agreed?"

"That was self-defense. Why should I care who finds out I'm the one that shot that piece of shit?"

"Because I'm the one that handles this shit, Si. Because Dad doesn't need that heartache on his chest. Because for some reason you love Matteo and I'm not so sure he could handle this type of knowledge. He gets scared, runs, and breaks your heart, then I'm going to show him just how strong he isn't. I will end that motherfucker so fast he won't have time to react. Don't force my hand, Sienna." Dom steps back, pulling air into his lungs as he continues to stare me down. "Besides, I don't know the extent of what Vin thought he was doing or if someone else was behind this. I don't need someone placing a bounty on your head, sister."

I stopped listening to Dom once he mentioned Matteo. What if my brother is right and Matteo wouldn't see this like I didn't have any other option? He wasn't brought up the way I was. He was sheltered from this life.

The insecure part of my subconscious rears its ugly head and I start to regret my actions. I waited too long for Matteo to finally notice me; to want me in the same all-consuming way that I've wanted him for as long as I can remember. I won't do something to fuck that up, so even though part of my brain is screaming profanities at me, I agree to Domenico's demand. "Okay."

"Thank fucking fuck!" Grabbing me by my leather-covered forearm, he pulls me forward. "If anyone heard those gunshots, we need to be out of here before the cops show up."

I spent a large part of my childhood and teenage years lying or withholding information about myself. The thought of doing that to Matteo again pains me in a way I'm not sure I'll ever recover from. But if it's the only way to keep him safe from my family's world, to ensure him and Brooklyn aren't tainted, then I have to do what I have to do.

Right?

CHAPTER 46
MATTEO

When I stepped into the ring an hour ago, I didn't know what choice I'd make; if I was going to bow out or come out swinging. All I knew is that the woman I want to spend the rest of my life with, in and out of bed, was in an unknown location with a madman holding a knife to her throat.

Then there was my daughter. The Russian prick showed up with my kid and she was scared, telling me she'd been involved in whatever had taken place with Sienna.

I was scared. I'm not so much of a son of a bitch that I can't admit that, but I was also raging underneath my skin. Tremors had started to wreak havoc on my body I was so angry. Then my opponent looked at me, stared me in the goddamn eyes with a smirk on his face like we both knew something no one else did.

He was in on it. Maybe he didn't know my girlfriend had been kidnapped or my daughter had been in danger without my knowledge, but he knew how this fight was supposed to end, and that pissed me the fuck off even more.

Seconds passed slowly as my body stilled, adrenaline amplifying, hitting a new high like those drag strip racing Christmas tree lights, readying the driver before takeoff. That's exactly what happened: the bell rang, my opponent stepped forward with raised gloves, and he was on the ground with his eyes rolling into the back of his head within five seconds.

The crowd roared. They lost their fucking minds over the outcome of the fight. I knew I had set a new record, one not even I would ever succeed at again, knocking out a boxer in the shortest match in history.

I stared out of the ring and into the crowd. I walked in a slow circle, hoping that whoever demanded I go out like a coward was watching me that very second. I seethed, and I made sure the cameras above the ring saw every ounce of lethal power I possessed. I wanted to frighten the Devil himself.

Once I walked off, the media swarmed like the flies they are. I ignored their calls, the shouts to hear my first words. I continued out until I saw Tony with my daughter still wrapped around him like he was her protector. He isn't, that's my job. I didn't have to pull her from his grip. He was handing her over to me before I stopped in front of him—and I only released Brooklyn long enough to change my clothes before leaving the venue.

During the car ride to Tony's, I sat in the backseat of an SUV I'd only seen once in his driveway. Apparently, it belonged to my uncle. The same uncle that's supposed to be behind bars.

Giovanni drove with Tony in the seat to his right and Brooklyn and me in the back. I assume Dad left in my Lexus. I didn't see him, but he had my keys from driving earlier tonight. I couldn't talk to him. I didn't know what to tell him; I still don't. Whatever is going on, I don't want my parents involved. Hell, I don't want them to know anything about the events of tonight. If I have to shield them by lying, then that's what I'll do. I don't like it, but I don't have to like it as long as they are safe.

"Pete can't know I'm out, Matteo," my uncle says to me from where he's standing next to the fireplace in Tony's living room, one leg propped on the brick hearth.

"Wasn't planning on sharing the news." Brooklyn fell asleep at some point during the drive, but I'm not ready to lay her down to rest, opting to continue holding her locked in my arms. "You get parole or something?"

"No," falls from his lips like I'm boring him with a mundane topic.

"From what I recall, you had a life sentence."

"Still do."

"Yet here you are." My eyes slide to where Tony sits at the end of the couch caddy corner from where I'm perched on a matching cream-colored plush sitting chair. When we got back to his house less than ten minutes ago, he filled a glass damn near to the rim with whiskey and has been sipping on it in silence.

As a father, I can somewhat relate to what must be going through his mind. He hasn't heard from Dom or Ren. I don't know if that's good or bad, but I'm praying for the former.

"How is it possible you're standing here, like a free man, if you're supposed to be in prison?" I finally ask when he doesn't elaborate.

"Matteo, someone is serving that sentence, it just isn't me; hasn't been for some time now. That's as far as this conversation is going to go, understood, nephew?"

"My dad said once that you two used to be tight, and then

one day you stopped being friends. Does this mean you're friends again?" I eye the two men, waiting for an answer.

"Matteo," Tony draws out, his tone a warning.

"Let the boy ask his questions, T."

"I'm no boy, *Uncle.*"

One corner of his mouth curves up, a chuckle sounding out. "You're an ignorant, sheltered boy, but that's going to change. You see, you being here, in Tony's home, dating his daughter, well . . . you stepped in something you can't get out of. Whereas I allowed my brother the illusion of being *out* of *the* family, you don't get that option," Giovanni announces.

Standing, I gently place my daughter down in the chair I vacated, her small frame curling up on the oversized cushion. In this situation, I'm grateful she's a hard sleeper.

Stepping around the square, distressed, wooden coffee table, I stride forward, only stopping when my feet are an inch from touching his. My uncle is at least half a foot shorter than I am, so this being close, my eyes cast down to look into a set of dark blue irises that match my own, but his are tainted with darkness that my dad and I don't possess. I may be *The Beast* in the ring, but even I don't house the demons lurking behind his hard stare.

"I don't care who you think you are, but let's clear a few things that up right now. Whatever family I choose to be part of, blood or not, is my decision and mine alone. You don't own me. And the person that does looks a hell of a lot better than you. Not even her father owns me, and never will. Understand that, Uncle. If you don't, I don't really give a fuck either." I lean in, crowding him. To my annoyance he still doesn't budge. Instead, his storm-filled eyes hold mine, taunting me to look away first.

"Matteo, sit back down," Tony says, his eyes remaining on the ice and liquid in his glass rather than Giovanni and me. "G, stop goading him. He's not a trained puppy yet."

Rolling my head in his direction, I say, "And I never will be. Sorry to disappoint."

"You're full of disappointment, De Salvo. Be glad you weren't one tonight."

Before I can respond, the chime from their alarm system sounds, signaling that a door has opened. I turn to face the entrance as Tony stands up, his chest shuddering as he inhales. Seconds pass, feeling like hours. Lorenzo is the first to appear around the corner, his eyes landing on his father's.

"She's . . ." he starts to say when his body is shoved forward.

"Move, dick." The sound of her voice is not only relief to my ears, but also oxygen to my lungs. Sienna's eyes find mine first, and the two of us speak in silence in the mere seconds our eyes are connected. *I'm back. Miss me, baby? I'm pissed at you, by the way*. Then her stare is gone too fast as it flips to her father's.

Tony makes quick work of his legs, practically running to where Sienna stands. Dom rounds behind Si, stepping around them both as Tony pulls his daughter into his chest, wrapping his arms around her like I held Brooklyn moments ago.

Domenico comes to a stop behind Ren, and that's when I take in the look on Sienna's twin's face. He's not staring at me, his eyes are looking past me, at Giovanni, like he recognizes him and is just as surprised as I was earlier tonight when I saw him for the first time in my life. "Someone fail to inform me of something?" Dom snarls, his eyes holding my uncle's.

"We'll discuss that later," Tony says. Pulling back only inches from his daughter, he asks, "Are you okay?"

"I'm fine, Daddy," she answers, forcing a smile on her lips.

"Don't look at me like that. I'm good. I swear it." Sighing a heavy breath, Tony presses his lips to her forehead.

Ren and Dom make their way to the couch, both sitting on each end, their gaze a mirror of caution and questions. Domenico isn't happy my uncle is present. Lorenzo is as confused as I was when I knew he was supposed to be in a cell.

Finally, Si pulls away from Tony to walk toward me, her stride increasing with every step. When she's in reaching distance, I snatch the front of her open jacket and pull her into an embrace. Cupping the back of her neck, I tip her head back and fuse my lips with hers, not caring who the hell sees my tongue fucking hers until I'm forced to let her go so that I can take a breath.

At some point Giovanni moved from behind me to take up residence on the other couch, the one Tony was seated in before Sienna appeared, relieving the anxiety we both shared. Taking a step back, I examine every inch of Sienna that I can see. Most of her body is covered with clothing, but the skin I can see looks unmarred.

"Matteo, unless your ears are busted, I'm pretty sure you heard me tell Dad I'm fine. Stop evaluating me like you're trying to find something that isn't there. I'm good. Not even a scrape." She purses her lips, daring me to challenge her. Her head turns from me as she takes in the rest of the room, her gaze stopping briefly on my uncle, her brows creasing, but I can't tell if she's wondering who he is or if she recognizes him the same as her brothers do.

Continuing her path, her breath is audible when her eyes land on Brooklyn. I still have questions. The only thing that Krishna told Tony was that my daughter had called Dom, and when they found her, she told them that a bad man had scared her and then Sienna told her to run, so that's what she did.

I don't have my phone to call my parents. I thought it was in my gym bag, but I must not have put it back in there after the call came through from Sienna's kidnapper. When I got into Giovanni's SUV, my black bag was sitting on the seat with everything in it except my smartphone. Right now, the whereabouts of that device doesn't even matter. I have my daughter and I have my woman. That's all I need. That's all I'll ever need to be a happy man.

When I imagined asking her to marry me, the last scenario I thought it would be was in front of her father, brothers, and a man that's an escape convict. I didn't know how I was going to do it. It wasn't planned when I bought the ring this morning. I feel like I've aged twenty years in the twelve hours it's been since I walked out of that jewelry store with a velvet box in tow.

Determined not to waste another second without her wearing my ring, I ease it from the pocket where I'd stored it after I changed, then I sink to one knee as her head swivels back around to see what I'm doing.

Her eyes round, growing in size, as air is sucked in through her opened mouth.

"Will you be my wife, my partner? Will you marry me, Sienna Caputo?"

The surprise in her eyes turns to something akin to worry. At the sight of tears pooling in her eyes, my skin prickles, and the organ in my chest seizes as a bead of liquid tips over the bottom of her eye, followed by another, cascading down her cheek on the opposite side. For a split second, I question if my spur of the moment decision was the wrong thing to do after what she's been through tonight.

"Yes!" Her face lights up and the breath I was holding finally releases. "Yes, I'll marry you."

CHAPTER 47
SIENNA

Matteo pushes off his knee, coming back to stand in front of me, ring box open for me to see. It's the most exquisite piece of jewelry I've ever seen. The diamond is a princess cut—go figure. But that's not to say he chose wrong. He most certainly did not. There is a halo of smaller diamonds around the larger one set in what I think is either a platinum band or white gold. Either way, it's a sight to behold.

Removing the ring, he discards the box by placing it out of the way on the mantle, then he pulls my left hand between us, slipping the perfectly sized ring on my finger. It's even prettier on my finger. Lifting my lashes, I peek up, smiling at the man I'm going to call my husband.

"Babe," I say. "I'm really excited about marrying you. In fact, I can't wait. Weird for me to feel that way but whatever, I'm going to roll with it. But there is just one little thing I need you to clear up for me."

“What’s that?”

“Did you let Brooklyn go to her mom’s?” I tilt my head to the side, waiting for an answer that can only go one of two ways.

“Yeah, about that—”

I hold up my hand, interrupting him. “There is no need for an explanation. A simple yes or no will suffice.”

“Yeeess,” he admits, slow and cautiously.

I nod in an equally slow performance, letting him know I heard his words loud and clear. Then I ram my knee between his legs so damn hard I feel a ripple effect up my own leg. Matteo’s knees hit the hardwood floor at my feet.

“Well, that went from lame as fuck to the highlight of my night in a matter of seconds,” my twin says from behind me where he’s seated on one of the couches next to Dom.

“Jesus, Sienna!” Matteo yells, cupping his crotch. “Fuck!”

“Let’s make sure that doesn’t happen again, okay?” I stare down at him with my hands on my hips.

“Don’t think you’re getting off that easy, De Salvo. My time is coming,” Dom adds, and I glance over my shoulder, pursing my lips at my brother.

“My fiancé, my problem to deal with. Go find your own person.”

“Tony, I like her already.” My gaze slides to the man taking up space in my dad’s house. He smirks when our eyes meet. “She’d give Arianna a run for her money in the how big are my balls department.”

“Dad, why is there an outsider in our home?” I ask, my eyes never leaving Matteo’s uncle’s. I do know who he is. The question is why is he here? Granted, Dad said he was falsely sentenced, but still, he was sentenced to life. So, what’s he doing here?”

"Baby girl, I am far from an outsider," Giovanni answers.

"She is not your baby girl or your anything. Do not call her as such," Matteo barks out.

"That's where you're wrong, nephew. Since you slid that ring on her finger, she is now my soon-to-be-niece. But"—he pauses, a curve to his lips forming as if he knows something we do not—"she's been my goddaughter for far longer. All three of them have."

"Come again?" Ren growls as my brows crunch together, confused.

Matteo starts to stand, slow in his rise, but I turn my back, searching out my father. Domenico and Lorenzo do the same.

"Giovanni, shut the fuck up." Dad shakes his head, his demeanor annoyed but not mad that his man is spewing lies. "There's the right way to do something, say something, propose,"—Dad's eyes land on Matteo, his announce growing—"then there is the way a fucking De Salvo does it."

"So, it's true?" I quiz Dad.

"It's a topic for another day." He steps forward, stopping before his black dress shoes collide with my boots. "Are you sure you want him? Has he not proven to be a complete fuck-up time and time again?"

"Thanks, Tony. Appreciate the love." Matteo snags me around my waist, pulling my back to his front. "She's already made her choice."

I'm starting to question if my father knows me at all, because if he did, he'd know his continued outspoken dislike of Matteo is only going to push me further to him. It's a good thing I genuinely love the man behind me and his fondness for showing possessiveness.

Daddy just better not try to stop me from marrying Matteo. I'll elope if I have to. Matteo is mine, now and forever.

Ignoring Matteo's words, Dad stares at me, a seriousness fueled by anger transforming in front of me. "What happened tonight? Who took you?"

"Also, a topic for another day, Dad." I force my eyes to widen the slightest bit, hoping he sees that we need to talk about this privately, and not because I'm going to spill the beans that I killed a man. I still agree with Dom. Dad doesn't need the knowledge that another one of his kids' hands are tainted in blood.

"It's been neutralized," Dom says in a much calmer tone than what mine would be if I had to admit what I did. I still believe he got what was coming to him. He deserved it, but I'm not sure I should have been the one to pull the trigger now that it's really sank in.

I didn't come to that resolve because I regret the outcome. The opposite actually. I liked it. I liked the powerful feeling the adrenaline rush offered. I killed a man that meant to do me harm. I could have kicked his ass or saw to it that he went to jail, but that isn't what we do. Right or wrong, I took his life, and I'd do it again.

He punched Kennedy in the face without so much as a kernel of guilt. Who knows if he's hurt other women before us? The likelihood is there, so what if I took one less pathetic excuse for a man off the streets. Dead men can't hurt women, or the innocent.

"Good. I wouldn't expect anything less of you, Domenico. But that doesn't tell me who took my daughter. Or who scared Brooklyn. Why he had her in the first place."

"I want the details too," Matteo chimes in, his arm tightening around my waist and his other going to my hip, anchoring my body to his.

"Sienna, I want to know if this was about Matteo's fight tonight or something else," Dad states.

"Fine!" I throw out. Pushing Matteo's hands off me, I step to the chair next to the one Brooklyn is curled up asleep in on the other side of the coffee table and sit down on the edge, my forearms braced across my knees. Then I spend the next ten minutes telling the room what I know, sans the small detail about my grandfather being the mastermind behind it all. I plan to tell my dad, but I can't do that with my brothers present. I made him a promise the same as I did Dom. I'll keep both a secret; at least for now.

I honestly don't know if Rafe's sole purpose was to take me out of the picture, or if it had more to do with Matteo's fight and I was just a bonus. I know my grandfather hates that I am so involved with the family businesses, that I handle all the finances. I do know that organized crime has always had a hand in professional fights, fixing them, and then betting on the fight to pull in revenue. I imagine before Dad took over, his father was heavily mixed up in those sordid affairs, and I'm sure a lot more than I even know about.

"You sure Vin never mentioned who he was working for?" Dad inquires for the third time, asking the same question in a different way; same as when he questioned if I was raped. Talk about awkward, especially with someone I don't know in the room.

"Positive," I lie. Standing, I say, "Daddy, can we pause this topic until later? I'm tired and dirty and I just want a shower and then bed."

"Yes. Dom, Giovanni, and I have things to do." Dad flips his gaze to Matteo's. "We may not return tonight, so you aren't to leave this house until I get back. Is that clear?"

"If Si is staying then I am too, but don't assume you can order me to do shit, Tony. That won't fly with me."

"Boy, you're about to get a crash course in this family," Giovanni directs to his nephew.

Dom stands, his eyes beating down on the man to my left. "Before we go anywhere, someone is going to tell me why he's here, why he seems to think he has any say in our family business. I can accept my sister's choice in a shit-for-brains husband. What I won't accept is someone walking in here thinking they run shit or have a say. Why the fuck is he here, Dad?"

"Domenico,"—my brother's name comes off Dad's tongue in a warning—"he's here because he is family. Maybe not through blood, but through other ways. Mostly, he is here because I allow him to be. Make no mistake, Son, I have the final say in everything involving this family. Giovanni is here because I appointed him as my consigliere."

"What happened to the other one?" The wheels in Dom's head are turning. He knows there are only a few reasons Dad would be stripping rank from a member of the family.

"He's being forced into retirement." Dad's voice can't hide the hatred behind his tone, or the blaze roaring in his eyes. He's planning on killing him tonight. I'd bet everything I own on that. Fuck! Should I tell him?

"Oh, I'm going for this. I want to see the look on that old fuck's face when you tell him he's been demoted to the old folks home." Ren jumps to a stand, a shit-eating grin on his face. Neither one of us, Dom included, have ever liked our grandfather.

Ren is in ignorant bliss.

Dom suspects something, but he doesn't know what our grandfather has done, and Domenico does not like being out of the loop.

"He's not going to a nursing home, stupid," Dom chastises. "He's going to a wooden box. Or the bottom of the ocean."

"Domenico . . ." our father draws out, his patience wearing thin. "Was that—" A chime sounds, stopping Dad's words. Someone entered the house without knocking or ringing the bell.

"Let go of me!" Sasha's voice pierces my eardrum before she and Krishna step into view.

"You're late," Dad says, his statement directed at Krishna as the lumbering Russian drags his sister into the living room.

Mischa is next to step into view. "That was my fault, Antonio."

Ren's body steels, his back becoming a steel rod. "I suggest you take your hands off her," he orders Krishna.

Raising from his seat on the couch, Dom places his hand on Ren's shoulder and forces his backside to meet the cushion of the couch. "Sit down. Mind your own business, little brother." Flipping his eyes to Dad, he says, "Care to enlighten us more? Why are they here?"

"What the hell is she doing here, Dad?" I push up from my seat. "Like Dom asked, why are they here?" She basically kicked my ass tonight. I don't care to see her face; not today, not tomorrow, not ever, unless it's meeting the flesh and bones of my knuckles.

Ren stands, and when Dom tries a repeat of his actions, my twin shrugs him off, elbowing him in the process. "Let her go or it's going to become a problem," he snarls, barely holding himself back from challenging Sasha's brother.

"Why do you even care, Lorenzo?" I ask, my anger getting the better of me. Suddenly, Sasha isn't the only person I'm itching to ram my fist into. Ren is right up there on the list, making his way to the number two spot.

He turns on me, his lips curling. He shoves Dom to move him

from his direct line of sight to me and Dom lands on the couch behind him. "Because she is my goddamn wife and no one touches her but me!"

I suck in a shocked breath of air, and I'm not sure if it's mine that's audible or Domenico's. He hasn't moved from where his tumble landed him, his mouth agape, his eyes wide.

"Ex-fucking-cuse me?" I say.

"Your fucking what?!" Dom yells.

"That better be a goddamn joke," Krishna seethes, his eyes taking on a look that's a cross between feral and lethal.

"Fuck!" Ren's head tips back, his eyes on the ceiling before his chin drops, his hand lifting, and his fingers pinch the crease between his eyes.

"Way to fucking go, Ren." Sasha's head shakes in slow succession, her lips pursed.

"Dad . . ." Ren says, his voice defeated.

"Sit down, Lorenzo." Flicking his dark eyes to where Krishna has a tight grip around Sasha's wrist, he says, "You go sit next to your husband."

When she doesn't move, Mischa's calm voice says, "Do as you're told for once in your life, daughter."

Snatching her arm from her brother's grip, she marches the couple of steps to where Ren and Dom are and takes a seat at the opposite end, across from Dom with Ren in the middle of them.

"Happy, father?" He nods but I swear he also rolls his middle-aged eyes. "Good. That's so my mission in life."

"Are you just going to stand there after hearing this and not do a damn thing?" Krishna directs his question at his father. "How about a bullet in the head? I think that's at least warranted."

"Motherfucker," Dom spouts. "Anyone so much as touches a

hair on my brother's head and their life will cease to exist before they know what hit them."

"Matteo, take Brooklyn upstairs before another curse word is dropped in this house," my father orders.

"If it'll get me away from this shit show, then yes . . . yes I will." After he picks her up, laying her head on his shoulder, he peeks down at me. "You want to follow?"

I stare up, not saying a word. Like hell am I leaving this room. I want answers, and then I want to beat someone's ass. Maybe more than one. Shaking his head, Matteo leaves us.

"No one is being killed," Dad declares once Matteo is out of sight. "They've been married for two years. At this point, it's a done deal. There is no undoing it, so all of you will have to learn to accept it. Capiche?"

"You knew?" Ren eyes Dad like he's seeing him in a new light.

"We both did, boy," Mischa answers instead.

"What?" Sasha and Krishna say simultaneously while Dom and I eye one another, both of us silently agreeing on our brother's betrayal.

"You're my goddamn twin and you kept that from me?"

"Honey, he keeps a lot from you," Sasha sneers like the bitch she is, and that's when I leap in her direction only for Dom to jump into action, catching me midair and then hauling me back to the seat I was in seconds ago.

"Sasha, shut the fuck up. You aren't helping this situation," Ren tells his ugly as sin whore of a wife. Jesus! Wife? Does she even know the meaning of the term?

"Kiss my ass, Ren. And go to Hell while you're at it," she throws back as she crosses her arms and looks away from us all.

"May as well get this out of the fucking way too," Dad voices, his eyes roaming to each one of us. “Welcome to the New American Mafia, kids. This is your new family; everyone in this room and the two that just went upstairs.”

Dad’s announcement stuns us all speechless. The room is so quiet you could hear a pin drop.

“Suddenly,” Giovanni speaks up. “I’m thankful I never had kids. I don’t know how either of you put up with all of their bullshit,” he remarks, his eyes going from Dad’s to Mischa’s, his lips curled in disdain.

“No one asked your opinion,” Dad tells him. “Now, I get that you all have questions, but I’m tired and I have shit to do tonight. Dom, you stay here. Giovanni, you’re with me. Mischa, you do whatever the fuck you want. Come or go home.”

“Tony, I have a plane to catch. I’m sure you can handle your shit without me,” Mischa informs him.

“Of course, you fucking do,” Dad says, his jaw moving from side to side.

“Whatever you’re doing with him,”—Dom says, his chin jutting in Matteo’s uncles direction—“I’m going too. He isn’t your second. I am. And that isn’t motherfucking changing.”

“I think I’ll come too,” Krishna adds.

“Fine, Son, I’ll allow it.” Only dad isn’t talking to Dom, he’s speaking to Mischa’s son.

“Not your son, Caputo.”

Dad throws his head back, a hard laugh rolling off his tongue all while I continue to sit where Dom placed me not having the first clue what to say to the most bizarre, fucked up night of my life.

Kidnapping.

Proposal.

My twin is not only married but did so in secret; two years ago!

Apparently two enemy families just merged.

Oh, and let's not forget Grandpa is getting taken out tonight. Can't forget that.

What in the fuck is going on?

"Sienna, do not start shit with Ren or Sasha while I'm gone. If I come back to blood all over my living room or anywhere else in the house, I may shoot someone else tonight."

"What in the fuck just happened?" Sasha pipes.

"You're coming home, baby, right where you belong," Ren answers her.

"Go fuck yourself, Lorenzo. I'm nobody's bitch to be ordered around."

"Actually . . ." Tony steps in front of her. Lifting his hands, he cups her face like the loving father I know him to be. "You signed your name on the dotted line then you sealed your marriage with a kiss. Welcome to the family, Sasha. You're Caputo property now." He leans down, placing a soft kiss on one side of her cheek, then the other. Her jaw drops and her eyes round. Dropping his hand to his side, he steps around her, walking away from all of us. "Ren, have your bride moved in by this time tomorrow. Dom, G, follow."

With those words, he walks out, the others following, including Mischa.

Matteo rounds the corner as they exit, our eyes locking. "What'd I miss?"

UNTIL . . . DARK PRINCE (REN AND SASHA'S STORY)

Also by N. E. Henderson

<u>SILENT SERIES</u>:

Nick and Shannon's Duet

SILENT NO MORE

SILENT GUILT

<u>MORE THAN SEIRES</u>:

Can be read as standalones but not recommended

MORE THAN LIES

MORE THAN MEMORIES

<u>DIRTY JUSTICE TRILOGY</u>:

DIRTY BLUE

DIRTY WAR

DIRTY SIN

<u>STANDALONE BOOKS:</u>

HAVE MERCY

<u>BOXSETS / COLLECTIONS:</u>

Silent Series

More Than Series

Dirty Justice Trilogy

ACKNOWLEDGMENTS

Writing acknowledgements are hard. I cry every time; the type of tears that forces you to blow your nose, but I'm going to try to keep this short.

Readers, thank you so much for reading my stories. Without you, I wouldn't be able to do something I enjoy so much. I love meeting and hearing from all you and I love reading your honest reviews. Thank you.

Charisse Spiers, with you I don't know where to begin. You're more than a best friend and editor. You're more than a fellow author. You're my soul sister and I thank God that he brought you into my life. I love you!

Tesha, you are always my first set of eyes, editing and beta reading the raw script. Thank you for doing this. Thank you for helping make this book better. Thank you for your friendship. It means more than I can say. I love you!

Maddy, thank you for falling in love with this story and your continued messages. You really are the reason I finished this book. I needed you for this story more than I can say.

Kita, Amber, Elizabeth, and Rosa, thank you for proofreading this books and being extra sets of eyes to help polish it to what this story now is.

With all of you, I feel like I've finally found my tribe. Thank you for the bottom of my heart. — Nancy

About the Author

N. E. Henderson is the author of sexy, contemporary romance. When she isn't writing, you can find her reading some form of romance or in her Maverick, playing in the dirt.

This is Nancy's nineth book.

For more information:
www.nehenderson.com
facebook.com/authornehenderson
instagram.com/nehenderson
tiktok.com/author_nehenderson

Printed in the USA
CPSIA information can be obtained
at www.ICGtesting.com
LVHW091552150724
785569LV00004B/95

9 781948 539142